Red Sand

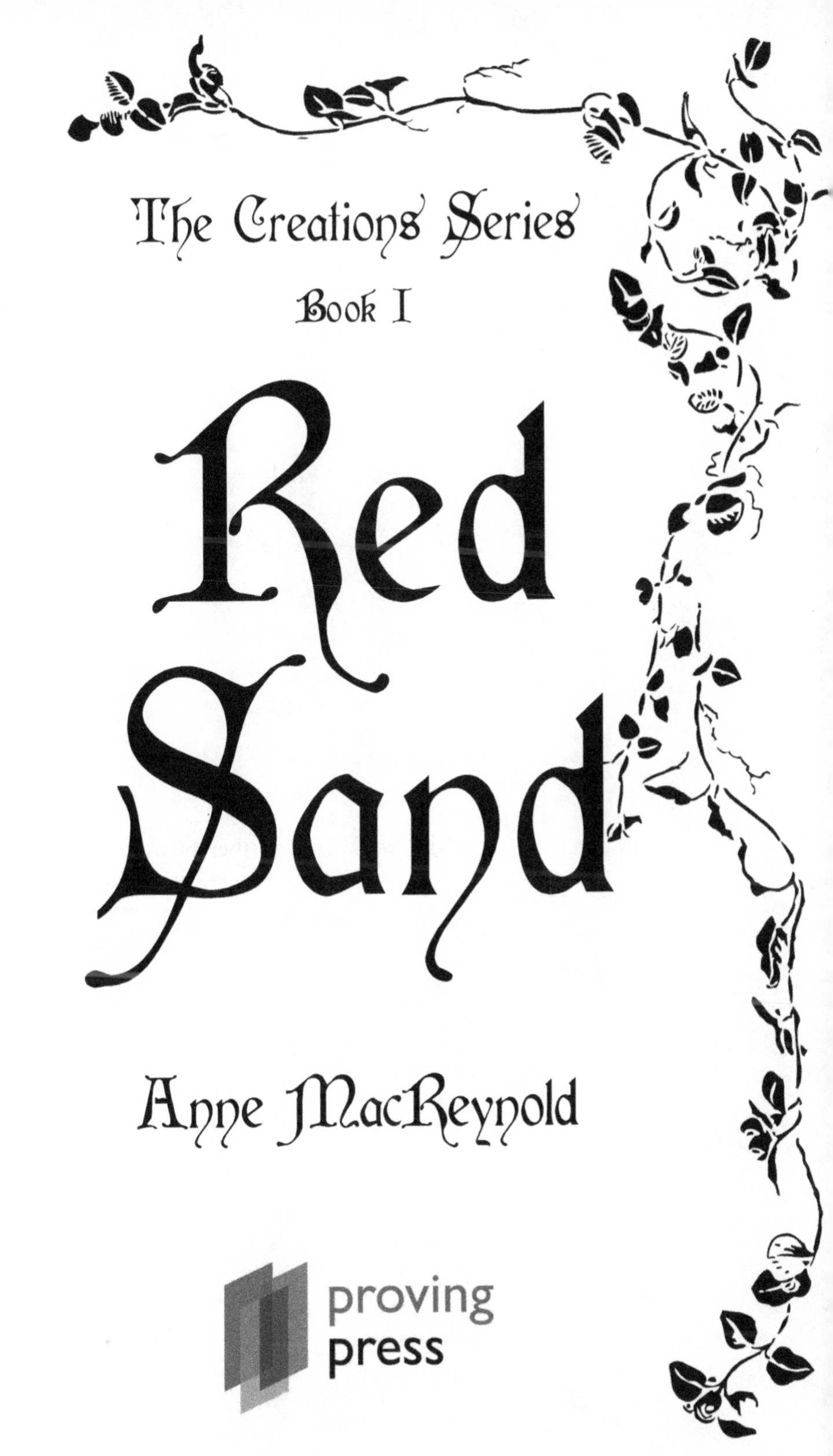

The Creations Series

Book I

Red Sand

Anne MacReynold

proving press

Book Design & Production
Columbus Publishing Lab
www.ColumbusPublishingLab.com

LCCN: 2019910380

Paperback ISBN: 978-1-63337-313-6
E-book ISBN: 978-1-63337-314-3
Hardback ISBN: 978-1-63337-317-4

Printed in the United States of America

Dedicated to a Hopeful Catholic, a Motherly Heathen,
a Drafted Christian Lion, and a Tenacious Freedom Fighter.
The parts you play in my life outshine any character
I could ever imagine in a book.

Thank you for the energy you've shared with me.

Contents

Part III: Pride and Greed

Part IV: Wrath

Introduction

This story is meant to be thought provoking. It's for philosophical readers, emotional readers, and any reader in between. The pages in this book are not meant to discriminate or judge. The story is simply that. A story. Because everyone has one. It doesn't matter what spiritual beliefs, political views, or cultures we stem from.

We all have a story and we all have a voice.

I chose the character of Lilith because of her origins in Jewish folklore (specifically *The Alphabet of Ben Sira*). She was demonized for speaking out against those who wished to control her, and instead of submitting she created her own path. One that was full of heartache and misery, but at least it was hers. She gave herself a voice, even if no one listened.

Even if she was viewed as evil.

Except evil is a concept. It is something we have named and categorized so that we as humans could find some feeling of control in a life we have no control over. And, as humans, that's what we want most—to be in control. To further that goal, humanity strives for knowledge. But the more we find the more we shun it away, unhappy with our own findings. Our discoveries become our enemies instead of our allies. We create our own cages so that

we don't need to work, to think, to accept. The cage is a place of safety and comfort, but it is a cage nonetheless. If we are to strive boldly forward on our own paths, we must break the lock and take control of our own selves. Even if that means accepting a world that isn't what we want it to be.

But of course that's *my* opinion and *my* philosophy.

I hope by the end of Lilith's story you will be able to understand why she does the things she does, and the events that led her there. None of us were born with blood on our hands, and none were born a saint. Our actions and our choices deliver us our own individual endings. Whether you see those as good or bad depends on the individual. The life we're given is the chance we have to tell a story, so make that story worth telling.

If you only take one thing away from this book, I hope it is this:

Keep trying. Because that is all we *can* do.

Sincerely,
A Teller of Stories

Prologue
Golden Light

My body burned, but it didn't hurt. The warmth covered my form and expelled the negative emotions that coursed through me. I couldn't remember why I had felt so sad. So lost. But now it didn't matter. The golden light that danced behind my eyelids calmed me.

My senses awoke and I could smell the sunbaked plants beside me. I felt a cold breeze pass through my hair, though the warmth from above quickly snuffed out the chill. My mouth was dry and begged to be moistened, but the sound I heard quickly distracted me. I opened my eyes to the noise.

The heat that radiated overhead was bright, and it took my eyes a moment to adjust, but I was soon able to see what had disrupted my rest. A dark gold creature stalked along the tree line. It hadn't seen me yet. Instinctually I kept low, only moving so I could keep the creature in my line of sight. The breeze drifted past me to the dangerous-looking animal. It lifted its head at the new scent. It was unsure, and scanned the clearing I hid in. The grass was tall enough to conceal me so long as I didn't move.

Satisfied with its solitude, the lion chuffed and disappeared into the dense undergrowth beneath the towering trees. Curious, I stood and followed silently. The grass crunched beneath my feet, and gold strands fell into my eyes. I was

wary entering the dark forest, but I hoped that whatever I found would answer the question on my mind.

Why was I here?

Part I
Gluttony and Lust

The emotions of our soul are many

So overwhelming they are to most

But to most they are rarely unheeded

Especially those of gluttony and lust

These wants are the meaning of pleasure

They feed the greatest of desires

Gluttony and lust create such happiness

So why discard such natures?

I

The Need to Run

Knowing the purpose of life means
having no life at all.
-A

Prehistory

I awoke to the cold. Not an unpleasant cold, but a refreshing chill that roused one's mind from a deep slumber. That was exactly what it felt like, too, as if I were waking from a dream. However, the dream didn't feel like a way to occupy my mind while I rested, but rather a way to revisit old memories, both the good and the bad ones. The memories drifted from my mind, as well as the chill, and were replaced by a bitter yet satisfied emotion. Only this emotion remained following the ancient remembrances. I couldn't recall any one thing anymore. Just a chaos of emotions ending in bittersweet happiness.

I decided not to question the mysterious happiness inside me. I let it envelop me until it spread electrical currents throughout my body, starting at my core and working its way outward. I reveled in it for what could have been mere seconds or several days, just enjoying the strange emotion, though all too soon I noticed my other senses establish themselves. The pleasant emotion was long forgotten and replaced with a new awareness.

I could now feel the ground beneath me; it was damp but soft and

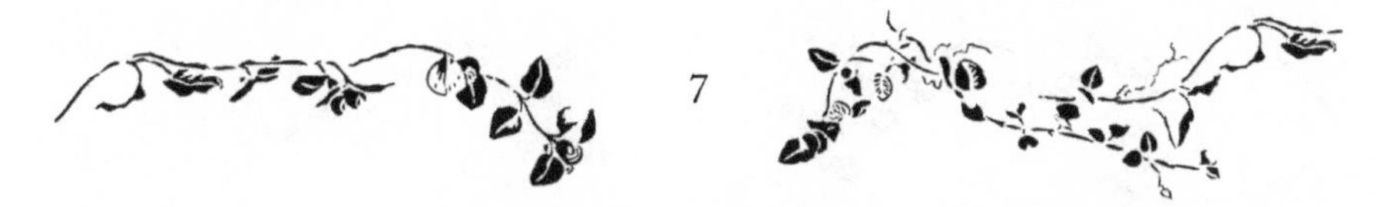

spongy. It was comforting. I could have drifted back into the abyss, completely satisfied due to the softness of it. I could hear the air moving around me; it was gentle as it caressed my shape, bristling the little hairs on my body. I could smell what surrounded me; it was pleasant and earthy and suited the quality of the ground and air perfectly, so much so that I turned my head and gently sniffed the moss beneath me. I could also taste what I smelled on my tongue, an odd sensation. It was different, yet I knew it was from my surroundings as well. Everything had a moist feel, but not so much that it was unpleasant. Lastly, I opened my eyes. This sense came just as naturally as the others, but the shock of the scene surrounding me made my eyes widen farther still. There was much to absorb in my environment, and I couldn't do it nearly fast enough.

The scene before me was enchanting. My breath ceased while I immersed myself in every detail that I could. Everything was covered in beautiful green. Not just one green, but several different shades of jade, emerald, olive, and mint layered the land. Mighty majestic trees of every kind towered over the landscape, and I soon noticed the additional colors of the spectrum dotted throughout the terrain.

I beheld every shade of daisy imaginable, strewn throughout a magnificent field to the north. Amethyst lilies and indigo forget-me-nots lined the trees all around me. Pale pink and blood-red petunias were spread through fluffy mint-colored bushes to the south. I moved my gaze upward and admired several twinkling lights strewn throughout the sky. Some were brighter than others, but each one was utterly unique and beautiful in its own way. Although, all these delightful images before me were completely outshined by the vast ivory sphere sitting separate yet within the same mass of darkness above.

The beautiful orb seemed to be gazing into my very being, and I gazed back. I felt a strange familiar comfort as I admired the sphere, yet the sight was brand new. It was as if I had glimpsed it before, but I was now seeing it

for the very first time, perhaps in a different light or from a conflicting perspective. I then noticed the feeling that laid within my chest. An unpleasant one. Like it was hollowed, waiting to be filled by some unknown source.

I was finally able to tear my gaze away from the orb when I heard the sound of gushing water. I scanned the area for the source of the alluring noise. To the west was a break in the trees. The sound beckoned me. I sauntered toward the undergrowth. The moss and flowers were cold and damp under my feet, but it felt reassuring, natural.

I broke through the line of expansive woodland and followed the sound of tumbling water. I traveled past several more trees and flowers; their scents overwhelmed my nostrils, and I couldn't separate one aroma from another. Some glowed in the dark of the night, and others turned toward me. There were mauve lupines, peach-colored tiger lilies, and the most beautiful rose bushes. I learned fairly soon that the roses protruded thorns in defense of their beauty.

As I crouched down to examine the tiny scratches the thorns left on my calves, I saw a small movement on the other side of the rose bush wall. Slowly, I crept closer to the twitchy motion. I reached out and parted the thorny branches to find a fluffy white creature with elongated ears and blood-red eyes: a rabbit. He stared at me a moment, startled due to having his mealtime disturbed. He nibbled on a radish, but soon discarded the vegetable and darted farther into the woodland. I decided to follow the creature's example and continue my journey.

Only a few moments passed before I discovered what I was searching for: an enormous waterfall that cascaded downward into a sky-lit pond. If it wasn't for the waves made by the waterfall, I would have mistaken the pond for the twinkling sky above. The white sphere, stars, and surrounding forest were so clear in its reflection I had to examine the pond at a closer distance.

I glided across the small clearing, over to the pond, and there in the

center of the reflective stars stood a young woman. Her effervescent emerald eyes were wide with the curiosity of a newborn, but were still somehow aged. They were held in a round-shaped face. A straight and narrow nose sat delicately above her heart-shaped lips. Everything was utterly proportional. Her skin was the color of ivory and looked as smooth as the still water along the pond's edge. The woman's face was framed with wild curls of crimson-colored strands, darkened, but at a certain angle one could see the vermilion hues in the reflected light.

The woman's dark red tresses spilled down to her hips, outlining the curves of her bare frame. Just as her face, her body was evenly proportioned. However, unlike her face, her body was built strong: muscles well-toned, sturdy thighs and calves, well-developed core, powerful yet graceful arms. These qualities created all within a tall frame. She was beautiful. I reached my arm toward her only to realize that she was me.

I stood there stunned for a moment, scrutinizing my new form. It was unrecognizable, but felt comfortable enough. I decided to ponder about myself later. I was more curious about the water that continued to send ripples toward me. I cautiously lowered my foot into the pond; it felt warm and inviting. Gradually I lowered my whole form into the giant mirrored pool. The sensation was wondrous, and my body trembled slightly.

I explored the pool's earthy banks and powerful waterfall. I even attempted diving beneath the reflective surface. I learned quickly that breathing was not an option under the waves, but I found I could hold my breath so I could further investigate the water's undergrowth. The greenery below differed from the light and colorful flowers above. The plants that grew beneath the water were dark and mysterious. They provided creative hiding places for the creatures that lived there. As I disturbed the plant life, fish of different colors, shapes, and sizes swarmed around me. Some were cautious and kept their distance, but most swam directly to me. They nibbled on my skin and followed my movements.

Occasionally returning to the surface to retrieve breath, I swam with the fish under the waves, amazed at the temporary weightlessness I achieved. There were creatures the size of my little finger that were shaded dark green to aid in their camouflage, as well as long, slinky ones that matched the length of my body and were pigmented the same deep hue of the indigo forget-me-nots I saw in the meadow.

My hand brushed against a bright crimson fish that hid in the dense greenery. He was as small as my hand. I startled him with my touch, and the creature grew five times his original size into a spiky sphere. The fish continued to float there, glaring at me for disturbing his home, yet he didn't seem to be able to do anything about his condition. The fish's disposition forced bubbles out of me. I returned to the surface to find myself shaking, and a chirping sound coming from my lips. The emotion that coincided with the sound was that of amusement and joy. I liked it and hoped it would continue.

Satisfied with my explorations, I rested on a warm and comfortable flat rock behind the waterfall. I observed the activity in the trees through a gracious gap between the tumbling water and the granite cove that hid behind it. I saw many creatures through my little window. Squirrels that constantly ran up and down the large trunks carrying pine cones in their mouths; some even carried minuscule versions of themselves. I saw small monkeys swinging easily through the branches with their long appendages; they seemed so carefree while they did this. My favorite was a gorgeous snow-white owl that perched herself deep within the branches. All the creature did was watch her surroundings, staring with her wide golden eyes at anything that moved. At one point that was me. The owl seemed to be waiting for something.

I heard a splash from the other side of the pond. I peered through the gaps in the waterfall to find a young man drifting through the gentle ripples. His eyes were full of the same curiosity I was sure mine had expressed when

I found the magical water. But my excitement was instantly replaced by caution. I could smell the scent of power emanating from him. It made my nostrils flare and shivers run down my spine. *Who was this man?* He looked like me. There were differences, but I knew we were of the same species.

All I let myself do was observe him; however, it was only a matter of time before he too would want to explore the waterfall. The man's patterns were very similar to my own, except he lifted the water in his hands to his mouth and drank deeply: thirst. As I had, he continued on to study the mossy banks covered in flowers, and he dove under the waves only to discover that air did not reside there. He was startled by the fish that swam comfortably by him, nibbling at his sides. However, he did not notice his reflection until after.

The man halted his journey through the water, staring at himself in surprise. The man was seeing his strong, uncovered form stare back at him with its pale gold complexion and nearly transparent blue eyes set in his diamond-shaped face. The man's eyes practically glowed in the light of the night sky. His features were sharp—deep-set eyes and high cheekbones. Wavy golden-colored hair framed his delicate facial features and tumbled to his shoulders. Though he had a strong wide jaw, this gave his lovely face a masculine charm. There was no doubt the rest of his body was masculine. The man held a tall and brawny form, but no taller than me, broad shoulders and chest, arms and legs as thick as tree trunks, sinews that etched his body to reveal every crevice and dip in his frame.

The man was beautiful. Maybe more so than my own reflection.

I was admiring the depressions on his abdomen when he suddenly charged toward me. I froze in fear. But just as he tumbled through the waterfall, clearly searching blindly, I dove beneath the waves to the other side of the crashing water. Right as I made my way to the surface for air, I heard grunting and yelling. He slammed into the boulder I had been resting on. It sat directly behind the falls and was nearly invisible through the spray if you weren't looking for it.

I quickly swam to the shoreline, climbed up the slippery moss-covered bank, and darted into the woods, the opposite direction I had come. I hurled myself through the forest, doing my best to avoid the thick trees and their branches. I used the spongy banks and flat rocks to catapult myself farther and faster through the immense foliage. Soon I could hear a second set of footsteps. As light as they were on the ground, they could not escape my acute hearing. I pushed myself faster. I finally thought I was going to outrun him when I tripped over something. It seemed to be a long vine lying across the ground. *It wasn't there a moment ago.*

I flew through the air. Once I landed, I was in too much agony to move. I had been charging so fast that I launched myself into a tree, but I was able to shield myself by turning to the left at the last moment. I was lying on my uninjured side, attempting to gulp in the moist forest air, when I heard the light footsteps I had been leaving behind draw closer. I looked to the tree I crashed into. It didn't fare any better than I had.

My breath refused to come; still, I forced myself to my knees. That's when I heard a low rumble. I had no idea where the sound came from, but the hairs on the back of my neck rose. I turned, and a sharp pain ran from my left side through the rest of my body, but the pain didn't last long, because I was staring face to face with another being. The golden eyes pierced me. The predator's elongated teeth gleamed in the light. I had crossed onto his territory.

I didn't know how I knew that. There was a small voice inside my head warning me of the danger. Still, this creature didn't frighten me as much as the one who continued to chase me through the forest. In this instance, injured and unsure of this angered predator, I chose the saber-toothed cat.

I moved to stand, and the throaty rumble increased. I bowed my head instead, hoping he would understand that I didn't want to fight. The giant cat took two deliberate steps forward; this brought the creature close enough for me to feel his breath on my face. The cat's breath smelled

rotten, his teeth riddled with the remains of his last meal. I quivered in anticipation of the attack.

I knew I should have been afraid, but somehow I wasn't. I was afraid *for* the cat. The footfalls in the distance drew closer. I wanted to scream at the predator to run, that he was in danger and that something worse was coming. But the words wouldn't form. And I knew that even if they had, the cat wouldn't understand. This was his territory, therefore he was in charge and ready to battle any challenger that dared cross his land.

The large cat continued to test me. I didn't move a muscle. I didn't even breathe. I felt his wet nose against my scalp. The cat inhaled my scent once more before grunting in satisfaction. He was ready to leave me when his ears perked up at the oncoming predator I had been running from. It was too late.

The man appeared then, and he halted upon seeing us. The great cat, sensing danger, moved to block me from the man's view. I was shocked. This creature was willing to protect me. Or, he had claimed me. Either way worked at the moment. The man, recognizing the protective stance, grew angry and territorial, much like the cat had not moments before.

Words formed in my mind, but still I could not utter them. My body had become rigid from uncertainty and fear. Fear for what the man would do to the creature to get to me. I had to stop it before it began. The man's virile scent mixed with the cat's to create one strong, horrifying odor, and I knew that meant a fight. My legs had gone numb. The prickly sensation hurt, and the pain shot through the rest of my body. I moved anyway. It was the worst mistake I could have made.

The cat turned his head to the noise that I caused. That's when the man struck. Instead of attacking head on, the way the creature would have, he coiled his way around the cat and straddled the predator's back. He wound his massive arms around the cat's throat and squeezed. But the cat was stronger than the man assumed, and the creature pulled away from

him. With nothing to steady his grip on the wild animal, he forced his thighs tightly against the cat's ribs. There were cracks and pops. Something had broken inside of the innocent being. I cried out in horror.

Once again I was a distraction, but this time it was the man who looked my way. His blue eyes bored into me. The iciness of them froze me over. My skin rose, though I wasn't cold. I couldn't get a handle on the emotion I felt. There was fear but also wonder. I wanted to know more.

The cat snapped his jaws at the man's legs. Focused once again, the man was able to end the brawl. When the creature snapped at him for the last time, the man gripped his massive fang and yanked back as hard as he could. There was a sickening crack, and the noble predator collapsed, taking my pursuer with him.

I stared at the horrific scene before me. I couldn't comprehend what happened, but I knew I couldn't stay. My wobbly legs were running through the woodland before I could think of what to do. I heard the struggle of the man forcing the heavy beast off of him.

I ran until all I heard was the wind grazing my ears.

II
The White Tree

To learn is to accept that you will
never have all the answers.
-A

Assured that I had run far enough, I stopped and took shelter in a hollowed tree. The night air was crisp, and I welcomed the chill. The panic and adrenaline I felt overheated my body. I was confident that I was safe from the creature chasing me, but that nagging voice inside me said it wouldn't last long. I heard rustling from above. Most likely more life. There was so much to see and explore, and here I was trapped by my own fear, unable to leave my sanctuary. *Where was I? Who was I? Why was I here?* I knew I wouldn't get an answer hiding away in a tree.

I crawled out onto the damp moss. The leaves crunched beneath me. The dust that flew from them smelled musty and lifeless. I felt oddly exposed because of the small noise. It echoed off the walls of the trees. Everything was silent in the forest, and if a sound was made, no source was visible. I had to become a part of it. I stepped out into the light of the white sphere. Its color enhanced my light skin. I glowed bright, much like the sphere itself.

I worked on my steps until I was as quiet as the breeze. Once I tried, I could see the path my feet should take. I could see the spaces in between crunchy leaves and snapping twigs, and I could distribute my weight

accordingly. My carefully placed steps had led me to a spot beneath a raised tree root. I was finally calm and comfortable when an owl hooted above me. In my surprise, I ripped out the heavy root from the ground simply by kicking forward. The mutilated limb bulged from the earth. The moss and flowers dangled from the crevice. The defiled limb spread all the way to the next tree. *Why had such a small movement caused such a catastrophe?* Frightened of my own presence, I moved even slower, hoping to find a place where I wasn't a threat.

My solitude was short-lived. They were as faint as my own, but I recognized the sound of human feet against moist ground. The man had found me. The ripping noise of the root had revealed my position. Not yet confident in my ability to travel quietly, I jumped upward and landed on a low branch. There I proceeded farther up until the flowers below were a minuscule dot in my vision.

It wasn't long after that I saw the gleaming golden hair of my pursuer pass underneath. The delicate breeze brought his scent to me. It was the same virile odor, but it left me strangely calm. As the night light brightened my skin, his hair had transformed into a snow white. It made it easy to follow him in the darkness, and I found myself mesmerized once again by his beauty. The man moved gracefully, reminding me of the cat he had fought.

My trance was broken at the memory, and my comfortable placement above was now unsettling. *What if he looked up and saw me? What would I do?* My body froze again, and my footing was lost. I slipped, and in my horror, I couldn't move fast enough to catch myself. I plummeted down the great tree, taking more of its body parts with me. I didn't cry out, because I didn't wish to be saved. I faced upward, and I could see the stars staring back at me. Strangely, I felt comfort in their presence. I didn't know what would happen when I reached the bottom, but my instincts told me it wouldn't be good. I braced myself for the worst.

That's when I felt warmth. My shivers calmed, and I looked up into

the eyes of a predator. Into the eyes of my savior. I was surprised when the language I wished to speak before came tumbling out of the man's mouth. "You know, you're very fast. Too bad you're not as graceful," the strange man commented with an arrogant smirk. Suddenly, out of instinct or something else entirely, I elbowed his rib as hard as I could. But he refused to let me go. He even started walking back the way we had come.

I protested with shoves and half-uttered curses when he offered, "I will put you down when we reach the water. There you can rest and tend to your injuries. Though if by then you decide you prefer me to hold you, and you surely will, I will not argue." His lips shaped a small knowing smile. Shocked and irritated by his confidence, I quieted. *What was happening?* The man acted as if I belonged to him, yet I didn't know him at all.

Uncertain of anything at that point, I let him carry me. I wanted to return to the water anyway, and maybe he could provide some answers. In turn I was able sneak glances at his glorious face during the journey back. Though what came out of his mouth both infuriated and confused me, I was very tempted to trace my finger along the outline of his lips…but I held myself back. I controlled the desire that was building inside of me, the desire for the strange man who carried me. But that was easier said than done.

The feral scent that I had come to know as threatening quickly became soothing. It made me feel safe and protected. As we traveled, I realized that this creature was the filler I needed for the emptiness living inside my chest. As if holding me that way was the way it was supposed to be, and there was an invisible tether between us, shrinking in length the longer we were together.

The man took his time on the way back to the pond. The slower pace made the journey longer than it had to be, but I didn't complain. His assured presence erased the memory of the cat and the events that occurred after. I let myself lean into his wide chest, enjoying the softness of his skin and

the security his arms provided. Soon I recognized landmarks I passed by hours ago.

By then the dark sky didn't seem so dark anymore. The twinkling lights were disappearing into the background of the sapphire and ginger-colored horizon. The ivory orb above had become nearly a shadow of itself, and it also disappeared into the changing colors, moving farther and farther away from me. The thought nearly brought tears to my eyes, but I knew somehow that I would see the magnificent orb again. *The moon.* Though the name had escaped me before, it would be impossible to forget it now.

As I let go of the departing moon, I turned my gaze to the east where the ginger colors grew brighter with each passing moment. Although it caused pain to my eyes to study the glaring horizon, I could not force myself to look away. The land around me was just as dazzling as the nighttime had been. Yet, I felt I preferred the comfort and protection of the vast dark blanket filled with a million lights and the ivory lunar orb to guide me, rather than this version of the sky.

I looked up at the man carrying me to voice my thoughts and found I could not. His face was breathtaking in the rays of the fiery orb. Not just his features, which were so much more pronounced than what I saw in the moonlight not hours ago, but the expression that was formed there. Blue eyes and golden hair were sparkling in the rays of the sun. The light seemed to bounce off of him and spread to everything around us. His seemingly permanent smirk was erased and replaced with a content and relaxed smile. The man was very much at peace in the light that shone upon him.

This made me reach up and stroke the hair that lay near his face. I moved it away from his eyes, so I could study the light that reflected off the pale blue. Though he did sneak a quick glance at me, he remained silent, letting us enjoy the moment in the sun.

The man's peaceful expression made me rethink my original opinion, and I turned my gaze to the sunrise once more. The sky turned lighter

blue as time passed. It was laced with several shades of ginger, violets, and crimson. White, fluffy puffs were floating lazily throughout the horizon. It reminded me of the previous night, while I had floated in the pond. I wondered if that was what the white puffs felt like, weightless and free. If so, I understood why they continued to laze about.

The best part of the new sky was the ginger orb that rose from behind silhouettes of the mountains. This was the source of all the magnificent new colors and shapes that I beheld in the landscape. I studied the scenery in the shadows of the night, but they were much more enhanced and vibrant in the gleaming glow of the new sphere.

I could not stare into the sun as I could the moon, but I could feel warmth coming from this one. As it grew higher in the sky, I grew warmer. It was only a little at first, which caused bumps to rise on my skin from the change in temperature. As the warmth grew and my body adjusted, the bumps descended, and I was completely comfortable in this new kind of light, especially in the arms of someone who already radiated so much warmth.

I had been so absorbed in the changing surroundings that I didn't realize when we reached the pond. Sun rays were bouncing off the surface, and it wasn't as quiet as it had been. The waterfall had increased in speed, as well as the waves it produced. The light seemed to bring more creatures out into the open. I could hear heavy flapping above and treading through the brush; they called to each other in many unique languages, and I couldn't understand any of them.

The strange man still held me in his arms, which I realized cradled me in a very gentle way. Careful of my injured left side, he had carried me with my right side against him. The man must have noticed me clutching it when he found me with the cat. Perhaps I had misjudged, and the pull I felt toward him was right.

Of course, he then ruined this quiet contemplation when he spoke.

"Comfortable?" He smirked then and pulled me closer. Too close. He was no longer worried about my wounds.

Panicked, I hit his rib as I did before, and smiled when he winced. I expected him to set me down after my show of distaste for his taunting. So I crossed my arms, looked away, and waited patiently for him to gain considerate behavior.

Apparently I put too much faith into that theory, because the next thing I knew I was under water. The water being shallow, all I had to do was stand to gather fresh air for myself. Once I did, I looked up at the arrogant man before me, the arrogance that I had mistaken for confidence beforehand. The man stood at the edge of the pond atop the mossy bank, a grin plastered across his disgustingly beautiful face.

I waded over to him, the water coming up to my waist. The first real words I spoke to him were, "You moron! Why would you throw me in the water? I'm injured, and I thought you wanted to help?" I berated him with several more curses and inquiries, all without him acknowledging a single one. He had keeled over on his side, cackling like the imbecile he was.

I recognized that he was laughing and found me humorous in some way. I thought back to the little red fish that had puffed up when I had startled him, and how he made me laugh. I felt instant regret for how I must have made that fish feel by expressing humor instead of kindness toward him. Because now I had become the little red fish, and this man had become me.

"Why did you chase me if you were going to treat me this way?" I questioned. The words flowed freely now.

"Well, because you ran from me, of course. And it's clear you can't defend yourself. That cat would have eaten you for dinner if it wasn't for me," the man stated as if it were obvious.

Anger setting in, I argued, "I can defend myself just fine. If you wouldn't have shown up I would have parted ways with the creature,

neither of us harmed. You are the one who startled him and crossed onto his territory." The level of anger I felt was more powerful than the fear or the shock of falling out of the tree.

"I doubt that, but in any case, it's my territory now, isn't it?" He seemed oddly satisfied with that realized fact.

"The land may be yours, but I'm not."

I went to crawl out of the water when he stopped me and said, "Oh no you don't. You're not running off again. I need answers, and you're the closest thing I have."

"Why would you think I have answers? I just woke up last night," I bellowed.

Disappointed but not surprised, he answered, "Well, I guess we need each other then, don't we?"

I realized then that despite his arrogant facade, he was confused. He was only looking for an explanation to this abrupt existence, just like I was. My anger fading, I nodded in agreement. My fury was replaced with understanding, and the hollowness in my chest was filled with the promise of his future presence. "What now?" I asked.

"Now we look at your injuries."

He moved to jump in the water when I shouted, "No!"

Startled, he asked, "And why not?"

Confused myself, I said, "I don't want you touching me." The image of the cat's head as it twisted unnaturally was conjured.

Completely unaware of my troubles, he stated, "Afraid you won't be able to keep your hands off me?"

I had no idea what his words meant, but I was angry just the same. "No! I just don't want you near me right now. I don't know you, and you've been chasing me through the woods the entire night. I'm tired." Which was true.

Amused with a mixture of another emotion I didn't recognize, he demurred, "I only want to help."

Panicked by the rising heat in my body, I splashed him and swam over to my rock behind the waterfall. He didn't follow, which I was grateful for. I needed to be alone.

I decided to check my own injuries. My side wasn't sore anymore, but I expected to find damage from the collision and fall. I did not. There had been some deep puncture wounds from slamming into the tree's branches, as well as falling through several more. But they had disappeared.

I smoothed my hand over where they had been, and all that remained was a powdery red dust that fell from my skin; it clumped due to the moisture. The fact that I was healed went against my instincts. But despite my surprising recovery, the warm water felt pleasing. It stole away all the aches I didn't know I had, but perhaps those were just mental.

I picked leaves and twigs from my tangled hair and threw them in the pond. The waterfall's current carried them away, and I watched as little fish mouths broke the surface to eat the remnants. I peeked between the waterfall's seams to see what had become of my pursuer, but I couldn't find him. I split the wall of water and swam to the edge of the pond. *He left me.* I felt irritation at the fact that he felt comfortable enough in his influence that he could leave me alone, trusting that I would wait for him. But I also felt oddly sad. The man's departure left that empty feeling inside of my chest again.

I had to tell myself that I didn't need him. Though I didn't quite believe it. *What was I supposed to do next?* The man was clearly no help, and the excitement of the new world was waning. Though I knew there was much more to explore, my inner voice was nagging me to do something else. Once I paid attention to the instinct, I became aware of my body. There was a low rumbling sound coming from my core, and pain followed soon after. *Did I hurt my stomach, too?* I inspected the area to find there was no outward injury.

I returned to my flat rock, unable to solve the problem. Lying on my

front seemed to help the pain. The fish beneath the surface were circling me, nibbling at the remaining bits of greenery floating on the surface. That's when my inner voice became clear. I needed to eat as the fish did. My mouth watered from the anticipation, but the fish food didn't look very appetizing. I swam back to the grassy bank and ripped out a handful of the plant life growing there. I sniffed the greenery in my hand. It smelled lovely; surely it would taste just as good.

I was very wrong. I wasn't even able to get it down my throat. The grass stuck to the inside of my mouth, and I couldn't break it apart with my teeth. Realizing the impossible task, I spit the grass back onto the ground where it belonged. I rinsed the remains out of my mouth with the pond water and decided to look elsewhere for sustenance.

I wandered into the woodland once again, in a different direction this time. I thought I might as well explore more of the land while on my solitary quest. And as I traveled farther into the undergrowth, I began to notice repeats of the greenery I'd seen the previous night, as well as new additions. Patches of sunlight leaked through the trees' canopy, revealing the details of the land in its yellow warmth. It reminded me of how the sun rays bounced off the strange man's skin, almost like he was a little sun himself.

The land was stunning. I often had to remind myself to keep going, as I would stop and stare at a certain flower or tree, just taking in the uniqueness of each one. I even discovered new creatures living in the branches above. They flew back and forth from their nests and sang while they did so. I attempted to mimic the beautiful sound, but it came out more of a wheezing noise, and I quickly stopped. I didn't want to ruin their song.

I traveled farther, testing different plants and flowers to see if they would satisfy my growing hunger. I found some eased the pain, while others made it worse. I cataloged each one to memory so I could use them in the

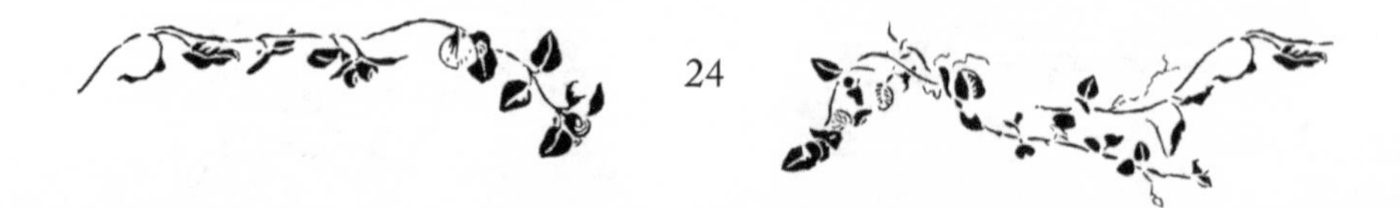

future. I was frustrated at the enhanced pain in my middle and becoming desperate. I began to eat anything I could get my hands on, no matter the look or smell of it. Upright lizards with long tails passed by. Their darting eyes glanced warily at my odd behavior but moved on uninterested. I was grateful and a little perturbed at their dismissive nature.

After hours of searching to no avail, I finally decided to lay down and await death's arrival. That's when I heard little pitter patter sounds on the squishy moss next to me. I turned my head to find the little white rabbit from the night before had come to bid me farewell from my current life. He stared at me a moment, then moved so close that I could feel his whiskers brush against my face as he sniffed me. The ticklish sensation made me sneeze, startling the rabbit.

I abruptly remembered that he had been eating a radish last I saw him. "Do you know where I can get food, little one? The radish you were eating last night? I would be most grateful." I tried to be kind and courteous, but it came out more like begging. How pathetic, if this was all it took to disable me. *What a weak creature I must be.*

The rabbit quickly dashed through a wall of rose bushes. *Perfect.* I had to deal with thorns again, as well as my hunger. I stood and strove to find a gentle route through the roses. Once I made it past the wall, scratches and all, I found the rabbit waiting for me. He made sure I could follow and lazily hopped away. His nose was twitching rapidly; perhaps he was searching for the scent he wanted. I attempted this, but I found I could only smell the earthy tones from before, though I didn't know what I was looking for anyway. Disappointed, I let the furry creature lead the way.

The journey was slow and excruciating, but the rabbit eventually did lead me somewhere helpful. We came into another clearing, except in the center rested a magnificent old tree. The wooden being was unlike anything I'd seen before. The color of it nearly blinded me. The purest of white shaded

the tree, from the tallest branch to the massive roots protruding from the ground. It was so thick it would have taken eighty of me to fill the width of it and two hundred to match the height. The tree's branches stretched out past the vast meadow that surrounded it, and its roots mingled with the greenery that shared the land. Only the dense canopy of its neighbors kept me from finding the grand tree sooner.

I forced myself to look past the blinding light and absorb every detail of its form. The trunk was rough with bark like the others but held no wear. No animal had marked its beautiful milky stem. The snowy leaves danced in the wind, and I caught one in my hand before it could escape. It was pure and undirtied by the earth below. Letting the leaf fly away, I saw what lived in its strange leaves. Apples.

My mouth watered.

I wrapped my hand around the red sphere closest to me and tugged gently. It let go from its home rather easily. The apple didn't have a very strong scent, but I would be able to find it again if I wanted. Its juice ran down my chin as I took a bite, and the taste had me craving more.

The second apple I pulled from the ancient tree caused a swarm of creatures to come flying from its branches. The top side of their wings were colored white to blend with the milky tree, but the bottom half revealed several different colors upon their fluttering. Their unique colors sprinkled the sky above. Rosy pink and sunrise-orange butterflies flew around where I stood. I could feel their little feet graze my skin, and their light wings fanned my face before they flew away to another part of the great tree, together as one graceful swarm.

Suffice to say, I remained in that meadow for a long while, eating my fill of the juicy food. The middle of the fruit was inedible, I discovered, and I threw the core to the grass. As I ate, the rabbit that led me to the meadow visited me and nibbled on the leftover apple carcasses. It was nice to have the company. I placed my palm against the unmarred bark of

the tree's trunk. It wasn't cold, but the temperature of it was cooler than its surroundings.

I felt a sudden pulse in my chest then. I looked around, expecting the man to waltz through the tree line and kidnap me again. Satisfied and a little agitated that he wasn't, I laid under the shade of the tree and looked up at the still, lazy clouds through the pale leaves. The sun had moved across the sky, and the blue wasn't as light. The darkened sky was making me drowsy.

I heard a noise to my right. An antlered being was munching on the crunchy leaves across the great meadow. The creature was delicate in stature, but I could see its muscles tense as it moved. They rippled under its soft, earth-colored fur. The white of its belly peeked out from its side. The stag's black pupils bored into me, warning me to stay away. But the challenge only thrilled me.

I stood slowly, stalking the wild beast instinctually. My steps were slow at first, careful not to alarm the creature. But this animal was smart and knew when it was being hunted. The buck bolted the opposite direction, afraid for its life. I pursued, quicker than I would have thought possible. I ran faster than I had the night before. The anticipation of the kill gave me the incentive I needed. The chase was intoxicating. I knew I could catch the creature any time I wished, but I stayed back. I wanted to enjoy it.

The stag, sensing its impending end, turned to face its hunter. It angled its antlers toward me, daring me to approach. I circled the angered beast and waited for it to charge. It didn't take long. I waited until the last moment, right before the tip of the antler pierced my chest. I swung myself onto its back as I'd done with the saber-toothed cat. The deer bucked and thrashed beneath me in hope that I would fall and be trampled beneath its merciless hooves. I grasped the deadly protrusions, intending to break its neck. But I paused, unsure. That was all the creature needed to fling me

forward. I turned in the air so my side would take the hit instead of my face. I was a hair away from hitting the ground when I woke up.

Startled, I leapt up. I was still in the meadow. I hadn't realized I had fallen asleep. The nature of the dream was disturbing and left my mind reeling. But the harder I tried to remember what happened, the faster the images disappeared. Emptiness and the overwhelming sense of dread were all that was left of the lost dream.

I decided to make my way back to the pond. The apples had filled my belly, but my body ached for water. The rabbit still rested in the grass, and I bid him farewell. I would have perished if he hadn't found me. I plucked one more apple from its bright home to take with me in case the hunger set in again. I glanced back at the great tree once more and promised myself I would return, for it was a magical place here in the forest. I saw the twitchy movements of butterflies on the far side of the meadow where they decorated their home in bright colors.

The journey back was quicker than the journey there, now that I knew where I was going. All I had to do was follow the trail of mutilated vegetation. Being no longer hungry and having a clear mind, I could see what I had attempted to eat. The remains of the partially eaten shrubbery, mushrooms, flowers, and moss nearly made me return the apples back to the earth. For I had done so with most of what I ingested, and it was not a good addition to the woodland, sight or smell. I said a silent apology to the vegetation and continued on. A horse galloped by me then. The two small horns protruding from his forehead were aimed downward. He looked to be charging at another being, though I didn't know what. The horse's white hide disappeared behind the dense trees, leaving me behind to wonder.

By the time I reached the pond the sky was dark, and I felt the blanket of protection on me once more. The moon and stars shone from that blanket and lit my path into the water. I set my apple on the bank in

a dry patch of grass and drank deeply from the pond. This sensation was better than filling my belly with apples.

Once I had my fill, I bathed in the waterfall to remove the evidence of the day. Now that I knew what to do, I wouldn't be reliving that harsh experience again. Hunger was not a pleasant thing to endure, but on the positive side I had learned a lot about the domain around me: what herbs and flowers were edible (and which were not), where a food source was, and that there were creatures who were willing to help if I needed it.

It was reassuring to know I wasn't alone.

Finished bathing, I laid across my warm resting rock behind the waterfall. The colorful fish swam around me, probing the air with their lips. As I was about to fall into a deep sleep, the emptiness that hollowed my chest reminded me that I had forgotten something important. Too tired to care, I ignored the thought and fell into my first blissful sleep.

III
The Nuances of Death

Life and Death are two souls
destined for one another
-A

I didn't wake until late the next morning and would have most likely slept longer if I hadn't heard the splash of water from across the pond. I peeked through the parting in the waterfall and saw it was him. The man from yesterday. My hollow chest was full once again, but I didn't know why. Instinctually, he made me feel whole, but intellectually he made me angry. I wanted him near and far away at the same time. It didn't make sense. I hadn't felt anything like that toward the other creatures who lived on this land. Perhaps it was because he was of the same species, and he challenged me in a way the others couldn't. His arrogant attitude didn't help either.

"Oh good, you're awake! That means you can help me," he exclaimed, while doing a rough wash of himself in the pond. He looked like he had been in the woods since he left the previous morning. *What had he been doing?* Maybe he had a difficult time finding food, too. Unsure if he found any, I came out from behind the waterfall to offer the apple I found. That was when I saw him. There, lying on the mossy bank, was the fluffy white rabbit that helped me when I was hungry.

I was glad he had come to visit me again. But the furry being wasn't moving and lay in an unnatural position. I waded over to him, not yet

understanding what had become of the creature. I pulled myself onto the bank to sit next to him. I stroked his fur to rouse his consciousness, but he continued to lie still. I then noticed crimson streaks stained his little mouth and whiskers, and his little red eyes were empty. "What's wrong with him?" I questioned.

The man looked up from washing himself and answered, "Nothing's wrong with it. I broke its neck so we could eat it. It took me a while, though. It was very hard to catch." He sounded confused, unsure of why he had to explain that.

I didn't question further, for I had to run to the nearest bush to relinquish my stomach. I saw the apples I'd eaten the evening before. I had to vomit yesterday to rid myself of bad food, but this time felt different. It wasn't a physical problem causing this; it was the emotions I felt. Shock. Sadness. Anger. Apparently it was possible to feel more that one emotion at once.

Thoroughly emptied, I turned around to face the killer. "How could you do that? What made you even think to? That's horrible. This rabbit was my friend. He helped me find food yesterday after you left me here." I sounded frantic. I had no idea how to control the anger I felt. I was shaking; I needed to hit something. I needed to hit *him.*

The man's shocked expression made it even worse. *Did he not know what he did?* I started toward him, planning on causing damage, when I caught sight of the rabbit again. Instead of being strong and holding my ground, I collapsed next to the little creature and water began pouring down my face: tears.

I stroked the rabbit's soft fur while I cried. The man then exited the water and sat next to me. He wasn't sure what to do, so he settled with a hand on my shoulder, which I wanted to shake off but felt too weak to try. I observed that sadness was surely a crippling emotion, and I would have to do my best to avoid it.

The man was suddenly on his feet and in the forest before I could even look up. Though when I did, everything was blurry from the tears, so the task itself was pointless. *Where was he going? Leaving me behind again?* I decided I didn't care, and I continued my silent grieving for my lost friend. His little body had gone cold and stiff. A peculiar form. *So, this was death.* I realized that's what had happened to the saber-toothed cat, though I hadn't acknowledged that until now.

The man emerged from the forest's edge holding two scarlet flowers. He crouched down next to my dead friend and placed a crimson rose on top of his form. He then proceeded to give me a single red lily and say, "I am sorry for your friend. I would have chosen another animal if I had known that. Will you forgive me?"

The tears finally clearing from my eyes, I was able to look up from the rabbit to the pale blue eyes across from me. They were not the eyes of sorrow, but rather uncertainty and maybe hurt? What would he have been hurt about? He's the one who killed the rabbit, not me.

Yet, the flower he offered seemed to soften my anger. I took the waiting lily from his hand, and not quite touching the flower with my nose, I sniffed. It was a strong, intoxicating smell. The pollen flew from its mini green stems and joined the breeze upon my exhale. It made me think of the rabbit sniffing out the pale apple tree, and if he would have been able to enjoy the scent as much as me.

The man spoke softly, "I saw this flower soon after we met that night. The brightness of it stood out in the dark. It reminded me of you. The crimson for your obvious anger toward me," he smiled, "and for the color of your hair. Though the beauty of it does not compare to you, it is the prettiest flower I have seen." These words halted my train of thought and brought heat to my face. *What was this emotion?* It was horrible and lovely all at once. Seeing my face, he panicked and asked, "Do you not like it?"

The question only seemed to make the heat worse, but I murmured, "No, it's beautiful. Thank you."

Satisfied with my answer, he went on to say, "What do I call you?"

"What do you mean?" I asked, confused by his change in topic. Was he trying to distract me?

"A name. The creatures around us and the plant life have names. Shouldn't we?" he fervently questioned.

"I suppose so, but I thought we did already. You're Man and I am Woman?" Perhaps the names that came to me were wrong? Did he see something else?

"Yes, that is what I see, too, but we seem to be different from the rest. Don't you think? We should name ourselves," he countered. The thought had not occurred to me. Probably because I didn't see us as different from the rest of creatures and plant life. *Was I wrong?*

I answered, "If you would like. What do you want to call yourself?"

"I can't think of anything. Would you name me? Mostly because I have the perfect one for you," he replied, nearly dying with anticipation at my next question.

The man's moods were as unpredictable as mine.

"What is it you have chosen for me then?" I asked nervously. What did I just agree to? What if the name sounded awful? It was hard to imagine anything awful coming out of those perfectly shaped lips, but it had happened before.

"Because you are so much like the lily you hold in your hand, I thought Lilith would be your name. Do you like it?" He didn't wait for me to answer. "Yes! That is your name. Lilith is perfect for you. Now, what name do you have for me?" *Lilith?* It had no meaning like the rest of the words that gathered in my thoughts. Perhaps it didn't have to, being it was just a name. But the concept that my name had no meaning left me a bit sad.

Despite the lack of significance, I did like the word. It sounded pretty

when he said it. Though it felt wrong to have a different title other than what was given. How were we different from the fish in the pond to sun in the sky? The man didn't give me much time to ponder this for he was anxious to receive his name.

I told him I was unsure and would decide later, because I couldn't think of anything in the moment, which was true, but also because I was worried that I couldn't create anything that described the feelings I felt toward him. It was a tug of war between desire and anger. A thought occurred to me then. "Why did you choose an animal to eat? Why not the greenery?"

The confounded look he gave me nearly made me laugh. "Well, other than the foliage didn't seem very appealing, I watched the lions hunt and eat the buffalo. I assumed the same would be for us, though more difficult, seeing we don't have their teeth or claws," he explained. "So that is why I decided to hunt something smaller." He avoided my probing gaze. Was he embarrassed?

"Why not eat what you have already killed? The cat? Surely that would have been enough for you." The thought made me want to vomit again, but it was better than killing another innocent being.

"The other creatures already claimed its corpse. I was too late." The man was clearly disappointed.

I nodded in acknowledgment. "I understand. We have seen different things and have comprised different ways of eating because of it. Surely now you will switch to my method and cease harming other creatures," I affirmed.

The man laughed. "Why would I do that? This is not my first hunt. Animal meat is delicious and eases the hunger," he recalled. "I will need to practice." The man rubbed his shoulder as if he was in pain, but there was no visible injury. The nausea continued, and I needed something to settle the churning in my core. I looked around for my apple. It was right where I left it.

The man studied me for a moment while I took small bites from the juicy fruit. I was about to tell him to look elsewhere, because his gaze was

making the heat return to my face, when he grabbed the apple from my grasp. "Is this the food you spoke of? It doesn't look very appetizing," he said with disgust.

I ripped the apple back from his large hand. It wasn't an easy task. If he hadn't let go willingly, I wouldn't have been able to do it. *Why was he so much stronger than me?* And his extremities were so much larger than mine, too. His hand covered the whole apple, while mine covered only half of it. Then I thought back to our chase in the woods when I ran from him. If I hadn't tripped, I would have outrun him. Perhaps that was what balanced us. The man had strength, but I had speed.

"Don't judge what you don't know. Have you even tried eating any of the greenery?" I questioned defensively.

He looked taken aback by the venom in my voice. "No, I haven't. It didn't even occur to me," he answered slowly, guessing what I was going to say next.

"Well, then, try it and you may be surprised," I answered stubbornly. Knowing I wasn't going let the subject drop, he motioned for the apple. I just shook my head and pointed to the woods.

"No, this is mine. Go get your own." I smiled sweetly, a plan forming. The man stood and began his journey for the food he thought was so disgusting. Finishing my apple quickly, I followed close behind and waited for him to make his choice.

"Where did you find the apple?" he asked, looking back at me. I noticed his gaze roamed everywhere but my eyes.

"It would take too long to get there. Why don't you try something else that is closer?" I suggested. He began picking things from different trees and bushes, sniffing and examining, but not eating. I was getting impatient.

"Try one of those." I pointed to a questionable mushroom. The man's blue irises peered at me suspiciously.

I decided to play innocent. "You don't have to. Try what you want.

That one tasted good to me is all." I comforted him the best I could. Whatever he saw in my expression made him relax, because he picked up the mushroom, sniffed it, and then ate it whole.

After he finished, he said, "That wasn't terrible I suppose. Meat is still much better." I couldn't contain my laughter anymore. It was rolling out of me in waves, the same way he had laughed when he threw me into the water.

His face went pale. "What did you do?"

Still laughing, I said, "Have fun with that. Those mushrooms made me very ill. Consider this vengeance for my rabbit friend. Enjoy!" I yelled over my shoulder while I ran back to the pond. I had to get away in case he decided to force the rest of the mushrooms down my throat, but I wasn't even out of range before I heard the sickening noises caused by the inedible plant.

On my way back to our watering hole, I found another fruit tree. This one wasn't white like the other fruit giver, and it grew pears instead of apples. I hoped my findings would make up for my previous mischief, because I found myself thinking of him while I gathered our meal—how his muscles bulged when he climbed out of the pond, and how the light shone off his wavy sunlit hair.

The man returned shortly after, interrupting my daydream. I had organized the fruits on a large leaf I found attached to man-sized sunflowers. They resembled the sun and the warmth it shared with us, but the flower also made me feel sad. The dark core expressed loneliness and wished only for someone to reciprocate the warmth it gave freely. *It reminded me of him.*

I couldn't even look at the man when he approached. I had time to reflect while he was gone, and I concluded that my escapade had been unnecessary. To my surprise, however, he was utterly cheerful by the time he reached me. Peculiar. *What was he up to?* He was holding something behind his back.

With a smile on his face, the man said, "Thank you for that wonderful experience. I will be sure to return the favor." He stepped closer.

"Now, wait, I only deceived you because you killed that innocent rabbit. We're even now," I said nervously as I walked backward toward the water. I believed myself to be a better swimmer than him. I could escape in the pond.

"Oh no. That isn't right. I only killed him to eat. There was no malice involved, unlike your little deception. I don't think we're quite even yet." The man then threw the hidden object at me. It took me a moment to find it. It had landed in my hair and was moving! I rushed to the water's edge to see my reflection. A giant spider was tangled in my mass of curls.

I shrieked and shook the creature off of me into the water below. I didn't know why this was my reaction. It's not like she was harming me; if anything, the spider was the frightened one. I believed it was the shock of seeing the creature for the first time. Her form was quite different than the other creatures I'd seen. The several legs, hairy body, and multiple coreless eyes startled me. I watched as she sank beneath the surface, my feet frozen to the ground.

"What's wrong? Is that one not your friend? Is that why you killed it?" the man questioned mockingly.

Realizing what was happening, I dove into the water to save the spider. I was searching the bottom of the pond floor when I saw movement out of the corner of my eye. The spider was floating in the midst of a group of fish. She was twitching rapidly, struggling to find her way to the surface. I began swimming toward the creature to save her when suddenly one of the bigger silver fish took a bite out of her leg. This action ripped it clean off. Soon, the other fish joined in on the feast. All the while, the spider fought and trembled until finally, without any legs left, she ceased movement. The rest of her body quickly disappeared.

I was too late.

After the scene I witnessed, I clambered out of the water onto the shore to sit and ponder. The man had found the pile of fruits and was examining them. Were all the creatures of this domain killers? Is that what we're supposed to do? *No.* The man had a point earlier when he said he killed to eat and not because of malice, but these creatures seemed to kill out of instinct to live. There was no choice in the matter.

Then there was the rabbit. He ate the vegetation instead of other animals due to the instinct to stay apart from the dangerous creatures that could harm him. One could eat the vegetation as an alternative, so other lives might be spared. *Yes.* That was the route I would take, and I hoped the man would too. He himself had said we were different. Perhaps it was because we knew we had a choice, which differed from the animals that did not know and could not conceive of choices. Just instinct to survive.

Still, that fact wouldn't stop me from trying to change their instinctual nature.

Determined in my decision, I walked over to the man and sat down next to him to enjoy the pears. Seeing that I was eating them, he took a bite of one himself. Obviously, the mushroom incident hadn't helped to build the trust that was lacking between us. As he ate, he commented, "These don't taste as bad as I thought they were going to. Thank you for gathering them. It has ebbed the pain in my stomach."

"The hunger you mean?" I wondered.

"No, the sensitivity left from the mushrooms," he corrected, but he smiled as he did.

He must have forgiven me.

"I know you won't like this, but we must eat the rabbit before it spoils." He said it so eagerly, but then composed himself and sent an apologetic look my way.

"Is that what happens after death?" I questioned, surprised that he knew so much.

"Yes, after a day the body begins to rot and is no longer edible," he explained.

That's odd. We hadn't been awake for more than two nights. Did he begin hunting that soon? "How long have you been awake?" I asked.

The man thought for a moment. "I believe two and a half suns. I observed the lions on the first and was able to catch a few small critters before the day was done. Then I found you," he concluded, staring at me again. So, it seemed we woke in the same day, except he woke first, during the daytime, and I woke during the night. I shared my results with him, and though he agreed it was strange, he didn't give much thought to the reason why.

While I continued to nibble on my pear, the man dove into the water. He returned to the surface quickly, the droplets glistening against the sunlight as they slid down his body. I eventually moved my gaze to his hand and saw that he grasped a pointed rock from below. The man headed toward the rabbit's resting place, grabbed the feet so the creature dangled in his grasp, and turned to me. The red rose that had rested in the rabbit's snowy fur tumbled to the ground. "I understand that you won't want to see this, so I will cut the meat from it elsewhere."

The man turned to walk into the woodland when I said, "Wait! What are you going to do with the rest of him?"

The man gazed back at me, puzzled. "What do you mean? No other part of it can feed us," he clarified.

His explanation unnerved me. "His fur can be of use. It would be a shame to waste it," I said sadly. I hated the thought of that soft white fur wasting away.

The man took a moment to answer. "Yes, I suppose it does get a bit cold at night. Though it is not much, it will help us keep warm." He smiled, creative notions weaving their way through his thoughts. I just opened a whole new world for him it seemed. The man was now ecstatic

and prepared to try our new discovery. Just what he needed—more encouragement to kill innocent beings.

"Just do your best not to waste any of him, please." My words helped him focus. The man considered what I said, and without another word marched into the undergrowth of the forest to carry out his gruesome deed.

The man was gone well into the night, and his absence continued to plague me. I had decided to gather as many provisions as I could while he was gone, as well as test more herbs and flowers along the way. Many of them made me ill in the same way as before, but I did manage to compile a good idea of what the forest had to offer. I took the man's idea of using the rocks from the pond and marked little notches on the trees.

Each mark had a different design for each trail that led to the intended purpose. I used an upward line to indicate the path to the pear tree and a sideways line to find several bushes of little elongated purple flowers: lavender. These flowers' leaves were the most effective in curing the multiple stomach aches I'd obtained. They had an intense but enjoyable smell. A creature flew above while I inspected the flower. I could see his wide feathered wingspan through the pockets of space in the canopy. His long golden-furred tail whipped back and forth aggressively, and his front talons carried a flailing fish. Water still dripped from the poor shark.

The more trails I needed to mark, the more designs I needed to create. I ended up capturing the likeness of the creatures I had seen. The trail to the radishes I marked with a crude drawing of the rabbit. As for the mushrooms, I drew the man. I wondered if that would make him laugh or anger him. Either way I found it fitting, for it helped me remember which trail to follow. Despite that the mushrooms we had eaten before made us ill, I did find some of different color that didn't do anything but taste good. I was sure I could get him to try again with different ones. Though after

carving my markings into the trees' sides, I realized I didn't need them. My nose did most of the work.

My stocking and organizing complete, I decided to pass the time floating along the surface of the pond. As the current nudged me in tiny circles, I looked upward at the night sky. Gazing up at the beauty of the twinkling lights made me wonder if they saw the horrors that befell Earth, and what they thought of it.

Of course, there was beauty too, but the carnage that happened daily was hard to adjust to. It took place even within the smallest of creatures. During my mushroom gathering, I uncovered the spot where the man found the spider. Her home was covered in sticky webbing; several insects had been caught in it. Unable to further investigate without risking being caught myself, I observed.

I watched as a beautiful butterfly with scarlet wings flew by my head and landed within the webbing. As soon as the spiders sensed the movement on their self-made trap, they attacked, one wrapping the poor creature in the sticky substance and the other tearing off pieces of the butterfly's wing to eat. It seemed that the nature residing in this realm had a certain order, circling until it came back around again. *Were we a part of that order?*

I was ripped away from my contemplations when the man jumped into the water with a loud splash. He hollered cheerfully and soaked me in his triumphant dive. My companion must have been successful in his… studies. Returning to the surface he shouted, "I have done it! Come see." Reluctantly I waded through the waterfall until I reached his whereabouts on the shoreline.

"Okay, what do you want to show me?" I grumbled.

"Oh, don't be so glum. You'll be happy to know that I spared no effort to use every part of the creature. It was a slow and grievous task, but I think I understand a bit more about the animals," he said triumphantly. For a moment I was excited to hear that he attempted to understand them. But

reality dawned on me, and I realized he spoke of their innards and how they could help us rather than how we could help them.

"And what is that?" I questioned. I lifted myself up and onto the shore's night-chilled grass to see better. A giant folded leaf was resting there. He must have found the sunflowers. That made me smile. The man opened the leaf to reveal a pile of fur, blood, meat chunks, and parts unknown to me. My smile disappeared. The odor that wafted up to me was rancid. Still, my mouth watered.

The man explained, "I was able to peel the fur and skin off without problem, and once the meat was removed, I found several different parts. Each one seemed to have a purpose to the rabbit's functioning."

The overly curious man sat down next to the pile of innards. "I tried to eat bits of the insides to see if they satisfied me, but it was the mushrooms all over again." He winced at the memory. "Though I did find these hard, pale sticks within. I used one in place of the rock, and it worked much better."

As I peered at the remains of the rabbit, the names of the pieces came to me, and I said, "The bones you mean? I suppose they can be useful." Blue irises glanced at me in agreement.

Once we finished discussing the different purposes for each part we went to work. I gathered the fur and bones and did my best to wash the blood out of the milky coloring. I wasn't able to remove it all, but the results were better than before. The man wrapped the fresh meat in a new leaf and stored them away next to my own findings.

Finding no use for most of the innards, the man tossed the pieces in the water for the fish to devour. This made me turn away and concentrate on other things like hanging the fur on the branch next to the hammock I had made for the fruits. I had hung my supply from a strong leaf in the air, and out of range of the little critters I found stealing my newfound supplies.

As I laid the stained bones onto the grass to dry, I felt a brush of skin against my arm. I looked up to find the man standing dangerously close to

me. The man's golden hair had turned white against the light of the moon, and his ice-blue eyes darkened upon seeing my close proximity. My stomach knotted in anticipation for something I was unaware of. He stiffened, but I moved closer. We stood face to face. My shaky hand rose to trace the outline of his delicate facial features, the curve of his shoulders, and the feel of his hard stomach.

I was entranced and a bit lost in the new emotion that overwhelmed me. But I woke from it with a start when he went to reach for me. The image of the saber-toothed cat's neck being twisted back, his hold on the rabbit's feet as its tiny form dangled helplessly from his strong grasp, and a new image intruded my thoughts. One where those same strong hands grabbed hold of my small neck and crushed it slowly in his palms.

I stepped away just before his blood-stained hand reached my neck. My abrupt departure confused him, but he didn't move to stop me. I hid my shaky hands behind my back, though they shook for a completely different reason now. The man was about to say something when I interrupted, "Do you think we look the same underneath as well?"

"What?" he asked dazedly.

"The same as the animals I mean."

Recovering himself, he explained, "I was curious about that, as well. I cut myself to see, and it wasn't the liquid that came out of the other creatures. It was more like the sand that lies at the bottom of the pond, but red. We have bones and muscles that are similar though." He paused a moment. "It hurt quite a bit, but the wound healed quickly. Actually, I had to keep reopening the wounds I gave myself to keep going deeper." He looked embarrassed while he explained, as if it was wrong of him to test the theory, but I would have done the same if he hadn't.

I was glad the change of topic distracted him from the mysterious moment we had. "Yes, my wounds healed quickly from the night we met," I recalled. "Still, I didn't get a very good look at the inside." As I considered

this, the man grabbed the mutilated bone that I had just cleaned from the ground and sliced my forearm open.

"Why? I could have done that!" I complained, holding my injured arm. The fear from before wasn't there as I expected it to be; anger had replaced it.

"You would have taken forever considering if it was worth the pain. We would have been here for days. Besides, it heals fast." Breaking my glare at him, I studied my arm. Red sand poured out of the opening at great speed. The red particles mesmerized me. It was billions of tiny granules of blood-colored sand. Each with its own unique shimmer.

Not soon enough I realized the wound wasn't closing. Panicking, I forced the cut closed with my free hand, but the pressure behind the injury was too much and bursting at the seams. I didn't know what to do. I just stood there watching as the life flowed from me to the ground. The man grabbed the rabbit's fur from the branch and wrapped it around my arm, sealing the wound within its clutch. He had tied the fur so tight around my forearm that I couldn't even feel my hand anymore. It seemed to work, though, because the sand stopped flowing.

"Apparently you don't heal quickly," he said, still holding my injured arm.

"No, I do, because whenever I get scratched by the bushes or branches the wounds disappear almost instantly," I said. There must have been another reason why this wound wasn't healing.

We stood there silently speculating for several minutes before the man said, "Maybe it's because I'm the one who cut you."

Rattled by the notion, I muttered, "Maybe." There was only one way to test the theory. I took the jagged bone that he had dropped, grabbed his muscled limb, and lightly scratched his forearm. If he was wrong, then it would have been mere seconds before the small wound healed.

The scratch continued to leak shimmering sand particles.

"You were right," I whispered. It disheartened me to know that there was someone who could cause me such permanent harm. Though he didn't seem worried. We looked each other in the eye and promised to take extra care around one another to ensure no accidents would happen.

Still, my stomach churned.

IV
Lost

Losing yourself to another is a most tempting instinct.
-A

10 Years Later

"Where are you going?" the man asked as I glided through the dense undergrowth.

"Where do you think?" I answered bitterly. My human companion and I had been searching non-stop for others of our kind. We explored all the directions available to us. The white tree I visited often, as we discovered, was the center of one giant landmass surrounded by water—a lot of it—in which we swam, but of course found nothing but more of it.

On our explorations we learned that we were much more powerful than our neighboring creatures, even the fiercest of predators. The man felt it was important to test our limits, but I was too afraid of harming the land or those that dwelled on it. So he did it for us, to my dismay. Our speed, strength, and senses were unrivaled. We were terrors upon the land we dwelled in.

I tried to move as delicately as the breeze through the trees, so much that there would be no trace of me left behind. That was all I asked for.

It became clear to me soon after we were brought into existence that we didn't belong here. Everything was too fragile. Too soft. *Too vulnerable.*

"I think that we need a break. We've been running for days now," the man said forcefully. When he said to stop, we stopped. When he said to run, we ran. There was no arguing with him and there was no persuading him. His overwhelming, superior presence snuffed out any light I could conjure for myself, and I found that I bent to his will because of it.

"Fine," I submitted. It was easier than fighting him. It was better than being miserable.

I stopped just short of a river where we could rest. I halted my long, delicate strides so my feet came to rest atop the moist moss beneath. The man swung from a thick tree limb, flipped in the air, and landed on the beaver's barely stable dam along the water. The tree limb was crushed within his grasp, he startled a passing bird, and destroyed the beaver's home upon landing. All this destruction happened in a mere blink of an eye, and simply because he was passing by.

The time with my companion had shown me his complete disregard for the life around him. We were more powerful, and he was vastly aware of it. And very happy in his realm of dominance. It wasn't as if he went around torturing innocent critters for amusement, but he didn't care for them either. The man reminded me of a tiger when it chased and devoured a deer. There was no malice, just simple instinct to consume. When he crushed tree limbs and obliterated homes, it wasn't because he enjoyed it. It was because he lived by a very simple rule: only the strong survive. *Nature seemed to agree with his hypothesis.*

What he wouldn't realize is that we *were* different, yet he was the one who pointed this out to me when he gave me my name. We didn't live purely on instinct. That was the reason he found me weak. He hadn't said as much, but I could see it in the way he looked at me. The man didn't see a challenge or a rival predator. He saw a weak-minded being

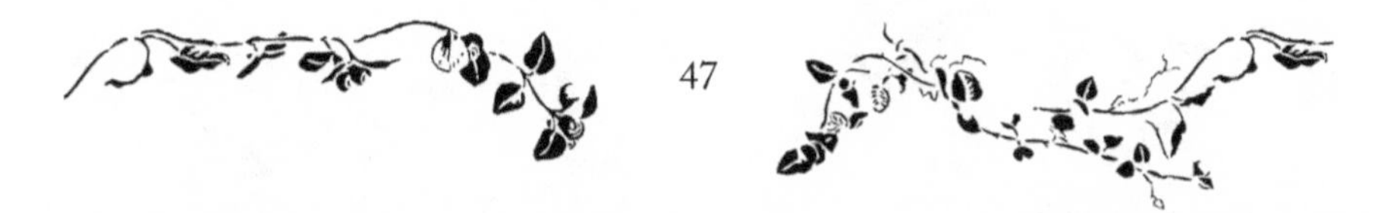

whom he had to care for. And yet, a predator wouldn't care for a weakling, would it?

The beavers barked at him in anger. The man yelled back territorially, and they swam away in terror. He laughed, mocking them.

"Don't laugh at them," I said quietly.

An irritated look crossed his face in the reflection of the water, but he twisted it into an apologetic one by the time he faced me. "Sorry," he grunted.

"It's okay." At least he attempted to look remorseful.

Seeing my troubled expression, he wrapped me in his comforting arms. It was easy to forget his aggressive nature when he did this. I felt safe and wanted. I felt loved—something that was unique to us as humans, or perhaps it was unique to me.

My companion released me reluctantly to say, "I'm going to find us some food. You get the fire started." And he was off to terrorize the creatures of the woodland once again, spear in hand. I appreciated that he said "find" food rather than "hunt" food. It showed that he cared for me, if only a little.

Unable to bring myself to steal the beavers' hard work, I ripped some dry branches from the nearest tree to burn. The guilt nearly crushed me every time I did so. The weather was pleasant enough, but why endure the chill when we didn't have to? The man made that point to me regularly. At least the tree could regrow its limbs, unlike the animals the man hunted.

They only had one life.

I gathered the dismembered wood into a small pile a short distance from the water's edge. I took two dry river rocks and brought them together aggressively, over and over again. It took six different rocks before I could light a spark without crushing the stones in my palms, but my labor soon produced the warmth we wanted.

I remembered the first time we discovered fire. There had been a rainstorm, which was normal; water was good. What wasn't normal were the angry sounds from above and the lights that lashed out toward us. The

lightning struck the tree I had been cowering in. I was cold despite the furs the man had made me wear, and he was gone hunting. Upon impact, the tree lit like the sun. The red waves burned hot and scorched my skin. Terrified, I remained paralyzed and was burning along with the innocent tree.

That was when my companion found me and pulled me out of my fiery prison. I could have done it easily myself, but I chose not to. Whether it was fear for myself or the tree, I didn't know. Either way I had been weak. The rains drowned the wicked flames soon, though, and we were able to mimic it later with rocks, striking them together like the lightning had struck the tree. The man's idea. I had wanted nothing to do with something that caused so much pain.

The present flames brought me from my reverie, and I stared into them. The reddish hues reminded me of the sunset, not the sunrise. There was something darker about the fire we created, something that exuded finality. I didn't like the color red. It was too aggressive. Dangerous even. But red was what animated us, and what flowed through the rest of the creatures that lived on Earth. *It was a part of us.*

The heavy sliding of footsteps brought me to my feet. A moss-colored, heavily scaled tail thumped the ground aggressively, splashing the angry current. Black beady eyes challenged me from the water's edge, only an arm's length from where I stood.

I kept our eye contact, but kneeled on the sharp, water-beaten rocks. I knew I should have been worried about her bite, but I wasn't. I needed to make her leave before the man returned and made her his meal.

I stretched my hand out to her snout to calm the enraged creature. I had done it several times before; most attacked, but still the option of peace was always given to them. The reptile's tail had stopped thumping. Right as I thought this one was going to choose the better option, her muscles tensed, and she struck.

The crocodile's jaw gripped my arm and started pulling me into the

water where she had the advantage. Saddened by the act, I grabbed hold of her lower jaw with my free hand and yanked it down; it didn't take that much effort. The crocodile roared in pain and backed quickly into the water, her jaw hanging loose. I had used too much force, and I cursed myself for it.

I saw the last of the reptile's tail disappear around the river's bend just as the man came marching through the tree line, a kill in one hand and my dinner in the other. The wounds from the crocodile had already healed, and my lost sand granules were kicked into the water, where they disappeared with the injured creature.

The man tossed me the scrumptious fruit and kneeled down with his meal. "Gets easier every time," he muttered. He lifted his head and sniffed, but finding nothing out of the ordinary, continued on to his bloody task. My companion turned his back to me, hiding the carnage of his bone-blade against warm flesh.

Downing the mango, I offered, "Let me help."

Laughing, he rebutted, "No. You can't handle it."

It was time I did. I hadn't realized until the crocodile bit me, but my wish for peace was a losing battle. Time and time again I tried. But nature was cruel and wanted only to fight, no matter the purpose behind it. *No matter what I wanted.*

Frustrated at his disregard for me, I argued, "Yes, I can. Now face me like the man you claim to be and show me how it's done."

The man's laughing ceased and was replaced with surprise. I had fought him when we first woke. Neither of us knew what to do in this new life, and we were on equal footing. But his willingness to hunt and learn about himself overtook my want to care for everything else.

His ignorance had become confidence.

My ignorance had become fear.

Turning, he handed me the sharpened tool and said, "Finally ready then?"

Stubbornly, I replied, "I have been ready. I just wanted you to do all the work is all."

Smiling, the man retorted, "Deceitful as ever, I see. Punishing me for something I didn't know I did? It's the mushrooms all over again."

"Of course. How could you think otherwise?" We laughed and enjoyed our time together despite the feeling of warm blood on my hands. It was a rare occasion. It was the first time we had really opened up to each other, and it was the first time I thought that maybe he didn't see me as weak.

"Lilith, are you ready to go home? There's nothing out here," the man said as we lay awake looking up at the stars. The moon was a thin slice of pale light.

"We haven't checked everywhere. We can't be the only ones." We had checked everywhere. Several times.

I had said those two lines many times before, but never had he said, "But what if we are?"

Startled by the abrupt realization, I stiffened. But maybe it wasn't as abrupt as I thought it was. Subconsciously I had been prepared for that answer. I had been prepared to accept our loneliness. But now that it was here, I didn't know how to react. I nodded in acknowledgment, unable to speak.

"Would it be so terrible if it was just us?" he asked.

Would it? Just the man and me. I really did need to give him a name, but still none came to mind.

"Lilith, I know it's been hard for you, adapting to this life. You have such a caring nature. It keeps you from making tough decisions. That's why I've done it for you." His choice of topic surprised me. We decided long ago that voicing our troubles to one another was a bad idea. It only led to fighting. *But quieting my voice had only made me unhappy.* "Today, you showed me that you can make those decisions..." the man stumbled through his sentence. It was unlike him to be so timid. So nervous.

"What are you trying to say?" I asked gently.

Frustrated, he blurted out, "I want us to be together."

Confused, I stated, "But we are together. *All* the time."

"Yes, but I want more…"

"More what?" *Was he talking about love?* He couldn't have. I had already decided that was something completely unique to me. Any hope that ever blossomed was quickly squashed by his disappointment in me over the years.

Vexed with my lack of understanding he roared, "I want more of you!" Unable to form the words he wanted, he leaned over and placed his lips against mine. My eyes closed instinctually, and my lips parted, welcoming the embrace. The emotion that overwhelmed me was completely new and confusing. I wanted more, but I didn't know why. He held himself above me on his elbows, unsure of the embrace.

I wasn't.

I pushed him off of me and he collapsed onto his back. The man's expression was hurt from my rejection, but the wounded look disappeared when I climbed on top of him. I straddled his waist. The fur from his covering tickled my thighs. I leaned down to him and deepened the kiss that he initiated. The passing thoughts I had over the years returned to the forefront of my mind. The times when I wondered if we should be doing what the animals were: mating and creating offspring. The times I suppressed the desires my body naturally hungered for.

We had spent so long searching for other humans that we hadn't taken the time to look at each other. I had been obsessing about the life around me instead of enjoying my own, and I was ashamed to say that he had frightened me. But he had never given me reason to do so. He was a threat to nature. *Not me.* That was most likely the reason he hadn't said anything before. He didn't want a weak, frightened mate. And I wouldn't be.

Our movements were natural. Instinct drove me to mate. To love. I needed him and he needed me. But the human side of me that rationalized wouldn't quiet. "Wait," I panted. He had rolled me onto my back again. Apparently he didn't like being underneath me.

"Why?" he breathed in my ear.

Shivering, I answered, "I don't want to do this here." Yes I did.

Wounded once again, he said, "What? You don't want..." The man was more sensitive than he led me to believe. It was endearing, and I loved him more for it.

"I didn't say I don't want to. I said I don't want to do it here." Smiling, I said, "I want to go home." Despite his wariness, he was delighted at my explanation.

It answered more than one question.

Kissing me once more, he said, "Let's go then."

We ran as fast as we could through the woodland. I didn't even care as I squashed some flowers in my haste. One thing was all I could think about the entire night that it took us to return to our home. Our hands were twined as we leapt across rivers and ran across vast plains. Closing in on the waterfall, he swept me off my feet so he could carry me in his arms, completely unable to remove his hands from me. *How had we gone so long without this?*

My mind had been lost in an ocean of obsession and self-loathing. He had freed me from it. I could only hope that I had freed him from his own ailments. We reached the waterfall in record time. The new motivation had increased our already high speed.

The man stood at the water's edge and our lips refused to part. I could feel his happiness spread and nurture my own. He set me down on my feet so he could crush me closer to him. I was barely able to breathe yet I wanted to be closer; he was the only air I needed. Then his touch became gentle. It sent shivers up and down my spine, and unfamiliar parts of me tingled. His tentative movements comforted me. The man was as naïve as I was. This was new territory for both of us.

I slowly turned us so that his back faced the pond. The hands that

had been exploring him halted their progress and rested on his chest. But I couldn't find the will to remove my lips from his; they were soft and warm. They beckoned me toward the light that was this man.

"Why did you stop?" he asked against my greedy mouth. Then I remembered. I pushed him abruptly into the water below. It wasn't a hard shove, just a firm nudge. His confused expression made me laugh as he fell. He resurfaced and shouted, "What was that for?" It was clear he didn't know how to react. His expression was a mixture of hurt and anger.

"You know you are more sensitive than you let on?" I teased. I stood over him at the water's edge, doing my best to hide the humor in my tone.

"No, I'm not." His jaw set stubbornly in protest. "I just live with a creature whose purpose is to torment me." I tormented *him*?

Going along with his theory, I said, "That may be so, but have you ever considered that you torment me, too?"

He scoffed in disbelief. Usually his stubbornness would be irritating, but at the moment I found it charming. "Are you going to tell me why you pushed me in here…at a very inopportune time I might add." It was his turn to be irritated with me; he didn't seem to find it endearing, though.

Determined in my goal, I said, "Yes. Ever since we woke in this world, you have been nothing but frustrating. You constantly order me around. And I am done with it." My tough façade shattered at the bewildered expression on his face. I looked away. "Or maybe it's just because you stink and needed to wash." I had much more to say but couldn't find the strength to express the words.

Understanding, he said, "Well, if the all mighty queen wants me clean, she'd better come do it herself." I looked at him skeptically. "That wasn't an order. It was a request."

I knew he had heard me then. He knew I wanted more, and I breathed a sigh of relief. Still, I was abashed by the new word he had created for me, so I sat and turned my head away from him. He swam up to me, close

enough to touch. Though I couldn't see him, I felt him immediately. The void in my chest was filled and bursting at the seams from his mere presence. He ran his wet fingers down my bare leg, leaving a trail of raised skin. "I think it's time you join me. I'm not the only one who needs to wash." Unable to escape in time, he pulled me in after him. But instead of drenching me, he held me close.

The sky was brightening from a pitch black to a sapphire blue. The temperature rose with the sun, and I could feel it in the water where I stood. All the words I said and had failed to say were there in his eyes. *He heard me.* He knew I wasn't happy with the way things were, and they needed to change if we were going to be together. But I had to change, too; my instinct to care had been nothing but a weakness and a blockade to our relationship.

The birds sang cheerfully in the emerald canopy. The sun rose over the snowy mountain peaks in the far distance. It warmed our skin and fed our desires. The fur coverings were no longer needed. The facades were no longer wanted. Our two halves became whole. Yet, I couldn't help but feel a strange sense of grief anyway.

V

The Seductiveness of Lies

Stay or leave the cage,
so long as you have the key.
-A

The air was chilled with the coming of night. My shivers were no longer pleasant, and I was swathed in darkness. The man was absent. Assuming he had gone to hunt, I continued to lie in the moist grass. The moon was bigger than last night; it was time for it to grow once again.

I recalled a passing thought right before I fell asleep in the man's reassuring arms. I had created a name for him. *What was it?* Finally, after so long of trying, I had one. And I couldn't remember. I felt like something was blocking my vision. Like something was keeping me from seeing.

That's when I realized there *was* something blocking my sight. Or at least adding to it. There was so much. There were so many colors that I had failed to see upon opening my eyes. They slowly formed in my vision, lines upon lines connected to one another. I slowly stood and scrutinized the scene around me.

Like the language that came to my mind, this knowledge was also given. The new lights I saw reminded me greatly of the stars and the infinite connections they made to one another. No one star was ever too far apart from the rest as to be disconnected. It could even be compared to

the intricate workings of a spider's web. All the threads led to one another, and each one shared its strength to help support the others, all in order to create the structure that it was. This was the same pattern I witnessed with my new eyes.

Everything from a single blade of grass to the bees that rested upon the flowers had a primary source and were in turn connected to those around it. Each source illuminated a different color, representing the soul within. The colors blended together as they touched and spread to the other, sharing and supporting each other with their own unique qualities. If I couldn't see it, I could feel it. The energy radiating from the worms below ground. I could see their tunnel patterns in my mind's eye. I could feel the roots of the trees growing slowly but surely beneath my feet.

My original theory had new meaning. Yes, there was an order to things and there was give and take of life, but I could finally see it clearly, the energy that all life shared. Energy, magic, aura, light, life force, spirit, soul: it had several names and several meanings. The sight brought tears to my eyes, clouding my new sight. I wiped the tears aggressively from my eyes. I needed to see. My obsession with the world was warranted after all. I was *right*. There was a greater purpose. There was a meaning. I just had to find it.

I sped off into the woodland. The plants and creatures were brand new to me. Even the dirt beneath my feet radiated energy. I spent my life alone. Seeing how every piece of the Earth connected gave me the hope that I wouldn't have to anymore. The man and I could be a part of something.

I frolicked through the trees. The nocturnal creatures stared at me in wonder as I passed by, probably because I was staring at them, too. The creatures of the day awoke and sounded in frustration at the disruption, but I didn't care. I soon found myself at the great apple tree's meadow, and it glowed in the night's dim light. I thought I saw a flash of white dash behind the even whiter trunk. But when I followed, there was nothing there. Just wistfulness it seemed.

I ignored my unhappy thoughts and tugged an apple from its home on the low branch. It was ripe and ready to be consumed. But I couldn't bring myself to do so. The white hue it exuded mesmerized me. I could feel its energy pulsating in my palm and into the tree it was birthed from.

I gingerly took a bite. Not only was my hunger satiated, but I could feel the power inside me grow. Each bite brought me closer to bliss. Soon the core was all that was left. The seeds fell into my hand, and I gazed at the lingering spirits. My euphoria diminished. The light that shone from the great tree dimmed, incrementally, but I noticed all the same. I tested my theory and downed another apple, taking care to pay attention to each bite.

The spirit dimmed again. I dropped the apple in disgust. But it wasn't the apple I was mortified at. It was me. *I* was causing the light to dim. For the first time since I woke with the new sight, I gazed upon my own soul. The light that emanated from me was a brilliant crimson. My hair was illuminated in its fire. I bent down to retrieve the dropped fruit and took another bite. My aura grew in brilliance as the apple's dimmed. My instincts had been right.

We weren't meant to be here.

It only took me a moment to notice why I didn't resemble the rest. Yes, I felt my own energy and saw its fiery hue, but there were no lines connecting me to that of the others. I was separate, disconnected. I had no place here. A lonely star. A thread of spider's silk that was doomed to hang alone on a branch, soon to fly away with the wind due to the lack of support from its peers. My tears of happiness turned into those of sadness, and I wept.

Panicking, I tore at the ground. I had to fix it. I placed the seeds in the moist earth, begging for the light to return. I covered and watered the seeds with my tears. The shared spirit of the Earth recovered slowly. I

assumed that meant I did something right. But the light brightened only slightly and not to the fullness it started with.

I had to tell the man what I discovered. I ran toward the waterfall. There, I could follow his scent. But I didn't have to retrace my steps. I crossed his path only minutes later. His scent trailed north, along with another creature's. I had to stop him. If what I thought was true, it was imperative that I find him before he completed his hunt.

I ran as stealthy as a cheetah and as quiet as a mouse through the foliage. As my feet bounced off the spongy moss, my mind reeled. The beauty that I saw before had turned sinister. The light haunted me as I chased my mate, taunting me with harsh words. *You don't belong. You don't belong.*

I pushed down the dark thoughts that threatened my sanity. I ran faster. *I had to find him before*— I heard a cry in the distance. A creature had been slain. I watched in horror as the surrounding light darkened, almost as if it was crying, too. It wasn't the same as the apple. This loss was more pronounced. Irreversible. The saddest part was that the natural creatures didn't even notice a change. They continued on with their lives as if nothing happened. They couldn't see the light like I could.

I walked the rest of the way.

I found my mate opening his prey with a knife. The black bear's flesh was fresh and steamed in the cold night air. The ripping of skin made me nauseated. The smell was even worse: partially digested fish.

My mate noticed me then. "What are you doing out here? I thought you would still be sleeping." His tone was suggestive, but I hardly noticed because of what I was seeing.

The bear's spirit left her physical form and the lines connecting her to her surroundings were snipped. I felt the pain of the forced separation, as if an appendage had been removed from the Earth's bodily spirit. The rosy soul lifted and absorbed into her killer's. The man's soul was as bright as the

sun. His golden light outshone everything around him, including my own scarlet hue. My soul was dull in comparison to his.

That fact brought a whole new wave of tears. They shed silently down my face as I compared our souls. I had always known he was better than me, but it still hurt now that I could physically see it. But as I looked closer, I realized that his was separate from the rest, too. We weren't even connected to each other.

"Want to help?" the man asked me cheerfully. Our intimate time together had gone a long way to improving his mood. Because of this, the man didn't notice my odd behavior. He was busy carving his trophy.

I turned and ran.

"Lilith! Where are you going?" he called after me. But I couldn't watch anymore.

Why had this happened to me? I was finally going to be happy. I was going to be with him. This new sight had obliterated any chance of that from happening. There was no possible way I could live the way he did if I had to watch the spirits die. How could I live *at all* in a world with so much pain?

I found our watering hole and dove in and under the waterfall. I hid behind the lazing rock, unsure of what to do. I felt panicked and helpless, much like the time lightning struck the innocent tree while I was still inside. What else *could* I do?

The fish swam around me anxiously as if they felt my despair. But even the safety of our waterfall couldn't shield me from the world's horror. A large, green, elongated fish darted swiftly to the rock's edge just in time to swallow a minnow whole. But instead of looking away in fright, I observed curiously. The spirits had been swallowed by our own souls when the man and I consumed. But it wasn't like that with the natural creatures. The light didn't dim. The killer didn't grow in power. The soul was immersed into the grand web. Everything shared. It was the circle of life.

They were not the ones who needed changing.

My panic ebbed, and I was able to pass the curtain of water to sit on the shore. I needed to explain this to the man. He would understand now that I had proof of my theory. *He had to.*

It took him longer to find me than I assumed. It wasn't until the sun rose that he entered the clearing. He set the wrapped meat in a dry patch of grass and strode over to where I sat dangling my feet in the rippling water.

"Why did you run from me?" he questioned.

"Why didn't you chase me? Isn't that what you do?" I retorted.

Wary, he responded, "Well, because I thought you didn't want that anymore."

I supposed I didn't. I needed to stop relying on him. I was stronger than I thought. Agreeing, I confirmed, "No, I suppose I don't."

"Was it the bear? I thought you were over this?" he questioned harshly.

"I thought I was. But I would have been only lying to myself despite what happened."

Confused, he urged, "And what happened?" I hated to ruin the progress we had made. It was wonderful, and I loved him. I wanted to be with him, but something greater was calling me.

"When I woke last night, I discovered that I could see."

"See what?"

Pausing briefly, I answered, "Everything." Instead of anxiously waiting his rescue, I had taken the time to observe. I watched the interactions of the natural world with new eyes and gained a new purpose from it. "I can see everything: how everything connects, where creatures go when they die, where they go when we kill them…"

I didn't have to look at him to know his face was twisted in frustration. "What are you talking about, woman! Didn't we discuss this yesterday? Things need to change if we are to continue on."

"Yes, they are," I agreed. He looked relieved until I stood and turned around. He saw something in my expression he never had before.

Determination.

"We are going to live differently. No more killing. We don't belong here. We don't have a right to take from it. Can't you see it, too?"

His confused demeanor said no. "Is this about us?" the man accused. My brows furrowed in confusion. "Because if you changed your mind, then just tell me. Don't make up more excuses to keep us apart."

I could not believe what I was hearing. "Us? This is bigger than us! How could you think that?"

"It's not hard to guess. It took this long for you to realize how I feel about you, and now you're spouting things that have nothing to do with us." He was getting angry. "I thought things were going to be different. Am I not enough for you?"

"Of course you are! I love you..." It was the first time I had spoken the words aloud. I didn't regret them, but they also confused me. If I loved him, why was I trying to change him? *Maybe there was something I loved more.*

The man closed the distance between us and gripped my face between his strong hands. "Then why are you doing this?" he whispered.

I didn't know how to answer. He didn't understand. I didn't understand. I removed his hands from my face and said, "I need time to think." I left him then. The hurt I caused was clear in his expression, but he quickly wiped it clean of weakness and set his jaw stubbornly.

The meadow where we woke was the only place he didn't come to, and his scent wasn't near enough to distract me. The breeze cleared my head of guilt and confusion. Now, what was I going to do with this new sight? Did I have to do anything? I knew the answer as soon as I asked it. *Yes.* I wouldn't be able to live with myself if I didn't.

What could I do? It seemed if I did anything I would be hurting someone else. The man was beside the point. He could handle himself;

he always had. My mere presence was harming the natural world, and despite my efforts, I'd come to love it. I respected how simplistic and wild they all were. None ever harmed the other out of malice or spite. They lived on instinct. None even knew that a choice for peace was possible. In turn that conundrum created its own version of peace. Everything gave and took in its own way. The natural world had perfect balance when left alone.

It begged the question, how did we even come to be in this land? Nothing that I saw with my new vision hinted at an answer. But if I was just now discovering this sight, perhaps there was more to find. But what would be the point? If I didn't have an answer now, I most likely wasn't meant to have one. I would only be wasting time searching for something that may not even exist. But that wouldn't stop me from trying.

There was one thing I could do, something that I had been prolonging. I doubted even my mate had attempted it. My fear was strong, but my determination was stronger. I needed to know why I was different. Why I was separate. If I was going to live a lonely existence, I needed to know why. I searched the meadow for the tool I needed. I then lay in the grass and stared up at the blue sky. I wanted it to be the stars, but I didn't feel like waiting. The key physical difference between us and the natural animals was the blood. I didn't have any; only crimson sand filled my veins. Though I had an aversion to cutting open creatures, I saw what pumped their blood. This aged, killed, and gave them life.

I took the pointed end of the rock and began to carve. The void in my chest filled when my mate was near, but I feared he was only a placeholder for what was actually supposed to lie inside. The pain was severe. A scream begged to be released from my lips, but I didn't want to alert him to what I was doing.

The muscles were finally weak enough for me to open the incision the rest of the way. I threw the rock and reached my shaking hand inside

my chest cavity. The sand felt rough and gritty against my skin. My furs were covered in the spilt dust. My hand roamed the opening, searching for the vital piece of life.

My hand closed over emptiness.

There was nothing there to pump blood, even if I had it. My chest was as it always felt: a hollow void of darkness. And my question was answered.

Part II
Sloth and Envy

It's easy to envy those who dominate

The ones who strike at your heart without regret

Who doesn't wish to be the strong instead of the weak?

But weak you are

Though why envy the dominator

When they haven't had the pleasure of being weak

Of knowing that it doesn't matter

Because the roles can reverse whenever the weak decides

To stand up and take on the role of strength

VI
Flicker of a Flame

We create our own
punishments.
-A

700 Years Later

I dashed through the undergrowth. I was following a group of cheetahs as they chased a separated wildebeest. Their speed was great, but not the fastest I'd seen. The cats had spotted and zeroed in on the unknowing creature. Typically, the hooved being would have a chance of surviving if it was just one predator chasing him. Cheetahs weren't very strong, and the wildebeest's hooves were a great defense. But his hunters had come together, fixed on a single goal. Chase and devour.

The long years had taught me much about the natural world and how to interact with them peacefully. And the most important thing I realized was that they were perfect the way they were: free. Free from the burdens that plagued me. Free from choices.

They belonged.

The coalition stopped in their tracks. My quick stride led me up the side of a tree, and I landed gracefully on a low hanging branch, watching as the three brothers paced back and forth restlessly. Something wasn't right. What could have caused them to forget their chase? The wildebeest had

been lucky today, but I couldn't say the same for the spotted cats. I listened for the heavy treading of a bear or the confident, lazy walk of a lion. But there was no sound at all, which was worse.

I heard it before I saw it. An elongated object tore through the air and penetrated one of the brothers. The sharpened stone peeked through the opposite side of the entry wound, and the cat collapsed. He died instantly. I doubted he felt any pain in his passing. It had been too swift, too accurate. The remaining two cats cried for their lost brother, then abandoned him to the superior predator that stalked them. Their sibling's sacrifice was the price for their freedom, and they took it.

The cat's once-diligent eyes stared at the moving brush where his executioner remained unseen. His eyes were glossy with death, and his spirit had already moved on to brighten his killer's aura. A small piece of the creature's soul was left behind as it always was, the residual energy that clung to the body it once inhabited. The leftover energy was what held the empty husk together. It was the price the soul paid for using the body, leaving a part of itself so its physical form could be consumed by another. Only upon consumption or decomposition would the remaining light join the rest. I could barely see the cheetah's residual spirit with how dim the glow was, but I could feel it.

"Didn't expect to see you here," I said, bored with the situation. The man emerged from the undergrowth. He was only seen when he wanted to be. But he couldn't hide his warm, earthy smell from the wind.

"The hunt takes me where it wants," the man responded, just as bored.

I reiterated as I had uncountable times, "Stay on your land. That's the only way this is going to work." *Why did he insist on fighting me?* It just made us that much more miserable. Not that we weren't already.

"You think this is working? That's funny." He didn't sound like he thought it was funny.

I sighed, "Fine, I will leave this time." I turned in the direction of the

waterfall. It was nearing sunset, though the clouds blocked out the sun's warm hues. I floated down to the mossy ground, my well-trained muscles only making the slightest impression.

The man quickly ran to block me. I could have darted ahead, but I let him stop me anyway. "Stay with me tonight," he demanded. I resisted his commands, but that didn't make it easy.

"You know why I can't." I pushed him gently aside, intending to leave before I gave in.

The man's tone became harsh. "Yes I do. And I'm asking anyway." He took the hand that still pushed against his chest.

My eyes wet with unshed tears, I repeated, "You know why I can't. We can't risk creating more of us. They would destroy this place, and us along with it." It could have been different, but he refused to believe me. Or he simply refused to accept responsibility for it.

I thought back to when I first received my new sight. I had finally accepted the violent life of the world and the fact that we needed to join it to survive. That day, the man and I had made love for the first time. And the last. I had been happy, finally. But something showed me I had no right to happiness when it came at the cost of everything else.

Alone in my discovery, I couldn't eat. I couldn't even drink. Everything I consumed disconnected from the natural world and absorbed into me, a selfish being with no other purpose than to destroy. I suffered for years. I thought I was finally going to die and be released from the existence I hated so much, but something about our anatomy wouldn't allow me to rest.

That's when it got worse. I was lying by a creek somewhere deep in the forest, away from my mate, when I discovered a new terrifying ability. I was staring at a blade of grass that rested in front of me; its only movement was from the wind that blew in and out of my lungs. I couldn't drink the water beside me, but it was comforting to listen to the light trickles that flowed downhill. My body was weak and frail. Muscles were no more, and

bones protruded painfully from my skin. My red hair no longer shone in the light, and my emerald eyes were deadened from sadness. The man wouldn't kill me, no matter how much I begged him at the time. But he wouldn't help me, either. My only choice was to exist.

My eyes lit for the first time in years when I saw it. My senses were awoken once again at the feel of magic coursing through my veins. My mind concentrated on the blade of grass. I watched as my weak crimson spirit surrounded the piece of greenery, shaping its form to my will. Then it was no longer small, green, or sharp. The soul now took the form of an apple, my favorite fruit. But it wouldn't have mattered what fruit it was, because I was starving and needed the sustenance. And there it was, taunting me.

My shaky hand took hold of the smooth fruit and bit down into its reddened skin. The juice ran down my chin, and the chewy chunks were forced down my throat. I hadn't eaten in several years, and my taste buds had not yet come alive. But the pain in my middle ebbed and my vision refocused.

I had lost my careful control. Control I thought I had honed. But this was proof of my weakness, and it was too late to turn back. I then realized what was different from before. I assumed the reason I didn't recognize the taste, and why I craved more of it, was because I had gone so long without eating. But I took a moment to inspect the apple. I raised it up in the air and into the light of the moon, seeing I had eaten the majority of it.

What I had mistaken for juice before was crimson, and what I had mistaken for cream-colored, soft insides were chewy and dark. Darkened pieces hung from the apple's innards, revealing their stringy texture, and its blood ran down my arm as I grasped it. I threw the abomination aside and crawled to the stream, desperate to remove the smut from me. I scrubbed my hands and arms roughly, and my unkempt nails cut into me. I looked down at the murky water and took in my reflection.

My hair was tangled and filthy. My once-rounded face was narrow, the sunken cheekbones hollow. My lips were dry and cracked and covered

in blackened blood from the apple. I looked dead. I supposed that was appropriate, because I felt dead. I reached into the water with a steadier hand. I cupped the cool liquid and washed the evidence from my mouth.

I knew at that moment in time that I was powerful. I could not only see the energy that flowed around me, but I could alter it. Whether it was my condition or the price I paid for the magic, my transformations weren't natural and weren't accurate. I was afraid, but the fear had never really left me anyway. I was used to the emotion by then.

"We don't have to have children," the man argued, interrupting the memory. "We can still be together. You didn't become pregnant the last time." *The only time,* I heard him say silently. The cheetahs were fast, but I could still hear their paws turning up the earth in their haste to escape.

"I can't risk that," I said quietly.

"Please," the man whispered. He pulled me close. I could feel his steady breath on my face, but still I refused to look at him. My mate asked me this question often, and every time it became harder to refuse him. I did love him after all.

We were a sliver apart. Our bodies yearned to touch. The scent he exuded was feral and made me want him that much more. I asked, my head spinning, "Do you believe me?" The man knew what I meant.

Hesitantly he answered, "Yes." My heart would have been pounding if I had one. But maybe if we had the beating organ, we wouldn't be fighting.

Surprised, I asked the next question. The most important one. "Are you willing to change for it?" I slid my arms up and around his neck. Our eyes locked and our lips parted in anticipation.

My mate answered, "No." His answer jerked me out of the lusty haze, and I let him go. He continued angrily, "This isn't worth it, Lilith. None of it."

Hurt, I turned away from him. He passed, careful not to touch any part of me, hoisted the dead cat atop his shoulder, and sprinted away. The

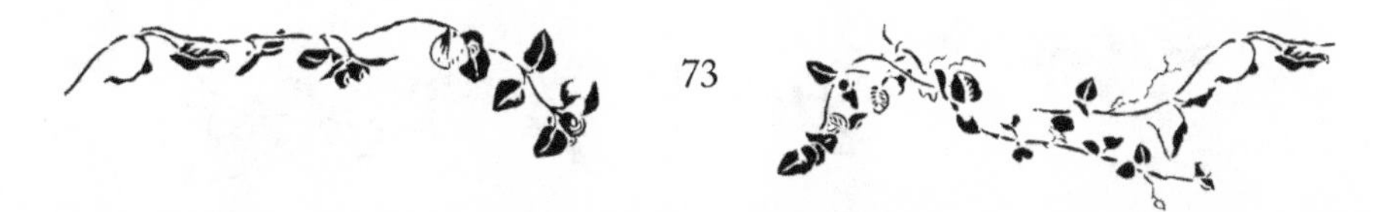

man's footsteps were quiet, but I could hear them as they ran north to his own land, past the waterfall that we shared. It divided our shared land, though we never roamed far from our watering hole. I continued to stare at the indent the cat's corpse had made in the spongy moss.

Keeping apart was best. There was no way to know when I would give in, but I would eventually. And that meant the end of Earth itself. Creating more beings like us would be catastrophic, especially with a mentor like him. I would be ignored, and my teachings outshined by his, because it was easier and pandered to the selfishness that defined us as humans. I had to fight that definition every day. But starving wasn't the answer. That kind of self-torture was behind me.

Unable to stare at the blood-soaked earth any longer, I ran the same direction he had. I slowed my pace so I wouldn't have to pass him. The cleansing water of the falls beckoned me. I needed to wash the feeling of disappointment and regret off. I passed the old apple tree, plucked a crimson fruit from its milky branches, and ate it quickly. I was careful to stash a glowing white seed in my rabbit-skin bag for safe keeping.

The ancient tree was and always would be beautiful. I could feel the magic that coursed through it better than anything else on this Earth. It was both calming and powerful, wise and fierce. Its roots would forever be embedded in the ground, feeding Earth's soul.

I could only think of one thing that could destroy it.

Despite our differences, the man shared his kill's furs and bones with me for warmth and tools. There was no need for them to go to waste, so long as I couldn't stop them from dying. I felt that I was honoring them by keeping a part of their physical form. And I always made sure to give the innards to a creature in need of food. Most weren't picky eaters.

I could have transformed the parts into something else with my unnatural magic, but from what I remembered of the meat-apple it was best to leave things in their natural form. I didn't have the right to change

the workings of nature anyway. I couldn't think of one being who did. But I had a feeling sacrifices would need to be made in the future.

The waterfall shimmered in the night's light. The sun had disappeared along with the clouds. I was grateful. I needed my steady companions to guide me tonight. Washing my tangled hair in the powerful stream, I gazed up at the unearthly lights, connecting patterns in my mind's eye. I saw a perching owl, a rabbit's feet, a horse's horns, and an elderly woman, at least what I thought an elderly woman would look like. What I would look like if time allowed it.

I floated on the pond's surface, ready to sleep in the soothing waves that the falls created. I was tired, though it wasn't possible for my body to be weary so long as it had nourishment. It was mental. My mind was tired from the sadness, the loneliness, the hate. Something needed to change. Soon. But how? I lifted my arm and looked at the elongated white scar on my forearm, the one the man had given me before he knew he could hurt me. It was the only thing that marred my smooth skin.

My lids closed, and I drifted into the freeing abyss of unconsciousness. At first I thought it would be a peaceful sleep, one free of images and worry. But that was too much to ask for. Out of the blackness came a white light. It glowed so bright it stung my eyes, but I couldn't find the will to look away. The light formed into the shape of a human. It called out, but the sound was unfamiliar.

Her hand raised and beckoned me closer. As I approached, her voice became clearer, but still I couldn't understand. The woman's mouth moved with the sounds, unable to relay her message. She didn't have any distinct features to reveal her identity; she was too bright. Finally I was close enough to reach out and take her outstretched hand. I hadn't realized how cold I was until I touched her. Upon my touch, her light dimmed. The once brilliant and enchanted spirit left her, and began its journey into my own crimson soul, warming me.

Panicked, I went to draw back, but my body had other plans. It gripped the woman's wrist firmly and sucked up more of her light. I absorbed it hungrily. My thirst wouldn't be quenched, and she was soon sucked dry of her light. But before I could see her face, the form crumbled. She collapsed into a pile of earth on the ground. I sank to my knees, but instead of feeling grief, I felt…strong. Flames licked where my heart should have been.

I woke with a shudder. I felt weightless. Untouchable. I thought I saw stars above me, but they were tiny beads of water. And then what I thought was rain were really delicate droplets suspended in the air, unmoving. I waved my hand through the ones above me. They rolled off my skin as if solid, but they left little wet trails behind.

I looked around for more strange rain and found myself staring at the peak of the waterfall. Confused, I looked down. The entire pond was suspended in the air, broken apart into small dewdrops. The fish floated in the air with me, completely unafraid and still able to breathe. Water continued to sustain them; it floated in and out of their gills as their fins swam to nowhere.

I was positioned with the horizon, just as I was when I fell asleep. Except now I was high in the air, floating with the water and fish. But I didn't feel scared like I should have. I knew I was the one doing this, and I knew I was now powerful enough to do what I had to. To change the fates that tortured me. I had the ability and now the resolve to make it happen. The energy that plagued my sight would listen and help me when I needed it. Selfishly, I reveled at the thought.

I prepared for the journey ahead. I wouldn't need much. Nature provided everything. What worried me was what I had to do beforehand. I hadn't attempted what I had in mind, and I was nervous about whether it was even possible. If it didn't work, all my hopes would be crushed, as well as the other part of my plan ruined. Although I could still leave if I wanted,

I wouldn't do that to him. Life was already lonely enough without me leaving, too. That's why I was going to make him a mate. One who would make him happy when I was gone. Someone to love and care for him since I could not. And last night was proof that I was powerful enough to do it.

We tried to make our relationship work for far too long, several lifetimes too long. We each had our own reasons for the way we lived, and I could accept that for now, but I refused to make it worse by having his children. The children who would literally suck the life from this planet. With us being separated from the circle of life and unable to contribute to it, that's what would happen.

The man's own spirit had become brighter. He was aiding his own selfish power and didn't care who it hurt. I aspired to substitute my needs in order to sustain the aura around us, but even with how disciplined I was, I still took. There was no way to replenish the water that I drank, and if I forgot to plant even one seed from the one fruit I took, the light diminished. Though incrementally so, it added up over time, and I didn't know what I would do when the planet's demise drew near, especially with the man speeding things up with his way of life.

That was why I needed to leave. I grew weaker every day I was near him. Eventually I would succumb and have his children. I couldn't prolong it any longer. I would travel as far south as I could. Far away from *him*.

I stopped and thought how life with him would be wonderful. I could just surrender to what he wanted and forget the rest. I could be happy being with him, but watching the life around us die would make me miserable and want to die along with it. I had to choose nature over him, and that meant sacrificing a part of myself and letting him go.

My love.

My very own ray of light.

Lucifer.

I chuckled to myself while I gathered my things. It took me long enough to think of a name; how fitting it was that it was at the end of us. I didn't get to enjoy calling him by his new name, and he wouldn't enjoy hearing it from me for more than today. I had to act out my plan quickly. I didn't want to give him too much time to think on what I was doing. I didn't want to give him a chance to stop me. And I didn't want to give myself a chance to stay.

I abruptly collapsed to the ground, dropping everything that was in my arms. I just sat there within my scattered supplies, crying. Crying for the life I was giving up. It hadn't been a very happy one, but the option was always there. To change my mind and pick him. It seemed I was taking that choice away from myself. The pain that came from that realization hurt worse than anything else I would ever experience.

Why was I the one who had to make a choice? Why did I have to be the one in agony? He never wavered or questioned his side. He was always so sure of himself. As much as I had come to hate that about him, I was also very envious of it. How nice it must have been to be completely sure of one's decisions. Well, I was finally making mine. I chose to save our home and the creatures in it the best way I could. I was giving a life with Lucifer away to do the right thing.

I continued to sit on the grass crying. There was no end to the tears. They kept flowing like the waterfall beside me, flowing over the edge of the cliff into the pond below. Perhaps if I cried enough, I would make my own sunlit pond, with the light glittering off the gentle ripples and the colorful fish swimming lazily below the surface. However, if I had the power to do that, I would have the answers I longed for.

I was inwardly bombarding myself with threats so I would get up and move when a pair of large muscular arms came from behind and wrapped themselves around me. The feeling of those arms felt so good and yet so horrible. Good, because my favorite thing in the whole world was to be

held by this man, Lucifer; bad, because of what I was going to have to tell that man. The knowledge of the pain to come caused more tears to spill out of me, adding to my personal pool of water. Too bad there were no actual fish to distract me in my pool. *Just emptiness.*

Lucifer held me until I was able to shut off my fall of tears and look up at him. He sat behind me, his head rested on my shoulder, and his arms were wrapped firmly around my waist. I enjoyed the moment a few seconds more before I turned around in his arms to face him. I opened my mouth to speak, but the look in his eyes stopped me.

They were so sad, mournful even. I had never seen that look on him before, but seeing my expression, he smiled, a small, sad, knowing smile. One that was meant to reassure me, but only made the pain inside worse. I made my decision. I was going to leave him. That would make him happy, and I wouldn't have to keep fighting my desire for him. Though, I hadn't left yet. *Couldn't I give in just once?* Just be happy once before my life of complete loneliness began?

Unsure, I moved close enough to feel his breath on my face. Lucifer's scent of sunshine overwhelmed my senses and drew me to him. I fought against the instinct and began to pull back when he closed the small gap between us. The man's hands grabbed my face and brought me to his. Lucifer's lips were eager and moved with passion against mine; passion that had been neglected over the long years. He lifted me so I straddled him, which surprised me, because he hadn't wanted me on top the last time. Perhaps it was his way of compromising and letting me have my way for once. It felt nice to be given something even as small as that. I felt Lucifer's smile against my lips as I let out a gasp of astonishment at his actions.

Our kiss grew desperate. My addiction to him needed to be satisfied. I needed to be closer. We were making up for all the time apart and all the fights we'd had. With each touch, they were forgotten and released. I ran my hands down the solid curves of his chest and stomach. Lucifer was

perfection, and I wanted to be a part of him. His hands gripped my hips hard and moved me against him. It had been so long since I felt his touch, but too soon he moved to fill me. This brought me back to sad reality. My legs locked him in place, so he was unable to move. I gave him one last kiss on his beautiful lips and slid off his lap onto the grass beside him. Lucifer didn't try to stop me as he had many times before. He just laid there with me, not saying anything.

"I'm sorry, Lucifer," I whispered. Though I wanted to, if he was to love me fully then I wouldn't have been able to stop myself, and then what I most feared would happen. Children. Children he would teach his ways, who would have our unfortunate disposition. It was best not to go that far, even now.

"Me, too," he whispered back. He turned his head toward me and questioned, "Lucifer, huh? Does that mean you have finally named me?"

"Yes. It means 'bringer of light.'" Though he already knew that. "I thought it fitting since you are the sun in my life. The light to my darkness. You don't have to use it. I know it took me a long time to create it, and I am sorry. My indecisiveness is a curse, and you've been the one to suffer from it."

The tears ran noiselessly down my face as I admitted this. What I said was true, and I refused to make him suffer any more for my hesitancy. I needed to tell him before I lost my nerve.

I turned my head to look at him. Lucifer was already staring in my direction. The love was clear in his eyes, and the lust leftover from our encounter was still visible. I closed my eyes. If I looked at him it would make it even harder to say. "Lucifer"—I loved the sound of his name on my tongue—"I need to tell you something. I've made another decision. One I've been avoiding." I tried looking at him again, and my throat locked up. I couldn't do it. Seeing my struggle, he laced his fingers through mine and squeezed gently, encouraging me to go on. There was hope in his eyes,

almost happy anticipation. Maybe he knew what I was going to say and was relieved to finally be rid of the constant nuisance in his life. Lucifer was happy to be freed of me.

I forced my eyes shut and said, "I am leaving. What we have together isn't working, and I think we will both be happier if I am gone. But don't worry, you are not going to be alone. I am going to make you a partner, and she will make you happy, because I know I can't." What I said wasn't completely true, but he would most certainly be happy if I was gone, even if I was alone in a strange new place far away from here. I waited for a response to my decision. I kept my eyes closed because I didn't want to see the joy that would surely be in his eyes as I said this. It would hurt too much.

He didn't respond, and I was worried that he hadn't heard me. Minutes passed before I let my eyelids open. But once I did, I regretted it. Lucifer was still looking at me, but all signs of love were gone and were now replaced with fury. Startled, I forced my hand out of his tight grip and backed away a few steps; he didn't move to stop me.

"Did you hear me?" I asked nervously.

Slowly he stood, glaring at me while he replied, "Yes, of course I heard you." The venom in his voice was like a punch in the face. Why was he so angry? He must have misheard me.

"Are you sure? I said I am going to leave you a mate. You won't be alone anymore. She will make you happier than I ever could," I said again as I stood to face him.

"Oh, yes. I heard that part. And you think that would make me happy?" he spat. In all the years of fighting with him, this was the angriest I'd seen him. It made me worried for my life. Except I wasn't as frightened as I once had been.

"Of course that would make you happy! Why would it not? I'll never be able to give you what you want! Don't you want children? A partner to be with whenever you want? Someone who doesn't reject you like I do?

Why are you so angry?" I was so confused. Where was the downside in this deal for him?

"I am *angry* because I thought you were finally going to give up this pointless fight of yours and finally be with me! But it seems that's not the case. You've just gone crazy! And yes, I want those things! But I want *you* to bear my children. I want *you* to make me happy. And if I can't have that I'd rather continue on with the way things are than be with someone else. Don't you see that?" he shouted at me. His hands shook. "I love you, Lilith," he said quietly, so that I nearly didn't hear it. His words broke me. I never knew that he cared so much for me. I had always thought I was a means to an end, someone to create his children and care for his needs, not someone he loved and cared for. Lucifer had failed to say those three words to me until now. Perhaps if he had said them before, things would have been different.

"If you love me, then why do you continue to live the way you do? I've told you before, the light I see diminishes with every kill, with every pluck of the fruit even. If you love me, then why not change your ways?" I cried. It didn't make sense. Why fight me if he cared so much?

"Do you love me?" he asked simply.

"You know I do," I whispered.

"Then why not change your ways for me?" That made my tears stop streaming. I understood then. "I have reasons for living the way I do, too. I don't do it out of spite for you. I just can't accept some invisible thing dictating my life and how I should live it. I won't give up my pride because of things that are uncertain and may not even pertain to us. Do you really not see my side of this?" he begged. Lucifer closed the distance between us. He wrapped one arm around my waist, and one hand brushed the hair from my eyes and held my cheek. My mate's gaze locked with mine, hoping to find some understanding or resignation to his argument.

He found none.

"I'm sorry, Lilith, but I won't give up my freedom. Not even for you." Those words cut deep. They made me want to cry again, but all that was left was emptiness. I didn't feel anything. Though he was standing right in front of me, touching me even, my chest was empty. Lucifer was my heart, and he couldn't make it beat anymore. He had nothing to fill it with. All that remained was a black hole that sucked me inward, hopefully into oblivion where I wouldn't be able to feel ever again.

Lucifer didn't notice the change in my eyes, so he continued to hold me until I finally removed his hands from my body and walked over to my scattered supplies. He didn't say a word while I gathered them; he just watched me as I moved about. Once I collected what I needed into my bag, I stood and looked at him expectantly. Realization dawned and he spat, "No." He stalked off into the undergrowth, taking trees down along his path. He would come back, and I would be ready when he did. Lucifer's words had given me the strength I needed and the confirmation that I was doing the right thing.

I called out to the animals I wanted. I learned and memorized the sounds of each creature, so I could communicate with them better; they responded quickly. A male monkey and a female snake—I chose these animals due to their characteristics. The monkey not only for being physically the most similar to us, but for his wisdom, generosity, and hilarity. The snake I chose for her intelligence, cunning, and seductiveness.

I believed that these traits together would make a great partner for Lucifer, hopefully making him happy for however long she could, and bear children for him, if possible. I was unsure if my new creation would be able to procreate with him, but if she could, then the children, no matter what they were taught, should be part of the great web connecting Earth's creatures.

Though she would look like one of us, she would ultimately stem from the animal she once was, thus pleasing him as well as keeping Earth's spirit bright. Everyone would win. Except me. I would lose Lucifer. The

feelings of loss and regret were clawing their way back to the surface, and a single tear ran down my cheek. Realizing this, I shoved those emotions back down into the abyss to deal with at a later time.

I began my spell; I found speaking out loud helped me concentrate on what I was trying to accomplish. I felt the energies in and around the two animals and the web that tied them to each other. I concentrated on the web line between them, bringing their energies closer and closer together. Reaching one another, their forms began to morph, and I said to them:

Thank you for your sacrifice
You will now become something different
Something more
A being of beauty and intelligence and generosity
You will be a mate
A mother
A brand new being on this Earth
You will be Eve

The words empowered my magic, and the creatures lifted into the air, twisting around one another as they did. I watched and felt their light transforming their original forms into the vision I wished for. It was actually going to work. I couldn't believe it. The power I wielded was greater than I had imagined. Though the thought excited me, I couldn't help but be disappointed. If I couldn't accomplish what I wanted, I wasn't going to leave, but it seemed I had.

She stood before me: Eve. Her name meaning "life-giver," I hoped it would aid the chances of them having children, and perhaps encourage his acceptance of her. Eve stood shorter than me by a head's length, had dark, honey-colored hair and amber eyes. Her pupils were that of a snake's, thin

slits that ran vertically instead of rounded. But it gave her a distinct gaze, as if she could read my thoughts. Eve's body was not as strong and toned, but rather dainty and delicate. *She was beautiful.*

I then heard the crunching of debris coming from the tree line. Taking no care to avoid stepping on the collapsed trees and branches he destroyed, Lucifer strolled right into the clearing. Once he broke through, he halted, surprise plastered on his face. Then confusion. Understanding. Then fury once again. It seemed the time he had taken to calm down had been for naught. How sad; I had hoped he would have been in a better state of mind when he met her.

"What is this? What have you done?" he bellowed. Lucifer was shocked at my power. I had told him before what I had done with the apple, and he hadn't believed me. But now that proof was right in front of him, he couldn't deny it. Lucifer marched the remaining distance between us, grabbed my shoulders and shook me hard. "Why are you doing this?" he cried. The pain he was feeling was obvious, but I refused to register it. The pain he caused me was far worse.

"This is Eve. She will be with you after I am gone, and hopefully will produce children for you. She will make you happy." I finished strong. He was not going to guilt me or force me into staying. If he wasn't willing to change for me, why should I have even considered changing for him? *I would no longer be the weak one.*

Lucifer peered into my eyes, still holding tightly to my shoulders. "Children? Doesn't that go against the whole reason you're leaving? Have you completely lost your mind? If you just don't want to be with me, then say it. Don't make up excuses and lie to me!" Lucifer shook me again and let go. I could feel the bruises he left on my arms, but I didn't look at them. It hurt that he thought that of me, but I could see he wasn't going to let me leave. That meant I'd have to hurt him more.

"Lucifer, you're right. This whole thing has been an excuse. I didn't

want to hurt you, but you leave me no choice." I grabbed his chin and yanked his face up to look at me. "I don't love you, and I want to leave. I'm only leaving you Eve because of the time we have spent together. I owe you some happiness for the pain I've caused you. Now please accept my offering so we can put an end to this." I had shoved all my emotions down deep into the abyss that lived in my chest. I felt nothing. That was the only way I was able to accomplish this act. So, when he looked into my eyes, he saw nothing there but coldness.

Lucifer slapped my hand away and stepped back from me, staring at the ground. I could see from his tense shoulders he was fighting the urge to hit something, probably me. I waited for him to accept what I had said. The man turned to Eve. "How did you create her?" he asked, jaw clenched. Once I explained the basics of what I did and why I chose them he said, "I don't want her to be funny. I don't want her to be smart. All a woman is good for is her body. Just make it so she can function to take care of herself and remove everything else. I have had enough of women who can think for themselves. It seems an independent woman does nothing but destroy things. So fix it," he spat at me. Though his words frightened me, I didn't show any weakness. I kept my face and body poised as I turned to "fix" Eve.

Eve looked frightened and confused by what was happening, and she ran to me and held on for dear life. I whispered to her, "I am sorry. Everything is going to be all right. I just need to make a few changes." She looked up at me and nodded. I pulled away from her, the words flowing in my mind this time. I didn't want Lucifer to know what I was doing. If he didn't want joyful and generous, fine, but she was going to need to know how to care for children and deal with Lucifer. I was not going to leave her defenseless. That's why I left her intelligence, cunning, and seductiveness: the snake. I would remove the rest.

Thank you for what you've done
But I need you to change once more
Remove yourself from Eve
Gather your core
And prepare yourself for leave

My words had taken effect, and the monkey's spirit revealed its hiding place to me. I used the magic to pull apart Eve's chest cavity, revealing her ribs. This spirit had transformed twice in one day and was tired; it wasn't meant to change at all. So instead of forcing the newly made rib to come to me, I went to it. I reached my hand inside Eve and retrieved the rib resting in her chest. I gently removed it and told the former snake's energy to form correctly around the wound once more.

While this process transpired, Eve's physical form altered as well. Her eyes were the same, but her hair had changed from honey to pitch black. She was still dainty and short, but her facial features went from rounded to narrow, making her look even thinner than she was before. I found I preferred the first version, but this was what he wanted. At least she didn't look frightened anymore. Almost comfortable, which I found odd, given the situation.

Without looking back at him, I said, "Is she acceptable to you now?"

He answered, "Yes. When are you leaving?"

"As soon as I know you're going to be okay," I muttered.

"Well, you can rest easy. I have an obedient woman to be with now. I'm happy, so you are released from me."

I stood there for a moment before I said, "She is made from the animals, so I don't know how long she will live, but the children she will bear for you should be fine if they come from us. Though I can't be certain because—"

Lucifer cut me off. "I get it." The pain was creeping back in. I needed to leave. I placed the rib into my bag with my other supplies and placed

the strap around my shoulders. I glanced at the meadow. My home for the past several hundred years, my whole life thus far. My sanctuary with Lucifer as well as away from him. I tore my gaze away to look at Lucifer.

Oh, Lucifer.

My light.

My love.

My *sorrow.*

I looked into his pale blue irises; though full of hatred, they were and would always be beautiful to me. I wanted to give him one last kiss. I needed to. I needed a goodbye. I stepped closer to him and reached out my hand. Seeing what I was going to do, he turned on his heel and strode into the woodland without looking back. His raging golden spirit thrashed at the space around him. I shouldn't have been surprised considering what I said to him, but it still stung.

I turned the opposite direction to leave when Eve came up to me and questioned, "Where did he go? Did he leave me?" There was no worry in her voice, just irritation.

"No, he will be back for you. You can wait here by the water." I took a hesitant step forward. The afternoon sun glittered off the still pond. The water that cascaded down the falls was important to me. It had become as much my friend as the moon and stars had. And now I was leaving it behind. *Just like him.*

But I was leaving knowing that I had tried. I could live with that. Without sparing another glance in his direction, I said, "I hope you and Lucifer have a wonderful life together." Then I darted into the familiar undergrowth, running until I felt nothing but the wind on my face and the moss beneath my feet. Until nothing was familiar, and I felt nothing at all.

VII
Metaphorical Hearts

One ending leads to countless others.
-A

The sky rained down cold water, but I didn't stop running until nightfall. I had run like an animal, purely on instinct. It felt nice; still my body would not tire. I headed south, following the river that flowed along the west side of the land. Lucifer and I had covered most of the Earth's surface when we were searching for others, but I was certain the land had more secrets to tell. I heard the winged lizards from above the canopy. Their heavy flapping echoed against the walls of the forest, and the fire they breathed out in puffs dried their wet scales. Though some didn't have such talents and continued on through the heavy rain.

I couldn't put enough distance between Lucifer and myself, between my old home and new home. The idea made me sad but strangely invigorated. I was free to do what I wanted. Go wherever I wanted to go. Do what I wanted without Lucifer's ridicule and judgments. I was free of him. I had no obligation to him or his way of life. I left him with what I could. Yes, I was disappointed that we did not end things peacefully, but I did the best I could. That would have to be enough. *Eve would have to be enough.*

Eve. I wondered what kind of person she would be. Since I took the monkey spirit from her, she wouldn't be what I imagined. Perhaps too

withholding for him, but he didn't want the kind of relationship that I wanted. Lucifer just wanted a body to keep him company. Fine, he had it. That didn't mean that I had to have the same thing.

I hadn't thought of it before. *Why did I not think to make a partner for myself? Why did I have to be alone?* I supposed that before our departure I had decided I would feel too guilty being with someone else, because I was the one who left and caused the rift; therefore, I didn't deserve to be happy. *Wrong.* I deserved it just as much as he did. His words cut me deep, and there would forever be a festering wound where my heart should have dwelled.

I took shelter in the protruding, mossy roots of a nearby tree. This tree was old, much older than the ones at home. One of the roots of the tree was so thick and large it made a spacious shelter for me, as well as hid me from anything and…anyone that could have passed by. I made a nest as comfortable as I could with moss and fallen leaves. I gathered a pile of dead leaves a few feet in front of me and influenced the spirit that remained inside. The energy traveled so fast that it sparked and became fire. I lined it with the few rocks I could find, so my small fire wouldn't spread. I didn't feel like making a fire the proper way; crushing rocks in my too-strong grip was tiring.

Once I was comfortable enough, I unpacked my lion-skin bag. The bag Lucifer had made for me from one of the deadliest predators in our… his land. I supposed that meant Lucifer was the deadliest predator. I hadn't truly realized that until now. The negatives I had been blocking from my consciousness were beginning to reveal themselves. The negatives I had blocked so I could make us work. But there was no need for that now. I could deal with those realities later.

I removed several different fruits and herbs and extra furs. Most of the herbs were medicinal, but I didn't need them with how quickly I could heal. Still, I made an effort to learn about them over the years. They were mostly for the injured creatures I came across. Now I knew I

could heal them easily with the way I could manipulate their energy, but natural was best. Safe.

I felt for the bottom of the bag and removed the rib that I had taken from Eve. I studied the crevices that marked the ivory bone. It seemed the spirit took more damage than I thought. Changing the natural form of a living thing was not difficult for me, but it did have consequences. That was why I would avoid making such drastic changes in the future. The new shape never formed completely right. There was always something wrong. *Incomplete.*

Eve's eyes. They didn't mimic a human's eyes; they were her original, perceptive snake pupils. Though the physical flaws didn't mean much, it made me wonder if there were also internal flaws, mental flaws. I put the bone down. I wouldn't be changing the newly structured rib bone any time soon. I would let the spirit rest for now.

I grabbed the last item out of my bag, a small bag made from the skin and fur of the rabbit that had helped me so long ago, at the beginning of our lives. Animal teeth held the creation together. The rabbit was my first friend and my first acknowledgment of death. There was something to be said about firsts. The first of anything stayed in one's mind permanently, carried through one's life as a reference for the inevitable repeats. Whether they were good or bad. In this case it was both. I learned how to make a friend and how to deal with the loss of one. *And how to forgive.*

I opened the soft white fur and pulled out its contents. I kept my most treasured items in this bag. The remains of the flower petals Lucifer had given me when we first met. The bright crimson was now a dull rosy color. Still pretty, but nothing compared to the fresh, vibrant color of the red lily. I loved the flower he found for me so much that I tried to collect more of it, but alas, I was never able to find where he picked it, and neither was he. It was one of kind, a lot like me: alone and dulled by the past.

I put the ancient crumpled petals onto the ground next to me and

retrieved the lock of hair I had taken from Lucifer. I had taken this piece of golden hair after we made love for the first and only time. He had been sleeping next to me that evening. The setting sun was bouncing shadows off the angles of his delicate face. Lucifer was beautiful when he slept. So peaceful. All the lines of anger and stubbornness were erased.

I kept the lock with me in hope for the bright future we would have together. Our brief time of happiness was all I had left. I poured those happy memories into the golden strands, wanting to preserve them. I gently scented the piece of hair; it smelled of sun rays. I placed it next to the petals. The last item I retrieved was a seed from the ancient apple tree. Resting underneath its bright canopy always relieved me of my burdens, if only momentarily. Maybe I could plant this in my new home, wherever that might be.

After a moment of regret that lasted too long, I put my treasures back into their proper place and lay down to sleep. Nostalgia was a heavy emotion, and after the difficult day I'd had, I didn't think I could handle much more. I lay on my back with the rib bone next to me. It was nice to have someone at my side. I gazed at the stars through the partings in the tree limbs in an attempt to drift peacefully away into nothingness.

The night dragged on. The breeze blew harder with every passing moment. The fire crackled and popped indecisively. The scurrying of rodent feet plagued my ears, and I could smell that they carried pieces of a rotting carcass in their mouths. I was restless as I floated in and out of sleep, until I heard the words, "*Rest now. Tomorrow will be better.*" In the midst of those few words a peaceful film wrapped itself around my tired mind and allowed me to sleep.

I awoke to the sun shining down on me. The air was crisp, but the warmth from the orb above made up for it. I didn't want to open my eyes and ruin the feeling. I didn't want to face what reality had to offer. I knew something

bad had happened, but I wasn't sure what it was. I lay there a few moments more, listening to the birds' songs and the cool breeze pass by my ear.

I realized then that I wasn't alone. I assumed it was the sun keeping me warm, but it was a body. A human body. *Had Lucifer found me?* My foot trail was nearly untraceable, and the rain should have washed away my scent. I stiffened, but the body next to me didn't seem to notice. From what I could tell, they were asleep too. The breathing was slow and steady. I slowly untangled myself from the arm and leg that wrapped over me like a heavy blanket. I was almost free when the arm tightened and brought me back. The breathing was still steady, but as much as I silently struggled, I couldn't break free again. My fear set in and weakened my mind. The arm tightened the more I willed it to release its grip.

I found my resolve then.

Enough! Lucifer thought he could track me down and take me for himself? Did he not understand the reason I left? What was wrong with him? I decided it was time to get mean. No more holding back. I brought my head forward and flung it back as hard as I could into the nose of the man behind me. That woke him. Once he let go of me, I elbowed him hard in the ribs and leapt forward to grab the bone knife I kept strapped on my thigh under the fur covering. Once the weapon was comfortably in my grasp, I turned to face Lucifer.

Except it wasn't him. It took me a moment to gather my senses and realize what I was looking at. The red faded from my vision as I scrutinized the being that held its face in pain. It was another human for sure, but not quite. Something was wrong. As my eyes roamed his body, I realized the man before me had a tail! *How did this happen?* I hadn't performed the spell to create him.

"Who are you?" I questioned sternly.

He looked up at me, rubbing his nose, and said, "What was that for? Don't you recognize me?" A bruise was forming where I had elbowed him.

I looked him up and down. Nothing registered, but then I looked into his eyes, the cinnamon-colored eyes of the monkey I had used to make Eve. I looked down to search for the rib but found nothing. I looked up again and saw that he had recovered himself and was smiling at me. How odd. Hadn't I just hit him in the face? Looking further, I observed that he was not the overwhelming ray of light I had become accustomed to; regardless, this man was still very charming. Not only his demeanor but his physical attributes, which were very handsome.

He was my height, maybe a smidge shorter, not so much that one would notice it right away. His sincere brown eyes were comforting. I trusted this man with my life, and I had barely begun to meet him. His features were rounded but strong. His jaw looked capable of biting through rock. Wavy, honey-colored hair tumbled down just past his chin. His waves were not as loose as Lucifer's, but definitely freer than my tight curls. The strength was clear in his physique. He could hold his own and could even challenge Lucifer; appearances could be deceiving, though. Then there was the tail, the length of over half his body's height and covered in the same honey-colored hair that lay upon his head.

"You are the monkey," I said.

"Yes, I am. Sorry if I startled you, but you looked cold in your sleep." He smiled his impish grin again. I couldn't help but return it. He was so different from Lucifer. This new man was open and welcoming, not defensive and controlling like my former mate. I liked him instantly. I put the knife away and lowered myself back into our nest. The monkey-man did the same. We sat across from each other, just smiling. I hadn't felt this excited in a long time. *Too long.*

"I'm sorry about your nose…and rib. I thought you were someone else." I looked away. My face turned rosy pink. I hadn't blushed in so long.

The new man reached over and placed his large hand under my chin to lift my face. "I am the one who's sorry. It's my fault. I shouldn't have

surprised you." His smile widened. "But I did enjoy sleeping next to you. You are soft to the touch. It is very pleasing." The monkey-man said the words slowly. He was adapting to his new language. The words must have felt very strange to him, compared to his previous existence.

My senses were overloaded. I didn't know what to do. So, I blurted out, "You have a tail." I mentally slapped myself. *Why did I say that?* The former monkey didn't look embarrassed though. He turned to see what I spoke of, grasping at the elusive appendage. Unable to grab it, he stood and did a few twirls before finally catching his own extra limb.

I couldn't hold in the laughter. The chirping sound flew out of me. I laughed so hard I collapsed onto my back. Too late I recovered myself. I expected a glare for humiliating him, but instead his face was one of delight. Seeing I had enjoyed his performance, he did it again, this time more exaggerated for my benefit. I hadn't felt so joyous before; the sheer silliness of his actions astounded me. The man then attempted to grab hold of things with his elusive tail.

I knew he was trying to make me laugh, but I could see the curiosity there, too. He climbed partway up the root we had lain under and grabbed onto a low branch. He hung upside down with his face in my direction. I noticed then how close he was to me, his playful smile still beaming with mischief.

The monkey-man looked into my eyes, and I gazed back. I breathed in his sweet scent. The moment grew long. His closeness felt uncomfortable, but I also didn't want it to end. I suspected he was going to kiss me when the branch he was hanging from snapped. The man landed with his head in my lap and body stretched out to the side of me. The fall shocked him, but he recovered quickly and said, "This was my plan all along, you know. To be here in your arms is wonderful. It's better than any shiny treasure or juicy fruit." He sat upright in my lap, so his arms were wrapped around my neck, and his posterior and legs sat

across my thighs. His actions were so impulsive and erratic that I wasn't prepared for his next trick. He planted his lips against mine. It only lasted a moment, but it left me breathless. Once he accomplished his goal he leapt from my arms onto the root above us.

Unable to speak, I watched him maneuver himself onto the monstrous tree leg. The monkey-man questioned, "Did you not like my kiss, my lady?"

Slowly I registered what he had asked and answered, "No, it was lovely. You just startled me. Why are you up there?"

The man's impish grin returned. "I thought I would put a safe distance between us in case you decided to hit me again." He laughed at his own joke.

Was it a joke?

"Well, you are safe for now, monkey-man. You can come down," I reassured him. Though I didn't think he needed my assurances. *Had he been teasing me?*

He hopped down and faced me. "Monkey-man? Do you still see me as a monkey?" The man's face was still cheerful, but I could tell this worried him.

"Well, it's hard not to with the tail, but no, I don't see you as the animal you once were." He moved his gaze to the ground. *Was he feeling self-conscious?* I assured him further. "Would you like a name?"

That perked him up. "Yes! What should it be?"

"Don't you want to name yourself?" I questioned. *Why did everyone want me to name them?* I wasn't that great at it. It took me centuries to come up with Lucifer's, and Eve's name choice was merely a means to an end.

"No, I want you to. It will make it that much more special," he stated. A flower blossomed inside me. My words mattered to him. *I had never felt that way before.*

"All right." I took a moment to consider, looking him up and down. I finally landed on his eyes. "Your name is Adam, for your eyes that are the

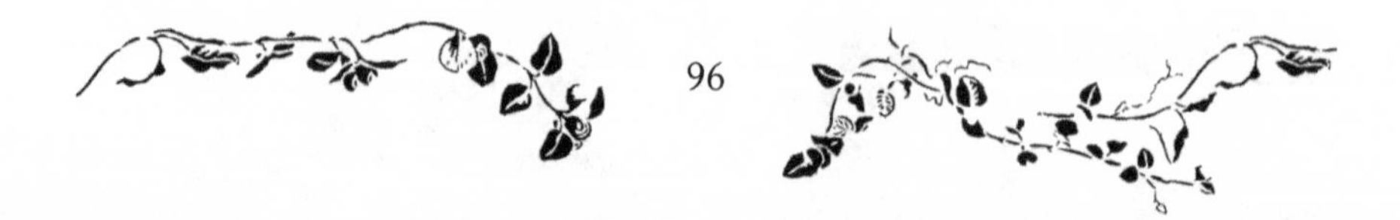

color of the earth beneath us. They are beautiful and warm. They make me feel safe." They complemented his aura's glowing bronze, and his spirit's surprisingly stable demeanor was comforting.

What was wrong with me? How could I have felt so much for someone I just met? Especially after going through the painful separation from Lucifer. *Perhaps my metaphorical heart had room for more than one person?* A tear streamed down Adam's face then. *Men could cry?* I thought that was something only my gender could do? Adam was so different from Lucifer. I hadn't decided if that was a good or bad thing yet.

"Thank you. You are beautiful as well. Your green eyes remind me of the forest. Looking into them means I am home." He said this to me with a straight and serious face. He reeked of sincerity. His voice, eyes, even his tail gave away his genuineness. I studied monkeys and their language. The man's tail revealed the truth in his words, and it would be a helpful tool for me so I could understand this new man better.

An obvious question occurred to me. "How did you come to be? I didn't use any magic to change you."

Adam thought on it for a moment. "Actually, you did. You said the words in your sleep. Before you gave me human life you seemed to be having a bad dream." The concern on his face was clear, and so was the look of fear on mine. "I suppose you needed my comfort, and I was happy to oblige." Adam smiled at the notion. *Was he thinking of our embrace as we slept?* It was wonderful. I hadn't slept so peacefully in such a long time, and it was because of Adam that I had. The realization made me smile back. But remembering the power I could wield quickly removed it.

3 Months Later

Adam and I made our way south, following the river's current. The journey was a joyous one, mostly due to the man who traveled beside me. The days

were kind to us as well. They were sunny and warm, and when the night came, we had each other to keep warm. Adam hadn't tried to kiss me again. Though I did want him to, I was glad for the space he gave me. I needed to let myself recover mentally from the loss of Lucifer before I could move on to another. It felt right to have a mourning period for my lost love. My lost life.

I attempted to educate Adam on his new body and how to care for it. Though he had a new form, he was much like the animal he used to be, weaker and slower than me, but I was envious of the heart he possessed. I supplied him with a fur covering for his lower half. He argued about the purpose of it, but in the end decided I was right, as he always did.

I explained that it was meant to keep him warm and protect…himself from his surroundings. It was a few days before he realized I also wanted to keep myself covered. The new man was constantly trying to remove my garments, saying that I didn't look comfortable in them. Adam learned how to lie quickly; this must have been a human characteristic.

Despite the lack of physical interaction, Adam was always happy, which I had grown to appreciate in the days following our meeting. He was constantly making me laugh whether he intended to or not. Adam was naturally just a joyful and fun person, and I needed that in my life desperately. I needed *him* in my life.

We traveled for many days and covered a vast length of land. And I had a feeling that our journey was nearing an end. It was hard to express, but I could feel that home was close. Maybe that was just my growing admiration for Adam, though. I had always viewed home as a place one lived, but my time with Adam showed me that home could be wherever one felt safe and loved. It was too soon to tell, but my home at the moment seemed to reside where Adam would be. Whether we took refuge under a tree or settled ourselves within a cave that rested along the hillside, each temporary settlement felt right with him near.

We were hiking through thick undergrowth. The sounds of the forest had been cheerful and lively for most of the day's journey, though it seemed to have quieted. The birds' songs had stopped, and the scuttering of small critters ceased. I was distracted from my suspicion by Adam's kind offering. He held out his hand to me as I made my way over a fallen tree; it was thick enough that we couldn't just step over it. He waited at the top for me, and though I didn't need it, he pulled me up into his waiting arms to steady my unnecessarily wobbly footing. Adam smiled his goofy smile and held me a moment longer than necessary before jumping down and offering his hand again. Lucifer would have never done that for me. Instead, I would have been forced into his arms and carried away against my will.

Regardless of my former mate's lack of empathy, I still loved Lucifer with all my soul. Our relationship had been up and down constantly through the long years. The "up" moments were brief, but the passion I felt for him was always there. Lucifer could bring the worst anger out in me. So much that, when I looked at him, his golden hue transformed into a blur of crimson waves, almost like fire. Then, not moments later, my anger would transform into incapacitating lust, and the crimson would die down to reveal his golden aura once more. The passion felt both amazing and horrible. It was exhausting.

It was not that way with Adam. I had lustful moments for him, but it was comforting, like I wasn't alone anymore. The emotion was gentle and reassuring rather than Lucifer's bewildering passion that left me lonely and craving more. I could grow to love Adam, if I didn't already. He was easy to love. Easy as breathing. This type of relationship was a welcome change, and something I could live with for however long either of us had left in this world.

Adam hiked in front of me through the dense trees. His tail always held the branches that swung back toward me after his passing. It was the

small considerate things like this that made me want to love him. Adam came to an abrupt stop. It took me a moment to realize why. My mind wandered often these days, even more than it had before. There was a black panther lazing on a low branch a short distance ahead of us.

"Don't move," Adam whispered. The new man never turned his back to the sleeping predator.

"It's all right. We can just walk by her," I said. He didn't even hear me. Adam's body had frozen, rooted to the ground, not unlike the trees that trapped us. The only movement from him was his shaky hands. *Why was he so frightened?* I shifted in front to question him. His eyes were locked on the cat. I understood then. As much as he had adjusted to being a man, his previous life as a monkey was still there. The same tendencies. The same *fears.*

I reached for him and held his hand. I walked ahead a bit and tugged gently, encouraging him to move forward. He budged slightly but refused to go farther. I pulled harder, hoping to force him out of his fearful daze. I regretted it. He instantly realized what I was doing and let go of my hand. We both fell backward onto the crunchy leaves and snapping twigs.

I didn't have to turn around to know the panther had woken, because as fast as Adam had fallen to the ground, he had climbed up a tree and disappeared into the thick leafage. I shouldn't have forced him. That was my fault. I was used to interacting with the creatures of the woodland, even the predators.

I turned around to face the panther. She had leapt down from her napping perch, and slowly worked her way toward me. She was unsure at first. The cat probably hadn't seen a person before. I did what I always did in those situations. I got down on my knees and looked to the ground, offering my outstretched hand as a gesture of goodwill. Respect was all nature wished for.

My previous experiences had taught me how to read and interact

with other creatures far better *after* I inherited my sight. I supposed all I needed was the realization that they weren't the ones that needed changing. Though it did depend on when her last meal had been. But even if she turned out to be hungry, the predator couldn't harm me. I didn't have teeth and claws, but I was much stronger and faster than her, and I could easily defeat her in a brawl. I had the ability to move her with a thought, but I considered that cheating—unnatural and unfair.

The panther stalked toward me. I felt her breath on my fingers as she sniffed them. My unfamiliar scent made her scoff. She circled me, judging if I was a threat to her and her territory. After a few moments of assessment, she decided I wasn't and sat down, allowing plenty of space between us. She sounded off a brief gentle growl to let me know. Sensing it was safe, I looked up at her. She had the most beautiful sapphire-colored eyes. Her fur was pitch black and shone like silk. She wasn't the biggest cat I'd seen, but it was clear her muscles were well exercised. A beautiful hunter. I wondered what it would be like to be taken down by such a creature, knowing your end was near yet entranced by the beauty she possessed. It couldn't be such a horrible death then, *could it?*

"Pssssstt…" I looked up to where the sound had come from and saw that Adam was hanging above me. The monkey-man's tail clung to a flimsy branch. He reached out and whispered, "Hurry! Grab my hand and I'll pull you to safety. Hurry! While she's distracted." In no hurry, I looked at the panther to find her cleaning her paws. Not at all concerned with us.

I moved my gaze back to Adam, "I don't think she's interested in us anymore. Perhaps you can come down and rest with me?"

Adam eyed me skeptically. "I don't think that's such a good idea. She could turn on us at any moment." I checked to see if that was a possibility. She had lain down and closed her eyes, continuing where she left off before we arrived.

"I think we're in the clear. Just come down." I then yanked on his

offered hand. This brought him tumbling down into my lap once again. It seemed he had not yet adjusted to the fact that he was heavier than his previous form. His branch choices would need to improve.

The sound of his fall didn't even rouse the huntress from her sleep, but Adam still felt the need to keep his guard up. Usually when he had the opportunity to be close to me, he would take advantage with his charming charisma, but the panther was too much of a distraction. Adam immediately got up and put himself behind me. Apparently, I was the shield against the dozing cat.

Lucifer would never have done that. He would have put himself in front of me, even knowing that I didn't need the protection. He would rather have taken the attack head-on than let one scratch mark my body. *No.* I had to stop comparing them to one another. They were two completely different people, Adam not even being a full human. I understood why Adam did the things he did. I was the one who forced him into this existence. I wouldn't change his character, too.

"Adam, it's safe. She won't hurt us as long as we keep a respectful distance." This seemed to relax him a bit, but he didn't let the panther out of his sight for more than a moment. "Here, eat something," I suggested.

I pulled out a mango I had in my bag and handed it to him. Still keeping his watch on the panther, he ate the fruit as I asked. Though the source of fruit was plentiful on our journey so far, we had yet to find an apple tree; though I wasn't surprised. The only one was with Lucifer, and it was utterly unique. I yearned for the taste of the delicious red fruit, my very first piece of food in this life. *I missed more than one of my firsts.* Shaking off the thought, I reminded myself that I didn't have the right to change the natural form of the fruit just because I deemed it so.

I had done enough already.

Hearing Adam bite into the fruit's skin, the huntress opened her eyes. She sniffed the air and sauntered over to where we sat. I immediately

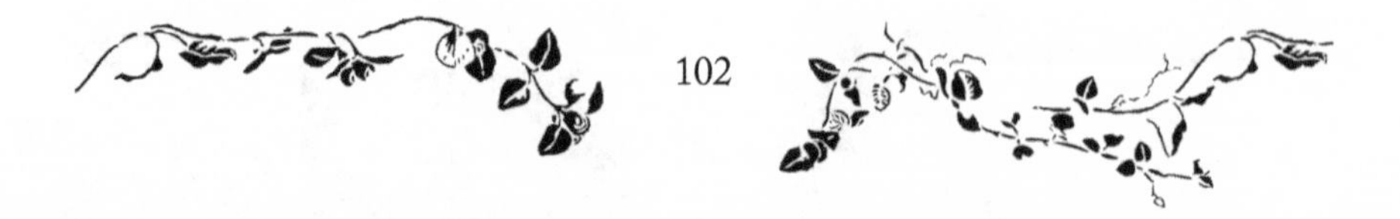

took hold of Adam's arm to keep him in place. I couldn't have him running off again. She might want him for dinner then.

I asked the cat, "Do you want something to eat, too?" Her response was a burbling sound. I reached into my bag to retrieve the other mango, and I set it in front of her. She looked at it with a cynical expression, then a disbelieving one toward me. "I know it's not what you crave, but it's all we have," I said. She gave the impression she understood, because she started to nibble awkwardly on the fruit, unsure how to eat it. I chuckled and grabbed one for myself.

We ate our small meal together in silence. I watched their interactions, doing what I could to withhold my laughter. The panther ate the mango whole, frustrated with the mess it was creating, and then undertook an intense cleaning job. She must not have liked how sticky the juice made her. Blood would have been worse, though.

Adam eventually relaxed enough to finish his mango, but I could see that he was shocked to still be alive. "Are you ready to continue on?" I asked.

"I suppose so." He then turned to the huntress and said, "Thank you for not eating us. Safe travels." We stood and headed south once more, Adam's hand clasped in mine.

We didn't have to travel much farther to find what we had been looking for. What *I* had been looking for. The river finally ended, and what resided there was enchanting.

The water emptied over a waterfall into an enormous lake. A stream continued farther on, but I had no interest in following it. It was nearing the end of the day, and it caused the sunset to dance off the surface. This lake wasn't like the pond at which I had spent the last several centuries. This lake was twenty times larger. The trees were taller and thicker even, as if they were fed better from the water that occupied this land rather than that of my old one. There was even a large clearing full of flowers that branched off at the bottom of the waterfall. The herbs and flowers I

gathered regularly were very close to here, too; we passed by them moments before we found the waterfall.

This was the place. This was our new home.

"It's beautiful," Adam said. I just nodded my head. Our hands still clasped, we continued to stare at our new home in wonder. The potential was there. We just had to make it our own. Suddenly, something leapt over our heads from the trees behind. It landed in front of us gracefully and silently.

"What are you doing here?" Adam shrieked. He nearly jumped into my arms, but seeing I wouldn't let him, he dove behind me instead. The panther responded with a clicking sound. She was excited.

"Did you follow us?" I questioned. She responded by rubbing against my leg as she passed. "You are welcome to stay if you like. This appears to be our new home." The huntress rubbed her face against my hand, then leapt onto the branch that hung over the falls. She meandered to the end of it and collapsed down onto her belly. The panther had claimed her piece of the land.

Knowing he would be uncomfortable with our new companion, I led Adam down the steep hill into the peaceful meadow that awaited. We stood at the edge of the tree line, amazed at our discovery. I looked upward at the waterfall and saw that the panther was still napping on her new branch, watching over our home with her vibrant magenta soul, and it spread to the tree she lazed upon. It always amazed me how the natural life of this world could so easily spread their energy from one to the other. Sharing wasn't even a choice. It was a way of life.

"Our new guardian should have a name," I said.

"Hmm…how about Man-Eater?" he scoffed. Clearly, he did not like the new addition to our family.

"No. She should have a noble name. One suitable for a huntress such as her." I thought on it a moment. "Shamira." Yes, that sounded right.

"What does that mean?" Adam questioned. He looked confused. *How did he not know the meaning?* Of course, I never questioned how I created words before. Lucifer just understood them. Obviously, Adam was different.

"It's another word for 'guardian,'" I replied. Shamira seemed to like her name, because when I looked at her again, her sapphire eyes were staring at me, and I could hear her rumbly purring from where I stood.

"If you say so," Adam smiled at me. Always so kind. He supported me no matter what. Even if he didn't like it, he would do it for me. Adam reached into my bag and pulled out the rabbit fur containing my treasures. "It's about time we marked this place as our own, don't you think?" He handed me my cherished rabbit fur, knowing what it meant.

On our journey, I had told him everything. Every detail about my life for the past 700-plus years. My views on how I chose to live. My unique sight and how it had changed me. Even about Lucifer. It hadn't taken long for the repressed emotions to spill out of me.

It was only a week into our journey, and we had lain down to rest for the night after a long day of travel. We lazed in the grass and looked up at the stars as we had the previous nights together. Adam was very talkative and energized during the day, but he remained quiet at night, as if he knew I needed to be there in silence, deliberating with the night sky above. *Trying to ignore the emptiness inside of me.*

The moon and stars had been the only true companions throughout my long time on this Earth. They didn't argue or belittle me. They just listened. It was that night that I realized Adam was the same way. He did his best to make me smile, and when all was said and done, he would wait for me. Adam didn't push me to reveal my feelings or force them to change once I did. He was much different than Lucifer.

That night, I made a decision. With the support of the lights above, I revealed my soul to Adam. I started by asking, "Adam, do you like your new life, or do you wish to be a monkey again?"

Adam contemplated for a moment before answering, "There are things I miss about my former life. The simplicity of it. There were no emotions. No obligations. The whole purpose was to survive." He looked from the stars to me. "But having the ability now, I would choose this one. Before, I couldn't even conceive of choices. The possibilities are almost overwhelming to think of now, but it's comforting to know that there are many different ways to live a life. Not just to survive, but to learn and…love."

I looked away from him, embarrassed by his comment that was obviously directed toward me. "Then you don't hate me for changing you?"

Adam turned his body toward mine and gently nudged my chin so I was looking at him. "I don't and will never hate you for that. I don't think I could hate you no matter what you did. It was fairly soon that I noticed my feelings for you. Not the basic instinct of an animal to reproduce, but the love for someone I care for. For someone I want to keep safe. I hope in time I will be that man for you."

"Oh, Adam." I began to cry, and not a silent cry, but horribly embarrassing sobbing. I couldn't help it. All the pain and loneliness that I had gone through came gushing out all at once. Adam just held me, not saying a word. He let me cry for far too long, and then listened as I told him everything about my life. Everything about me. It was a relief to confide in someone after so long. The peace that came with it ebbed the pain in my chest.

We made our way to the center of the clearing and kneeled down. Adam dug a small hole in the earth, just deep enough so I could place my apple seed in its new home. I covered the seed with the disturbed earth, leaving my hand on top. Adam then placed his hand over mine and said, "This is our new home now. You don't have to be lonely anymore. I am here and will be here as long as you will allow it." His words gave me hope that maybe this life could be worth something after all. I leaned across the seed's home and placed my lips gently against Adam's. It felt nice, like lying

in a field of soft grass. Like comfort and companionship. I would never be lonely with Adam at my side.

The kiss deepened, and the yearning I had felt for him since our first encounter took hold. We rolled through sweet-smelling flowers. The sunny day had left the ground warm and dry. The sound of the waterfall was reassuring and brought me back to an older time. I had fought so hard all my life to resist my most basic desire, trapped by the responsibility. Now, Adam was setting me free.

VIII
Burdens

Mothers are helpless to the will that
lies in the womb.
-A

9 Months Later

"You're doing great, my love. Keep going," Adam encouraged. I was giving birth to our first child. Finally, a child. I was going to bring life into the world instead of take from it. I was going to have someone to love and care for. Someone to pass my knowledge on to. The joy I felt almost filled my heartless chest cavity. *I was going to have a family.*

It had been too many hours. The pain was nearly unbearable. I must have been doing something wrong if it felt this agonizing. Sharp pain shot through my body. My nerves pinched and my hips ached. My back arched in anguish. My body was covered in sweat. Veins that I had never seen before showed through my skin. I had never hurt this much. I begged that our child didn't feel this way. But I couldn't do anything about it until the baby was in my arms.

"You are so close. I can see the head!" Adam urged excitedly. I could have delivered on my own, but I was grateful that Adam was there. It was easy to stop and wallow due to the pain I was in. My lover kept me

motivated, constantly reminding me why I was putting myself thorough the torture. "One more push!" he coaxed. As I cried out in pain, I wondered if it would have been this horrible with Lucifer's child.

The pain suddenly ebbed. I heard crying. I lifted my head to look at what lay in Adam's arms. A tiny creature was there, wailing for no other reason than to let us know it was here. Its tiny arms and legs flailed helplessly. Adam kneeled down next to me and placed the child in my arms. So soft and delicate. I had never been more self-conscious about my unnatural strength than in that moment. One wrong movement and she could die.

I nestled the child in the nook of my arm so I could look at her. Surprisingly, she was coated in blood like that of Adam, but my crimson sand had been a mixture in the womb it seemed. The blood and sand blend had created a paste-like substance. But it was easy to see past the birthing fluids and gaze into the emerald eyes that stared at me. The green stood out prominently against her pale ivory skin. There were tight curls of dark, honey-shaded hair poking out in every direction. Our baby. *My beautiful baby.*

"What do you want to call her?" Adam asked. I forced my eyes away from my child to look up at him. His expression was proud. Happy. *Human.* Adam really had adapted well to this life.

I moved my gaze down toward the tiny creature. "Naavah," I said. We had created something beautiful for this world. She should be named for it. I continued for Adam's sake, "Beautiful."

"That's perfect. She is beautiful. Just like her mother." A tear streamed down his beaming face. The new father stroked the dark blonde locks on his child's tiny head.

"She has your hair," I said.

Refusing to remove his gaze from the newborn creature, he said, "She has your eyes." We laughed silently together, but then Naavah closed those familiar irises and fell asleep. Adam took her from my arms, seeing I was fading. "I will clean her up. Rest now. You did wonderful, my love." Before

he stood, he placed a kiss on my forehead; it felt nice. Knowing Naavah was in safe hands, I did just as he said and drifted away from reality.

The next day came all too soon. I had a dreamless night, and it felt as if I had just fallen asleep. I was tired. The sun had risen and shone down through the moss insulation on our wooden hut. I never had the luxury of a self-made shelter before, because of the limits I put upon myself, and Lucifer never seemed to care enough to build one. But so long as Adam did the killing, the light would remain bright.

A refreshing breeze drifted through the cracks in our home's openings. It was a peaceful feeling, like the wind was connected to the rhythm of my own breath. It blew in and out of the shelter in time with my lungs. In and out, east and west.

I remembered then.

My breathing and the cool breeze ceased movement. "Naavah!" I forced myself to sit upright on the grass-lined bed.

"Take your time, Lilith. Naavah is sleeping again." I turned my gaze toward the west side of our home. Adam was lounging next to his child. My daughter was wrapped tight in a bundle of furs in her own grass bed. The furs had been from Shamira's prey. Now that she lived with us, she brought us her meals to share. Although, instead of eating the meat she offered, we made use of the rest of the creature and gave the meat back to her, just as I had when Lucifer brought me his prey's remains. I was grateful Adam didn't want to eat the meat, either. It made it easier for me.

Naavah slept deep, and her little fingers curled in frustration at the dream she was having. Due to our unnatural union, I feared we weren't going to be able to conceive. So, when I found myself with child, the fear that it would be taken away was unbearable. The delivery was painful to endure, but the results were perfect. Naavah appeared to be healthy. *That was all that mattered.*

Comforted by that fact, I took the time to inspect myself. Adam had done his best to clean the mess from me, and he replaced my furs. My lover always took care of me in whatever way I needed him to. I truly loved the man he had become.

After a few unsure moments, I stood. I must have healed quickly from the previous night. It was good to know that hadn't changed. I walked the short distance over to my lover and newborn child. I ran my finger down Naavah's rosy cheek. *Beautiful.* This notion made me smile, and that smile spread to Adam. The last year together had strengthened our bond. We knew what the other was thinking without even uttering a word. We understood and appreciated one another. *How it was supposed to be.*

"Naavah slept most of the night. She's so calm. I stayed up all night watching her." Adam glanced in my direction with eyes full of happy, unshed tears. Adam was going to be a wonderful father. He cared so much for Naavah, and he'd only just met her. It felt unreal to have a partner who felt the same way as me.

We laid there next to Naavah most of the day, until she woke hungry. I wondered if I would ever get used to the volume of her cries, but she was easily satisfied. Once I brought her to my bosom, she went silent and drank the sustenance I provided for her. I stared down at her as she fed. Her perfect little face brought tears to my eyes as I enjoyed the alone time we had together, mother and daughter. Adam went to gather food for us and medicinal herbs for Naavah in case she needed something later we were unaware of.

I hummed a tune I heard the birds singing when I woke for the first time in this life. I remembered I'd had trouble mimicking their sound, but after practicing, I soon found a way. The sound was not as lovely, nonetheless it seemed to placate Naavah. I was nearing the end of my tune when I noticed something wrong with my daughter.

I double-checked her physical form. Ten toes and ten fingers. Two

eyes and two ears. One nose and two lips. *What was it?* The outward appearance inspected, I listened to her heart and her breathing. Thump…thump…thump. Her heart sounded like Adam's and her breathing was steady. I noticed she had a dimple in her stomach from the umbilical cord that attached her to me in the womb; Lucifer and I had no such scar. Not even Adam and Eve had a navel. Though that was to be expected since I had created them in my image. I couldn't help but envy the strange feature. It represented birth, a mother and a father.

Shying away from my selfish thoughts, I concentrated on the nagging sense that something was wrong with my child. This was going to drive me crazy. Maybe I was being paranoid. The worries of a mother, I supposed.

Naavah's aura was a lovely cyan. It reminded me of the ocean.

I stiffened then. I wished I could have looked away. I didn't want to acknowledge what I saw. She was supposed to be like him, like her father.

Adam walked through the hanging leaves I had strung together for our door. "I couldn't find any peppermint, but I found the bananas and…" He stopped mid-stride to stare at me. I wasn't faring well. My breathing was irregular, and I even began to sweat, which rarely happened. Before the panic could completely take me, I removed the baby from my breast and placed her back in her bed as gently as I could. Naavah didn't like that. My daughter began wailing again and flailing her arms. She was still hungry, but I couldn't hold her—not this creature that I had plagued the world with.

"What's wrong?" Adam demanded. He had never been so forceful before.

"It's not like you…" I couldn't get the words out. *What was wrong with me?* I had to tell him. Before he could question me further, I turned to him and said, "The baby is not like you. It isn't meant to be part of this world. The child is separate…like me."

"No," was all Adam said. He immediately went to the child and cradled it in his arms. The wailing subsided, but it was clear it wouldn't last

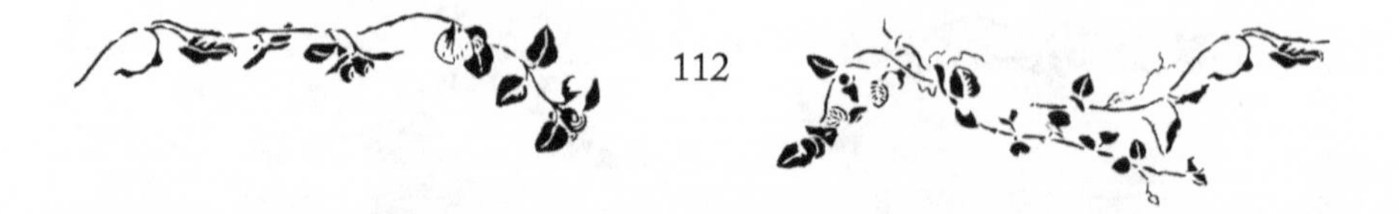

long. We stood there for a long while, unmoving and silent except for the stifled cries of the baby. Sensing there was something amiss, Shamira sauntered inside our hut, the constant guardian of this domain. She sniffed the air, tasting the tension that resided there. The panther took a step toward me, but then changed her mind and went to Adam and the child.

The worst thing I had ever seen happened then. Shamira's life force leaked from her physical form. She grew weaker and weaker until she collapsed to the ground, breathing hard. Her spirit stopped waning, but by the time it was done there was barely any left for her. The piece of spirit that abandoned the panther went directly to *it*.

To the abomination I created.

Adam did not see this take place, but he did notice that something had happened to Shamira and squatted down to stroke her side. In doing so, he inadvertently shared his own spirit with the panther. While his dimmed, hers grew, though not as bright as it once was.

It took a moment before she had the strength to stand again. I stood frozen and in shock. That shock soon became fear, then blinding anger. Seeing the only option I could, I lunged at Adam and the child. "It's an abomination! It cannot live!" Adam dove out of my reach just in time and ran out of the hut. So blind with fury and sorrow, I didn't hear anything he said. I kept chasing and attacking, but the fury made me sloppy. I was unable to catch him as he maneuvered out of my grasp with the monstrosity still in his arms.

This dance continued for a short time, but I grew tired of the chase and grabbed hold of her energy and brought her to me. Adam tried to grab her in midair, but I threw him back in the same thought. The red overtook my vision. I snatched the floating child, fully intending to end its life. The magic that coursed through me had become stronger with my age. Spells were needed less, and the power had become instinct, no matter how much I repressed my will to act on it. I had the spirits I consumed daily to thank for that.

Cradled in the nook of my arm, my free hand gripped the small creature's neck. The little form in my grasp was colored red just like its surroundings. My spirit had taken me over and controlled my actions, driving me to defend the life I had always strove to protect. But as my hand tightened, two small emerald green circles penetrated my crimson vision.

The baby wasn't crying anymore. She didn't even look afraid like she should have been. Naavah looked up at me curiously, her honey curls blowing softly in the breeze. She was wondering why her mother was trying to hurt her. *What was I doing?* This was my daughter, and I was about to kill her. It went against every instinct I had.

My soul was engaged in an inward battle with itself once more. Except this time, the battle was with my child, not a mate. It was so much worse this time, because I knew which side would win, and that broke my metaphorical heart. But not as much as it would have if I had killed my own child. Naavah would come first. Always. It didn't matter if she needed to swallow the world whole to satisfy her hunger. I would gladly give it to her, because that was my job and my deepest desire. To care for her and love her, no matter the cost. That was why I had fought motherhood for so long. *There was no longer a choice.*

Yes, the battle was won before it had even started. I realized this, and the red faded from my vision. My daughter's green eyes calmed my angered soul. I brought Naavah to my bosom so she could finish feeding. Adam continued to lay on the ground where I had thrown him, the hurt clear on his face. How was I going to apologize to him? How would he trust me with our daughter after this? *Could I even trust myself?*

"I won't hurt Naavah. I know I don't deserve it, but please forgive me. The fear I felt blinded me, and I wasn't thinking clearly." I exhaled a painful breath. "Not only is Naavah like me, but she is worse. She doesn't need to kill to steal the spirit from another. She absorbs it whenever another is near. She sucks it in—a succubus." The name came to me without even

searching for it. A succubus: a being that takes the life force of others. What a horrible name for something so beautiful.

Shamira stalked over to Naavah and me, obviously wary after what just happened. In the same moment, Naavah finished feeding and fell asleep. She was completely at ease, the incident long forgotten. Just then, the light she had taken from the panther seeped slowly back toward Shamira and Adam. Steadily, their full strength returned, and their light shone bright once more. So, she could give back what she took. I breathed a sigh of relief. *There was hope.*

Adam cautiously made his way toward us. The returned energy must have given him the strength to approach his emotionally unstable lover, or perhaps it was the worry for his child that gave him the courage. "What did you see?" Adam asked, gently this time. Nothing escaped his notice anymore.

"Naavah returned the light back to the Earth. Back to you and Shamira. It was incredible and terrifying," I explained.

Adam, careful with his words, said, "That is a good thing, Lilith. It means that she has a choice to give back, in a much easier way than you, even. We will teach her. And being your daughter, I am sure she will choose to do the right thing."

I nodded. Adam and Shamira forgave me for my shameful outburst and sat with me. Yet Adam continued to watch me with cautious eyes, not wanting to touch me, but unable to leave his daughter's side.

The shame I felt was brutal, but only because of the hidden reason behind it.

20 Years Later

Twenty years and twenty children. And time passed all too quickly. For someone who didn't age, the time with my children was swift. They grew rapidly and learned even quicker. I taught them what I could. But I found

that the less they knew, the better. The less I had to use my powers, the better the world would be for them.

"Mother, why is it you don't use your magic?" Kun, my second eldest, asked me. We were lounging in the grass by the lake. The day was sunny but there was a chill in the air that left my skin rough and made my spine shiver.

Confused, I asked, "Why do you ask? You never have before." Kun didn't know the extent of my abilities, but he did know they were greater than Naavah's.

Hesitating, he answered, "Well, you have told us of a world that none of us can see, besides Naavah. You have taught us to give back to it…so what I'm really asking is why? Why give when you can take from it?" My son's face was relieved once the words tumbled out of him. Clearly this had been on his mind for a while.

This question was something I hadn't expected from my offspring. I had never wanted to take from the natural world, even before I could see it. And his father, Adam, was a part of that world. I found myself angered by his thoughts and rather afraid.

"Kun, you give because it is what's right. Because we are guests in this land," I said sternly.

"But…I'm not," Kun said quietly.

"What?"

"I'm not a guest in this land. I was born here. Even if you are, Father belongs here, and I am a part of him. We all are." Kun was on the verge of adulthood, a young man who questioned the world. His dark honey waves blew angrily against the gust of wind that passed through the clearing, and his brown eyes bored into mine.

Exasperated, I replied, "It doesn't matter. The light wanes whether you think you're a guest or not, Kun. You have to accept that or doom us all." I stood to flee from the horrid topic.

Kun was becoming braver and stood to fight against me. "How can you expect me to accept that when I can't even see it? Maybe you're just crazy and are trying to control us to do what *you* want."

His words were a slap in the face. None of my children had ever spoken to me in such a way. It hurt and I was scared of the outcome.

Before I could say something even worse to him, Adam appeared, my constant savior. "Kun, don't speak to your mother that way. Ever. Now sit down and listen." Adam gestured for us to sit, and we did with furrowed brows and heated glares.

Kun turned his glare to the earth beneath him. Adam started, "Son, do you love your family?"

"What kind of question is that?" Kun said. He still stared at the grass, his lips thin from frustration. If it wasn't for the topic, I would have laughed. Kun was an exact replica of his father, but I could see that Adam was older; the laugh lines around his mouth revealed as much. I often found myself avoiding my reflection, unable to accept I looked the same age as my oldest children.

"Answer me."

"Of course I do," Kun answered.

"And you wish to have children of your own one day?"

Kun blushed. I knew he was thinking of Naavah in that moment. He had been in love with her since they were small. Naavah, so absorbed in the unseen world, rarely paid attention to the only one her siblings *could* see, and hadn't realized this about him. "Yes," my son admitted.

"Think now of their children, and their children in turn. Do you want them to be able to live in a peaceful world? One full of life?" Adam questioned calmly.

"I don't see what this has to do with—"

Adam stopped him there. "If you want your future family to have a happy existence, you have to start by taking care of their future home. Or

else what will be left for them?" Kun finally looked up at his father, appalled at the realization forming. "It's the small things we do for our home that matter: taking care of our animal neighbors, for example. The more we sacrifice now, the better future generations will live. That is the one thing that will last the test of time, the one thing that will be left of *you*."

Kun was abashed, but knew his father was right. I could see in his expression that he regretted his harsh words. "I never looked at it that way before." He breathed out a crestfallen sigh. "I'm just frustrated with the constraints on us. I feel...trapped. We have to worry about so much, and I feel like I can't handle it at times."

His words brought tears to my eyes. I had never wanted my burdens to fall on anyone else, but I couldn't find a way to avoid them. Adam's job completed, he left me with Kun without saying another word. *How would I have survived without him?*

"Kun, I never wished for you to feel this way. Even *I* have a hard time with our way of life." I paused and took a breath. "You say you can't understand because you can't see it. But I am grateful that you can't. The light I see is amazing, but it haunts me as well. There is no escape from it, and there is no hiding from it. It will always *be.* Even when I close my eyes, I can feel it." Realizing that I was revealing too much, I ended with, "Be glad that you cannot see it, because Naavah doesn't have that freedom. And it is your job to relieve her from the burden."

I didn't want to disclose the extent of my powers, because I didn't want to explain why I thought things were best left natural and untainted by my touch. I feared for the land if I tested it. I saw myself as too much of a monster to trust the untamed magic within me. I had already explored more than I should have. I created completely new beings simply because I wanted to—beings that were never meant to be.

No one should have that power, yet someone did.

My son nodded dutifully, and I knew he would do what I asked.

Content, I said, "Now go, enjoy the day. I believe Naavah said she was gathering herbs above the falls." His sky-blue spirit danced excitedly at the thought, and though it was beautiful to see my child's spirit happy, I forced myself to look away from him.

I didn't want to see the spirits.

I didn't want to acknowledge their existence if I didn't have to.

Kun kissed my cheek before departing, a new determined gleam in his eye. Adam came to me then, his eyes on our son as he clambered up the hill and disappeared into the undergrowth of trees. "Our children will learn. Do not worry." He took my hand in his and kissed my palm. My lover's lips were warm from the sun.

"I know. I just don't know the right things to say to them like you do. I never had to go through childhood. I just…was," I muttered. I stroked my flat belly distractedly.

"You have such a way with words, my love. Unlike the rest of us." He was referring to the fact that we had to teach our children how to speak, and I just knew language instinctually. Even he only knew the words I'd spoken aloud before. "You just have to…be patient," he said carefully.

I smiled. "You don't think I'm patient, monkey-man?"

He scowled at my teasing, but the grin came soon after. Changing the subject, he said, "Do you want more children?" This had been the question on our minds since the last child was born. Shortly after, I saw the Earth's spirit wane drastically, even more than it already had. Lucifer's family was growing. Only time would tell if my decision to leave him was worse than if I had stayed.

Watching the ripples of sunlit water on the lake, I replied quietly, "No." I didn't have to explain for Adam to understand. Lucifer was something I could not control at the moment, but I could control us.

Our way of life was careful and reserved, the same way I had always lived. I taught my children to give back what they took, and they did so

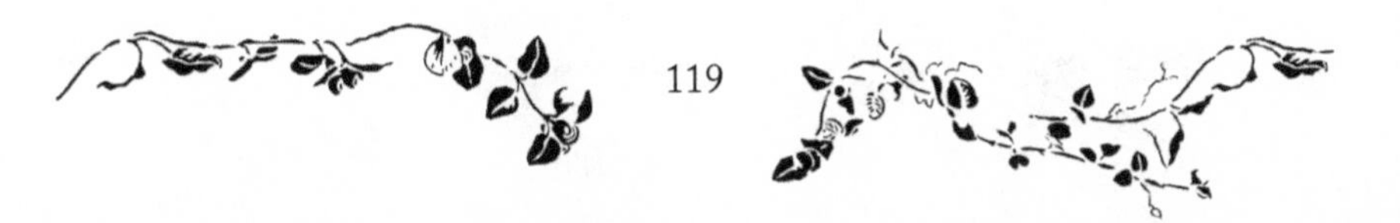

beautifully. Meditation and the will to give was all it took. But despite all our sacrifices, we still stole something from the spirits. That would only grow as time went on. My children would be adding more members to the family soon enough, and our species would multiply because of it. It was only natural. My time for creating life was over. I now had to lead the next generations to the light.

I only hoped they would continue to listen.

IX
The End of an Era

One only learns by trusting
the untrustworthy.
-A

500 Years Later

It became more difficult to keep the light alive. Not because of my children, not because of Lucifer's thievery, but because I had lost the will to live long ago. Time was never-ending, and I wished constantly for a way to end it. Seeing each child die, seeing each descendant die, was torture—so much so that I removed myself from their lives. But I still lived near, a constant guardian watching over them, waiting for the day I would either have to save them or kill them. But I knew I would never be able to complete the latter. I was their mother.

The knowledge I had passed on of the Earth and the intricate ways it weaved itself kept me from leaving them completely. I trusted my children to continue on living the right way and to pass it on to their own, but it was my duty to watch over them. Once in a while, a child was born with the gift of sight, like my first child, Naavah. My grown children always made the ones able to see the magic their leader and guide. This made me very happy.

My children's need to create was stunted due to the limited lives they

led, the life I had made them live. It didn't allow them to kill, other than taking the minimum food they needed from the greenery, therefore they couldn't build or create. Though this rule was broken to make simple shelters from the plant life. Adam couldn't do everything. But the predators they shared their lives with offered remains to them, as Shamira did for us. So they had tools and clothes. My offspring brought all kinds of creatures into our lives and into the village we built. It didn't matter what species or gender they were; there were always natural creatures willing to be a part of something other than themselves. Seeing the natural world adapt to humans was reassuring.

The village Adam and I built was now full of my descendants and animals, all contributing to the peaceful lives they led. I watched as they died, one by one. Naavah, Kun, Shamira—but not Adam. I believed once that it was his sheer will that allowed him to live so long, his will to stay by my side. I was very naïve. I tried to prepare for the inevitable day he would pass on and leave me here to walk alone on this Earth once more. But there was no need to do so, and I was grateful.

Death hurt every time it took a loved one, just as much as the last. There was no way to build a tolerance. There was just sadness and the longing to see that being again. And due to my immortality, I never would. Whatever awaited us upon death was never to welcome me, to relieve me from my loneliness. Of course, there was one way, but I had an obligation to guide what I had created.

Naavah was the last out of my twenty children to die. Her children and the children of her siblings were grown and had children of their own by that time. I thought of that day often. Naavah had lain in her grass bed, the same one she was born in, its only change being the size as she grew. She said to me, "Mother, please don't cry. My time here was wonderful." My daughter let out a painful breath.

"I only wish I could see Kun one more time before I go." A single tear

streamed down her wrinkled face. Naavah rarely cried in her life. She had been so strong. I envied that.

Naavah had aged, but her beauty remained. Her hair, once the color of dark honey, was now the brightness of snow and waved down past her hips. The skin around her eyes had wrinkled, but the color of the emerald green forest remained within, a constant reminder of her relation to me. My daughter. My firstborn.

I sat by her side and continued to weep. I was her mother and needed to be strong for her, but I couldn't. Naavah's children were in such despair they couldn't stay in the hut longer than a few moments to say goodbye. Adam sat quietly in the corner, staring at nothing. His age showed in his silver hair and the laugh lines that rested around his mouth and eyes, but he still held the leftover strength from the young man he once was. Adam spent most of his life laughing and smiling, but when his children began to die, I saw less and less of that playful grin. That thought brought on a whole new round of tears.

Naavah lifted her frail hand to my cheek and wiped away the tear that ran down. "Lilith, you have been a wonderful mother, and Adam a wonderful father. I couldn't have asked for better parents. You gave me life knowing the risk, and I am thankful for it. I just hope that you can learn to forgive yourself and continue to help your children. Even if they forget your name. Even if they forget you." She then added, "But that won't be for a long time, if it ever does happen."

The thought had never occurred to me at that point in my life. I assumed I would always be part of the family, but Naavah had become a very wise woman, far wiser than I would ever be. She knew I wouldn't be able to watch my loved ones die forever. She knew they would grow to forget. My little Naavah had truly become someone extraordinary. If only she had the immortality I possessed so she could have passed on her wisdom instead.

I couldn't make myself speak. All I did was grip her tighter, willing her to stay with me just a few moments more. Her cyan spirit struggled,

dimming and growing in brightness sporadically. Naavah had another round of painful coughs. She wouldn't last much longer. "Father, please come here," Naavah urged. Adam looked up for the first time in hours at the sound of his daughter's voice. Naavah's father did as she asked and kneeled down on the other side of her to grasp her hand.

"Yes, my child?" Adam questioned. My lover was far better at concealing his emotions than I was, but I could see in the way he held his breath and the way his tail twitched anxiously that he was close to falling apart.

Naavah continued, "I love you so much. Both of you. I want to give you one last thing before I go."

"Naavah, you have given us everything. There is no need to give more," Adam said. I just nodded my head, still unable to speak.

"Even so," she smiled, "I would like to give you and Mother more time together. You need each other." She looked to her father. "You need to help her get through this." Naavah and Adam exchanged a knowing look. "You will die not too long from now. I have done my best to share my energy with you, and it has granted you more years, but your time is not yet done."

This was news to me. *She had been giving her own energy to Adam?* It explained why he outlived his children, but I imagined how much longer Naavah could have lived if she hadn't given her life force away. *How much longer could I have had with her?*

"Naavah..." Adam muttered. The tears streamed freely down his face; he hadn't known either. That comforted me.

"Take care of each other, however long you have left. It goes by so fast. Don't waste one moment." Naavah's breathing hitched again. I expected her to cough as she had been, but all she did was exhale. It broke my spirit knowing that her last breath was a painful one, but she hadn't seemed to mind. My daughter's spirit remained calm and content. Her lips held a smile as her heart beat once...twice...then nothing. Silence was all that remained. My Naavah was gone. My beautiful child.

My tears finally stopped. I stared at my daughter. I waited for her chest to start moving again, still unable to accept her death. I actually thought my wish was going to come true when I saw movement come from her, but it wasn't her body moving. It was her spirit moving on. The thought passed through my mind for only a moment, but it was there all the same, just like it had been with the rest of my children. I could have used my powers to heal her. I could have extended her life. But Naavah wouldn't have wanted that.

Immortality was a burden, not a gift.

I expected her spirit to lower and disappear into the ground as my other children's had. To my dismay, their spirits never became part of the web that connected everything. They would simply disappear and become… nothing, at least as far as I could see. But this time was different. Naavah's spirit glided toward her father instead. Once Naavah reached Adam she was absorbed into him, making his light shine brighter than it ever had before.

The absorption forced more tears out of Adam. My lover's once controlled persona had finally let go, freeing him to grieve for his lost child. His physical form also altered. My lover's silver hair had returned to its original deep honey, but his temples were still shaded white, similar to the snowy mountain peaks in the distance. The wrinkles on his forehead and eyes all but disappeared, leaving the laugh lines around his lips. I realized then that this was the only way he could have stayed with me. My will to fight against my magic was too great to heal anybody. At least this way our child was still a part of us and perhaps the natural world.

We grieved together for the remainder of the day. At sunset we decided it was time, and Adam went to dig a grave for Naavah next to her siblings and her life love, Kun. We had buried them under our apple tree. Nearly one hundred years had passed while the tree had grown into itself, though it was not the pale beauty its predecessor had been. It looked like every other green-leafed tree, but at least it grew apples

for us. It was our place to remember our children and the happy lives we had together.

By the time Adam finished unearthing her grave, I had prepared her body. It was my belief to not waste any part of a perished body, but I was never able to desecrate my children's bodies that way. It would have been too difficult, and I would never have asked Adam to do that. I gave their bodies to the Earth to absorb on its own. That would have to be enough. Our species were separate from the rest anyway.

We carried our firstborn's body to her place under the tree. I wrapped her in Shamira's skins. Naavah had a close friendship with Shamira. I thought it fitting that they would rest together. Once we buried her, our descendants joined us and said their last goodbyes to their mother and grandmother.

It was the end of an era. And so it went every time one of our loved ones died, again and again and again and again. For five hundred years Adam and I repeated the cycle, slowly distancing ourselves from our family and from the home we created.

We shared what Naavah had done for Adam, and they passed on the knowledge to the next seer who was born. Because of this, they discovered how to absorb the spirits of the departed, so they weren't lost to the ground below. They remained home in a different form. The seers were the only ones able to accomplish this despite the efforts of my other children. I was curious to know if they could have given their energy to the natural world as well, but I never said anything because I wanted them to continue giving it to Adam. In a way he was a part of it.

Adam kept in contact with our descendants, and each time the seers passed on, they did as Naavah had done: they bestowed their spirit upon him. With each absorption he gained another lifetime. Though they were unaware of our parental connection to them, the seers gifted their spirits anyway. Something about Adam called to them. Whatever the reason, I was grateful. I could not have continued on without him at my side.

Adam was not the man he once was, the comical monkey-man who always did his best to make me smile. Adam was now a man hardened by grief and a life lived for far too long. Yet, each time the offer presented itself, he accepted the seer's spirit. For me. So I wouldn't be alone. Each time he did, he withdrew himself further and further from me. Physically, he continued to stand by my side, but his mind had long left me. Still, I refused to free him from this long and lonely existence that he had never asked for.

The self-hatred grew in me each day for what I was doing to him, but I never found the strength to let go of him and the memories that were attached to him, the memories of discovering our new home and building a family. Those memories were the most precious in my life, and also the shortest. I wouldn't let go unless he forced me to, and he knew that. Yet I always asked myself, *would he?*

I gathered herbs for my garden. I didn't know why I bothered. I didn't need them. Adam never got hurt anymore due to his lack of ventures, and any sickness he developed in his first life had long disappeared as a result of the absorption of his children's spirits. My descendants were well aware of the medicinal properties of plants and how to grow the crops they needed, and they no longer required my skills. I supposed it was just something to do. Anything to keep my mind busy.

It had been centuries since I had been needed by anyone. My children had grown in number and had formed a society and culture of their own. I was proud to have been the source of it, not only because of my part as the first mother of this land, but because of the lessons I had passed on. My descendants would be a kind and caring people for a long time to come. I was just here to ensure it stayed that way.

I took my time on the journey back to our hut. Adam and I decided to live away from our offspring. Not so far that we couldn't help if they

needed it, but far enough that we wouldn't be tempted to visit every day. That was best. Not only because it was difficult for us to see them, but because they needed to live on their own. I needed to be certain they would follow my practices even if I wasn't around. I needed to be certain Earth would be safe if I died. Although it might have been eons from now, Lucifer was still out there, and the surrounding light waned every day. And every day it dwindled more quickly.

I would have to step in eventually.

Despite the fact that I traveled at a pace a turtle would have been ashamed of, I reached my garden too quickly. I usually took herbs from my garden if I was in need of them, but for some unknown reason my plants had begun to die. It wasn't as if I wasn't caring for them. I had too much time on my hands, so they were very well cared for. I didn't understand why they were shriveling up as if the sun had singed them. I carefully removed the deceased herb plants and replaced them with the new ones I had gathered.

Finished placing the greenery in their new homes, I sauntered over to the pear tree that rested next to my garden. I slid down the trunk to sit in the moss below and scrutinized my current dwelling.

Adam had made a small hut for the two of us. It wasn't as spacious as the one our first children had grown up in; we didn't need that much space anymore. All we really did was sleep there, whether during day or night. I mostly slept during the day and did my work at night. I loved the crisp night air, the stars that shone down on me, the moon that guided me. Guiding me to where, I was still unsure, but I always felt it was trying to relay a message. Hopefully I would figure it out someday.

The hut's structure was built from the bamboo trees, and the roof was covered in a mixture of earth, moss, and grass. It wasn't the best it could be, but it was enough for us. The ancient trees that towered over us provided enough cover from the ever-changing weather. I didn't remember

the weather being so unpredictable before a few hundred years ago, but perhaps I hadn't paid enough attention.

I decorated the shelter with assorted flowers to brighten the gloom that seemed to exude from it. Most of these flowers were those I had first seen when I woke up in that meadow from so long ago—the indigo forget-me-nots, the multicolored daisies, and the red roses. The roses that had pricked me several times throughout my long life. The roses that constantly hurt me, but I continued to love them. Their beauty compensated for the pain they caused me.

I decided that I had sat there brooding for long enough, and I went inside the hut to check on Adam. He was curled up, sleeping in his moss bedding with a jaguar's skin covering him. The jaguar had been Kun's companion. Kun had insisted his father keep the skin, and he did not want to be buried with his jaguar. He wanted his father to have something to remind him of his children, of his son. Adam had watched as Kun grew and aged and died, something that Adam wished to do—join his children in the blissfulness of death. Regardless, he would never say that aloud, especially to me.

I noticed my rabbit-skin bag was tucked away safely in the corner of the hut where it continued to hold my ancient crumbling treasures. My lion-skin bag had withered over the years and lost its use. Quietly, I curled up next to Adam under the jaguar's skin and hugged him with his back facing me. I listened to his heartbeat and watched his chest rise and fall. My lover was always so warm, even if the weather was cold. His heartbeat used to be a steady rhythm that I could fall asleep to, but since his life had been extended, his steady beat had become an irregular drum. As if his heart couldn't support his body anymore. As if it were struggling to endure his continued life.

Still holding onto him, I wept silently. It was a tearless endeavor. I felt the sadness within me at every moment of my existence, but I couldn't

produce the tears anymore. Losing Naavah had dried my tear ducts. I had told myself I would be strong from then on. I never taught Naavah how to be strong, but of course she didn't need me to. She taught *me.* All I could do now was go through the motions. It wasn't as satisfying as the water that bled down my face, but it allowed me to relieve some of the confined emotions I held.

It was the only way I could handle the constant hollowness in my chest.

No noise sounded from my silent suffering. Even so, Adam sensed I needed him, as he always did. Removing my tight grip on him, Adam turned and wove his arms around my body. He held me while I grieved yet again. "I am here for you, my love," Adam consoled me.

"Adam, you don't have to comfort me. You are in as much pain as I am, if not more. Doesn't it hurt you to do this for me? Do you not hate me by now?" I questioned.

Not skipping an irregular heartbeat, he answered, "Lilith, I could never hate you, no matter what you do. I have told you as much several times. I would think you would believe me by now." I looked up to see the smile that played on his lips. It was not as full and lively as it had once been, but it was nice to see just the same. I didn't get to see it very often.

"I love it when you smile. It gives me hope that there is happiness awaiting us somewhere in the future," I said.

Adam looked away as he answered, "There is happiness for you, Lilith. You just have to find it." My lover held me tighter. I didn't like the way he evaded my comment, like he wasn't planning on being with me in the future. That couldn't happen. Adam had to live on. I would find him happiness, even if I had to sacrifice my own.

I took his face in my hands and proclaimed, "I love you." Adam returned my adoration with a kiss. And another. And another. We soon felt the spark we once had, the spark that had ignited us with passion nearly every day in our first lifetime together. After our family began to dwindle,

our spark diminished to merely a smolder. It made this moment all the more special, even if he didn't release inside of me, even if we couldn't have any more children.

The heat grew fast within our hut and we no longer needed the cat's skin. Adam rolled on top and rubbed himself against me. He caressed my face, neck, shoulders, and bosom with his kisses. His hand moved to my hip while his other was knotted in my hair. My hands roamed the sinews of his chest and shoulders, feeling all the hard years of labor he had spent building our home. I wrapped my arms around his neck to force him closer to my waiting lips. Once our lips touched, he thrust himself inside my waiting chasm. The sensation was the most wonderful I had felt in a long time. One by one, each worry was banished with each thrust. The rest of the night was undeserved bliss.

It was just before dawn when he said, "Do you want to watch the sun rise?"

"Yes," I said, with one last kiss on his beautiful grin. We dressed and hastened to our destination. It was a considerable distance away, and if we were going to beat the rising sun, we would have to run.

It felt good to sprint. I had been so preoccupied, filling my time with my many chores and deliberate unhurried movements, that I had forgotten what it felt like to push myself. The early morning wind bit my cheeks as I flew past trees and waking birds, past the nocturnal creatures bedding down for the day, past the dew-soaked plants that grabbed at my legs. I had forgotten how it felt to be free, to be merely one of the creatures that lived in the woodland and not an abomination that stole from it.

I slowed my pace for Adam, but we still reached the river falls in record time. The sun danced off the waterfall's waves as it crashed down to the lake below. We climbed onto the low-hanging branch that led out to the peak of the falls. It was Shamira's chosen spot when she had first been accepted into our family. She gladly shared her perch with us on many occasions.

The panther would lay her head in one of our laps as we sat and dangled our feet over the edge. Even Adam had grown to love her despite his initial instinct to hate her. The monkey attributes he once possessed disappeared slowly over time and left only the man—the man who shared my life and fathered my children.

Adam and I sat on the old branch and watched as the sun rose over the tree-lined mountains and spread its warmth to the village below. No one had woken yet, so it was silent except for the gushing of water. We held hands and I leaned on his shoulder, remembering times long past. I could almost feel Shamira's heavy head resting on my thigh.

"My love, I can't be with you for—"

Adam began to speak, but a loud noise interrupted him. It sounded like thunder. The sky was clear though. *Where was it coming from?* The more I listened, the more I thought it was a herd of—*antelope? Rhinos? No, bigger than rhinos. Mammoths? How did they get this far south?* They dwelled in the north.

My thoughts were confirmed. The scent of thick, dirty wool wafted on the breeze, and I could see the trees shifting and falling before I saw the giant creatures. Adam and I dove down the falls and into the lake. The fall was a long one, but Adam came out unscathed. We swam to the shore and sprinted for the village.

"Wake up! Stampede!" we hollered as loud as we could. Our offspring woke immediately. The villagers grabbed their children, and the strongest carried the elderly upon their backs. They ran into the forest opposite of where the thundering sounded. Adam and I had almost evacuated everyone when the first mammoth appeared. He pulverized the ground he ran across, taking the trees with him. Soon, I saw the rest of the herd. The giant creatures came hurtling down the hill that rested next to the waterfall. Our path made by my years of travel was lost to their enormous foot impressions.

Seeing everyone was out of the clearing and into the safety of the

trees, I told Adam, "See that everyone keeps going. I am going to try and divert their path." Adam nodded and dashed into the undergrowth after our children, his tail twitching nervously. Now that I had no distractions, I ran toward the oncoming mammoth. Usually, if I stood my ground and challenged the stampeding animals, they would change their direction. This time was different. The creature clearly saw me but was going to choose to trample me anyway.

I waited until the last moment and jumped onto the beast's tusks. I used my unnatural strength to pull the giant tooth in the direction I wanted. As the mammoth called out in frustration, I noticed something attached to the tusk I gripped. Plant fibers were wound together to form a long thick string. The rope was wrapped around both tusks and led up past the back of the creature's large skull. I followed the trail of tough string before he could shake me off, and I used his upward momentum to jump onto his head.

Once I reached the top, however, I found I was not alone. There was another creature directing the crazed mammoth. A human. A man. However, he was not one of my children. I knew every one of my children who were born to this Earth, and he was a stranger. *It couldn't be.*

I immediately recognized his features. The man had golden hair and pale blue eyes. He had a strong physique, though not as sturdy as the one I was thinking of. His face was beautiful, but narrower than the one I remembered. It was not the man I feared it was, but it was clear he was akin to him.

I was stunned. I didn't know what to do. Seeing I wasn't going to attack, the man said, "You're the one he spoke of? You're not so impressive." He smirked, a facial expression that was familiar to me. The man raised his arm. I thought it was a defensive pose, but then he snapped it forward and hit me hard across the face. I tumbled down the front of the mammoth and landed directly in front of his large stomping feet.

My breath was lost from the landing, and I wasn't able to move fast enough. That was all it took. The angry mammoth brought down his front foot and planted it on my lower half. My hips and legs were crushed beneath the weight of the creature. I couldn't feel it right away. I laid there waiting for the pain to come. I heard the crunch of my bones, so I knew it was coming. By the time the mammoth lifted his heavy foot again, I felt it.

The injuries were excruciating, but I couldn't make a sound. My body had shut down, leaving my thoughts to silently scream. There was no escape from the pain, but it was worse because of my fast healing. I could feel my body already attempting to stitch itself back together; slowly and agonizingly.

I felt and heard bones reconnect with their counterparts. I could feel the stretch of muscles and tendons as they morphed back to how they were supposed to be. I inwardly cringed as the crimson sand filled my body; it was rough against my sensitive injuries. All I could do was lay there and wait. Thankfully the mammoth had moved on, but to where I didn't know.

During my partial unconsciousness I heard footsteps. They crunched on the dropped branches the mammoths had brought with them on their fur. Once the steps reached me, a voice said, "Is she dead?"

"No. She will wake again." *Another voice?* I must have been further gone than I thought. I hadn't even noticed the second pair of footsteps. "Just throw her in the lake. That will keep her down for a time." *Keep me down? Why would they want that?* I felt hands on me then, one set holding my shoulders, the other my mangled legs. The movement made me want to cry out, but I was still paralyzed.

They made their way to the lake with me in hand. I could hear the waterfall in the background. "All right, toss her," the second voice said. It was oddly familiar. *Where did I know it from?* The person carrying my upper half smelled of sunbaked earth.

Soon I found myself underwater, still unable to move. I sank to the

bottom and rested there in the sand and lake-grass. I felt the fish bump me as they swam around my healing corpse. I tried to force myself awake, but not even the constant feeling of drowning could rouse me. The sole task I could do was lay underwater and wait for my body to heal, hoping that my family had run far from this place.

X
Necessary Sacrifice

One's savior
is another's monster.
-A

The spider's web is wildering
And so it remains unclear
Why the spider's web is glimmering
With that of our fears
As long as we remain dear
To that which shimmers
The web won't grow dimmer
And we will all continue to cheer

The rhyme I created for my children played in a continuous loop in my head as I drowned over and over again. The now disturbing words were the only things that distracted me from the horrific torture I endured. The water entered my lungs as my chest lunged for air, only to find none. Once my body processed that there wasn't a purpose to the repetition, I would lose consciousness. My body was forced to the edge of death. When I finally reached the point where I thought, *Yes, it's finally time to let go*, my senses would awaken once more. This brought on the struggle for air again…and twice again…and fifty times again. Something wouldn't let me rest.

I just wanted to rest.

After an unknown amount of time, I noticed a change. I could feel my legs again; I hadn't realized I couldn't. I tried to move them, only to fail. I was still paralyzed. Memories started to flood back to me. Mammoths. My descendants fleeing for their lives. Two men who were not of my kin. I had to get up. My children were in danger. *Where was Adam?*

If I could only breathe. If I could breathe my healing would be much faster. I needed air. The sweet relief of the wind in my lungs was all I wanted. My body still refused to obey. I knew then what I had to do. I had to hurt myself further if I wanted to make it to land. I tried to relax and concentrate on what I wanted. I only hoped I would have enough strength to do it.

The water grew warm around me. It felt nice, but only for a moment. *More.* I had to do much more. I willed the water's energy to speed as fast as it could. I felt the push and pull of the tortured lake. The burning tides nearly tore my crippled half from me. The water was boiling now. The pain was horrific. *Faster.* The water that molested my lungs caught fire. *Faster!*

I thought I was going to lose consciousness again when air entered my lungs at last. My whole body was on fire, and it convulsed with the pain. But the air I breathed was a welcome exchange. I had forced the energy in the lake's water to travel so rapidly that all that was left was the steam rising from the ground. With air in my lungs, my crushed pelvis and legs healed faster, as well as my self-accumulated burns. I felt skin regrow and cover my mending muscles. My hair tickled my arms as it grew down past my hips. The life in the lake had been extinguished, to my regret, but my children were more important. *Necessary sacrifices.*

Only partially healed, I stood and stumbled my way out of the deep crevice that rested in the Earth. I hoped the water would return someday. I looked around for the mammoths and strange men. They were nowhere

to be found. The mammoths had destroyed everything we built. The village was nothing but a pile of rubble. The crops were trampled. Our apple tree had been ignited and it continued to burn, despite the lack of life. I could see blue flames licking its charred trunk. That apple tree had represented our home and held our deceased children within its roots. *This would not be forgiven.* I stumbled to one of the demolished huts and donned the furs that were left behind. My new skin was hot and simmered with anger, but I needed something to hold myself together, even if it was only clothing.

Scanning the area, I saw the path the beasts had taken. It was the same direction my children had gone. I sprinted as fast as I could in their direction. I stumbled only a few times before I adjusted to my new limbs. *How long had I been unconscious? Who were these people? Why were they attacking us?* I gazed upward as I ran and scanned the sky through the towering trees. The sun was well overhead. Midday. I had been asleep too long. If these people weren't my own, then they must be his. But why were they here? My children were peaceful and hadn't crossed onto his land. There was no reason to attack. *So why did he?*

Even at my incredible speed, I followed the trail of destruction for what felt like hours. Where was everyone? Adam? My children? Lucifer? I halted. I heard the slightest crunch of a leaf. I stilled and listened. I didn't even breathe.

"Lilith…" a whisper in the wind.

"Who's there?" I called out.

"Have you forgotten the sound of my voice already? That's disappointing."

"Lucifer. Why do you hide? Come out and talk to me." I shook with anger, but his presence only seemed to weaken the emotion. My chest felt full for the first time in centuries.

"Of course, *my love*," he snickered. *My love?* Only Adam called me that. Lucifer entered my line of sight from the opposite direction I thought he would. I had forgotten the stealth he possessed.

"Why are you here? Where are my children? Where is Adam?" I demanded.

"I guess you don't feel like catching up. I thought you would be happy to see me after all this time." His arrogance had only grown in size. It made me feel small, like a minnow next to a shark. I hated it.

"Catch up? If you wanted to talk to me all you had to do was ask! You didn't have to destroy my village and harass my children!" My anger flared, and I enjoyed the wary look that crossed his face.

"Oh, right, your children. How did that go? I remember you being so adamant against having *my* children, because it would harm the 'Earth's spirit.' Yet, you ran off and had children with—what was he before? A monkey?"

I gasped. *How did he know that?*

Lucifer continued, a smirk plastered on his face, "The tail gave it away."

How had he even seen Adam? Did his people find my lover and children?

"Where is he?" I questioned. I meant it to sound strong and demanding, but it only came out as a whimper. Apparently, all these years apart had not numbed me to his authority. Lucifer could still defeat me with only a few words. That realization brought a tear to my eye. It seemed I had some water left in me after all. That tear suddenly seared my face. I felt the burn, and the tear disappeared in a miniature cloud of steam. *Had I done that?*

Still pondering the tear, Lucifer said, "I never liked seeing you cry." I stiffened. "You're not the only one who commands the energy anymore. You should have stayed around longer."

I stuttered, "How? Did—"

He cut me off. "You did. The punishment you gave me for loving you is what did this to me." It was obvious he wasn't going to explain further. "Knowing it was what you spoke of before, I began to experiment and found that I could do a lot with the light I saw." He smiled, but not the smile of someone who finally understood me. It was the smile of someone who wanted to hurt me.

I still asked, knowing the answer, "Then you see that the light wanes when you take life from it. Have you changed your ways?"

"Not even for a moment."

My stomach dropped to the ground. "Why? Do you not care what happens to your home? To my home?" I finished rather pathetically. There was just no talking to him. I could feel a fight coming, and it wasn't going to be good.

"As I said before, I will not live by the rules you invented. There is no way of knowing if the light diminishing is a bad thing, and I honestly don't care if it is. I have lived a long life, and if my time ends with the light, then so be it," he said indifferently.

"What of your children?" I found my strength again. "You may want death, but don't take them and everything with you. You're being selfish and monstrous." I breathed out an angry breath. "How could you?" How could I have loved someone so horrible? How could I *still* love someone so horrible?

"How could *I*? How could *you*? *You* are the one who left me. *You* are the one who chose a life with an animal over me. *You* are the one who created these mutated children. And look at you now. Did it bring you happiness? Did you finally find what you were looking for?" My former mate moved closer. "No, perhaps not. You don't even live among them anymore. Did you outgrow them like you did me? Did you discard them like you did me?" His words brought me to my knees. How could he have thought that of me? Didn't he know I left because he told me he wouldn't ever change? That his *pride* was worth more than me.

The words that came out of my mouth were small and vulnerable. "You should realize that I left because I didn't want to create more of us. I thought that if we mated with ones who were part of the natural world, our children would be part of that light you see now, connected to it like the rest of the world is." My hands balled into fists. Sand poured from

the cuts my nails made. "Clearly, I was wrong, but I didn't leave because I outgrew you, or I didn't love you. Leaving you was the hardest thing I ever had to do." The tears were still dry, but that didn't stop my weeping. "You wouldn't change your ways, and if we had children you would have taught them wrong. Without your interference, I was able to guide my children to live the right way, despite the fact that they turned out worse than either of us." Hopeless, I asked, "Did Eve bring you any happiness? Any at all?"

We were silent for a few moments. Lucifer wouldn't look me in the eye, but I could see he was torn. The man wanted to believe me, or maybe he already did. But his pride got the best of him, and his beautiful golden face filled with hatred yet again.

Not answering my last question, he said, "Our children *are* worse than you hoped, but no worse than you. You brought this upon yourself, Lilith. There is no one to blame but you." I looked down in defeat. "I will continue to suck the life from this planet, Lilith. There is nothing you can do to stop me. I have been very busy these last five hundred years. My numbers are far greater than yours, and they have already spread across the entire land. You were our last stop, and I have accomplished what I came for." Lucifer wasn't smiling anymore, but he was still exuding arrogance.

"And what did you come for?" I asked.

"To see you in pain," he replied bluntly. My nails dug deeper into my palms. I refused to believe he meant those words. "You hurt me, Lilith. No matter the reason, you still chose to leave me, and I will never forgive you for that." He started to walk away. "Oh, and I couldn't have your children interfering. So I got rid of them." That roused me. My strength returned with a vengeance. The violent tendencies I fought returned so I could carry out one final task.

I ripped the thick branch from the tree next to me and closed the distance between Lucifer and me, fully intending to end his life. If he wanted to die so badly, all he had to do was ask. The man had taken my children.

They were all I had in this miserable existence. Lucifer was going to regret his actions, even if it came at the cost of my own soul.

I blinked and I was behind him. My former mate turned to face me just in time for the pointed end of the branch to press against his chest, where his heart would have been if he had one.

Lucifer just stared at me. He didn't fight back or try to stop me. "What are you waiting for? Do it. I took over this land to bleed it dry, and I killed your children. End me."

The green of the forest and the gentle light that caressed it were no more. All I saw was red. All I saw was the sand that would pour out of him. The man knew the anger I felt. Lucifer could now see my spirit, and it consumed me. The crimson light clouded my vision, urging me to end him.

I pressed the wood farther into his chest, piercing his gaze with mine. But I didn't see hatred there as I had a moment before. There was just nothing. Lucifer was empty. He cared for nothing and felt nothing. The man didn't even flinch as the wood pierced him. *This was wrong.* I couldn't kill him, even if he had done those things. I loved him, and nothing would ever change that. This was a man who wanted to die, and he was doing everything in his power to make that happen by forcing me to murder him. I wouldn't let him do that. I wouldn't let him die. He was going to face the consequences of what he'd done. Lucifer was going to face me. And I refused to be afraid of him anymore.

"Why do you hesitate? Do I need to finish off your precious Adam as well before you will kill me? You are weak. I can't believe I ever loved you." The man swatted the branch out of my hands. Red dust flaked off the end of it as it fell to the ground. The anger faded from my vision and panic soon replaced it.

"Where is he?" I demanded.

"Mourning over your lost succubus children, I assume," he said coolly. I flinched at the word he used to describe my children, remembering

when I had called Naavah such a thing. I couldn't look at him anymore. If I stayed any longer, I was going to kill him, and I didn't want to give him the satisfaction. He didn't deserve the peace that came with death. *Not yet.*

Not looking back to see if he followed, I left Lucifer behind to search for Adam. I didn't hear his footsteps, but that didn't mean much. For both our sakes, I hoped he ran in the opposite direction. Upon request, my heartless chest cavity ached, and I knew then that he was no longer near.

I called Adam's name over and over again, and after an agonizing amount of time, I heard his erratic heartbeat. Though I wished I hadn't. I wasn't prepared for what awaited me. I entered a freshly made clearing where the mutilated bodies of my children lay dead.

The mammoths had crushed most of them, but the ones who were able to outmaneuver the beasts were struck down with spears and arrows. Adam was holding one of them, the current leader of the village, Frode. He was a wise leader, and it wasn't right that his life had been cut short. I slowly made my way over to Frode and Adam. I made sure to burn the scene into my memory. Though I didn't know how, I would learn from this horror. The smell of blood filled the air, and its metallic odor infiltrated my nostrils.

I collapsed next to my lover and child. "Where were you?" Adam questioned. He wouldn't look at me, and his voice was barely audible. Adam had broken, and I didn't know if I'd ever be able to fix him.

"I'm sorry…" I couldn't think of anything else to say. I had no words of comfort to give. A spear protruded from Frode's abdomen, and his hands grasped at it helplessly. The village leader's face was pale, and he coughed blood. My child was suffering…because of me.

"Frode, my son. I am so sorry. This is all my fault," I whimpered. The tears still wouldn't come to relieve me. I looked down at my descendant. I could see a little of Adam and me in every child who was born. Frode had my red hair and Adam's strong jaw.

Adam responded for Frode. "This isn't your fault. I failed to protect

them, all of them…against that monster," he spat. I didn't know if he was speaking of the mammoths or Lucifer, but I supposed it didn't matter. I took notice that there were none of Lucifer's children decorating the ground. My children weren't taught to fight back.

Frode was no longer able to speak. All he could do was stare at us, crying silently, pleading for help. "Adam, take out the spear. It will be easier for him." I could see Frode had absorbed as many of the dead as he could and was now waiting for release.

Adam looked at me then. "No, I will not speed his death along," he cried out.

"Frode will only suffer longer if we don't," I said, but he already knew that. Adam simply didn't want to watch another son die. I understood perfectly.

Adam nodded but gave no sign of movement. "Let me," I said. Adam didn't move. Taking the initiative, I grabbed onto the spear's stem and pulled as quickly as I could. Frode coughed more blood. It splashed across Adam's face. He didn't even flinch as the red liquid dripped down his cheek.

Once I removed the spear, Frode's passing came swiftly. It was all I could ask for. We watched as another one of our children died. We held Frode's hands and I whispered comforts in his ear. Once more the spirit of the seer offered itself to Adam, responding to its centuries-old duty.

I expected him to absorb it as he always had, but when the rainbowed spirit touched him, he simply said, "No." The soul then preceded to sink into the ground below. The moss and earth blocked our view, and I could no longer feel him. I settled my hand on the blood-coated grass where the spirits disappeared. Frode was forever lost to us like the rest. I had hoped a seer would have the power to join the natural web, but Frode proved my theory wrong. Or maybe he and the others didn't *want* to join.

"Why did you do that?" I asked quietly.

"You know why," he said.

I couldn't look at him. *Why was he doing this to me? Hadn't I lost enough? He was going to leave me, too?* That was his last chance to absorb our children's offered spirit, and he rejected it. Adam didn't have long left as it was. Another few years maybe. That was nothing to an immortal.

"I can't go on anymore, Lilith. You've known that for a long while, and now this…" His voice failed him, but he recovered and continued, "I had a wonderful life with you. Those first hundred years with our family were amazing, and I thank you for giving me this life, but I wasn't meant to live this long. You know that. My body can't handle it. I'm not like you and…him." I averted my gaze. I didn't even want to think his name.

Shoving down my emotions, I said, "I understand. I have put a burden on you, and I have been selfish. I am sorry for that." I took a breath. "At least we still have a few years together." I gave a small smile but the look on his face wiped it away. "Don't we?" I questioned.

"My love, please don't make this harder than it already is," Adam pleaded. I could see how this event had altered him; his spirit barely glowed. It was only a matter of time before it dimmed to nothing.

I lost my temper again. "Me? Make this harder? We have lost our children, Adam. You have refused the last chance you will ever have at another lifetime, and I accepted that. But now you're telling me that you can't even finish this one? How can you leave me after *this*?" I stood and motioned around us, showing the complete destruction and carnage that befell not only this forest, but our very own children. Bodies were strewn everywhere. The elderly and small children were cut down where they stood, their crushed corpses left to haunt us.

"Lilith, it doesn't matter when I leave, because you will never be ready. I wish I could change our fate, but you will have to continue your journey without me," he said sadly. *What was he saying?* He always said he would never leave me, that he would always be there for me. The loneliness

crushed me once more, as if I were being sucked into a vortex of black. Forever alone in the nothingness.

I decided not to say anything. If I opened my mouth something awful would come out. I began gathering the bodies; Adam helped as much as he could in his rapidly declining form. I lined my children up and cleaned them the best I could, which wasn't much. I wrapped each child in sunflower leaves. Each leaf was big enough to wrap half a body. It was morbid of me to wrap them in these flowers, the ones that reminded me so much of Lucifer. But since he had killed them, a piece of him should lay them to rest. It was the least he could do.

The miserable task would have gone much faster if I had used magic to move the bodies and wrappings, but working with my hands was something I wanted to do. I had expected as much from them. I owed my children the hard work that came with this job. I wouldn't cheat them out of that, like I had their lives.

Adam and I worked through day and night. We decided to bury them where they died. Adam wanted to lay them to rest under our apple tree, but once I told him what became of it, he agreed to do it there, in the place where our children's lives and lineage ended. Though I kept it to myself, I knew my lover wouldn't have been able to make the journey anyway. We buried and said goodbye to each one of our descendants. My mind had gone numb by the time we finished. I couldn't let the pain in. Not yet. There was still the worst to come.

Adam and I sat in the moss next to the graves. The smell of freshly dug earth clung to the moisture in the air. Neither of us said a word as we were both mentally preparing for the next onslaught of emotions. The sun rose above the mountain peaks. That was something I could count on. The sun always returned, as did the moon and stars. They were my constant companions in this life. My only companions. Though the sight of the sun now reminded me of death.

"It's time, my love," Adam said. He went to stand, but found he no longer had the strength. I went to him and took his outstretched hand, the hand that always offered support to me. I didn't want to take it this time, but this was something that he wanted, and I was going to give it to him no matter what it did to me.

I gripped Adam's hand tight and cradled his head in my lap. I ran my free hand through his still soft, wavy hair. My lover's face had aged, and his hair had greyed, but I couldn't help but see him as he was, the energetic and funny monkey-man who always made me smile even when I didn't want to. I hadn't noticed how muddied his bronze aura had become. There were so many colors. So many spirits shared his body. His earthy eyes were tired.

I placed my hand on his cheek and whispered, "No matter how long I live, you will always be in my thoughts, and your love in my soul. You gave me something to live for. Thank you." The smile I gave him was genuine, but it ached to mean something different.

I held him tight, unable to let go. Adam raised his calloused hand and tucked a wild crimson curl behind my ear. "Try to find happiness, Lilith. That is all I ask." I nodded my head, but I knew that would never come to be. Not after this.

The bronze of his spirit pulsed with the irregular beating of his heart. It wouldn't be much longer now. Adam's body was not meant to carry so many souls. His prolonged existence was a temporary one. I suspected he knew that if he had absorbed Frode and the others, he would have died right then and there. Even in great despair, he granted me these last few moments with him. I squeezed his hand tighter, begging the tears to stay in.

I didn't break eye contact with my lover for a second. He needed to know I was with him until the end. Once his irregular beating ceased, I closed his warm eyes and kissed his forehead. I could feel the relief in his spirit as it was released from his frail husk. Adam's soul departed his body and united with the rest of the surrounding light, taking Naavah and our

other descendants with him. I only wished Adam could have carried *all* our children to peace.

The realization that I would never see those welcoming brown eyes again nearly crushed me. But as I had before many times in my life, I shoved the pain down deep into the abyss that dwelled within. I lifted my lover's body into my arms and carried him to our hut so I could wrap him in Kun's jaguar skins. Adam would have liked that. I didn't want to bury him where our children died, where there was only heartache for him. I saw my rabbit fur lying in the corner of the hut as I left, but I didn't feel the need to retrieve it.

I found myself back at the recovering lake. The water from the waterfall crashed down angrily into the seared pit. The apple tree was nearly gone, but its low limbs still burned hot. The earth around it was charred and blackened. I placed his wrapped body on top of the blue flames that licked the tree's ancient roots. Upon his touch, the flames grew and engulfed his soulless form. I watched as Adam turned to ash and blew away in the wind. *My lover deserved more than a simple burial.*

Nothing was left for me now. My children were gone. Adam was gone. Everything that I had built for myself was destroyed. Lucifer was determined to extinguish this planet and him with it. *Wasn't the solution simple?* I could have just killed him, and it would have been over. But his children were still here, and if what he said was true, they had taken over the land. Even so, I wouldn't have been able to anyway. I still loved him, but I also wanted him to suffer for what he'd done to me. He wanted to die; perhaps living would be his punishment, just as mine was.

Separating the children from him would be their only chance. *Earth's only chance.* I had to believe they would find their own path, and hopefully that path would be the right one. I jumped into the lake's crevice and sat; the water from the falls puddled in the burnt muck. All I had to do was let it in, let in all the emotions I'd shoved down and the magic I'd shunned.

The power was there; I only had to access it. My thoughts roamed the course of my life, making sure to feel every bit of the long existence.

My love for nature. My love for Lucifer. My shock and disgust at the carnage of the world. The wonder of seeing Earth's light for the first time. The realization I was separate from it. The confusion I had for Lucifer. My loneliness. My hatred for Lucifer. The joy for my newfound freedom. My happiness for Adam. The excitement for our new home. The anger toward my creation. My rejoicing as I accepted it. My love for Adam. The despair for my children's deaths, each and every one of them. The guilt for Adam's suffering. The pride for my children's accomplishments. The terror of seeing Lucifer. The anguish I experienced at my descendants' forced demise. The hopelessness that I couldn't fix it. The bitter sweetness of letting Adam go. The determination to fix my mistakes.

I let it all in.

The chaos was what released my power. I let myself grieve for the first time. Even if it was only for a moment. It raced through my veins and spread outward. The fear that masked my emotions for centuries was accepted and added to the mayhem. An inner fire fed my soul. I basked in the energy it granted me.

I willed my soul to feel for the cracks in the Earth, like I was growing my very own roots in the ground. I grabbed hold and made the Earth my own, further than I ever had before. Under rock and dirt and tree roots, I went deeper and deeper. Further and further until I felt the land wholly and fully. Once I had hold, I pushed. I pushed as hard as I could against the weak points in the land until they broke apart. The one united land mass broke into seven separate parts, slowly but surely moving apart from each other.

The ground shook, and water crashed over lands, filling the crevices that remained, and I was right in the middle of one of those cracks. Rocks tumbled down from the waterfall, and soon it was no more. I looked to the

black smoke of the apple tree and said one last goodbye to Adam before allowing myself to be washed away by the forceful current. I let the water take me where it willed, not caring if I could breathe or not. I was sorry for the life that would be lost from this, but they would continue to contribute to the cycle—the natural animals and plants at least. As for the humans, I wouldn't know.

A necessary sacrifice.

The water had entrapped me once again, and so soon after the last time. The current carried me far. The Earth didn't settle or calm. It was a constant storm of earthquakes and tsunamis. The only creatures that were safe were the fish. Even that was questionable at this point. The water began to taste of salt. It burned my throat and lungs, but I continued to suffer. It was what I deserved.

The weeks grew. It was a constant cycle of drowning, being crushed by debris, healing, and nearly dying again. The salt became overwhelming. It burned my skin, eyes, lungs, mouth, everything. I was in water, yet I was on fire all over again. But this fire was worse. It was slow and ate at me. I preferred the quick boil and release I had done to myself rather than this. My thirst grew worse and worse each day.

After being tugged back and forth between the harsh currents, I decided my punishment should evolve. I slowed the water that surrounded me so much that the energy hibernated. The water became cold. Soon I couldn't move. I couldn't even gasp for air. There was no need. My lungs had frozen, along with the rest of my body.

Finally, the fire stopped. Everything stopped. I couldn't feel anything anymore. Body or mind. The currents continued to tug my frozen bubble back and forth, fighting for the right to kill me. I guessed it didn't realize I couldn't die. Just as I submitted to the water, I submitted to the abyss that called to me. Down, down I went into the bottomless void of nothingness.

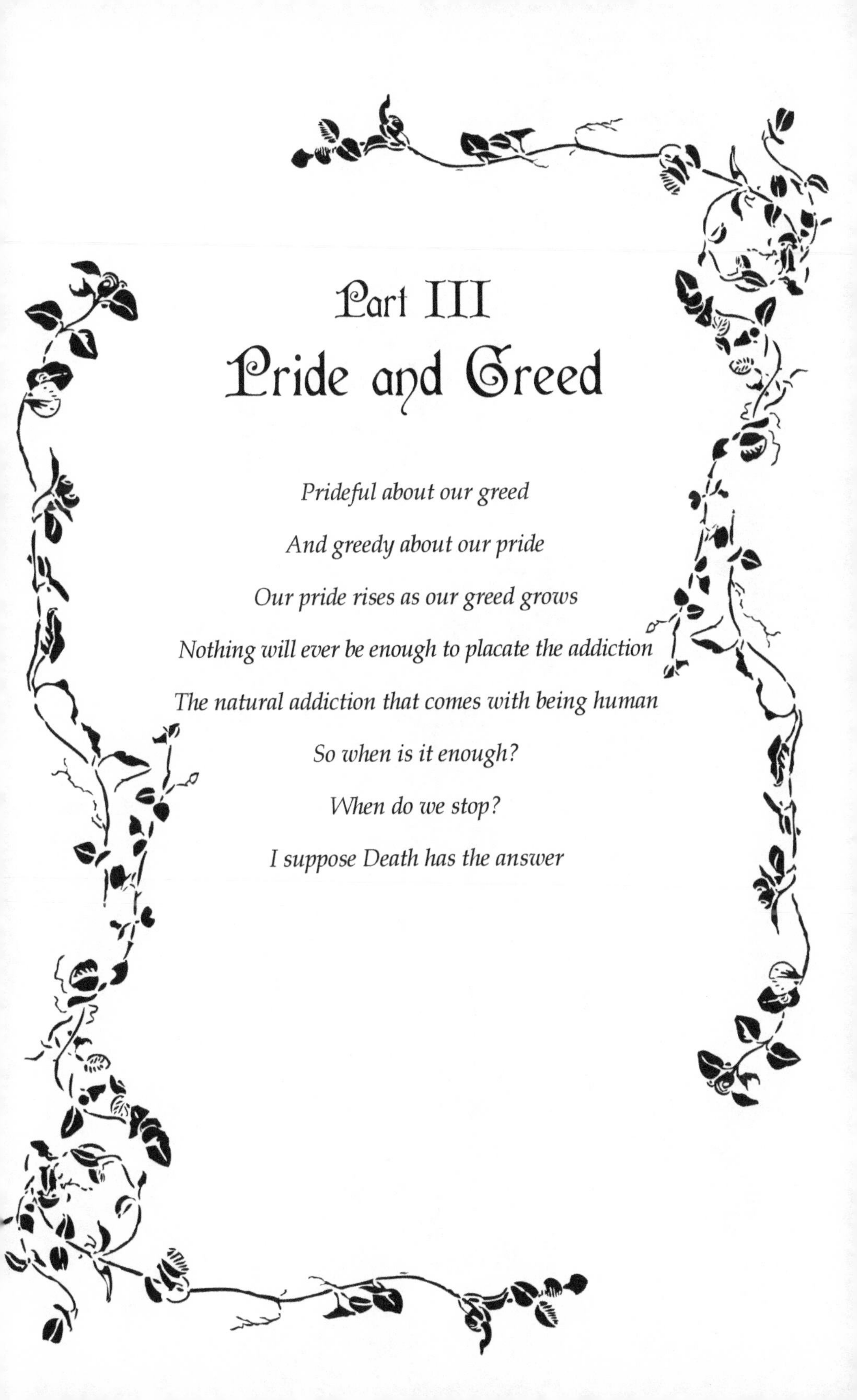

Part III
Pride and Greed

Prideful about our greed

And greedy about our pride

Our pride rises as our greed grows

Nothing will ever be enough to placate the addiction

The natural addiction that comes with being human

So when is it enough?

When do we stop?

I suppose Death has the answer

XI
An Unfortunate Time

The strangeness of a place can make us question our normalcy.
-A

1194 BCE

It was so dark. It was so empty. There was nothing. Nothing to occupy my mind except my thoughts. But those had left me long ago. I remembered being sad. No, angry. No…what was it? I gave up trying to remember. There was no point. What good would it do to remember? Here in this darkness, alone and unchanging. Nothing ever changed. Not even the fish swam by me anymore. Were they fish? Or were they mammoths? The confusion would frustrate me if I bothered to care anymore, but I didn't. The lack of incentive didn't give me any peace despite this fact. Something wouldn't let me rest, even in this state.

Occasionally I would unwillingly receive flashes of memory. Or was it my imagination trying to stimulate me? Didn't matter I supposed. The images would be gone soon enough. There would be an emerald forest that bled blue fire. A white rabbit that chased an ebony panther. Children who ran around me as I laughed and cried. A man with a tail and cinnamon-colored eyes; he held out his hand. A warm golden orb in the sky that

came to Earth and morphed into a monster with icy blue irises. I couldn't make sense of any of it. *Were the images I saw real?* Then I remembered.

I didn't care.

I continued to descend into myself, reveling in my silent isolation. I would go so deep that I would never be able to come forward again. I was so close. So close to shutting off. There would be no memories or delusions or emotions in this dark oblivion. There would just be nothing. This was the way to peace. *It had to be.*

I was a sliver away from everything disappearing when I was disturbed by a bright light. Would nothing let me rest? I was so tired. *Leave!* Anger. I felt again. It had taken so long to turn that off. So long to feel nothing. *No.* If it left me alone now, I could recover before the rest of the emotions flooded in. *Please. Go. Away.*

Of course not. Why would this thing called life listen to what I had to say? I was only the one who experienced it. I was only the one who suffered for it. Why should my opinion matter? The earth and grime fell from my human-sized bubble, causing the light to grow brighter. It pained my eyes to see it. Were my eyes open this whole time? I thought they had closed long ago. Even my body wouldn't allow me to sleep. Fine. *What did life want from me now?*

My eyes adjusted slower than I would have thought, but adjust they did. It didn't mean I understood what they were seeing. There was rope. The rope was attached together and encased my bubble. My bubble seemed to have shrunk in size. Sad. That meant I would have to leave it sooner. I didn't want to abandon the safety of the ice yet. The rope drug me higher and higher into the blinding light. Fish swam away from me, escaping from the unknown being that levitated upward.

It had been a long while since I had seen them. The creatures were different somehow. Like they had morphed into something new, but I still recognized them. I could see the form they had stemmed from. Their auras

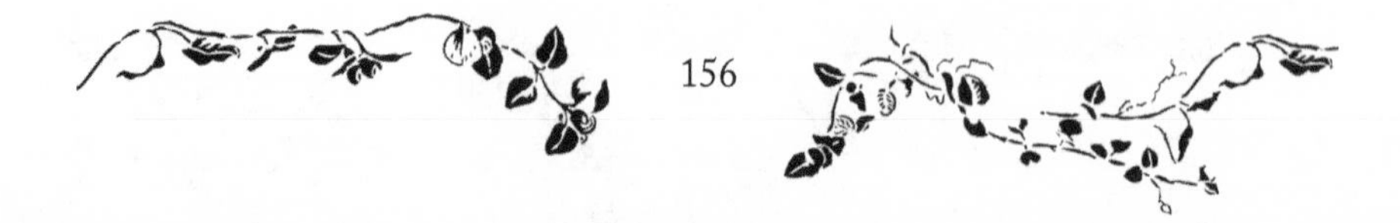

were still there, too. It was good to know that hadn't changed. But I unwillingly noticed that their light was drastically dimmer than before. Their once brilliant colors were nothing but a soft glow now. The sadness inside me was also beginning to show its colors. *No. Push it down.* I worked hard to shove the pain down. I would not relive the horrible emotion.

Whatever disturbed my silence continued to bring my anger to the surface. It made my frozen bubble steam. *Stop! Keep in control.* I could still salvage this. I could deal with whatever was up there and then go back to the darkness. It seemed to take ages, but I eventually broke the water's surface. Now that I could see properly, I saw that the netted rope encased all of my bubble. How did that happen? Was I so withdrawn that I hadn't noticed someone swim down to surround me in this handmade prison? How did they find me? I was buried deep in the muck along the water's floor.

I didn't have time to contemplate these questions because I was soon being swung through the air from a piece of wood. The rope that held me let go, and I presumed I was going to be released back into the depths when I landed on something solid. Being frozen I could only see so much, but I could tell I was on a large piece of wood that had its midsection carved out. An enormous piece of cloth was attached to long, cut trees. The name came to me then: a boat. It seemed the continent's separation had spared the people after all, and they had gone on to imagine and invent. I wondered what my children could have accomplished if they had been allowed to live on; perhaps nothing if I had continued to rule over their lives.

The memories were coming back and becoming harder to ignore. Soon people surrounded me. Their faces were blurred from the ice, but I could still see the shock and wonder on them. Had they been looking for me? Had Lucifer sent his children out to find me? Had he decided to kill me after realizing I wasn't going to grant his wish? If his life goal was to kill this planet to spite me, then hopefully that was the intention. I wouldn't watch that happen. I *couldn't* watch that happen.

It couldn't have been very long that I was encased in ice. I had barely begun to forget. Maybe a few hundred years. It took him long enough to find me. Too bad his children were only pawns in his sick game to ruin everything on this planet. I wondered if they knew what they were doing. Did he train them to follow his commands, or did they simply not care? Or both? I had to remind myself that *I* didn't care. I refused to let any emotions in, especially if it was about him. My first love. My *only* love now.

I stayed in my frozen bubble. It would take days to melt, even in the sun above the water's surface. Let them gawk. What would it get them? All they could see was a frozen corpse. They had no idea I was alive in here. Lucifer could have warned them, but if he had they would have been more cautious. Where were the weapons? The guarded eyes? No. These men simply brought me aboard to study me. Fine. I had nothing else to do. I could always shut down later.

The men appeared to be fishermen and were similar in appearance. Not only were they all dressed in the same clothes, but they possessed the same olive skin and dark hair and eyes. They looked like kin. Their energies varied widely in color though, from the palest orange to the deepest blue. My children's energies always remained within themselves, and they were unable to share with the others around them. This wasn't a bad thing, but it would have been nice to see them interact as the natural world did. Even if they were separate from it, they could have shared with each other. But we never did discover the secret to that.

It seemed these beings had; however, it didn't look like sharing. *What was it?* My mind was still fogged from the lack of use over the centuries. Their colors intertwined with each other. That was good. *No.* Frustrated, I forced my senses to come forth. It was difficult to accomplish this, as I was trying to keep my emotions from turning on with them. My eyes cleared, and I could finally understand what I was seeing.

I should have just gone back to sleep. Why did I continue to do this

to myself? What did it matter to me what they were doing to themselves? *It didn't. Just a quick look and then back to the abyss.* Focusing, I was able to see through the cracks in the ice. These people had managed to interact with each other's energies. But they were not sharing. They were fighting. The physical forms of these men were merely speaking calmly to each other, smiling even. Yet, their spirits were raging on in an invisible battle. One man's spirit would nearly absorb his neighbor's, and then, at the last moment, the weak spirit would pull back into its own self and battle on. They all fought each other simultaneously, none knowing what was actually happening around them. It was…morbid. It was worse than watching Lucifer absorb his kill's light.

These creatures didn't need to kill to absorb one another. They did it naturally, as if that was their very own instinct. Their very own purpose. My children had the same disposition, but I never saw one of their spirits attempt to steal from their own kind. Only the natural life, and even then they gave it back right away. Splitting the children apart from Lucifer was apparently in vain. They never learned the right way to live. It was obvious Lucifer had created something far worse than I had. And it was all my fault. I could only hope that there were ones out there who did learn.

The humans lost interest in me soon enough, and I was left alone. We traveled for a short time. The sun set only twice. A couple of men would wander over from their posts to look at me; the rest stayed clear of my bubble. I guess a frozen corpse staring at them made them feel uncomfortable. Understandable. It made me wonder about those who did continue to gape at me. What were they thinking? Were they simply curious, or was something wrong with them? Perhaps they had seen death too many times to worry about another corpse reminding them of their mortality. Perhaps they had accepted the fact they would die someday.

I wondered what that would feel like.

I often had to comfort my children about the idea of death. It was

something I hadn't been prepared for. How could I, an undying being, comfort another about their mortality? Adam gave the advice that I couldn't. "Life and Death are two souls destined for one another. There's no point in trying to keep them apart. Their love is too strong." Simple and comforting, and he always said it with a smile. Adam was very wise for a monkey. He was very wise for a man. It had been a long time since I had thought of him as an animal.

Stop thinking about him! He's gone. They're all gone. I wouldn't allow myself to grieve. It would be too painful. I had to concentrate on what was happening now. My sleep would come soon enough. But all I had to look forward to was the journey back down into the depths. All I had was the hope that no one would find me again, and that I would remain within the bowels of the Earth, undisturbed and alone.

I heard muffled shouts beyond the layers of thick ice. The noise goaded me from my dark thoughts, and I was able to see the light again. The sun had risen. I saw then what the men were clamoring about. They had conveniently placed me to face the bow, and there I was able to watch the blurry image of a land mass grow in size. I wondered what their land would be like, what the world would be like.

I wanted to hope for the best, but my metaphorical heart wouldn't allow it.

The next hours were agonizing. The anticipation and dread whirled together into one complex emotion. I was anxious to see what these creatures had built for themselves. It was clear they possessed creativity, and watching the men interact with one another on the physical plane was comforting. They treated each other with respect and companionship. They worked as a team to sail the boat they guided. That was all I had hoped for my own children.

But these weren't my children. No one person on this planet was my child. They were all gone. They were replaced with beings who sucked the

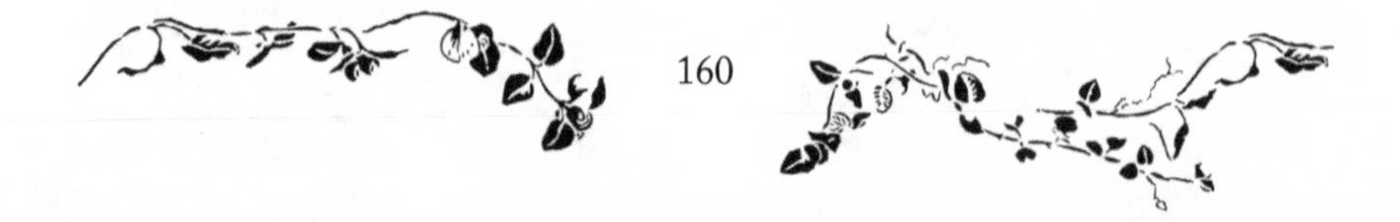

life from one another without a thought. These children of Lucifer and Eve were never taught the ways of the unseen. They probably wouldn't have listened even if they were. There was something different about them. The camaraderie on the surface was misleading. Deep down, could they be trusted to deal with turmoil? If they knew they had the power to remove another's life force, would they give or take it?

My musings were broken when my frozen sanctuary shifted. The fishermen rolled my misshapen bubble back into the netting. They attached it once more to the wooden crane that lifted and swung me onto the boardwalk beside the boat. This was where they loaded me onto another contraption: a wagon. The design fascinated me. My metaphorical heart ached, knowing that I had held my own children back from such creations. Still, it was odd how fast Lucifer's children progressed. The more I thought on it, the more I worried about how much time I had actually been dormant.

The numbers had grown since we docked. Humans swarmed to either help transport the sea life the sailors had gathered or gawk at me. Men and women pointed and spoke amongst themselves. It felt odd to be seen. Not only because I had been at the bottom of the sea for an unknown amount of time, but because although my children were different, they never made me feel separate from them. I removed myself from their lives, but I always knew I would be welcomed if I wished to be.

Here in this strange land, I was not natural. I was separate. I was the strange one, and I had no claim to these people. I had accepted this fact with the natural world, but it felt awful to realize this about my own species. I was a lonely star among a galaxy of many. My only comfort was my ability to understand them. Their words were different from my children's, but I had many words at my disposal and easily understood the meanings behind them.

Once the fishermen were finished distributing provisions, they shooed away the curious bystanders and boarded the wagon alongside me.

They slipped a thin sheet over my sanctuary, but I could still see. My eyes had plenty of time to adapt to the darkness. Curious, I peered past the threads that draped me to the scene beyond.

The wagon suddenly shifted. But how? The only clue to the mystery was the faint clomping sound of hooves. I was placed facing the rear of the structure and was unable to identify which animal hauled us forward. Clever humans indeed. Besides eating the animals, these beings forced the natural creatures to work for them. *What atrocity was next?*

I shouldn't have asked. I watched the town's life as we rolled through the streets. There were joyful people. They traded goods and exchanged pleasantries. But there was also fraud and deception. I watched as a man traded oranges for a small, glittery item. The man smiled and laughed at something his customer said. Then a small boy slinked to his side, begging the fruit man for a measly rotten apple that resided in the corner of his cart. This boy looked as if he lived in the earth and muck. Instead of helping the child, the man struck him across the face, forcing him back into the grit of the street. *Why did no one stop him?* There were several witnesses, and yet no one moved or even flinched upon the sound of a hardened fist colliding against weak flesh.

I saw a little girl slip past that same fruit cart and swipe three apples, tucking them into her dirt-covered clothes. She did this while the fruit distributor was busy beating the weak little boy. The girl didn't even look his way. She had taken advantage of his misfortune to help herself. She couldn't have been older than ten. *What had this world been reduced to? Were people so cruel that children were forced to steal to survive?*

Seeing the crimson fruit, I wondered where the ancient white tree rested now.

The scene reminded me of my early years in this life when I studied the woodland creatures. I would watch tigers hunt the antelope, and the predators would always aim for the weak. Easiest target. Fastest meal. It

was only logical from an instinctual perspective. As the tiger bit down into the young antelope's neck, the defending mother would move on and join her herd, accepting that her child had been taken and had contributed to the circle of life.

Yes, I understood the natural world despite their horrific dispositions. I respected that they had only instincts to guide them. A simple purpose to fulfill: survive. I could see it in the people who dwelled here, the need to survive, no matter the cost to another. But wasn't knowing that fact what kept us from living in such a way? The fact that we knew the difference? The fact that we *could* be better? People were content acting like wild beasts, it seemed. That saddened me. They could have been so much more. *Perhaps they still could.*

I continued to study the people and their interactions as we ambled past them in our wagon. It didn't take long for us to reach our destination. They brought me to a small home made of tan stone. There had been a garden at one point beside the front door, but the years of neglect showed. All that remained of the greenery were the ruins of rotted vegetables and moss-covered stones that lined the small area. The roof was made of clay tiles that oozed fungi.

Despite its lack of care, there was clearly someone living there. Smoke drifted through a hole in the roof. *They must keep warm by fire inside. Ingenious.* My children had not created an indoor fireplace. We had no use for them. Even in winter, the weather was pleasant enough that our shelters were all we needed. Perhaps the weather had changed in the time I was away.

I attempted to spread my invisible roots through the ground as I once had. I needed to know where I was. I didn't get very far. The farthest I could go was just past the port at which the men docked their boat. I was so weak. So cold. I hadn't noticed how cold I was. I had spent so long in my bubble, trapped within myself, that I never noticed. The sensation of temperature was foreign. Numbness was all I had known for a long time.

The fire inside the home called to me. I just had to wait a little longer. I wanted to see what they planned to do with me.

"Bring her in!" An old man sauntered out of the stone cottage. He was wrapped in clothes made of wool, comfortable and warm. Currently that was all I could think about. Why was the cold bothering me so much *now*?

They unloaded me from the wagon. It took all the men to lift me, but my frozen shell fit easily though the opening in the cottage. They set me by the fireside, facing the men. Couldn't they have faced me toward the fire? It had been so long.

"Where on Earth did you find her?" the old man questioned. The man plastered his hands to my shelter, as if his mere touch could melt me.

"Our net was caught on her. We thought she was a rock until the debris was knocked away. We definitely didn't think there would be a woman trapped inside when we pulled on it." The man who explained this was the same one who had stared at me throughout the journey.

"Amazing," the old man said. He never removed his hands from the ice.

"How long has she been in there, you think?" the curious fisherman asked.

"A long time," he answered.

"How can you tell?"

"Besides the fact that her beauty doesn't compare to any of the women from our time," he smiled, "her clothes give her away. She wears furs that are unknown to me. I couldn't tell you what animal they come from. They must be long extinct by now."

Extinct? That could only mean that Lucifer's children had destroyed those animals. Even with great numbers, it would have taken them years to do so. *How could I have slept for so long?* The time spent away was pointless. If I couldn't find peace within thousands of years of solitude, how would I *ever*?

"I brought her to you because I know you like the…oddities of the world. I thought you could learn something from her," the fisherman said.

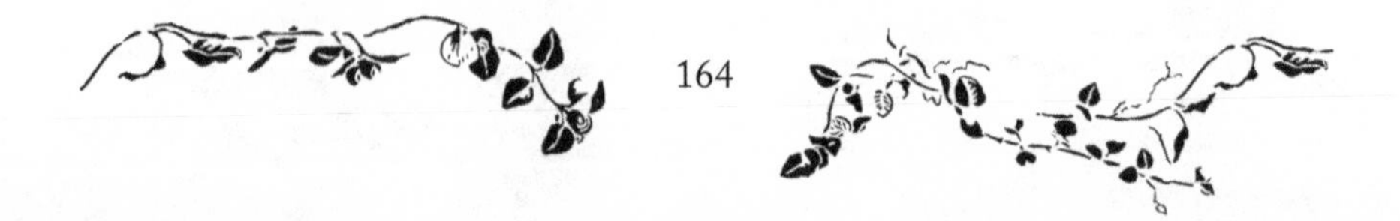

"Yes, indeed. Thank you. This is a great discovery. Now I will only have a short time to study her once she melts, so I must be ready." The old man wandered off into another room and came out with an armful of tools. They were created of bronze and iron rather than bone. Some looked new and others old. *How long had he been "learning" from things?*

"To everyone here. Please keep this quiet. I don't need people interrupting my work," he said to the group of fishermen. The boat crew gave their agreements and left, leaving only the old man and the fisherman who watched me. The old man began to clean and sharpen his pointed tools. I could almost feel their cold metallic touch.

My time was up. I needed out. Now. The fire aided me in my task, but I needed it to be hotter. I stretched my roots and grabbed hold of the energy that surrounded me. I forced the water's spirit to awaken once more. The spirit moved slowly at first, but I soon accomplished what I wanted. The ice turned to water, then nothing at all. It evaporated, joining the air.

I collapsed. I gulped in fresh air for the first time in ages and it burned my raw lungs. The years of immobility left me weak and cold. Even after relieving myself of my ice prison, I still felt frozen. I pulled myself closer to the fire. So close I was sure I burned myself. The shivers finally subsided, and I was able to turn toward my captors. The fisherman hadn't moved. Was he in shock? The old man was the only one who showed change; his eyes were fearful as he clutched his chest. I hoped I hadn't given him a heart attack.

"Hello," I said politely. No response. This wasn't going to be easy. "I am Lilith. I know you are probably surprised to discover I am not dead," I laughed nervously. Speaking felt strange. My lips were still numb. "But don't worry, I won't harm you. I can explain—"

I was cut off by the fisherman. "Are you a god?" He was shaking now.

I turned toward the old man. "God? What is that?" That was the first word I had not understood. Was it a word they created all on their own?

"A powerful being that rules over us and this world," the elderly man stuttered. He clutched his chest harder.

I replied, "I know not what a god is. I am human, though I am unable to die."

The two men continued to stare at me, mouths gaping. I could hear the fire crackling beside me. The sizzling pops were the only thing that kept my eyes from closing.

"I am not sure how long I've been frozen. I have nowhere to go. Would you help me?" I asked. I didn't know how these people would react to me. I was unsure of their world and what aspects of life they were aware of. It seemed they thought there was a higher being than them, and that being resembled me. *Was it Lucifer?* Still receiving no reply, I continued, "Do you know of Lucifer?"

"No," the fisherman muttered. I was happy, but also disappointed. As much as I hated him, it would have been nice to see a familiar face. "You must be a demon then?" he continued.

I shook my head in confusion. It was surreal to be ignorant of the words they spoke. It made me feel even more disconnected to them than I already was. "Is a demon like a god?" I questioned.

The elder man answered, "Close enough. They have little differences." The wrinkles on his face relaxed. "Do you want something to eat?" he offered. The old man recovered and released his chest, looking rather excited. He was a man who strove to learn about the world, and he knew this was his chance.

I smiled. "Yes."

He then proceeded to his counter and removed several items from the cupboards. The old man brought me dried fruits, nuts, and meats. I took them graciously but acknowledged that the food barely had any residual energy to hold the form together. That was due to the nature of the succubus humans, I assumed. Despite my aversion to it, I ate everything, including the meat.

Once I finished, which didn't take more than a minute, I looked up to see the men watching me, both in fascination and something else. I couldn't place the expression. "Is there somewhere I could sleep?" My will to stay awake was waning. It had been so long since I'd done anything, yet I hadn't found a moment's rest in my bubble.

"Of course. Come this way," the old man said. I stood too fast and nearly collapsed, but the fisherman caught my arm with his hand. The warmth of his hand was nice; to be touched felt nice. I could feel the callouses on his hands rub roughly against my chilled skin. The fisherman helped me into the room while the old man led the way. They laid me down atop warm, soft bedding, and that was the last conscious thing I remembered. I slept as the sun set and rose again, all the while dreaming of gods and demons and what they might be.

XII
Gods and Demons

The drink of knowledge is meant to be sipped, not gulped down thoughtlessly.
-A

"It's impossible. She can't be a goddess. She's too human. She eats. She sleeps for hours. The woman even said she doesn't know what gods are," the fisherman whispered. They were unaware that I had better faculties than that of a hawk, and so they continued on.

"Yes, I know it seems rather odd, but how do we know that gods don't eat and sleep?" the old man rebutted, less careful about his sound level than his companion.

"Because gods are supposed to be perfect beings. Eating and sleeping is a sign of weakness. It shows that we need the support of other things rather than ourselves." He paused. "That's the whole point, isn't it? The reason the gods are the gods? They're perfect."

"Oh, please. They are better than us, yes. But perfect? I don't believe so. They just have different problems." I could hear the smile in his words. "Frankly, I would love to discover the limits to their so-called perfection." So that's what they were. *Perfect beings.* I didn't think there were such creatures. I lifted myself into a seated position on the edge of the cot. The sun streamed in through the window and warmed my skin. Bumps rose, making my skin rough and the soft hairs on my arms rise. My plan was to join

the others, but the light rays felt so nice I didn't want to move. I had spent too many years without the sun.

Craning my neck to warm my hair, I noticed a table at the foot of the bed. There was a bucket of water and rags to clean myself with. I investigated further to find a long linen garment with a woolen cloak to drape over my shoulders. These must be the new adaptations for clothing in this era. The linen was designed to cover the majority of my body, but it hugged my form, revealing its shape. It was a welcome change from the still-wet furs I wore; they clung to my skin desperately, much as my memories clung to my thoughts. I discarded them immediately.

Once cleaned and changed, I turned to find the fisherman standing in the doorway to my room. How long had he been there? "Hello. You're finally awake. If it wasn't for your snoring I would have thought you dead." The fisherman leaned against the entrance to the small room. I was too distracted to notice before, but he was quite handsome. Tall and sturdy. He worked to live. His eyes were so dark you could barely see the pupil within. Ebony waves were contained in a leather band held at the nape of his neck.

"Yes. Sorry for sleeping so long. I needed it." It was more than a need. My body forced it from me. There was no possible way I would have continued on without passing out.

"No problem. The old man was happy to oblige. He doesn't get many beautiful women to stay here, let alone sleep in his bed," the friendly man joked.

"You would be surprised," the old man called from the other room. I couldn't help but giggle. The sound surprised both me and the man in front of me. That made us both laugh.

"My name is Aegeus. Yours is Lilith, right?" he asked.

"Yes, that's right. Aegeus." I tested the name on my tongue. "Are you a protector then?" Aegeus looked surprised that I knew the meaning of his name.

"I suppose I can be. How did you know? I thought you'd been frozen for a long time?" His suspicious gaze pierced me.

"I have. I suppose it's a gift of mine. I know the meaning of words. But not the ones you said last night: god and demon. Those are the first I have not understood," I said. Not including my own name, of course—I still didn't know its meaning. Perhaps it didn't have one.

Aegeus interrupted my pondering. "Hungry?"

I looked to him and nodded my head appreciatively. I liked Aegeus. He was kind. There was something familiar about him, but I didn't know what.

"There you are, beautiful," the old man said. "Did you get enough sleep?" he asked as he poured a bowl of stew for me. He placed it in front of where I sat at the table. He was tall like Aegeus. His eyes were not as dark, and his hair had greyed, but one could see he had been handsome in his youth.

"I did. Thank you for lending your bed," I responded.

"No problem at all, my dear. Someone ought to use it. I don't sleep so well anymore. My back isn't what it used to be," he confessed. "My name is Ambrose, by the way. I know Aegeus calls me old man, but I would hope a young lady like yourself would call me by my given name, the name many ladies have called out before." He winked suggestively. Seeing my startled expression, he chuckled. Then all three of us were laughing. I had forgotten what it felt like.

"Ambrose? Peculiar that you were named for something that can never be," I said.

Just like Aegeus, this surprised the old man. Ambrose recovered quickly though. "Indeed. The name hasn't given me immortality. I age more every day. I keep finding new problems with the decrepit body I was bestowed."

"Aging isn't a bad thing. It means you can spend the time with your friends and family, and then rest when you have done so. Imagine if you outlasted everyone you loved? It's a lonely endeavor. Immortality is not

a gift. It is a curse." The words spilled out of me. *Why was I confiding in these strangers?*

Ambrose looked to Aegeus, then to me. "It seems you have experience with immortality," the old man said. It wasn't a question.

"I do."

Aegeus offered, "Perhaps you could tell us about it?" The look in his eyes was enough for me. I trusted this man. I should have been more cautious, but after years of isolation, I needed this. I needed companionship. Even if all I got was a conversation.

The three of us spent the rest of the day talking. I told them of my past. Not all of it, just knowledge I thought they could handle. I told them of Adam, another human, and our children. I relayed how I outlived them, and wished to drown at sea, but couldn't. I didn't want to talk about Lucifer or my magic.

They exchanged stories about their lives, as well. Aegeus was the son of the old man's sister. Ambrose's sister passed away when Aegeus was young; he was then raised by Ambrose. He never met his father, and he lived a simple life as a fisherman, working as much as he could. The fisherman's crew was his family. Aegeus was not married and had no children, which I found odd. How could he not have found love by now? He was kind and generous, and someone I would wish for myself.

Ambrose had a wife and child during his life, but only for a short time, though. Once Ambrose and his wife married, they had a son who died of sickness as an infant. His wife killed herself soon after, leaving Ambrose alone. He never remarried. He spent his life working and studying the "oddities" that life offered. Ambrose said he enjoyed learning new things, especially if his discoveries would give answers to ancient questions.

The two men I spent the day with were very interesting people. Despite their simple existence, they were interested in more complicated aspects of life. Ambrose especially was very philosophical; he questioned everything and strove to answer those questions. He inspired me. But I couldn't help

but notice Ambrose's spirit was at constant battle with his nephew's—his deep forest green to Aegeus's cobalt—more so than what I saw with the crew. More aggressive.

Of course my spirit was left alone.

I had planned on returning to the depths, but after talking with them about their culture and what humanity had built for itself, I wanted to know more. I could always return to the sea if I wanted. There was no harm in walking among them, if only for a short time.

The sun was setting, and we had just finished dinner when Aegeus said, "I better get home and make sure it wasn't ransacked by my crew. They tend to get careless when I'm not there." He smiled at me.

"You live with your crew?" I questioned.

"Yes. Those of us who don't yet have a family stay together. Less lonely and more productive that way." Aegeus stood and handed Ambrose his bowl. "Thanks for the meals, old man." He turned to me. "And thank you, Lilith, for sharing your story with us. Most fascinating thing I've ever heard, and probably will ever hear. Goodnight. I will be back tomorrow." Aegeus bent, grabbed my hand, and placed a small kiss on my inner wrist. He released my hand and exited through the front door.

I stared down at the place Aegeus had kissed while Ambrose cleaned our dishes. I suddenly knew why he was so familiar. It was his scent. He smelled like Adam, like a storm that rained flowers. The scent was strong and masculine, but sweet. I could feel the tears forming around the rims of my eyes. *Stop.* I promised myself I would never cry again. I didn't deserve to cry, not after what I did.

Naavah would have been ashamed.

I stood.

"Ambrose, I am going to sleep now. I don't want to steal your bed again, though. Is there somewhere else I can rest?"

"Oh, none of that. You will take my bed again. I am much more comfortable out here anyway."

I looked around the small room. There were four chairs for the table we ate at, a small counter with cupboards to hold his food. There was an iron slab placed above the fireplace, holding a heavy kettle; the water was boiling. The only place I could see that was suitable for sleeping was the few woolen sheets laid next to the fireside. That could not have been comfortable, especially for an old man.

Following my gaze, he said, "I don't want to hear another word on the subject. Here, I'm making tea. Take some in with you." Ambrose lifted the kettle from the fire pit and poured some hot water into a waiting cup. He then filled that cup with some plants I didn't recognize.

"What flower is that?" I questioned. I thought I had discovered and learned about every plant, but of course time had passed. Things had changed. I needed to stop being so arrogant. There were always new things to learn.

"The petals of the blue water lily. It helps relax the mind." He handed me the hot cup. It felt wonderful.

Upon further inspection, he had put a lot in the small cup. "Is there need for so much?"

"Oh, yes. The petals work wonders, but it is very subtle. You need to use quite a bit to feel anything," he answered, looking away from me. Ambrose concentrated on pouring his own cup of boiling water.

Trusting his knowledge, I said, "Well, thank you. Goodnight then."

"Goodnight." Ambrose didn't look at me. I made my way back into the small bedroom. I gazed out the window at the little town. There were no fires to be seen. The town must go to bed early. My children would stay up well into the night, if only to watch the stars appear. The moon was full tonight, but the usual comfort I felt under its light never came. I was unsettled. I gulped down the scalding cup of tea and laid down to rest. Perhaps morning would be better.

I awoke to pain. What was causing it? My stomach hurt. Was I hungry again? No, it was the muscle. The skin. Something was ripping my skin apart. I opened my eyes. It was so dark, still nighttime. I still should have been able to see, though. My head swam. My vision blurred. I attempted to sit upright and found I couldn't. Something held my wrists and ankles. It was cold and hard.

"Help!" I cried. "Adam!"

"Hush now. You'll only make it worse."

"Ambrose?" I questioned.

"Yes, dear. Sorry, I didn't think the tea would wear off so fast."

"What are you doing? Let me go!" I demanded.

"I can't do that. You are the solution I've been looking for. You are the key to immortality. I just need to figure out your secret. Now stop squirming; it will only make the pain worse. Drink this," he instructed. He brought the teacup to my lips. It had been refreshed with new hot water and petals. I threw my head forward, causing him to drop the scalding cup. The boiling water splashed onto his hand as well as my face, but I didn't care.

"Ow! You ungrateful bitch! You owe me! I saved you from that block of ice, fed you, and gave you a warm bed to sleep in. You *will* submit to my demands!" Ambrose shouted at me. He was a different person. What happened to the friendly old man from yesterday? The one who shared about his family's losses, the one with whom I shared my losses. Was it an act? *Did he not care?*

"I don't owe you anything! And Aegeus is the one who saved me, *not* you!" I growled.

"Aegeus doesn't know what he found. If he did, then he wouldn't have given you away so easily."

"He wouldn't do that. He's not the monster you are!" I refused to believe otherwise.

"It doesn't matter. I'll take it anyway." He dug farther into me. "You're just as difficult as my wife was," he snarled.

His wife? He did this to his wife? What kind of monster had I come across? If he did this to his mate, I feared his child must have met the same gruesome end.

Ambrose continued to dig into my flesh. The red sand spilt out of me. I could hear it falling to the floor. He pulled at organs and bones, unable to keep up with my rapid healing. "Incredible. You heal so quickly. I need something to keep my incisions open." He dashed into the other room. I could hear him digging through his tools. They clanged against one another, a horrible sound.

The panic I felt cleared the remaining drugs from my head. Finally able to see, I saw that he had restrained me with chains. The chains were attached to bronze spikes in the floor. Had they been there before? Anger pulsed through me. How dare he treat me this way. *Had all mortal humans become this cruel?* Certainly Aegeus couldn't be. Ambrose had waited for him to leave. That must have meant he knew Aegeus would not approve.

"Damn it! Where is it?" Ambrose grumbled in the other room. I still had time. I pulled as hard as I could against the thick metal. The spikes came free before the chains, and they dangled from my limbs. As soon as I was free, Ambrose walked in with a new tool. It was wide and had clamps on either side. He had meant what he said. He was going to hold my stomach open so he could examine me.

"Ambrose, I don't want to hurt you." I did. The world needed to be rid of this creature, but I vowed long ago to do no harm to any living being out of malice, for any reason if I could help it. "Put your tools down and let me walk out of here. You won't see me again," I said.

"Let you leave? I don't think so. You are my only clue to immortality, the only way I can be saved," he said. His answer was disappointing. I liked him before this happened, and I didn't want to hurt Aegeus by taking his only family away.

Ambrose lunged at me, knife in hand. *Where had that come from?* I

must have still been groggy. Disoriented, I fell back. He took advantage and plunged his knife into the place where my heart would have rested. The pain was excruciating and just what I needed. I had been numb for far too long. Frozen. I needed to feel again.

With my resurrected senses, I was able to throw him off me. Ambrose collided with the wall in the next room. I yanked the knife out of my chest and threw it aside. Crimson sand spilt to the ground. I ripped the metallic cuffs from my wrists simultaneously; I freed my ankles next. The chains clanked noisily to the floor, leaving dents in the wood. I placed a hand over my wounded chest just as the gash closed.

I ambled over to Ambrose. He had slid down the wall and crumpled at the bottom. I threw him too hard. I didn't need to touch him to know he was dead. I no longer heard his heartbeat. Ambrose wasn't the first being I'd killed, but he was the first human. The others were all accidental, plant and animal. They were just as important, but I found this so much worse. It was another of my kind.

The spirit rose from his corpse and made its way toward me. "No! I don't want you!" I scrambled to get away from the oncoming spirit, knocking the table and chairs down in my panic. But there was no escaping it. I had killed him. The spirit belonged to me now.

Huddled in the farthest corner of the room, the spirit reached me. It absorbed into my own light, my own spirit. It felt awful. Not because I had killed it and taken it for my own, but because it felt good. The power that it gave me made me feel strong. His dark desires were mine, as well as his fears. They masked my own. The realization scared me. It paralyzed me. I stayed in that corner for hours. I didn't even notice when the sun rose above the horizon.

"Lilith?"

No. Not yet.

"Lilith? Are you okay?" Aegeus asked, worry in his voice. It made it

that much worse to look at him.

"Please, don't come any closer," I whispered. Aegeus stopped, then turned his head.

Aegeus looked at what had become of his uncle, broken and crumbled on the ground. "Uncle?" It took him a moment to understand. "No! Old man, wake up!" He grabbed his last remaining family member, begging him to wake. The fisherman bent his head to listen for the dead man's heartbeat.

"He's dead, Aegeus. I'm sorry. I am so sorry." My small voice barely carried itself to where the fisherman swayed back and forth, his uncle in his arms. I couldn't feel my face or what it expressed. I couldn't feel anything but dread. Aegeus looked around the room. He saw the knife and tools and chains that had fallen to the floor, the red sand that rested in mounds throughout the two rooms, and he saw the dent in the stone wall where his uncle had been thrown.

"What happened?" he demanded. He was a strong man. He held his emotions together, even while holding his dead uncle's corpse. Aegeus didn't deserve this. It was obvious when he spoke with his uncle how much he cared for him. I couldn't take that away. He had lost his only family. I wouldn't steal away his memories of him, too.

From my corner of the small room, I explained, "Ambrose was trying to discover the secret of my immortality. The man wouldn't stop questioning me and wouldn't let it go. I got upset and pushed him. I pushed him too hard, though. I am sorry." Aegeus didn't say anything. The fisherman's eyes roamed around the room. He was going to figure it out.

I stood and marched over to where he sat with his uncle. The corpse was already beginning to rot; my nostrils flared in disgust. "No one has the right to my immortality. Only I deserve it, and your uncle couldn't accept that. It was his fault this happened to him."

The fisherman finally understood my words. "So you killed him? Get

out! I don't want to see your face ever again," he said. "If I see you, I will find a way to kill you, immortal or not." Aegeus meant it. That hurt, but it was the reaction I had hoped for. "I should have never brought you here." He looked down at his lost uncle and whispered to the corpse, "I should have left her in the sea. I'm sorry."

I couldn't say I didn't wish for the same.

The memory of Adam holding a dying Frode invaded my vision. Against my better instincts, I reached out to him, if only to sweep the hair out of his red-rimmed eyes. Aegeus grabbed my hand before it reached him and said in a low, terrifying voice, "I hope your immortal life is filled with misery and sorrow. It's what a *goddess* like you deserves." With wet eyes, he threw my own hand back at me. "Now leave." If he knew the extent of my history, he would have realized his wish had already come true.

I breathed in his familiar scent one last time and ran. I didn't know where I was going, but I had to get out. I had to run in case he changed his mind and attacked. Not that he could hurt me, but I didn't want to harm him in the process. I had to run to escape the memory of what happened. Another memory to regret.

If there were such things as gods, I hoped they enjoyed watching me sprint.

I stopped running when I saw a row of clothing blowing in the wind; the clothes were attached to a rope behind a cottage. Removing my torn garments, I grabbed the dark chiton that hung there and a full-length, loose-fitting cloak. I fitted the chiton, wrapped the cloak around myself, and pinned it where it was supposed to be. It flowed across my form and cinched at the shoulder. The cloak was ebony and embroidered with gold designs. It reminded me of nighttime and the stars. I didn't want to steal, but my disheveled clothing would have drawn too much attention. I only

made it that far because of my speed. I was merely a blur to those passing by. A gust of wind. But I couldn't run forever.

I knew I should have left, but I stood there motionless, disgusted with myself. I had judged these people, but I was no better than them. Ambrose's face was there when I closed my eyes, and lifeless orbs stared back at me. I thought I could even feel his spirit writhing inside of me, like it knew it didn't belong. And it didn't. *Was it a necessary sacrifice? Or another mistake?* In that moment, I wanted nothing more than to be someone else, to have anyone else's life but my own.

Wallowing in my self-hatred, I didn't notice until I took a step how close I was to the ground. A strand of golden hair whipped back and forth in the wind, stinging my eyes. I raised my hand to remove the strange strand and saw that my skin had darkened. Panicked, I stole into the cottage. No one was there, but the scent of boiled meat was strong. My mouth watered involuntarily, and I knew whoever lived there would be back soon.

I didn't have to travel far. A reflective piece of wall was conveniently placed in the entryway, as if whoever lived there was inclined to check their appearance before being seen by the outside world; or perhaps they merely enjoyed their own beauty. And that's what I saw when I gazed into the dirtied reflection of the mirror: beauty. But it wasn't me.

My hardened muscles and lengthy form were now small and delicate. My facial structure had changed to that of a young woman I saw selling jewels, my skin to the olive tone the majority possessed. The hair length was the same, but the shade went from that of a dark crimson to a golden silk. The texture waved smoothly like the sea instead of the terror of a tornado. Many of the women I saw here had naturally dark hair, but they colored it blonde. My emerald eyes were now shaded dark, like Aegeus's. Exploring my new form, I discovered I now had a navel. Accepting that I had unknowingly discovered another ability, I tied my long thick waves

into a massive braid and wrapped it atop my head. I had noticed a young girl in the market wearing it that way.

Tending to my hair, I took a moment to look beyond the new face. My spirit rested calmly despite the recent events. Like flares from the sun, it would lash out at a certain painful thought or memory, but otherwise it was content. I had mastered the art of repressing emotions, so much so that even my own spirit was oblivious. It matched the shade of my natural hair now, a dark crimson instead of a bright and warm red.

Aegeus might decide to hunt me down during his grief. I couldn't allow that. So I had shifted my own energy to take the form I wanted, and it only made sense that I could. I had altered the forms of different species before; why not my own? It was easy, having the power of the additional spirit within. The thought made me nauseous, but I did what I had to do, consciously or otherwise.

My appearance disguised, I was ready to leave. *But to where?* I wandered along the main road, hoping to find an answer.

The surrounding town was much larger than my children's had been. There were more people, more shelters, and more need for inventing and creating. The larger the populace, the harder it would have been to feed and care for everyone. I could understand that. But despite the humans' advances, there was still a lot of work to be done.

I could smell the grime of the town, the bodily filth of the ones who had no home, the neglected animal carcasses that were unable to be distributed to the hungry souls, the moldering fruits and vegetables of the carts. Even the shiny trinkets sold by the clean and fed held a strong metallic odor and left a rusty taste behind on my tongue. The only reprieve my nostrils had was the scent of the sea brought by the wind. Even that wasn't pleasant anymore. Several millennia surrounded by the water had sullied the natural scent.

Soon, though, I discovered that I was in a town called Gythion, a very popular place for travelers and traders. I reprimanded myself for not asking more questions about where I was yesterday when I spoke with Ambrose and Aegeus. After talking with the locals, I learned there was a great river nearby. That felt like a good place to start. I found a paradise last time I followed a river. Perhaps I would again.

I made sure to visit that man with the fruit cart before I departed. Of course, he was very polite and kind to me. He even gave me an apple at no cost, simply because I was pretty; my nausea returned. Despite my rooted love for the red fruit, the man's cart of delicacies held no interest for me, though there were others who would have disagreed. I thanked him and left with my spoils. As I walked away he ogled me. The tradesman was promptly distracted by a gust of wind that knocked over his cart, leaving his neighboring traders unscathed and his fruits scattered in the muck.

The housing and businesses created a large maze that was Gythion. It was intricate in design, and I often found myself lost before picking up the scent I was following again. The paths I walked were coated in brick and dirt. The brick had been painted to match the sunset with saffron, pink, and red hues. The beautiful creation it had been was clear to me, but the more people treaded upon the man-made stones, the more they crumbled and became part of the grimy ground.

The wind eased enough that my nose was able to locate the boy the tradesman had beaten before. He was sitting in a dank corner behind a cottage with the same girl who had stolen the apple. She was sharing her bread with him. The boy had fresh wounds on his face, still bleeding. I understood then. He distracted the traders while the girl stole from them. They were a team.

I walked over to where they huddled, frightening them. *What had humanity done to these poor creatures?* I stopped short. I didn't want them to run off. I set down the multiple fruits I had stolen from the horrid man,

turned, and left. I heard their rushed footsteps as they scrambled to gather their gifts.

There had to be a solution to help humanity. They needed guidance. They needed to see that there could be peace. Witnessing the travesties that befell the daily lives of these mortals awoke something in me, something I hadn't felt in a long time.

Determination.

I had a goal for the first time in thousands of years. We were not the instinctually driven animals we shared this Earth with. We were more. We had choices. We had knowledge. Humanity only needed to be shown the way.

XIII
Glittering Temptations

No one can blame the beasts when
the creator walks among them.
-A

What to do, what to do?
The dawn of life
New ideas to ponder
Uncertain of one's purpose
Plenty of time, no need to worry

What to do, what to do?
The prime of life
Many days pondered
Purpose remains uncertain
Minimal time, need to worry

What to do, what to do?
The climax of life
Too many days pondered
Purpose undiscovered
Out of time, worry no longer

This poem carried on the wind as I walked along the side of the river, traveling against the current. There was a well-used route on the other side of the water, but I chose to walk alone, hidden within the cover of trees. It was best not to attract unnecessary attention. I was still unexperienced in this new world and traveled with caution.

Despite my attempt to stay unseen, I encountered an old woman who followed the same path I had chosen. She chose to walk the difficult path through the brush and prickled bushes rather than the flattened trail of earth that most had before. It didn't make sense, her being so fragile. One would think the popular path would be more comforting to her, but alas, she wasn't a normal elderly woman. She repeated the poem several times to herself on her way to me.

The river raged aggressively, and it drowned out most of the sounds of the forest. I noticed then that the creatures from my time didn't fly through the sky anymore. Their bursts of random fire could always be seen, but now the sky was vacant. Either they had been hunted into extinction or they hid for safety. I concentrated on the woman's footsteps as she approached. The breeze passed by me, bringing with it the scent of freshly dug earth. I breathed it in, hoping to clear my jumbled thoughts.

"Good day, lovely lady," the elderly woman said.

"Good day," I replied cautiously. The old woman could be no threat to me, but I couldn't help but be suspicious. She walked so confidently through the undergrowth, even with a cane in hand and milk-covered eyes.

"Where do you travel from?" she asked.

"The sea," I answered bluntly. If I answered with confidence, there would be no reason for her to suspect anything amiss with me.

"Oh, a foreigner, huh? Travel far?" she said with a smile on her lips. Her snow-white hair was caught in the wind and tangled in a hovering branch, but she didn't seem to mind.

"Indeed, and I have much farther to go. If you don't mind, I will be on my—"

"Ah, the sea," the woman interrupted. "A wondrous place, isn't it? So much life. Just as the land we stand upon."

Life? If only she saw what I could, she wouldn't have said that. "I suppose. Though it wanes as the time passes." True, but I didn't need to say that to her. She wouldn't understand anyway.

"Is that so? What do you mean?" she asked, curious.

I might as well; it wasn't as if I'd see her again. "I witness as children are starved and beaten, as neighbor steals from neighbor. Even the animals are not only used for food, but as slaves. Life is declining. Slowly, but declining it is." This woman would not understand my ramblings, but she needed to know not all was as it seemed.

"Yes, those things that you speak of are indeed the truth. But hate is not all that humanity has to offer," she said. She then proceeded to unwrap the crimson scarf around her neck and place it in my hand. "You look cold, my dear. Here, take this."

I took a moment to gaze into her clouded eyes. There was something there I had not cared to notice before. Kindness. I saw it in the eyes of Aegeus, as well, but I had chosen to ignore it. I had been so concentrated on the horrors humanity developed that I had rejected the good they did.

I never took the time to appreciate the families as I passed by in my frozen cage, yet they were hard to forget. There were mothers and fathers, sons and daughters, brothers and sisters. Most of the families I observed were happy and enjoying the life they followed. I saw a mother smile and braid her daughter's hair. I caught the look in a boy's eyes as his father praised him for a job well done. I saw as a man and a woman kissed behind the cover of hanging bedsheets. There was love within these humans. It only took a stranger pointing it out to me.

"Yes, I suppose there is. I shouldn't be so skeptical," I admitted.

"Thank you for the scarf. I often find myself cold these days." I weaved the long scarf around my bare neck. Much better. Due to her frailty, I would have offered to give it back, but she looked completely comfortable. She wasn't shivering like I was.

"Of course. It matches your hair quite well, don't you think?" the woman commented.

I froze. I pulled a tucked strand from behind my ear to inspect. "Actually, my hair is blonde," I said. *How did she know?*

"Really?" She leaned forward to confirm my words. "Ah, my eyesight isn't what it used to be. Well, I better be off. Safe travels, young lady. Stay warm." The elderly woman passed by me then, heading deeper into the undergrowth. For an elderly woman, she could move fast. She was out of sight before I could finish a thought, and she had given me much to think about. *Did I need to save them?* The fiery determination I felt before in Gythion had smoldered.

Though I was unsure, I had to learn as much as I could. Not only about my human comrades, but about myself. I'd been alive a long time. Too long, yet I still hadn't fully explored my magical abilities, or my physical attributes for that matter. I had been too afraid to misuse them. That time had passed. If I decided to help the humans I would need to learn to survive in their world. I needed to master my gifts so I could protect others. That meant using every advantage I possessed, including my power to influence energy, the one I had been afraid of the most.

Lost in thought, a stray twig snapped beneath my weight as I walked along the river's edge. *What did I know?* I could alter my form to look like other humans. Could I transform into other animals? Was there a need to? I was already physically stronger and faster than any human on the planet, though I was unsure how much more. Perhaps there was no need, but it was something I would be willing to try someday.

I could alter the forms of others, but they never turned out quite

right. There was always a flaw in my design. Maybe leaving things in their natural form was best. But of course, there was Lucifer to think about. What if he wanted me dead? How would I defend myself against him? I didn't have to alter the energy to control it, though. I could move things or beings that held energy with only my will. I passed by a small rock and kicked it absentmindedly across the raging river. It skipped across the surface, creating little indents in the waves.

Before, my whole existence revolved around ignoring and pushing down my powers, even then they slipped through once in a while; now that Ambrose was a part of me, the power ached to be released. The wind was a part of my very breath. The earth beneath me shifted to my will. I could force the clouds to expose their woeful tears. I was able to persuade fires to rage or smolder. But like most of my powers, I had chosen to ignore them. Lucifer had those same abilities now, and I was sure he had been practicing, unlike me.

Just then, I heard the low, pained yowl of an animal. I turned and saw nothing. I followed the sad sounds deeper into the trees. I could hear the rapid beating of her heart and the ragged breaths she took. There in the midst of the greenery was a wolf. She sat on her haunches, unable to lay down properly. The creature's front leg was covered in dark dried blood. I watched as the vulnerable being put pressure on her injury, only to cry out in pain. The creature was much smaller than the noble predator I remembered from my time.

The wounds on her front leg were not like any injury I had seen before. Its bite was wide and deep. The smell of metal mixed with the animal's odor of distress. I knew then that it had been the humans who did this. It was surprising that the wolf escaped from their clutches, but she was suffering for it.

I stepped closer, distracted by my curiosity and worry. I watched the wolf's muscles flex as she turned, intent on destroying whatever disturbed

her. I automatically kneeled and bowed my head. It had been many years since I had come in contact with a natural animal, especially one that was hurt. But I had mastered the art of their languages and communicated well with them by the time I was forced to freeze myself. My throat made the high-pitched whine I wanted that spoke of trust.

My years of study and trust-building were lost to the passing of time it seemed. The wolf's soft grey fur ruffled at my mannerism. She growled, untrusting. But knowing she couldn't fight anymore, the wolf backed away slowly. When she was a safe distance from me, she turned and ran as fast as she could. Her wound reopened. I could hear the droplets of thick liquid falling to the ground below.

I found myself back at the river's edge. I could have followed to help the creature in need, but I would have only made it worse. The animals of this time didn't trust humans, and I couldn't blame them. The humans enslaved, tortured, and consumed anything they could. Animals were merely the easiest target. All my hard work was lost, and it was my fault.

I needed to be stronger. For everyone.

Rocks were the strongest things I could think of. I waded over to a boulder resting in the gushing river. I squatted and grabbed at the river's floor, digging until I found my grip. I lifted the giant boulder above my head with ease. No mortal could have accomplished such a task. *But what was my limit?* I put the boulder down and rammed my fist inside it. If my arm had been long enough, it would have penetrated straight through to the other side.

I wandered over to a monstrous tree. The trunk was thicker than the boulder I had punctured. Wood was brittle compared to rock, but the roots that held the tree in place would be much stronger. *Necessary sacrifice.* I needed to know. I had spent too long ignorant of my own body, simply because I was afraid. My fear had cost my loved ones their lives and Earth its peace. *No more.*

I wrapped my arms as far as I could around the base of the massive trunk and pulled. I could hear the cracking and moaning of the forced movement. I apologized every time I heard a rupture. The process seemed slow, but in reality it had only taken me a moment to relieve the tree of its ancient home. The roots drug across the ground as I carried it against the current of the angry river. I walked a ways with the tree, hoping my limit would come soon. I couldn't hear any people traveling nearby, but of course the snapping of branches and the groan of the bending trunk drowned out most of the forest's sounds.

Feeling no resistance in my body, I ran. I couldn't travel as fast as I could otherwise, but the foliage around me swayed from the wind I created. River water splashed up into my eyes. I gave up before too long; there was barely any change. I could have gone forever. I set the tree down across the river. It would make a useful bridge for those who wished to cross. I collapsed onto my back in the cool water and unwrapped the heavy scarf from my neck. I held it up as the wind blew against it. The scarlet fabric twirled and danced in the breeze.

My physical strength was vast. I thought that would scare me, but I felt empowered. A familiar flicker of heat scorched my chest, but it was gone before I could register it. Fear had prevented me from being happy for so long. I didn't want it to be a part of my life anymore. Perhaps the misguided humans had given me the opportunity I needed to change that. A fish fought its way against the violent current. It had pale blue eyes that scrutinized me.

It had been ages, but I could still remember how Lucifer's eyes looked when I pierced his chest, only the tip of the branch within him. Empty. I could see that he wanted to die. Whether that was due to my departure, or our extended life, or something else entirely, I didn't know. And that made me sad.

I knew the hardships of an extended life. I had lost my family one by one, and I was sure Lucifer had too. But there was something else to it. We

were able to keep our bodies busy with tasks of our choosing, but the mind was entirely different. Our children were able to concentrate on the past, present, and future. They had goals and steps to follow throughout their lives. Their minds were filled with the worry of tomorrow, because they had limited time to complete what they wanted.

Immortality was different. The past, present, and future had little meaning when time was endless. There was no distinction between yesterday and tomorrow. We would still be and always would. It was exhausting, the constant fight to keep going, to find something that mattered, anything that gave purpose to the endless existence. Never-ending time was a very good excuse to give up on life.

Perhaps there was someone else who needed saving.

Seeing that my scarf was still wet, I willed the wind to travel faster. Its dancing increased. The water droplets returned to the raging river, no longer burdening the garment. I stood to warm myself once again with its soft fabric. I breathed in the scent of the previous owner. It was nice. Comforting. It was what I imagined a mother would smell like.

Only stopping to sleep a few hours, I found what I was looking for the next day. The sun shone down on the bustling city of Sparta. I gathered as much information as I could before I left Gythion. The town port was intriguing, but I had already created too many bad memories there, and it was small compared to the rest of the world. I needed to be where the majority was if I was to learn about them. There were many people who strove to trade here, so I would be among travelers, as well. Sparta was a good first step.

I traveled down streets and alleys. Large glittering abodes decorated the walkways. I saw at least three enormous golden temples. Each one had a large statue of a man guarding its entrance. The man was clad in ebony metal and golden skin and held a spear in his hand, challenging anyone who tried to pass him. I shivered.

I looked to the people. The materials they wore were shinier. Embroideries were bolder. Here, was where the highest of the mortals resided. I heard as much from passersby in Gythion. I caught the envy in their voices as they spoke of this great city. Despite the shininess of the city, the aroma was nearly the same as Gythion's: rot and filth. *What was the real difference?*

I didn't have time to contemplate my own question. The answer came to me in the form of a large man with dark wavy hair and beard walking down the city's path. He was covered in gold. Both his jewelry and clothing were the color of the sun. The only reason I noticed him was because of the surrounding men.

The warriors were dressed in bronze coverings and thick leather garments, with helmets adorning their heads. The helmet formed around their eyes, nose, and mouth. There was a strange design sitting directly on top of the head covering. It was thin and stretched the length of their skulls, end to end, eyes to nape. It didn't seem to have a purpose. More bodily decorations.

I moved my attention back to the heavyset man. Despite his short stature, he held himself tall and confident. His head was tilted so that he had to look down his nose to the people who bowed before him. The man's superiority didn't sit well with me, but I realized what it meant. He was their leader, their king, as the crowd proclaimed.

Living within the same city as their leader must grant these people privileges others did not have. I saw it in the way they dressed and acted. They were all properly bathed and healthy compared to the people I saw at the town port. The king continued his stroll down the street, making his way toward me. Though it hurt me to do so, I bowed with the others. No need for unwanted attention. *Necessary sacrifice.*

The king stopped in front of me. I kept my gaze down. He waved his men aside so he could approach me. "What is your name?" the arrogant man demanded.

What was my name? I already told Aegeus my name in Gythion, and I didn't know where Lucifer was. "Helen, my king." I hated to submit, but I mimicked the words of the city's people anyway.

"Helen. Where are you from? Your hair is most unusual." He reached out to stroke my hair, but I pulled away. He didn't like that. The king grabbed harder than he should have, pulling me closer for examination. He smelled of sweat and the city, nearly making me gag.

I panicked at my choice of hair color. I had thought following the trend of the women here would help me fit in, not make me stand out. But it was too late now. "From across the sea, my king. I have only arrived in your beautiful city today." I was going to be sick. His hands caressed my locks. I could feel his touch on my collarbone through the strands of hair.

"Welcome then, Helen. Perhaps I could give you a personal tour of my great city." It wasn't a question.

"You don't have to waste your time with me, my king. I am not worthy of your presence," I said. Hopefully he would believe my lies.

The warrior standing closest to us scolded, "You will not refuse King Menelaus, woman."

The king waved him aside. "Indeed, she will not. But Helen was only being gracious. Weren't you, my dear?" he said, sliding his hand down my bare arm.

I swallowed what I had left of my pride. "Of course, my king." I bowed for visual effect, but mostly to get away from his traveling hands.

"Wonderful. Come." The king then grabbed my arm and tucked it underneath his own. Menelaus was unaffected by the surrounding people who wished to praise him, and the warriors took their original formation. I was trapped against his side. I cringed. How was I going to handle this? I could escape easily, but not without causing a stir. I would have to wait it out and hope he didn't want more than a walk.

"Helen, what do you think of my city? Isn't it much greater than your own?" he asked.

"Oh, much lovelier than any I have ever seen, my king." The words that ran through my head begged to chastise his presumptuous behavior.

"And where is it you come from?" the king asked, not at all interested in my answer.

I knew this would happen, but I didn't think so soon. I hadn't learned anything about the neighboring lands yet. "A land far from here. It's a dismal place. Always dark and cold." I recalled the darkness of the sea from my bubble.

"The north then. But that does not require the aid of a boat?" He was growing suspicious of my vagueness. *Lie better.*

"No, indeed it doesn't. But I have traveled to and from several different places, and I have only recently come from across the sea to visit the great land I heard so much about. Could you tell me more? How far does your land expand?" *Please take the bait.*

The king stared at me a moment. "Yes, of course. But tell me, why do you have the hair of a northerner and the complexion and eyes of a Greek? Are you mixed?"

Greek? Was that where we were? I thought it was Sparta?

"Yes, I am. Very perceptive of you, my king. My father was of this land and my mother of the north. My father traveled there on exploration, and that's where he met my mother and had me. He died soon after. That is why I made a point to travel here, to my father's homeland. There was a reason my mother named me 'shining light.' She didn't want me to stay in the darkness forever." I waited anxiously for his response.

The king smiled. "Well then, welcome home, dear Helen. There is no greater light than here. You will be shown the best that Sparta has to offer," he proclaimed. I bowed in thanks. He continued to lead me around "his" city. Menelaus boasted about the temples he had built, the wealth he'd obtained, and the size of his army.

"Army?" I asked, curious about the new word I somehow already knew.

"Of course. Every great king has an army to defend him." He winked. "Surely you know that, being the traveler that you are?" I nodded my head in agreement. I needed to learn more. The biggest concern on my mind was why his aura was similar to mine. It was a duller crimson, but it worried me just the same.

Did that mean we were similar people? I found that was often the case with my children, but they always grew into something different from their source color. Two may have possessed the same shade, but their natural qualities adapted as they made different choices through their lives. Two souls that resonated a blue shade could both be wise but become wise in different aspects. They could both be sensitive but reveal it in different ways.

Still, I despised the notion that we *could* be the same.

I spent the afternoon with King Menelaus. The man shared more than I thought he would, especially with a stranger. His pride was his weakness. The king was so proud of his land and everything in it. That could have been a good thing. I was proud of my children when they were alive. I still was. But his pride stemmed from greed. He demanded to have everything and anything he wanted, and then he hoarded it and refused to let it go. It was a sickness, and something I hoped I wouldn't have to deal with much longer. Surely he would tire of me and send me away.

"Helen, this will be your room," the king said. He had taken me on a tour of his unnecessarily magnificent home.

"My room?" I questioned.

Apparently that was not what he wanted to hear. His face grew angry as he said, "You will stay with me as long as I wish it, Helen." The king's gaze bore down on me. "Rest tonight." He then turned on his heel and strode back down the great hall.

I faced the door to my new room. *What was the harm?* If he became

too difficult I would just leave. He was a great source to have around, wandering hands aside. I'd learned so much already. The land of Greece was nothing compared to the lands that were connected to it, and those that were connected to those. And then there were the lands across the water. The humans had formed societies and separated themselves from each other. It had not been what I intended when I separated the great land, but at least Lucifer wasn't able to influence all of them, if he was even still trying. *Where was he?*

Right before entering my room, the scent of blood drifted past me. But before I could turn my head to investigate, I caught sight of something that shone, blinding me. The setting sun bounced off a gold vase that sat next to the window. The rest of the room was just as beautiful, beauty that I had never seen before. The stone walls were colored white. Gold was laced in intricate designs along them. They told stories, mostly of the great battles the Greeks had fought and won.

There was a bowl and linens to clean myself with. On a chair next to the linens was a golden tunic embroidered with ebony floral designs. It was beautiful, but the thought of King Menelaus giving it to me ruined its allure. There were gold ornaments inlaid with gemstones of every kind beside the garment. I wasn't positive how to wear them, but I was sure there were enough to cover my entire body. Though lovely, they looked heavy and uncomfortable.

Thankfully, someone had also set out a simple woolen garment to sleep in. I washed and changed quickly. Sleep was calling me. I climbed into the large bronze foundation meant for resting. It also had golden designs. Apparently gold was the symbol for prosperity in this land. The bedding I lay upon was the thickest and softest I had ever felt before. It made it easier to accept the king's offerings. Though the task ahead was burdensome, I allowed myself to rest and prepare for the inevitable onslaught to come.

XIV
The Unkindness of Others

The siren song of fate is
difficult to ignore.
-A

The next morning I awoke to a woman setting food at my bedside. She was Greek and had been one of the few I'd seen who kept her natural dark tresses. She was dressed in a simple white tunic. No embroideries or jewels decorated her frame, yet the natural beauty she held was worthy of their so-called goddesses.

"Good morning. I have brought you your morning meal, and I'll dress you when you are ready. King Menelaus is waiting for you in the garden," the maiden said.

"Thank you. I won't be needing assistance dressing myself. I'd like to think I've mastered that task by now," I responded dryly. I had nothing against the young girl. She was only following her king's instructions, but the idea that people were pampered this way merely because of the title they gave themselves was shameful.

The girl was taken aback by my tone. I softened my voice and asked, "What do I call you?"

She looked as if the question confused her, but she responded with, "Agnes, my lady."

My lady? No one had called me that except Adam, and he merely

meant it as an endearment, to show that he would love and serve me just as I would him. This context was different. She somehow thought I was more important than her.

"Call me Lil…Helen," I said. Another confused expression showed on her face. Had she always been a servant? Did she know that she wasn't any lesser than her king? Her nervous spirit told me she did not.

I had to remember this world was different. It was not like the life I created with Adam. Everyone in this world lived differently due to their invented status. "You can call me whatever you like in front of others if it makes you feel more comfortable, but know that when it is just us, I would like to be called Helen." Agnes bowed her head and swiftly left the room. *Skillfully done, Helen. Spectacular way to integrate into society.* But perhaps my alternate perspectives were just what this place needed.

As I stripped off my nightgown, I heard voices from outside. The opening that let light into my room was darkened with the silhouettes of men. From what I could see, they were warriors. The sun bounced off the shiny armor they wore; it reminded me of the trinkets Menelaus wanted me to wear. They spoke to each other in hushed tones, not realizing I had seen them. Though I didn't think they would have cared anyway.

I breathed out a long, irritated sigh, and the wind outside fought against the men who ogled me. Unable to stand their ground, they tumbled toward cover. I could hear the ungraceful steps and falls of the noble men through the thick walls. They ran far from the unknown windstorm.

After eating and then dressing in the golden clothes King Menelaus provided for me, I went in search of the garden. It wasn't hard to find. All I had to do was follow my nose. Ironically, he kept my favorite flowers among his vast variety: red roses. I pulled one to my nose, pricking my finger in the process. Despite my previous irritation at the thorns, I found that I had missed their refreshing scent and bright color. My time under

water had not provided such things. I would take the sting of a rose's thorn over drifting seaweed any day.

Though an ugly man claimed it, the garden was beautiful. Not only was there an immense arrangement of wildflowers, but there were matured deciduous trees spread sporadically throughout the maze of emerald hedges. Some bushes were cut into the shapes of natural beings, predators mostly. Some were of women. Clearly there was a theme.

There was an enormous bowl in the center of the maze. It held clear water, and there were several species of brightly colored fish swimming lazily about. I saw this through the small gaps in the complicated greenery. I had a suspicion I was the only one who could, due to my enhanced sight. There were two servants who appeared to be lost in the labyrinth. Or was it due to their lack of sight? I was unsure of which. The entire garden was trapped within tall borders of cut wood, caging the wild plant life within. Flower petals were strewn about from the recent wind gusts.

I was taking note that no birds dwelled in the man-made landscape when the king strode up to me and grabbed my hands. He was adorned with even more gold than the previous day. It was surprising he could hold himself upright. "Oh, my dear Helen, those colors suit you." The king scrutinized further. "But where are the jewels I gave you?"

"My king, they are the most beautiful I have ever seen. I am unworthy to wear such godly trinkets."

Please let it go. I was trying to blend in. Those jewels would have made me shine like the sun.

"Nonsense. Even unworthy, the woman who stands beside me must take on the appearance of godliness, especially when she is beside such a being as me."

Really? He was comparing himself to the perfect beings these mortals worshipped? How much more arrogant could he be? Even Lucifer didn't compare to this man's ego. Menelaus motioned for his servant to

bring the jewels from my chamber. The young boy returned promptly, out of fear, I suspected. There was bruising along his jaw.

The boy held the jewels out to his master. King Menelaus then began to decorate me with his forced gifts. He slid several golden-ringed bracelets up and down my arms. They clanked together, making a musical sound. He continued to add layers of necklaces that held rubies, sapphires, opals, and many gems I didn't recognize. Even a thin golden chain was woven through my hair by the maiden from my bed chambers. When had she arrived? Lastly, the king kneeled to adorn my calves and ankles with ringed anklets. Of course, he took his time, slowly moving his fingers along my chilled skin. It took all the patience I had to refrain from kicking him across the garden.

Luckily, I was saved from his advances by another young boy. He carried something tan, and it had dark inscriptions written on it: a parchment containing written language. I had noticed the traders in the city writing on such parchments, recording information about their products. This was my favorite creation yet, besides the material it was made from. Regrettably I was unable to read such symbols. I would have to take the time to learn.

"Sire, I have an important message from your brother, King Agamemnon." The child bowed low as he held the message out to the king. Menelaus swiped the message from the poor boy's hands. His fingers were crooked, as if they had been broken and healed misshapen. I didn't know when or where, but King Menelaus was going to atone for his actions.

How far was I willing to go to make that happen, though? *Was I prepared to kill him?* In close quarters it was easy to see why one would kill. It almost seemed logical to do so. The world would be better without a person like him in it. But did that make it right? Wouldn't that make me just as horrible as him? Perhaps. But maybe my morality had to be sacrificed in order to maintain humanity's integrity.

"That fool! Does he think that I will just drop everything and go to him whenever he pleases? The nerve. He isn't the only king of Greece,

despite what he thinks." Menelaus threw the parchment back in the boy's face, and the child ran off. The king was fuming. The king's spirit flailed with anger. It was almost amusing as his face turned red and sweaty. *So much for maintaining a god-like appearance.*

"Are you well, my king?" I questioned, barely containing my laughter.

Hearing the amusement in my tone he moved his gaze to me, but all he saw was a woman concerned for her king. Menelaus relaxed upon seeing my face. "Yes, I suppose I am. My brother infuriates me is all. He arranges unnecessary meetings. Regardless of the fact that he knows the answer I will give him." The king's face reddened at the thought, and his hands balled into fists.

"And what is it that he wants, my king?" I questioned sympathetically.

"It is no business of yours, woman. Only kings and men. And you are neither," he snapped at me.

Containing my urge to throw him, I said, "Of course not, my king. I only wished to unburden you."

Menelaus stood there a moment, considering me, and waved the servants away. Once they were out of earshot he continued, "My brother, Agamemnon, wishes to conquer Troy. I see nothing to gain from it besides loss of men and time. But my brother is a hungry man. He wishes to see the great city fall. And if that ever was accomplished, he would then proceed to claim it as his own. I know my brother. There would be nothing but trouble if we attacked the Trojans." He paused then. I could see the king regretted sharing that information.

Conquer? Why would his brother want to attack another land? Did he not have enough already? These rulers were hungry men indeed. They strove to take as much as they could without a thought to others. But it was also the greed of King Menelaus that kept him from sacrificing his warriors, and the worry his brother would have more than him. Greed could be good at times.

"I am sorry for your troubles, my king. Perhaps this gathering will convince him your way is better. You are a wise ruler. Surely your brother can see that," I said.

Menelaus's cheeks reddened again, but not from anger. Maybe there was something kind in him after all. Maybe all he needed was my guidance, as limited as it was. The king cleared his throat with a grunt. "Indeed I am. He will see my side soon enough." His expression changed from amusingly uncomfortable to hungry, and his eyes roamed my body. I could feel the unwanted touch with his mere gaze. The king moved toward me.

"My king, when are you to leave for your brother's land?" I asked quickly.

"Immediately." The question didn't distract him. He closed the distance between us and groped along my hips.

Menelaus's hands were sliding inward when I offered, "King Menelaus, would you not prefer me to remain untouched? You yourself said you favored a goddess at your side. Would a goddess not be untouched and pure?" The man's hands halted their progress just in time.

"A clever woman you are." The king slowly removed his grip on me. "You will remain chaste. For now." I was half relieved that had worked. I wasn't quite ready to beat him yet, but the thought still enticed me. I needed him to get to his brother. It surprised me how quickly I adjusted to the idea of violence. I had never been a violent person. Or maybe I told myself I wasn't. Even if I hadn't been before, I couldn't hold it back now. The chaos that came with the humans required it.

"Am I to travel with you?" I asked.

"Of course! I must see the expression on my brother's face when he sees you—the envy he will feel at seeing such a beauty at my side." The Greek king roared with laughter as he dragged me back into his home. "Prepare for travel, my darling. We are going to Argos."

We traveled by carriage along the main paths of the woodlands. The journey felt long, being in such close quarters with King Perversion, as I'd come to call him, but in fact we made it before nightfall. In between speaking with Sparta's ruler, I had time to contemplate what I'd learned.

Interacting with one of humanity's leaders encouraged the notion that they needed guidance. I needed to lead them down the right path, but it was difficult to accomplish this, for I didn't know what the right path was myself. Though *something* had to be done. The violence and poverty I witnessed, as well as the way these people constantly attempted to steal one another's life force, had to change. They did it without even knowing, because they couldn't see it like I could. The best way to teach them to share their energy with each other and the natural world was to change the way they lived on the physical plane. Their leaders were a good place to start, and I had an unlimited amount of time.

King Menelaus rested his hand on my thigh as the carriage jostled over the bumpy terrain. I had been lucky, despite my aversion to him, that King Menelaus had taken an interest in me. Now I could infiltrate their system and learn how they ran their kingdoms. I could find a way to teach them and change their outlook on life. From there, the ripples would travel all the way to the abandoned children who thieved and struggled to survive. At least that was what I hoped. I had to try, no matter how difficult; I owed these people my time and attention. I caused their existence. I was responsible for their lives.

The carriage pulled up to the front entrance of a grand abode. I hadn't expected to see anything greater than the one I had stayed in the previous night. I was wrong. King Agamemnon's home was much larger and had many more statues that decorated the massive entrance. The setting sun's rays lit the snow-colored home so it glowed against the darkening sky. The comforting scent of a garden was there, but it was masked by something I couldn't identify. The inside was even grander. There were displays of gold,

jewels, and erotic art. There were several servants maintaining the unnecessary trinkets.

The servants were all beautiful women, each one unique and foreign to this land. The ability to influence energy flowed through their veins, and must have allowed the humans to evolve and harmonize with the ever-changing environment they resided in. The unnatural energy I saw daily was unfamiliar to the people from what I could understand. The knowledge had been lost.

The servants bustled about, preparing for some unknown event. A man entered the room then; he strode in confidently with guards at his sides. "Menelaus!" the King of Argos exclaimed. "It has been so long." The eldest king walked up to his younger brother and grabbed hold. It was supposed to be a hug, but soon became a strength competition. I could see their forearms bulging from the embrace.

Once their battle ceased, Menelaus replied, "Not long enough, brother. What have you brought me here for this time? The same, I assume. I hope you don't expect a different answer," he said.

"Can't I simply want to see my brother? I have missed your company," King Agamemnon said. The elder king didn't adorn himself with gold and jewels as his brother did; he was simpler. He wore a long black chiton with only red rubies decorating his neck. The chains they hung from weren't made from metal though; they looked like soft, multicolored fibers.

King Perversion scanned the room. "Why do you need my company when you have so much at your disposal?" He gestured to the awaiting young women dressed in fine threads and jewels.

Agamemnon scoffed. "They indeed make great company, but I speak of real conversation with a fellow man and king. There is no greater company than that. We are rulers, dear brother. We must communicate if we are to better our lands." His gaze moved to where I stood behind Menelaus. "I see that you have been keeping company of your own.

Where did you find this treasure?" I watched as he closed the distance between us. A small, elongated metal object that hung from a leather string protruded from the collar of his clothing, dangling with the rubies. He noticed my gaze and moved to conceal it. The king continued toward me. *Another admirer? Didn't these men have more important things to do? For example, rule a kingdom.*

King Menelaus grabbed his brother's arm before he could touch me. "Ah, brother. This one is mine. You may look, but do not touch." His tone was firm, but I could see that he enjoyed it, having something his brother didn't. Too bad it didn't seem to affect the King of Argos as much as Menelaus had planned. It was not only Agamemnon's outward appearance that was composed, but his aura as well, his too-dark spirit. Nearly black. But his was not the first of this color I'd seen. I saw many figures that possessed the strange inward darkness prowling the streets of both Sparta and Argos.

King Agamemnon patted the hand that gripped his arm. "Of course. I wouldn't dare to take something that belonged to you. I have plenty of my own anyway, plenty to share, if you grow tired of yours." Menelaus's face fell slightly. He removed his grip on his brother's arm and balled it into a fist behind his back.

"Thank you for your generosity. I will be sure to keep that in mind," he said through gritted teeth.

"Wonderful. Let us feast then. I am sure you are hungry after your long journey. Your woman is welcome to join us as well." *Was I not welcome before? Oh right, I was a female.* My gender was looked down upon here. I kept forgetting because I was so much *more powerful* than either of them!

I kept my face pleasant. "Thank you. It is a great honor, my king." *Arrogant pricks.* Since interacting with mortals, many new words were integrating themselves into my vocabulary. Most I hadn't even acknowledged I knew. I didn't need them before now. But I had to remember why I was

doing this. I was trying to save these men from themselves. I had to be more patient. I had to be above their petty faults. But it was easier said than done.

"Indeed it is, woman," Agamemnon condescendingly returned.

The elder king turned to lead the way when I said, "My name is Helen." I heard the muffled gasps of the servants around us.

Agamemnon turned back to me. "Helen then." He eyed me suspiciously. King Menelaus stifled a laugh. He didn't enjoy it when I voiced myself to him. I guessed that seeing someone else deal with it made him laugh, especially when it was his brother. "This way then," the elder king said.

We made our way to the dining room. It was just as glorious as the rest of the rooms. Delicate workings of art were painted on sculptures of women and animals. Regardless of the obvious notion that my gender was considered on the same level as the animals they disrespected, I enjoyed the art. The details were very real. I felt as if I were really in the battle that was portrayed. I could see every weapon and corpse that lay upon the large field. It thrilled me. *Strange.*

"Sit here, Helen," Menelaus instructed. I sat to his right while he sat to the right of his brother at the head of the table. For how much I disliked Menelaus, I appreciated how territorial he was. It prevented me from having to ward off other admirers, including his brother, whose gaze explored my body when Menelaus was distracted. The looks repulsed me, but I was comforted by the fact that they couldn't touch me, regardless of Menelaus. I could overpower them easily. It made me worry for my fellow sisters. They had no such advantage.

The brothers spoke of the current trade in their respective lands and where they deployed their military. Apparently, there had been trouble keeping the northern "savages" from crossing their borders.

"You are from the north, Helen. Why don't you tell us why they keep trying to ravage our lands?" Menelaus asked.

What kind of question was that? Why did your brother want to invade Troy?

"Brother, don't be so hard on her. You can't expect a woman to know anything about that. I'm sure she wasn't even aware there was a problem," King Agamemnon said.

If there was such thing as a god, it was not me. I was far from perfect. A perfect being would have patience for these creatures. "Actually, I was aware." I wasn't, but that was beside the point. "Perhaps these 'savages,' as you call them, are only trying to seek refuge in a better place than their own. Or maybe they strive to overtake you as you would strive to overtake another." I said too much, but once I began I couldn't stop. Pride was contagious.

"Silence, woman!" Menelaus stood and slapped me across the face. I was more surprised than injured. In fact, I think I hurt his hand more than he hurt my cheek. The king rubbed his hand discreetly and sat down. I remained where I was, unsure of what to do.

"I see you have been giving away secrets, Menelaus," Agamemnon said. "Would you risk a Trojan becoming aware of our plans? Shame, brother. Just because you fancy this woman does not mean you have to speak to her." That was it. I went to stand when a man entered the room, halting the impending beating I planned.

"Ah, Achilles. The great god Ares has blessed us with your presence at last." The expression on King Agamemnon's face did not reflect his words. He clearly disliked this Achilles. But for him to be so formal to someone, he had to be important.

"Indeed, he has," Achilles replied bluntly, but I could see the corner of his mouth lift in amusement. I stifled a laugh. He was even more arrogant than the kings if he acted as such in their presence. The man even took the seat opposite of Agamemnon at the head of the table. I was still learning the subtle customs of the "people of importance," but I already knew that this was not acceptable. I was actually surprised Agamemnon hadn't seated his brother across from him. The elder king didn't want to share the power, it seemed, even at a dinner table.

"What is he doing here?" Menelaus accused, clearly thinking what I was.

"Why, he's just here to discuss strategy. Aren't you, Achilles?"

Achilles didn't even look up from the large plate of food the servants had brought him. He merely nodded. I liked him already. These "kings" needed to know what it felt like to be looked down upon. It was apparent that this man did.

Menelaus interrogated, "Strategy? For what? You said the matter was ended? That there would be no more discussion?" The younger king knew for sure then that his brother had not summoned him for a pleasure visit. The King of Sparta grew red and sweaty again; his spirit floundered.

"Brother, there is no harm in discussion, as I also said. Man to man. King to king," he said.

"He is no king!" Menelaus bellowed. The laughter was becoming hard to contain. I just couldn't see Menelaus as serious when he was angry.

The king's fuming was interrupted by Achilles. "I have no desire to be king, and I have no desire to discuss strategy with you. Attack or don't attack. I could care less. I simply came here because you have the best food." Achilles scooped another piece of roasted bird into his mouth. "When you decide to attack, then and only then will I respond to you. And that response will depend on if I feel like fighting that day or not. Lucky for you, that is most days." Another bite was shoved into his mouth.

The silence was deafening. I could see the king's energies as they attacked back and forth, more urgent than before. Agamemnon was clearly winning, though it appeared he held back. His spirit was just as composed as his demeanor. This was a man who bided his time and waited for the perfect opportunity to strike. This was a man to fear. *For a mortal to fear.*

I paused my dark thoughts. Where was Achilles's spirit? I looked down the table to where he sat. His golden hue was still and calm within

himself. Golden hues were bound to be possessed by others, weren't they? The man from my past didn't have to be the only one. The man's aura wasn't even completely gold. It was exceptionally brighter than normal, but there was a greyish hue outlining the spirit. Though it didn't fight like the others did. I looked harder.

The man was well built, but that was only expected if he was a warrior like they said. Achilles's eyes were emerald green and his face was shaped narrow, but he had the same golden locks and skin as the man I wished to avoid. My ancient mate had been honing his skills, as I had. But he'd had much longer to do so, and I was not yet confident enough in my magic to stay in his presence.

"May I be excused? I need to use the lavatory," I whispered to a still-fuming Menelaus. He nodded his head, and I hurried out of the room as fast as I could without running. I didn't know where the relief room was, but I needed to get away before he noticed me. I was surprised he hadn't already, but I could guess why. My appearance was as changed as his was. As for seeing my familiar aura and its obvious withdrawn disposition, he probably didn't pay much attention to it. If he held the same opinion as before, he didn't care. So why would he look? I even found myself ignoring the light in front of me at times, simply to relieve myself of the obligation, if only for a moment.

My run had diminished to a slow walk. I circled the large halls, keeping my head down. I needed a moment to figure out what I was going to do about Lucifer. What were the odds he was here? The fates were toying with me as usual. Was I ready to see him? What would I say? What did I *want* to say? I knew then what words would come tumbling out of my mouth, and I cringed.

I was a sick human being. How could I possibly still love him? I told myself I spared him because it was the opposite of what he wanted. I told myself it was his punishment that I let him live. And it was, to some

degree. But I knew deep down that I couldn't kill him no matter what he did. Lucifer was the only other of my kind, purely anyway, and I was in love with him still, after all these eons.

It wasn't the same love I felt for Adam. True, I loved and treasured my time with my self-made partner. He was a devoted lover and father. Adam's love meant everything to me, but it wasn't the passion I felt for my first mate. Adam had been comfortable and secure, always a guarantee. I saw now that I had used his loyalty as a crutch on which to lean my insecurities. That was why he had suffered. It was wrong of me to force him to watch his children die and to constantly care for my neediness. Like my strength, my cruelty was vast.

A servant passed by carrying shiny round cuffs. They reminded me of Ambrose.

My thoughts returning to Adam, I promised myself I would never do that to someone I loved again. I would no longer be a creature of weakness. I would no longer watch the ones I loved die. I would stand and protect those who needed me. These human beings weren't my children, but they had a guardian nonetheless. I would become the beast that tamed beasts. And I had yet to discover what kind of beast Lucifer and his children had become.

I passed by a crimson vase with gold warriors on it for the third time. I could still hear the angry bellows of King Menelaus shouting at his brother from down the hall. I wasn't ready yet. One more round.

I had time to reflect on my actions while I was encased in the frozen depths, but I had wasted the opportunity. I should have used the time to grieve and acknowledge my emotions. I should have used the time to become stronger. The whole time I had been in my solitary prison, I pushed down my emotions and memories, desperately seeking a way to forget and die. I thought I had been close until Aegeus found me.

But life had other plans for me. It wasn't going to let me go. The

cosmos was forcing me to atone for my actions. I deserved worse. Maybe the same could be said for Lucifer. I wanted to forget, but it was clear I couldn't, and shouldn't even have tried. It was selfish. I would learn from the tragedies that I'd lived through. And if I had learned anything from them, it was that life wasn't worth living afraid and alone.

I turned a corner and rammed into something hard. Was it a wall? No, it was warm. But I should have sent that person flying back. I looked up from my daze. *Shit.* Yet another word I learned and had used numerous times already.

"Hello, Lilith. Nice to see you." I could only stand there and gape at him. I didn't know what to say. That's why I had left the dining table. We had an audience for one, but I also hadn't decided if I was ready to speak to him. The man decided for me, as usual. It looked like eons of time hadn't changed that aspect of him.

Lucifer chuckled. "Have you nothing to say to me then? You've kept me waiting for a long time. I would think you would have some words for me." My former mate was reserved, but I could see how his spirit thrashed about.

I swallowed. "I suppose I haven't had a chance to think of what to say to you," I replied quietly.

"Haven't had the time? How much do you need?" he questioned. Disbelief plagued his face.

"I have only just seen you at the dinner table. I didn't expect to see you so soon after I woke." It felt like my heart should have been pounding. I was grateful I didn't have one, or else he would have heard it.

"Woke? Where have you been, Lilith? I searched for you. For a long time. I thought you were running from me," Lucifer whispered. He grabbed my hand. I pulled away out of instinct. He was hurt. I hadn't been able to look into his eyes before, but I could see it now. Lucifer was in pain. I empathized.

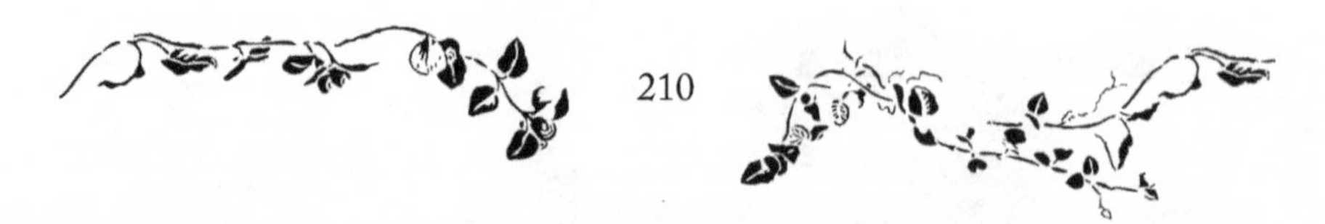

I needed to take action if I wanted to be happy. I had promised Adam I would try to find a way to do so. I owed him that much. Or else what was the point to his sacrifices? I always felt there was a flame inside of me waiting to burst, a fire that wanted to be released. I knew it was the key to my happiness. Perhaps it was the beast that was shown in the core of these humans, or maybe the determination in their characters. Whatever it was, I needed to give it life. *But what could light my internal flame?*

"In a way I suppose I did." I averted my gaze to the floor, afraid of my own thoughts. The ground was lovely and white, more depictions of battles detailed in gold. "After what happened…I was taken by the water's current and decided to freeze myself rather than continue to suffer."

"Why didn't you just swim to land? You didn't have to suffer," Lucifer questioned, concern in his eyes.

"It wasn't only my body suffering, Lucifer." It was nice to say his name out loud.

The man understood then. "Was it you who caused the land to part?"

I nodded.

"I thought so, but I had to make sure." He didn't ask why or how. "What about Adam?" he said through tight lips. Apparently he still held hate for him, though I didn't know why. Adam never hurt him.

"Adam didn't want to continue on without his children," I said. I didn't need to say that I hadn't wanted to continue either, but I'd had no way to join him.

"And you only found your way back to land now? What was the wait?" Lucifer gave me a small encouraging smile. He radiated warmth. I had missed it so much. My former mate was making it very hard to hate him. I wanted to desperately. If I didn't, I would be a horrible mother. If I did, I would be alone again. But perhaps this was the start I was looking for. A way to be happy. That's what I wanted to believe at least.

"I didn't actually. I was found by some fishermen. They brought me

to land." I returned my gaze to his green eyes. "It was time to wake anyway. I was gone far longer than I thought. Time was irrelevant under the waves. A millennium felt like only a moment." My eyes itched to tear up, but none came. Still empty. Lucifer embraced me then. I was enveloped in his wide chest, and he scorched like the sun. I needed the sun after so long in the dark.

"I never liked seeing you cry," he said. I fought it at first, remembering the last time he had said those words, but I returned the embrace. It felt nice. No one had held me like this since Adam. *Don't think about Adam now.* I wasn't ready to accept his absence yet. I let Lucifer comfort and hold me.

I looked up at his wonderful face then. "What's with the disguise? You hiding from someone?" I questioned. I could feel the familiar weight in my chest. It had been a long time since I had. I was so used to the hollowness that the weight nearly dragged me down.

The man smiled. "No, I was just tired of looking at myself every day. I thought a change might help." I closed the small gap that parted us and felt the hard lines of his chest and stomach against me.

"And the green eyes?" I wondered as I traced his brow line.

"I'd rather look into the eyes of someone I loved rather than someone I hated," he confessed. A familiar yearning was there in my thoughts, but I couldn't consciously acknowledge it yet.

"Why would you hate yourself?" I asked absently, completely forgetting my original want to loathe him. I continued on to trace my fingers along his hairline and jaw.

"Because of what I did to you. For killing your children." The man gripped me tighter. "Don't you hate me?" Lucifer's spirit was fighting now, but not with mine. It was an inward turmoil. It writhed and struggled against itself. I had never seen Lucifer's spirit lose control like that before, even when I left.

Of course, I tried not to pay too much attention to the lights I saw before I woke in this new land. I did as much as I could to repress the spirits, even when I lived among my children. When I wasn't training them, I looked elsewhere. Every time I witnessed the natural light dim, or a person's spirit flutter helplessly, it killed me inside. To be able to see the problem and have no way to fix it—it was torture.

Lucifer's eyes bored into mine as I contemplated his question. The battle within myself waged ruthlessly. Which side would win? Light the flame or let it smolder? "I hate what you did. That moment in the woods when you asked me to kill you: I wanted to, very much." My soul exploded in a hailstorm of anger around me. I could see the bloody shade on the outskirts of my vision as I remembered that moment. So much hatred and despair. My grip on him tightened. "But I don't hate you, Lucifer, and I think I know why you did it," I said. Weak but plausible reasoning was budding, as well as the resolve to let go. My crimson spirit no longer obstructed my sight.

"You do?" Lucifer looked away.

I explained, "The gift you were given scared you, and you lashed out at it. You finally realized that I had been right all along, and you were horrified with what you had done already." His forehead creased. I smoothed out the worry lines with my touch and continued on. "So instead of trying to make it better, you attacked, because you thought there was no way to correct what you'd done." I wound my hands tightly around his nape. "But, Lucifer, there is always hope, no matter how far you go. There is always a way to make it better." Lucifer had stilled while I spoke. I couldn't read his face anymore. "Lucifer? Is that why?" The man's golden soul danced excitedly.

Expressionless, he asked, "Do you remember what I said to you when you saw me for the first time in over five hundred years? Do you remember why I was there?"

Confused, I said, "I think so. I don't know. It was a blur." I tried to

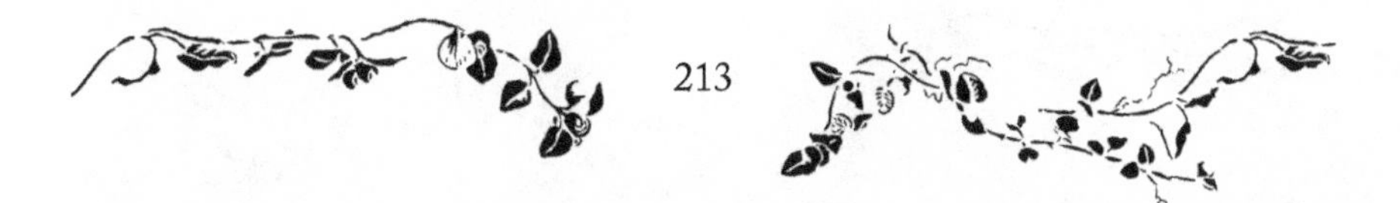

remember, but all I could conjure was the image of my dead children lying crushed in the forest floor. Lucifer's dead eyes. I remembered that he wanted to die, and he was saying anything he could to make that happen. The rest didn't want to come to the surface. "Why?" I asked.

Instead of responding with words, he brought me close enough to coerce my lips apart with his. Despite my reluctance, I responded naturally. I could almost taste the desperation on his lips. Without breaking contact, he led me through a doorway into a bedroom a few steps from where we stood. Lucifer picked me up so my legs were wrapped around his hips as he walked. We made it to the bedside, but instead of putting me down on the soft blankets, he pressed me against the wall beside the frame.

He mumbled the words, "Stay with me." Though I didn't know why he felt the need. I was clearly spending the night with him. Our spirits danced around each other, but still they did not mingle. *Forever separate.*

Lucifer pushed the sleeves that held my golden tunic off my shoulders, and it fell from me. The man caressed my curves, and I traced the muscles that rippled through his body. Each touch was like a licking flame; it stung where it grazed, but the pain of it felt too good to resist. Our one union had not been enough to quench my undying thirst. My soul encased his golden spirit and I discovered, to my surprise, that it outshone his.

We immediately shed our disguises and beheld each other's true forms for the first time in several millennia. I was able to look into his piercing blue eyes again, and I was lost in them. We soon grew irritated with the clanking jewels I wore. The man placed me rather indelicately on the bed and aided me in removing them. I worked on my upper half and him on my lower. Soon I was free of my chains, and I was able to love him fully.

My inward battle ceased, and I allowed him to reciprocate my love. We were completely and utterly in sync. Our bodily rhythm played the most beautiful song. It didn't feel as if we'd only made love once before.

Our movements were too natural, too right. I wondered as I kissed him if time *was* capable of healing our wounds.

I knew I should have been worried about King Menelaus. He was bound to be searching for me, but I didn't care. All that mattered was the man in my arms and the time we had to make up for. The fear of children didn't cross my mind as it had before. I knew that whatever happened, I would survive. I had been through much worse.

The hours passed too quickly. It was early morning when we fell asleep, our limbs tangled together, and I had a lot to consider about Lucifer, as well as the kings. *Would Lucifer help me save his children? To save Earth? Would he finally stand by my side?* If so, I thought I could find it in my metaphorical heart to forgive him.

My questions worried me, but I soon found myself drifting away, thinking of my time by the waterfall, of a time with children's faces and of a man who *had* stood by my side.

XV
The King of Kings

A world without lies would be a
world lacking imagination.
-A

My dreams were happy as I slept. My children played in the lake by the waterfall, and Adam held me as we watched over them from Shamira's perch, her head lying heavily in my lap. I was thinking to myself that my life couldn't get any better, when suddenly the lake began to steam and the happiness was gone.

The water bubbled from the extreme temperature. My children screamed for me to save them from the scalding water. The pain was too much for them to escape to the shoreline themselves. I couldn't move. Adam held me in place as he said to me, "It's all right, my love. This is what you wanted." *What was he talking about? Those were our children!*

I was paralyzed in Adam's grasp. Even Shamira did her part to hold me in place. *When had they become so strong? Or had I become weak?* All my children had sunk beneath the boiling waves. All but Naavah. Her skin puckered and reddened, and her hair singed off to reveal more burnt flesh. My daughter held her mutilated hand toward me. She didn't call out for help, though. She just looked at me with disappointment in her eyes, as if she were silently relaying a message to me. *You did this, Mother. This is all your fault. You should have done better for us.* Once Naavah joined her

siblings, Shamira dove in dutifully after her, only to meet the same fate. I cried out in anguish, but I couldn't ignore the relief that came with my children's absence. The burden no longer plagued me.

The heat grew. Soon the grass along the shore lit with flame. A trail of fire led right to our apple tree. Soon it was nothing but a charred reminder of what it once was. Adam continued to incapacitate me, whispering comforts in my ear. Why was he doing this? *It was all my fault!* Why didn't he toss me in after them? I finally found some of my strength and threw myself off the branch where we sat, tumbling down into the boiling water. Adam didn't let go of me.

We entered the fiery lake together. I held his hand as long as I could, but he forced it out of my grasp and swam to shore. I watched as he walked willingly into the blue flames that tortured our apple tree. Then he was gone, and I was alone. My lover didn't even look back at me.

I begged and begged to die. *Please take my life. I failed.* But of course I couldn't. I burned over and over again. The cycle never waned, and it never stopped. It was an endless circle of misery and regret. I eventually came to embrace the heat that tortured me. I made sure to feel every singe and every blaze on my skin. I forced myself to feel every bit of the pain my children had felt.

I laid at the bottom of the lake. I could still breathe. That didn't make sense. *Wasn't I under water?* Then suddenly I was awake. I had been dreaming. I subconsciously knew that fact at some point, but I had forgotten it in the turmoil of my imagination. The heat wasn't invented though. *Why was it so hot?* I was lying tangled in thick blankets, and the sun was beating down on me through the window.

I had complained about being cold ever since I was dragged from the sea, but that was no longer an issue. I rolled to the cool side of the bed and tossed the blankets to the floor. I was still undressed from the night before, but it didn't help. I turned to face the other side of the room and discovered the problem.

Lucifer was sitting in a large chair in the corner of the small room. The man wore nothing but an angry expression. Even angry, he was beautiful. I admired the perfection of his body so long it took me a moment to realize his soul flared around him like a deranged wildfire. At least the grey was gone from the brilliant coloring. I wondered what it had been. Maybe I had imagined it.

I followed his gaze. Lucifer was staring at his hand where it rested on the arm of the chair. He kept igniting and extinguishing a sphere-shaped flame that extended from his hand. It explained the excruciating heat, and I couldn't help but envy the skill he'd honed.

"Lucifer? What's wrong?" I asked. It felt good to say his name. For how long it had been since I'd given it to him, I hadn't said it aloud to him more than a handful of times.

Lucifer didn't seem to share my thoughts. "What's not wrong, Lilith? There is always something wrong. Something always keeps us from being together." The flames in his hand extended well past his head before he abruptly extinguished them in his fist. The man closed his eyes as if he couldn't bear to look into the images reality provided for him any longer. "Sadly, I know what it is. I've had a long time to consider the possibilities, and last night confirmed it." Any moisture in the room was quickly being burnt away.

I was at a loss. *What was he talking about?* Last night was wonderful. We needed it. *I* needed it. We needed to reunite after what we'd been through. All the hate and anger needed to be set aside, if only for the few hours we shared together.

"What do you mean? I know we have a lot to talk about. I mean… we've been apart for a long time, and we need to discuss what's next," I stuttered. *Why was I so nervous?* I had forgotten how Lucifer made me feel. The man's confident and authoritative influence always snuffed out any light I managed to shine.

The man looked up at me then. I thought I recognized the emotion as pain, but it quickly transformed into the anger I remembered so well. "You."

Me?

"You, Lilith. You are what's wrong. You are the reason we separated. You are the reason we never had children. You are the reason for the monsters that now infest this planet."

What was he saying? I thought he had forgiven me? I thought that's what last night was: forgiveness.

"As I said long ago, I hope these abominations destroy the planet. Not only will I be able to finally die, but it will be the greatest revenge on you, *my love*."

Why did he use Adam's name for me?

Any happiness I felt had disappeared, almost like he sucked it into himself and destroyed it. "Where is this coming from? I thought last night was special? I thought it meant…" I couldn't finish; my throat closed.

"You thought what? That I would be with you again? That I would follow you around as you tried to save everyone? Wake up! There is no saving this planet, Lilith, let alone these hybrid humans." Lucifer stood as he said this to me. His anger was growing. The golden hue he exuded nearly burnt the pupils out of my emerald irises.

"How did you…" I started. I hadn't even spoken of anything relating to his descendants. We hadn't done much talking last night.

"How did I know you want to save them? You talk in your sleep, my dear. And that wasn't the only thing you spoke of." He looked down at his feet. I was surprised his gaze didn't set them aflame. The man didn't let me question what else I mentioned in my sleep, but I could guess. Adam was in the dream with me. "You plan to leave me again. Just like you did before. You left me because you outgrew me and wanted more." That couldn't have been what I said in my sleep, because it wasn't true.

"Lucifer, I didn't leave because—"

He cut me off. "I don't care what your excuse is or was!" He turned his glare on me then. "Whether your excuse is the cursed light that we see, or simply due to your own selfish endeavors, you chose something else over me. You chose *someone* else over me. And you always will. You will always leave. No matter how much I want you to stay…" He finished quietly, so I nearly didn't hear his end remark.

I stood and walked slowly to where he stood in the middle of the overheated room. "I didn't want to leave you, Lucifer. I've told you as much. I haven't had much time to think about now, but I certainly don't want to leave you again." I took his hand and he clung to it desperately. "I want to stay with you. I love you—so much it hurts. I want us to be together. It's been long enough, don't you think? Don't we deserve to be happy?" I probed his eyes, begging him to give in, to give in to what we both wanted.

"How can I be happy when you hold this planet's welfare above me? When you hold the welfare of these creatures above me? I will never be enough for you. I will never be a priority for you, even after all this time. Do you not realize that no matter what we do, it doesn't matter? Could you really be with me? *Just* me?"

I took a moment to think on what he said. *Did* it matter? He had a point. It seemed no matter how much I tried to prevent further damage to our home, it happened anyway. I left him because I didn't want to create children who drained the Earth's light. Being with Adam, even as a creature of the natural world, this problem was still an issue. Worse even. Then I taught my succubus children to follow the natural order. This not only didn't work, but it prevented them from truly experiencing freedom. Without my constant guidance, they would have strayed from their teachings. It was bound to happen. Their natural instinct was greed. It showed in Lucifer's children. He gave them free rein, and they basked in it. They reveled in it. It was their basest of desires to take. *But at least they were free.*

I looked to the ground where the sunlight hit my feet. Maybe it

wouldn't be such a terrible thing to give in and just be with Lucifer. We were not only immortal, but powerful. We could live grand lives, full of the things we longed to take. Things that *I* wanted to take. Even something as small as eating meat would have been a gift. Could I really ignore the voice inside of me that told me it was wrong? *Could I be free to be human?*

Lucifer still had not learned patience in his time away from me. "Well? What is your answer?" he demanded. His hand still gripped mine.

"Do I have to answer right now?" I asked, my eyes still on the ground. I needed time to consider. I couldn't just uproot my whole ideology at a moment's notice.

The man dropped my hand. "If you don't already know, then I have my answer." He dressed quickly and left the room. The only thing that remained of him was the cloud of steam that encased the small bedroom.

I made my way over to the window in a dreamlike state. The sun had shifted in the sky, and no longer irritated my overheated skin. But the wooden frame that held the delicate glasswork still radiated warmth. I opened the clever opening as wide as it could go. Humans were very artistic. I wondered if my children could have thought of such an invention. The steam that hovered in the room departed with the breeze. I thought I caught a whiff of rot, but it quickly disappeared.

Though the window's natural elements emitted only pleasant and comforting warmth, the tips of my fingers still burned at the touch, sensitive to the unwanted heat. Not unlike the words Lucifer spoke to me moments before, except his words didn't radiate pleasant warmth. Lucifer's accusations felt more like a blazing…core. That's what it was. His anger reminded me of the heat I felt when I explored too deep into the Earth. It scorched and mutilated my wandering spirit. I always stopped my mindful roots from spreading further when the heat became too much, even though I knew there were several more layers to explore, even though I had yet to reach the center, the core of the world I claimed to love and

protect. As much as I hated the notion, Lucifer was right. The world *was* a mystery to me.

I reached my hand outside and stroked the daisies that rested beyond the opening. Lucifer said he already had his answer, but I hadn't answered him. *What did he expect?* My whole life had been dedicated to protecting the life on this planet. Regretfully, that was also the humans, or hybrids as he called them, a mix between natural animal and us. At least they had some connection to the natural world. It was our half that made them horrible, the human half. That was my theory at least.

In reality, there was no way to actually know for sure if it was the mixture that made them monsters, the human side, the animal side, or simply the fact that they were misguided. Despite this, I was still considering leaving them to their chaotic lives. For Lucifer. So he would be happy. *No.* That wasn't completely true. I would be doing it just as much for me as I would be for him. I wanted to let go and indulge in what our lives had to offer without constantly having to worry about the consequences. In a way I had already allowed myself some breathing room in my abilities, but it was for a greater purpose, not just selfish indulgence. I slowed the harsh breeze outside. The daisies' petals were spared because of it.

My mate said that I was the one who always caused the rift between us; he was right. I couldn't ignore the voice inside of me telling me to help. Harassing me. Haunting me. I wouldn't be able to relax and enjoy my life while everything suffered. That basically meant I'd suffer either way. If I helped Earth, I suffered because I lost Lucifer. If I stayed with Lucifer, I suffered because I would watch the planet die. But only one option would cause Lucifer pain. A question that he had asked me the night before infiltrated my thoughts: *Do you remember why I was there?* Sadly, I did.

Ignoring my dark thoughts and procrastinating in my decision about Lucifer, I transformed back into Helen. I dressed in the godly adornments King Menelaus insisted upon and made my way out to the

hall. I hadn't noticed last night, but the grand structure we slept in had a myriad of window openings. Sunlight streamed in through the painted glass, embellishing the white and gold inlay of the decor.

I knew that these "kings" only surrounded themselves with such beauty to express their power, but it was quite lovely. One day, I hoped to inhabit a home that exhibited such elegance, but not for the mere purpose of dominance. It was simply because I loved beauty. If humans could create things as lovely as this home, certainly there had to be beauty within themselves. I only had to bring it out into the light.

I was not looking forward to seeing King Perversion and explaining my absence. So I took my time admiring the structure and art that King Agamemnon collected, mostly depictions of battles. Didn't the artists have anything else to paint? Why not a dozing panther or an enchanted meadow? I knew of a couple that would inspire the artists.

Lost in my thoughts, I didn't realize that someone had approached until an arm was wrapped around my waist. It pulled me in close. My peripheral vision went black. Panicked by the darkness, I pushed it away too hard. The man next to me stumbled back. I turned to face the black spirit and immediately composed myself.

"King Agamemnon, I apologize. You startled me." I hoped he didn't notice the strength that I had put behind that push.

Righting himself and discreetly rubbing his arm, he said, "I'm sure you are. Now, what is a beauty like you roaming my halls all alone for?" He looked me up and down slowly, inspecting me. "Ah, yes, you're that girl my brother brought with him yesterday. He was quite angry when you didn't come back to dinner." The king chuckled. "You embarrassed him tremendously. He claims you as his, yet you don't even follow his orders. What kind of man can't control his woman?" He rubbed his short patch of beard as he smirked at me; his narrow face reminded me of someone.

"That question is of no consequence. A man who can't control his woman is every man. There are only women who decide to follow and men who believe they are being followed, my king." *Why did I say that?* I kept my gaze down; maybe that would keep me from hitting him. I detested Agamemnon from the instant I saw him, but I wasn't the only one. I saw how the servants avoided him. I recognized the fear in their eyes. I had the capability to see the nature of his aura, but one didn't need to possess my power to realize this was a terrible man. Even his own brother disliked him. As much as I loathed King Menelaus and his advances, he was a daisy compared to his older sibling.

The elder king closed the distance between us and whispered, "What did you say, little girl?" My pride would kill me if it was possible.

"My name is Helen, my king, and I believe you heard me just fine," I said under my breath. It wasn't his arrogant expression or his words that angered me. It was his aura. Usually when people were angry it flailed and fought to be released from its physical prison, but his was different. It was eerily calm. Silent. A black void of darkness. The man wasn't upset. That was how arrogant he was. He merely thought of me as a bug beneath his boot. What I said didn't matter.

If words didn't invoke a reaction out of him, perhaps action would. I turned my gaze upward and met his stare. Agamemnon was taller than Helen, but I still found a way to look down at him. This didn't even rile him. Instead of anger, it was curiosity. The king was looking at a bug that wouldn't be crushed beneath his heel, and he was considering a different approach. Perhaps fire? Drown it?

"You have a tongue, don't you? I would watch that. Even if my brother allows it, I don't." His expression turned dark. The man grabbed my wrist and yanked me into him. He wasn't an unappealing man, but he stank of death. How many had he killed to obtain that scent? The king's other hand wrenched my hips against him. I felt more than I wanted to in that

movement. This man enjoyed a challenge, and defeating that challenge by any means necessary, so long as he was the victor.

"Get off me!" I gave him a chance to let go on his own. He didn't, and his hands roamed my body mercilessly. I had enough. He thought he could overthrow me physically since he didn't win with words? These mortals needed help. I became surer of that every day I encountered men like this. I didn't want to reveal my powers, but what else could I do? I wasn't going to allow him to handle me like this.

Before I could make a decision, the king fell to the ground. Agamemnon cried out in agony. The once calm man clawed at his chest, but that wasn't enough. The king's nails raked across his skin, attempting to peel it from his own flesh. *What was wrong with him?* I knew as soon as I asked myself the question. *I* was what was wrong.

In my attempt to find a subtler way to release myself from his grasp, my influence over energy stepped in instinctually. I could feel it now. A tiny piece of my mind was working on reversing the direction of his blood flow. Agamemnon was dying. Slowly. His heartbeat grew erratic, confused. He scraped at his skin violently, unable to fix what was occurring within.

I hadn't meant to, but perhaps this was a good thing. The elder king would die, and his brother would rule; Menelaus was much easier to control. But that wasn't my purpose. I was here to help these people, even the kings. In order to do that, I needed the authority of *both* rulers. Their constant distrust would keep the other from becoming too powerful. If they were questioning each other, they wouldn't be questioning me. I would keep Agamemnon alive as long as I could, until he proved to me that there was no saving him.

I concentrated on righting his blood flow. Now that I was doing it consciously it was more difficult. The fact that I had subconsciously done it frightened me. *What else was I capable of?* The king laid upon the ground unconscious, his wounds completely healed, though I was sure I had caused

permanent damage to his heart. I knelt down in front of the haughty man. Even in his sleep he looked conceited. I slapped him hard across the face. The king woke with a start and immediately stood. His confused expression gave me some satisfaction, but it was short lived.

"What did you do to me?" Agamemnon demanded.

In the sweetest voice I could muster, I said, "My king, I assure you I don't know what you mean. We were speaking and then you collapsed to the ground. You must have fainted." I averted my gaze downward so he wouldn't see the humor hidden there.

"Liar! What did you do?" Apparently he wasn't going to be misled that easily; he wasn't his brother. Fine by me. I didn't have the patience anyway.

I dropped the sugared tone, revealing the true age in my voice. "I wouldn't be blaming me for your faults, *my king*. You have complete control of your actions, and those actions have consequences. I suggest you learn from them." I hoped those words would make him think twice about forcing himself on another woman, but I mostly enjoyed the flash of fear I saw cross his face knowing he wasn't the superior anymore. It was satisfying. It was…disturbing. *Why did I enjoy that?*

Nevertheless, he composed himself, mimicking his original demeanor. The king fearlessly strode the short distance to where I stood. I held myself tall and confident. I would not be swayed by him. The man knew this. Agamemnon smiled. He enjoyed this? Did he not realize he almost died? Or was that the part that excited him?

"You, my dear Helen, are going to be fun." Seeing my confused expression he continued, "You are just the distraction I need."

The king turned to leave when I argued, "I am not meant for your entertainment. Besides, I travel with your brother, and I am sure we won't be staying long." There were a couple reasons I wanted to leave this place.

Without turning around he answered, "I wouldn't be so sure about that. I have ways to keep my brother busy."

"Menelaus is a king, as well. He has duties to attend to in his own kingdom. You cannot keep us here."

"Ah, lovely Helen. Do you not see? I can do whatever I please." He chuckled darkly. "Because I am the King of Kings." King Agamemnon left me then.

I stood there, pondering what he said. Agamemnon might have been the King of Kings, but according to the ancient spiteful words of Lucifer, I was The Queen, and I ruled above them all.

XVI
Mind Games

Sins surpass the heavenly docile.
-A

I crossed King Menelaus's scent. I needed to make amends with my "captor" if I was to help his subjects. I wound my way up the wide staircase, down the grand hallway, and to a bedroom occupying the corner. I felt a fresh breeze coming from beneath the doorway. The perfume of roses and sunshine wafted through. King Perversion and I shared a love for roses it seemed.

I knocked twice. I heard another door close inside. I thought he hadn't heard me, but right as I was about to knock a third time I heard his heavy steps. He paused a moment. *What was he waiting for?* He reluctantly cracked the door open and peeked out. The man's face turned from expectant to angry in an instant. The king opened the door the rest of the way and yanked me inside, slamming the wooden frame behind him.

"Where have you been?" he bellowed. His trademark red and sweaty face made an appearance. Menelaus was dressed in his sleeping gown. None of the gold he loved so much adorned his body. It was a nice change.

"I apologize for my abrupt departure, my king. On my way to the lavatory I passed a room where a woman was giving birth. She wasn't coping well, even with her handmaids. I have a lot of experience with

laboring women, and I stayed with her through the night. She finally gave birth this morning. Both baby and mother are healthy." I did hear a woman giving birth somewhere in the residence last night; that part was true at least. Hopefully he wouldn't need to confirm my story and go looking for her.

The king's face lightened a shade. "Hmph. Despite your intentions, you are not to disappear without approval from me. Also, if you are to remain at my side, you will not sully yourself with deeds such as that. My brother has plenty of midwives to tend to the pregnant." King Menelaus grabbed my arm roughly and continued, "You will *not* do that again."

I gently placed my hand over his tight grip on my arm. "Of course I will not leave without your approval again. But a man such as yourself must realize it is the duty of every woman and goddess alike to tend to the births. We must do our utmost to birth healthy baby boys to provide for your kingdoms. Is that not true, my king?" I bowed my head, awaiting his answer.

Menelaus loosened his grip on my forearm and took my face in his other hand. "I suppose it is." His hands moved from my jaw to my collarbone. "Just not without my consent. I don't need to give my brother any more incentive to disrespect me." King Perversion traced his fingers down my collarbone, past the skin between my breasts, and settled on my hip.

I despised his touch, but he seemed to have his own boundaries, and stopped before I had to force him. Perhaps he was saving me for a special occasion. I would have to avoid such an event. It was going to be difficult, as his attention to my words seemed to be connected to caressing my body. It was the only mortal power I had over these men. Despite my aversion, I would have to continue to use it if I was going to reach my goal. The king's heart was pounding. His fingers lightly traced the curve of my hips.

I could simply have changed my form into a man. It might have been easier. Even so, they would have seen another man as a threat and a challenge to them. A woman, on the other hand, would not be seen as a challenge, and I could make subtle changes to their outlooks. Also,

for my own prideful reasons, I didn't want to. If they were to change, I wanted them to change because of me, a woman. That was another factor I needed to alter: the world's perspective of females. Sadly, that included changing women's perspectives, too. They knew they were treated unfairly, yet very few did anything to stop it. Ignorance and fear were powerful weapons these men wielded.

"As you say, my king." I took his hands in mine and bowed. There was no need to tell him of my encounter with his brother, and I was sure Agamemnon wouldn't say anything, either. What occurred between us was private, and surely the elder king wouldn't want to share that he was nearly killed by a woman.

Menelaus's heart slowed. "Now, my dear, why don't you accompany me into the city? The staff here will be busy preparing for the council tonight, and I need to stretch my legs," he said.

"Council? What is the gathering for?" I asked with innocent curiosity.

Not answering me, the king gathered his gold adornments and robes and began to undress right there in front of me. I turned the other direction to give him privacy. In my life with Lucifer, Adam, and my children, we wore coverings simply to keep warm. So nudity wasn't abnormal, but this was different. They dressed themselves in decorated clothes to not only beautify themselves, but to cover their bare forms. It was seen as immoral to walk among others undressed. I didn't understand the origin of the custom, but I could see the advantages for the women; it was a way to protect themselves from further scrutiny. On the other hand, it could be used as a weapon for humiliating someone, as well. If nudity was the normal way of life, there would be one less way to shame one another by uncovering them without permission.

Regardless of my opinions, I followed their customs. It was clear that the king was unashamed of his naked form and wanted me to see, but it was all about what it meant, and I knew the meaning behind his actions.

Seeing I was uninterested in watching him undress, he quickly decorated himself with his heavy robes, jewels, and gold. The king took my hand and led me toward a secluded entrance behind the home.

We passed by a large room on our way to the hidden doorway. The floor was marbled white and swirled with the intricate gold and black patterns of predators. A raised level sat at the back of the room, and at the top rested a grand throne. It shone despite its dark ebony coloring. The material reflected as if it were glass, and its sharp, pointed design made it look even more so like shattered remnants of a mirror that had been put back together. The chair had been placed on a pool of hot gold, making it a permanent fixture. The now-solid gold leaked out onto the marble and down the white steps. The throne was not besmirched by jewels and stones other than three rubies. One rested on each of the arms and one at the peak, above where the king's head would rest. The throne beckoned for me to take my place upon its harsh surface.

Seeing where my gaze rested, the king pulled me toward the doorway and through the garden and trees beyond, four guards trailing us as we departed. King Menelaus took his time regarding the roses as we passed the flowered grounds. Every time he did something like that, it made me question him. How could a man as power-hungry and dominating as him enjoy anything that had to do with nature? *Could he really be as terrible as I thought?*

We walked among the city goers as the king led me through the trader's market. He offered to buy me clothes, jewels, and treats. There was no denying him. When I tried he only reddened. Then I came across something that actually interested me. It was a small wooden board with eight rows of squares in length and width. A bag of small colored rocks accompanied it.

I asked the trader about its purpose, and he explained enthusiastically, "Ah, you must be an intelligent young lady if you are interested in something

such as this. This is the game of Petteia." *Pebbles.* "Two players. One king survives. It is a game of strategy and cunning. Are you up to the challenge, miss?" It was clear he just wanted to make the sale, but it was nice to hear he wasn't against female intelligence. I was also intrigued by the concept, and he included a parchment that listed the rules.

I gave the salesman the gold Menelaus allowed me. The amount the man asked for was most likely not what I ended up giving him. I could see the excited flutter of his spirit and the wry grin upon the exchange, but he said nothing to the extra payment he received. It was odd to trade something for another instead of sharing among everyone, but I could see its purpose. With greed and deception infesting the masses, the only way to keep people honest was to attempt fair trade.

A small black cat sauntered past the tradesman's stand. I reached out my hand to the unnaturally tiny creature, and she responded by swiping her delicate but deadly claws in my direction. The cat then ran as quickly as she could from me. Disappointed, I weaved my way through the crowds back to Menelaus. When he saw what was in my hands, he said, "Ah! The game of Petteia! My brother and I grew up playing this with our father. It is a useful tool for learning strategy, both as a ruler and a leader in war. But why on Earth did you buy it? Wouldn't you have preferred something prettier, like those colored silks over there?" The king pointed over to another stand where a woman advertised her shiny clothes.

"They are very beautiful, but I think I would enjoy something that we could do together instead. Would you teach me how to play?" I touched his arm as I said this. I wanted to learn from someone who had played before. Also, I still could not read, and wouldn't be able to learn the rules on my own.

Blushing quite different from his angry crimson, he responded, "Well, of course." He changed the subject quickly. The king was done shopping and wanted to eat. We made the short trek back to his brother's home and had the servants prepare us a meal. While we waited, he showed me the

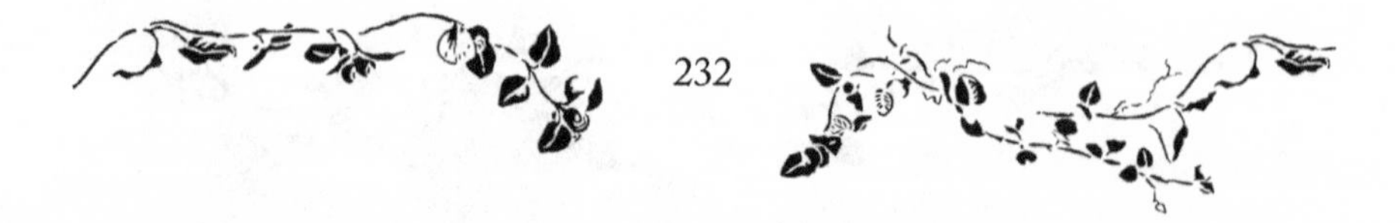

basics of my board game. I loved it instantly. It exercised my mind and helped me focus. I used and sacrificed pieces as I needed, and I found to his and my surprise that I was very good at it. I defeated his king my first time playing. I quite enjoyed the power the queen pebble wielded.

King Menelaus's pride wasn't hurt like I expected it would be. He actually asked me questions on my thought process when I made one move or another. The fact that he listened was very enlightening to me, and it gave me hope. We played the rest of the day, even during our meal. The king was determined to defeat me, and he became frustrated after the fifth time he lost. The seventh time, I allowed him to win. Menelaus didn't seem to notice the lack of wits on my side of the board that time around. He was simply satisfied that he had won. To his benefit, he wasn't a bad strategist, he just had trouble making tough decisions. I suspected he viewed the board as his actual men and didn't want to sacrifice needlessly. But to win, sacrifices must be made.

After my thrown game, a servant came to collect us for dinner. She led us to the same dining room I had escaped from the night before when I saw Lucifer posing as Achilles. Luckily he wasn't anywhere in sight. I didn't need the distraction while I worked. Unknown to Menelaus, his guidance in Petteia gave me ideas on how to handle the council meeting. Guidance I desperately needed. I knew I had to change things, but how? Agamemnon was out of the question, unless I could discover a way to use his demented game against him. But Menelaus was kinder to me now that we had spent time together; he led me gently by the arm rather than forcing me to follow.

I would meet the other kings of Greece tonight, or at least observe them. I had overheard our chatty guards today at the market say that this was a big gathering, and it only happened when something important took place. They said something about visitors from across the sea, but not much else about the mysterious newcomers.

Menelaus took his proper place opposite Agamemnon at the head of the table, me at his right. The fellow kings took their own seats. There were fewer than I thought there would be. The two brothers must have ruled more of the vast land than I assumed. The table was bursting with delicious food. Meats of every kind, vegetables, fruits, and treats filled the room with their lovely aroma. My mouth watered despite my guilty conscience.

Women entered the gathering dressed in bright colored silks and jewels. They didn't sit to eat with us, but rather took the time to coddle the men and feed them the delicacies. If these men did have wives, they weren't permitted to come, and I understood why. Their travels were not only meant to meet and discuss leader-like duties; they were also meant for pleasure. But perhaps that was the purpose. Agamemnon might have arranged these "comforts" for his fellow leaders as a way to win them over for whatever venture he had in mind. The elder king was a skillful strategist. Menelaus mentioned before that he had never beaten his brother at Petteia. I believed him. The King of Kings thought of every last detail.

I looked away from the lustful intentions of the men before I lost my appetite. I ate what my guilt allowed and waited for the kings to finish their meals. During this time, I noticed King Agamemnon and Menelaus were the only ones not basking in the beautiful women who paraded around them. Menelaus seemed disinterested, but his brother was another story. Though I kept my gaze from roaming over to him, I could feel his eyes on me. He was hungry for another taste of what I had given him this morning. The elder king's lust to break me from my rebellious state seemed to overtake him, and he concentrated solely on me.

I grew tired of his gaze and willed his blood to pump faster than necessary, hoping to distract him. Agamemnon began to sweat, and his breathing became difficult. The men around him didn't notice; they had their own distractions. Despite my intention, he never removed his eyes from me. Agamemnon knew I was the one who caused his heart to fluctuate

with pain, yet he still refused to back down. Finally, I gave up the small battle and went back to conversing with Menelaus.

Seeing our battle was at a stalemate, the eldest king stood and wiped the sweat from his brow with a dinner cloth. Agamemnon proclaimed, "Friends, brother," he gestured to Menelaus, "I have gathered you here for a great purpose, but before I reveal it..." He paused and dismissed all the glittering women. He looked to me then. "That includes you, my dear." Agamemnon's smile was spiteful. This was something I couldn't openly contradict him on. Seeing my rebellious demeanor, Menelaus patted my arm and encouraged me to go, more gracious than he had been before today.

I reluctantly stood and left the room. I could hear the gasps of the men as I stood. They had failed to notice me before and were now in awe of Helen's beauty. Menelaus silenced them instantly with threats to their lives if any one of them touched his property. I wasn't his property, but I appreciated the gesture just the same.

I snaked around to the adjoining room and listened. If I couldn't interact with them, I could at least hear what they had to say.

"Fellow rulers of Greece, thank you for traveling so far from your homes to see me. The time taken away from your duties will be well worth your while," Agamemnon proclaimed.

"Get on with it, brother. What is it you want this time?" Menelaus remarked, clearly bored with his brother's antics.

Agamemnon must have harassed them often with ambitions of war. From what I remembered, Menelaus said that Agamemnon's recent target was Troy, and he intended to take over its bounteous land and trade. Sadly for him, he not only needed to win over his brother, but the other rulers of Greece. He still hadn't made it past his brother, so I was unsure of why the others were brought here, if that was still his intention. Agamemnon might have been the King of Kings, but he still couldn't ask his fellow rulers to launch an unprovoked attack on a city as powerful as Troy. The risk was too great.

"Patience, brother. It is not my former aspirations that bring you here. It is a new and glorious one. One that will benefit us all." I heard footsteps enter the dining room. "Give welcome to the eldest son of Troy, Prince Hector." The footsteps halted and the room went silent.

After a few uncomfortable moments, Hector asserted, "Thank you for having me. I believe this peace treaty will benefit us all and bring an age of calm to both our lands." The prince cleared his throat inconspicuously. "I apologize for my brother's absence. Young Alexander tends to run off whenever he deems it so. I am sure he will be along momentarily." I couldn't see Hector from where I hid, but I could hear that his voice was kind and strong. The prince comforted those around him. My initial judgment said that he would make a respectable leader.

"No matter, make yourself comfortable. Let's discuss details, shall we?" Agamemnon ushered him to sit.

The dining room erupted into a chaos of voices. I couldn't distinguish between one man or the other. The tones were harsh at first, accusing the elder king of acting without their consultations, but they were soon soothed by Hector's pleas for cooperation and peace. The prince's arguments were unrivaled. There was not one negative outcome that could stem from the treaty for either side. Both would live in peace. Both would have the opportunity to expand their trade. Hector was well trained in diplomatic words, but I suspected most of his talent came naturally. No one could sound that convincing without truly caring.

The only thing that concerned me was King Agamemnon. This was out of character for him. Why would he want peace when his whole existence revolved around taking and conquering?

"Hello there, beautiful. Can I help you find something?"

A male's silvery voice startled me from my concentrated ear on the wall. I really did need to pay more attention to my surroundings. I turned to see a young man staring at me; a friendly smile played on his lips. Though

he was still growing into a man, he was well past my height, but that was expected for how short Helen was. The boy wasn't burly like a warrior, but muscles were developed within his lean build. He was similar in appearance to the Greeks, but his hair was lighter, as if he spent a lot of time in the sun, and he kept it shorter than most of the men. The waves hung only to the bottom of his ears and were parted to the side. Instead of dark eyes, they depicted the grey-blue of the sky on a stormy day. Handsome, but young. It was hard to dismiss the adolescent gleam in his eyes. They reminded me of my son, Kun. He always found a way to cause trouble.

The young man's marigold aura flourished in excitement while he waited for my response. *Definitely young.* "No, sorry. I was just exploring. Thank you anyway."

I turned to go when he stopped me by saying, "Exploring, huh? That's exactly what I was doing. Would you mind if I joined you?" *Persistent.* I would give him that much. I was about to dismiss him again when he said, "My name is Alexander, but you can call me Paris."

I turned back to face him. "My name is Helen. Pleasure to meet you." I bowed slightly. He bowed back. How kind—cut from the same cloth as his brother, Hector. This was my chance. I couldn't interact and ask questions as I wished with the Greek rulers, but maybe this young prince would give me some insight.

"I would love it if you joined me. I can show you the garden if you wish?" I offered. I didn't have to pretend to be nice to him. Unlike the other men, Paris expected nothing of me. The prince's presence indicated that he didn't want to be part of the king's meeting anyway. Best to leave things to the older brother, it seemed. I wondered if that meant he didn't have anything to offer me after all, but it wouldn't hurt to try.

I led him out the hidden entrance Menelaus had shown me earlier that morning. Paris was impressed with my knowledge of the structure, especially since I told him I only arrived the day before with King Menelaus.

Hearing that I was the king's consort put a damper on his mood, but he perked up quickly when I showed him the grand pool that rested in the center of the blooming grounds. There were no colorful fish in Agamemnon's pond as there had been in Menelaus's, but it was still lovely.

"How did you come to be in King Menelaus's graces, my lady?" Paris asked innocently.

Best to tell the same story I told Menelaus. "I traveled from the north in search of adventure. I have been to many places, but this was my father's homeland. I had finally decided to visit Sparta when King Menelaus spotted me among the traders. He immediately claimed me. We were summoned here the next day. I haven't traveled with him too long." Had it really only been a few days? I had learned so much in that time. So much had happened.

"Traveled with him? Do you not plan to stay with him?" He was a clever young man. The prince picked up on my choice of words effortlessly, but I felt I could trust him.

"Between you and me, I suspect he doesn't plan on letting me leave at all, but there is no way I could stay with him. The people he surrounds himself with are dangerous, and I have no wish to be a part of it." I stiffened at my words. I hadn't realized this was how I actually felt. I did want to help them, but deep in my old bones I knew it was a lost cause. Menelaus might have a chance, but not with the influence of his brother around to ruin any progress he would make. I could kill the elder king, like I thought to before, but that was the easy way, the way of these hybrid humans. I didn't want to do that unless absolutely necessary. But were these doubts that Paris roused merely caused by my fear of being alone? Lucifer's ultimatum wormed its way into my thoughts.

Observing my thoughtful gaze, Paris said, "How do you expect to leave then? If he won't allow it?"

Confused, I responded bluntly, "I would just leave, of course. There

is nothing to stop me but his words. I just have to pick the right time to sneak away quietly."

Paris was in awe. "You are a very brave woman, Helen. I have not met someone so courageous as you besides my own brother."

I chuckled at the sincerity in his tone. "It is not courageous of me to maintain my freedom; it is expected."

My words seemed to resonate with him. Perhaps my ramblings inspired a new scheme for him to take on. I hoped he didn't torment his brother too much. The rebellious glint in his eyes returned, and Paris stood to face me where I sat along the stones lining the pond. He offered his hand.

"It is getting quite late. My brother is sure to be waiting for my arrival, and I don't want you to get into trouble with King Menelaus." The prince's worry was unnecessary on my behalf, but I returned his kind gesture with a smile and took his hand. Our venture was shorter than I thought it would be, considering the way his heart raced when he took my hand. The young man walked me to the room I was supposed to have slept in the night before. Paris then kissed my hand and left me to my thoughts. I watched the prince as he disappeared down the hall, a happy rhythm to his steps.

My research had been cut short due to the child, and I hadn't even had a chance to ask him the questions I wanted to. Paris was busy asking me instead. The thought made me laugh. I needed that little bit of companionship, one without pretenses, wandering hands, or chaotic mood swings. Just a friendly face to look at and a pleasant voice to listen to, because they were few and far between on the land where I had been dragged ashore.

XVII
Choices

Truth is revealed in our souls.
-A

I didn't sleep much through the night, despite the friendly companionship Paris had given me. I tossed and turned restlessly. *Stay and help, or leave with Lucifer?* I knew it was selfish, but I didn't want to be here. Hector and Paris were here. Was it possible that they could take my place as the saviors of this land? I wanted to believe it was true, but doubts plagued my selfish desires.

I was always so afraid to use my powers that I crippled myself into living a small existence. I forced my children to live limited lives due to my own beliefs. I even neglected to prepare them for the dangers of the world. I knew Lucifer was out there and what he believed. I shouldn't have assumed he would leave me alone. My ignorance cost them their lives because I didn't prepare them. They didn't know how to defend themselves because of me. I wanted peace so badly, I became obtuse to a world that wasn't peaceful.

I heard a bee flying near my balcony door and could smell the pollen it carried.

Even the natural world wasn't conflict-free. The intentions were different, but there was still death. There was killing and fighting, and there

were creatures struggling to survive. My own idealism of the natural world had glorified them, blinding me to the reality. No matter if the creatures were natural or not, the world demanded balance—both good and bad. This was what I had failed to realize before.

I understood now. All it took was a young man demonstrating kindness and a prince who wanted peace so badly he sailed across the sea to convince a room full of hateful men of his just cause. When I was brought to this new world, I blinded myself once again with the notion that everything was in chaos. I saw the poverty and violence, the deception and greed, the spirits that fought constantly. What I had failed to see was the kindness and generosity and hope. I dismissed that old woman along the river too easily before. She had brought this to my attention, and I had smothered its light and basked in the remaining shadow.

I heard the bee drop to the ground and slide across the floor.

Who was I to judge what this world needed? Indeed, I was the first woman, but I had done nothing but add to the chaos that now congested this world. Being around these kings had sullied my mind. The worst traits I saw in them, I now saw in me. I enjoyed the challenge and fight just as much as Agamemnon. I showed impatience and anger as Menelaus did. If only Lucifer would just put aside his own pride and help me through this. Perhaps if I had someone to confide in I would be able to see more clearly. But that would never happen.

Our conversation from the night before nagged me. *Do you remember why I was there?* he asked me. I cringed. I was blinded yet again by his beckoning light, no matter the words that were spoken. Except it was love that blinded me this time, not fear.

I would have to do this on my own. It was almost ironic, that notion. Since the beginning my fear had been that I would be left alone. After all that worry and sorrow, I ended up alone anyway. I blew out a breath, and the breeze carried the dead bee out the doorway and off the edge of the

balcony where it could rest in the soft grass. It was no good to die in a place where evil men ruled.

The day was still early, and the sun had not yet risen. I swung my legs over the side of the bed and sat there, unsure of what I could accomplish at the premature hour. I bent my head to stare at the floor. My blonde hair fell loosely in front of me. I had come to despise the sunlit color. It had brought me nothing but trouble, and it reminded me of someone who tortured my lonely soul.

I walked over to the mirror that hung on the wall above my basin. The oval surface was rimmed with silver and detailed with black floral designs. It was a nice change from the constant gold tones of the rest of the home. It reminded me of the night sky with its silvery stars and ebony blanket. I missed gazing at the stars.

I studied my appearance in the reflection of the starry mirror. I could see why everyone gawked at the beauty of Helen. She was comely, delicate, exotic, and graceful. But I missed Lilith. I did my best to stay in Helen's form for fear I would be caught by surprise by unexpected visitors, but I needed to see myself. I needed to remind myself who I was. Playing the part of Helen was strenuous, and I often lost myself in the role.

My limbs lengthened and my body filled out. My strength never waned, despite the petite body of Helen, but it was nice to feel the force of my natural muscles as I stretched. My face rounded and my lips filled to their natural shape. My irises became the color of the forest, and my hair blended with the surrounding soul. Lilith stared back at me.

I had to remember that I was not a helpless human girl. I was an ancient immortal being who had been through travesties no other could comprehend, and I was stronger because of it. I had an advantage no one else did: time. I had time to learn. I had time to grow. I had time to finish what I started. I splashed cold, stale water on my face that pooled at the bottom of the basin. I longed for the feel of the waterfall to cleanse my face

and hair. I longed to doze on the flattened rock behind the curtain of water that always managed to maintain the warmth of the departed sun, even at night when the moonlight chilled the forest.

What was my purpose during that time, when I had nothing to worry about but myself and Lucifer? When there weren't children to care for and there wasn't a devoted partner to feel guilty over? A simpler time without the chaos of humans, and a history without pain. The time when I simply cared for Earth. When my only task during the day was to watch as its light dimmed and grew again with my efforts.

It was unclear then, but the solution was simple, even if I didn't see it. But my age would aid me now. The solution I neglected to act out then needed to be done. I needed to stand and fight for what I believed. Life was a constant game of catch up, and I needed to catch up now. The cold droplets of water from the basin dripped from my face onto the cold stone floor.

I would stay with the humans. No more running.

I was wiping away the remaining water from my eyes when a sound at the balcony startled me. Two ebony ravens were perched at the railing. They dispersed at the sounds of struggles below. I quickly reformed into Helen and ran over to investigate. "Paris? What are you doing?" I whispered into the darkness; my eyes found him immediately, yet he struggled to find where I stood at the balcony.

Paris was in the midst of climbing up a tall tree that lived outside my second-story room, and he was failing. He must not have had much practice climbing trees in his adolescence. The prince struggled from branch to branch. I aided him discretely by willing the winds to lift him upward. To him it would feel like nothing more than a random wind gust.

"I have come to speak with you. I apologize for the unorthodox entrance, but there were guards posted at your door, and I didn't want my visit to travel to the ears of King Menelaus," he explained between breaths. *Guards?* Menelaus must have been concerned I'd run off again,

or our guests would be tempted to sneak over to my room for a visit. It appeared he posted guards at the wrong entrance.

"What is so urgent that you need to speak with me this early in the morning?" I questioned, attempting to hide my amused smile from him. Although I doubted he could see me very clearly in the dark.

"One moment, my lady." My eyes could see his bright yellow aura making its way down the long thick branch of the tree closest to my balcony railing. Paris jumped the distance that remained. The prince was definitely the rebellious youngster I thought him to be, because if it wasn't for another gust of wind he would have fallen to his death.

Once he recovered from his climb, I persisted, "Would you now grace me with an explanation of your presence? Isn't it inappropriate to come to a lady's bedchamber while she's alone?" I didn't mind really, but it was fun to watch his face redden from embarrassment. I giggled when he realized I was in my nightgown, which wasn't much. It was a sheer white dress that hung to the floor.

"I apologize for my rudeness, my lady. I felt I had to see you as soon as possible."

"And why is that?"

All humor dissipated with his serious expression. "My brother says we leave in two days' time to discuss the terms of the peace treaty with our father, King Priam." He paused a moment, unsure of how to phrase his next words. "I would like you to come with us at that time. You said you wanted a quiet way to leave King Menelaus. What better way than to sneak aboard our carriage and sail with us across the sea to Troy? He would never know, and even if he sent his men to find you, you would be long gone by then." The prince's unsteady breathing was all I could hear.

This boy's gallantry touched me. The risk he was taking to free a woman he'd only just met from the clutches of the very king he was meant to be discussing peace with was dangerous and foolish and very brave. "Paris,

you are very kind to give such an offer. But I would not want to risk your treaty in any way by involving you in my woes. Does Hector know of this?"

The prince averted his gaze and guiltily ran a hand through his wavy hair. "Not really. I didn't plan on telling him, either. The less people who know, the better. I wouldn't want to risk someone discovering our plans and taking you away from me." He blushed at his own words. "I mean take you away to a place you can no longer escape."

I took his hands in mine and said, "Thank you for your kindness, but I wouldn't be able to live with myself if you jeopardized your kingdom's chance at peace because of me. I can take care of myself anyway; I have survived this long on my own, after all." I kissed his warmed cheek.

Hands still clasped with mine, he knelt on one knee and decreed, "Helen of Sparta, I proclaim to you my undying loyalty and servitude for the rest of my days. You are unlike any woman I've met before, and I wish for you to be my wife."

My appreciative smile disappeared, and a confused expression replaced it. Didn't I just tell him *no* to the escape plan? What made him think I would say yes to this? "Um, Paris, did you not just hear me? I said that I didn't need your assistance." I was flabbergasted.

"I did indeed, my lady. It was your selflessness and strength that sealed my love for you." Despite the ridiculousness of the situation, I was moved by his proclamation. It was my first proposal. Yes, Adam had declared his love to me countless times, but the custom to bind one another in written words gave my metaphorical heart a jolt of joy. It was more than the mere promise of spoken words; those could easily be broken.

I imagined my arguments with Lucifer would have gone a different way if our words were written. I could have said, *"See here. You said that you loved me on this date and time. Do you want to take that back? Do you wish to remove it from our contract?"* That would have made him think twice before toying with my emotions. I needed to learn how to write.

Paris saw that I was lost in thought, and his face lit in delight. The prince didn't realize that I wasn't considering his question; I was just lost. "Helen, you do not have to answer now, but a decision must be made soon. Give me your answer tonight. That will allow me enough time to make the preparations for your escape." He bowed and went to leave in the direction of the balcony.

"Wait, Paris. Go out the main entrance. I think I heard the guards leave." I had willed a large painted vase to tip off its stand around the corner down the hall. Alarmed, the guards took off toward the sound. With one last mischievous smile to me, Paris exited my room and ran the opposite way of the guards down the hall and stairs as quickly and quietly as he could. Once I was sure he hadn't been seen, I closed my bedroom door and sank to the floor.

How did this happen? I had enough to worry about without adding a persistent admirer to the mix, one who could harm his own kingdom by helping me. Paris was thinking like a lovesick young man, not a ruler. That might have been due to his lack of incentive, since he wasn't next in line to lead. Still, I couldn't lie and say his offer didn't entice me.

Someone knocked on the door I leaned against. Another visitor so early in the morning? I stood and cracked open the door to see Achilles, or rather Lucifer. I didn't open it any more than I had to in order to speak to him. "What do you want? Come to set fire to my room?" I questioned ruthlessly.

Lucifer rolled his emerald eyes in annoyance. "You going to let me in or not? The guards aren't going to spend too long looking for the culprit who broke the vase, especially when she's hidden in the very room they're guarding." I frowned, but opened the door wide enough to let him inside. He didn't waste a moment. Lucifer strode over to my bed and sat down, completely at ease in his surroundings.

Unexpectedly, the flowers that rested in a vase beside my bed caught fire.

"Lucifer! Why did you do that?" I ran over to the blazing greenery and submerged them in the water that once sustained them. I twisted to glare at the man, only to find a grin on his face.

"That wasn't me, Lilith," he said, amused.

Realizing my mistake, I growled, "What do you want?" I transformed back into Lilith, and he followed suit with his own form. The ripple of change through my body was instinct now.

My mate avoided my question and asked his own, "What was that boy doing here? Replace me already?" His amused smile became an arrogant smirk. I loathed that smirk. I wanted to slap it off his face every time I saw it.

"No, I have not, and it's none of your business why. But if you must know, he came to proclaim his love to me. He's just a lovesick child in love with a beautiful girl. Nothing more." I waved, disregarding Paris.

Lucifer laughed, "I hope you let him down gently. It's not easy mending a broken heart."

I countered, "How would you know? You don't have a heart."

"No, I suppose I don't. Feels like someone yanked it out of my chest long ago." I avoided his probing gaze. Lucifer's expression became serious. "I'm not sorry for what I said." Lucifer paused.

"Oh, is that all you came to say? Lovely. You can go now." I was so angry with him. I could have lit the whole place on fire.

"Woman, let me finish," he said, exasperated. Satisfied I was only glaring at him now, he continued, "I'm not sorry for what I said, but I am sorry for forcing you to decide so soon. I've known you long enough to know that you need time to think about what you want to do." Lucifer scrunched his forehead in frustration. "I am willing to give you that time." He rose and held my face firmly between his hands. "I love you, Lilith, and I want to be with you. *Only* you."

Lucifer's words pierced my soul. I wanted to give him what he wanted. That was the second time he said those three words to me. I often

wondered if he meant them. Lucifer was a man of action, not words. But his actions were sporadic and just as confusing as his words. I was never able to understand him, but that was only because I refused to acknowledge what he was. I hadn't *wanted* to.

I knew what I had to do.

The fire that flared from my anger dulled and burned with a different kind of heat. "Lucifer, I love you. I want to be with you, too." He didn't let me finish what I was going to say. The man forced his lips against mine. I tried to fight it at first. I needed to finish what I was going to tell him. The man misinterpreted my hands pushing on his chest and pulled us closer together. Lucifer then backed me into the bedroom wall. He kissed me with fevered passion before moving his lips slowly down my neck and along my shoulders, and I didn't stop him from doing so.

Separated from his lips, I was able to breathe. This gave me a chance to clear my head and speak. "Lucifer, stop."

"Why?" he breathed against my skin. Shivers ran up and down my spine.

"Because I wasn't done talking, Lucifer." I mustered the strength to push him away. Gently, so I wouldn't hurt his feelings. I began to lead him to the bed to sit when I thought better of it and directed him to the balcony instead.

The cool morning air calmed my overworked senses. The sun was rising over the jade trees, the sky a mixture of plum and orange hues. Birds sang to one another as they awoke and flew away in search of food for their young. I felt envious of their simple lives.

"What is it you need to say, Lilith?" Lucifer questioned. He was wary but waiting patiently for the moment.

"I want to be with you, Lucifer. I always have and always will." I stared at the horizon. "Our early lives consisted mostly of fighting, due to our own opinions on the light. I have seen the downfalls of limiting myself for its sake, but I still want to save it, regardless. And I want to save your

children, too. They need help, and it's our fault they are the way they are." As long as I didn't look at him, I could say it. "You see the spirits now, and you have lived among your children longer than I have. I don't know what you've done in that time, but I hope that you will continue on with me. I hope that you continue living among your children and help me better them and guide them." I swallowed. "With that said, my question is…will you choose to be with me and care for Earth in the process? If not, then we will have to part ways again. I chose last time. It's your turn, Lucifer." I took a breath for the first time since I started speaking.

I was terrified of what he would say. When I left him he had been furious, and he nearly destroyed the forest in his rage. I hoped this time would be different, because now he was the one making the choice, not me. "Lucifer?" I couldn't make myself look at him. I feared what would be revealed in his eyes.

After a long painful moment, he said, "You're not giving me a choice, Lilith. You're choosing for me. Don't you see that you can't love both? Not really. One will always take priority over the other, and that would never be me." The tone of his voice frightened me. I faced him, expecting to find the familiar rage there, but it was nowhere in sight. His expression reminded me of the time he asked me to kill him. There was nothing in his eyes, no emotion to tell me how he felt. There was nothing to prove a living being was in front of me. I still didn't know if it was true, or if this was what he wanted me to see.

Lucifer's usual golden shine dimmed, and the grey I noticed when I first arrived appeared once more. This time the dull shade overtook most of his spirit. *What was happening?*

"Lucifer, of course you have a choice! Why can't you accept what I have to do?" I knew that he was never going to change, but it still made me angry. Crimson overtook my vision and I lashed out. I hit him hard across the face.

Thankfully, my hit sparked something in him, but not the emotion

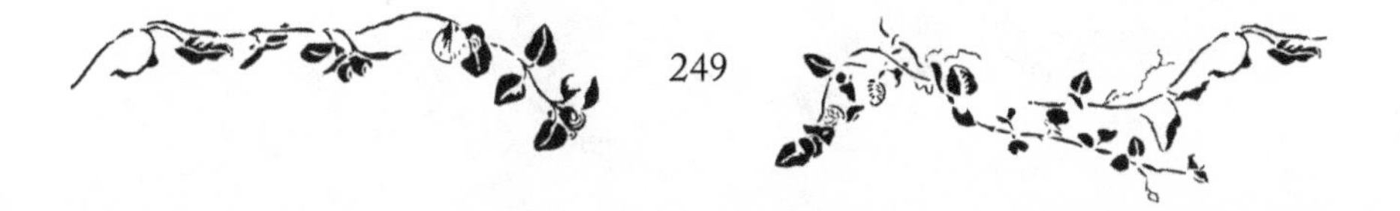

I wanted. His rage was back, nevertheless his eyes continued to be empty. "Me? I am not the one doing this to us!" His rage died down as fast as it was given life. "Why won't you choose me?"

"Because I can't," I growled. The red still fogged my vision, but I stared into his dead eyes nonetheless.

"Why?" he demanded.

"I wouldn't be happy with just you." The words that came out of my mouth were true. I had never acknowledged them before, not even to myself. Lucifer's previous accusations had been right. I expected him to yell or at least look hurt, but the void was a permanent fixture. I couldn't look at the deadened version of Lucifer any longer, and I moved my gaze to the rising sun.

I heard the faint footsteps of him leaving and closing the door. I had expected this outcome. My mate would never do what had to be done. The words he said to me all those years ago rang in my ears.

I will continue to suck the life from this planet, Lilith. There is nothing you can do to stop me. I have been very busy these last five hundred years. My numbers are far greater than yours, and they have already spread across the entire land. You were our last stop, and I have accomplished what I came for.

And what did you come for?

To see you in pain.

I had ignored those words and the many that came before and after them. I was blinded by my love for him. I didn't realize the person he had become and the person he still was. The man would do anything in his power to force me to love him. *Just* him. If I didn't, there would be nothing else left to love. Earth was nothing to him, and Lucifer was lost to me. My tear ducts begged to release the water that would bring my relief, but none came. At least I had kept that one promise to myself. It was the only thing I could do to exhibit the will I'd obtained over the eons.

The only thing I had to prove that I was strong.

The sun had risen high enough that I could find King Menelaus and hopefully have him answer my questions about the leaders' gathering. Dressing in my glittering decorations, I stared at myself in the mirror. As my crimson hair lightened to the corn silk coloring of Helen, I found myself smiling, not because of my appearance or the sun that warmed my chilled skin, but because of the tremendous weight that no longer lived in my chest. The emptiness where my heart should have been was hollow once again, how it had been when I first awoke in this world. My suppressed internal flame lit and burned away anything of him that lingered in my chest. Lucifer had filled it with his love and his hate and his burdens. Now, for the first time in eons, those emotions were gone, the connection was gone, and I was free to live.

Part IV
Wrath

Wrath is the destroyer

Wrath is the conqueror

Wrath is the devourer

Wrath is the executioner

Wrath is the motherless

Wrath is the childless

Wrath is the fire

Wrath is the satisfier

XVIII
Hope

The fury that consumes is the death
that will devour.
-A

Menelaus had risen early, to my surprise. He was sitting at our spot by the window in the lounging room where we had played Petteia the day before. My game board was out, and he had the stones arranged in different formations on each side of the panel. King Menelaus of Sparta was practicing.

"Good morning, my king," I said. Usually I wouldn't have been so cheerful knowing I would have to spend time with him, but he had grown likable since we first met. And my recent discussion with Lucifer had put things in perspective for me. I felt empowered by the knowledge I had admitted to myself and to him.

I didn't need Lucifer. My inner flame could be lit without him.

Reciprocating my good mood, the king returned, "Good morning, my dear. Fancy a game? Of course, I would be wary. I have been practicing." His smile was contagious.

"Of course." I sat across from him and placed the stones back into their preparatory squares. "I have nothing to fear from you, my king. I am sure you will care for me regardless of the outcome."

"Yes. Yes, I suppose I would."

The king stared blankly at the board for a moment before making the first move.

We played into mid-morning; I allowed him to win most of the rounds. My tactic seemed to work, since his lips became looser with each win. "I am surprised by my brother. I could not have foretold his arrangements with Troy." He took one of my warriors with his queen. "Despite his secretiveness, I am happy with the outcome. We drew up a worthy contract, one that benefits both lands." I took his queen with my pawn. Menelaus frowned. "All we can do now is wait. Hector and his brother will bring the contract to their father for approval. Once that is done, they will come back here to finalize it."

I allowed his king to take my pawn. "What happens if their father does not approve of it?" My warrior had the opportunity to take his king, but I moved it recklessly, and he was able to steal my warrior with his own instead.

Smiling, he explained, "I doubt that would happen, but if not, that would give my brother ample excuse for war." A suspicion seemed to worm its way into his thoughts as well as mine. Could that have been the purpose? King Agamemnon was the one who initiated the idea of a treaty and arranged the meetings. It wouldn't be difficult to start a war with the Trojans if they couldn't come to an agreement. But even with a peace treaty, Agamemnon could attack. Troy wouldn't be expecting it.

After a few questionable moves from me and long contemplative moments in between, Menelaus took my king with his own. "Ha! I win again, my lovely Helen. I have to admit, I miss your competitive fire from yesterday, but a win is a win."

"I have no idea what you speak of, my king. I played just the same as yesterday. Your skill must have grown since then," I said in a consoling manner. The king blushed at my words; he was easily pleased.

Menelaus went on gathering the stones into their bag when a dark,

ominous voice behind me said, "Don't put that away yet, brother. I would like to try my hand against your Helen. Yesterday, you claimed her such a skillful opponent." Chills ran down my spine. I wasn't frightened of the elder king, but I didn't enjoy his company either.

King Menelaus's demeanor changed immediately. He sat straighter and his voice deepened. "Of course. I am sure Helen would enjoy that. Wouldn't you, dear?" I nodded my head in agreement.

"Lovely," Agamemnon replied.

Looking uncomfortable all of a sudden, Menelaus stood and said, "I have business to tend to anyway. Brother, I leave Helen in your capable hands." Menelaus's tone conveyed that he believed otherwise, but he couldn't argue against his eldest brother about something as trivial as a game of Petteia.

"Of course," Agamemnon agreed. Menelaus departed the room with one last worried look in my direction. Then I was face to face with darkness.

"Oh, don't look so morose, Helen. It's unattractive. I watched you play, and I am sure you will make for an interesting game." From the tone in his voice, it was clear he wasn't talking about Petteia.

"I lost almost every turn this morning," I said derisively.

"And I am sure my brother appreciates your kindness in that respect." I stiffened. The dark cloud gazed up at me as he arranged the stone pawns. "Oh, please don't give me that confused expression. I watched your last game. Your moves were placed carefully and strategically, even your bad ones." He finished resetting the board and sat back in his chair, completely at ease despite what I had done to him the day prior. "It takes an adept strategist to place their own pawns in calculated positions to win, but an even greater strategist to guide their opponent unknowingly to victory."

"You think too highly of my skills, my king." I smiled innocently at him. The king wanted a game. He was going to get one. And I refused to lose. The board game or otherwise.

"Let's test that then, shall we?" The king gestured that I should make the first move. And so I did.

The game lasted until Menelaus returned from his unknown business hours later. Agamemnon was a skilled player. He was bred to be so. The elder king had years of practice with the game, as well as actual experience ruling and commanding armies. He was a master of strategy and manipulation, but all that experience and natural talent wasn't enough.

Agamemnon took his time with his last move. My queen had cornered his king, and he had few pieces left while mine conquered the board. Our kings were in opposing corners; my warrior and pawn stones blocked their path, waiting for the chance to take his ruler. Yet, his spirit didn't flutter in the slightest during our time together. Not one move of mine surprised or angered him. The blackness of his spirit was unwavering and patient. That might have bothered me if I hadn't known I was winning. I didn't hold back like I did with his younger brother.

The elder king smiled, and his spirit did a slight dance, like a breeze had blown through its thick mist. "I win," he claimed.

Confident, I said, "How so?"

Agamemnon then grabbed hold of his king and drug it across the board, taking warrior and pawn alike in its wake. The departure left my queen to rule her lonely side of the board. Finally it reached my king, and with force unnecessary, he knocked my ruler to the floor. The pebble clanged against the painted stone ground. The impact of the small rock caused part of the gold design to chip, leaving a gap in a woman's detailed lips.

Shocked, I said, "My king, surely you aren't one to break rules simply for a small victory?"

Agamemnon leered at the disbelief in my tone. "My dear, of course not. But I am one who takes advantage of loopholes."

Boldly I countered, "Show me these loopholes then." I handed him the parchment that held the guidelines to our game.

The king read through it quickly. "Well, it's right here, lovely Helen." I took the paper and pretended to read it. The elder king didn't seem to notice my dilemma. Remembering that Menelaus arrived moments before, I gave him the parchment to inspect.

"He's right, Helen." Menelaus looked away guiltily; he had failed to mention that rule before. From where Agamemnon had pointed it was at the bottom in tiny lettering. I assumed the move he made was situational and not a normal tactic of the game. And something I was unaware of.

"I wasn't aware of that rule," I said. I didn't relish the fact that he had defeated me. It had been a battle of wills, and I had lost due to my ignorance.

"It's best to know all the rules before you play the game, darling." Agamemnon sneered once more and strode out of the room, his dark cloud circling him.

Ego bruised, I kept silent. This forced Menelaus to initiate the discussion. He cleared his throat discreetly before saying, "Helen, we are to have a midday meal with our guests. Come."

The king pulled me from my seat and guided me toward the dining hall. Menelaus rattled on about the incompetence of servants. He had spent the last several hours trying to organize them and their duties in order to design a grand event. The King of Sparta didn't reveal what the event was for, but he seemed rather thrilled by it.

To be honest, I didn't pay much attention to his ramblings. I was still seething from my loss to Agamemnon, but my anger wasn't due to the loss. That was unavoidable, considering I wasn't aware of all the rules of the game, similar to how I felt in reality. I was angry at myself. I had allowed my ego to overcome my new freed self and rule my decisions. Rather than accept it and move on, I had been angry and petty. Just like these mortal humans. Every day I recognized the odious traits they

possessed and the existence of those same traits in me. Being around the mortals shined a light upon the qualities I wished to darken. It was a continuous battle, and one that I lost often. It made me wonder how different I actually was from them.

Still babbling, Menelaus seated me at his right at the dining table. It was then that I was finally released from my mental chastising. Paris sat directly across from me, Hector to his left. Agamemnon sat at his usual seat at the head of the table across from Menelaus. The rest of the kings sat in between. The women who gushed over the Greek kings the night before were nowhere in sight. Agamemnon had gotten what he wanted.

"Good day, King Menelaus," Hector said as we settled. He shot a warning glance at his young brother, most likely due to Paris's lack of subtlety. The young prince hadn't removed his eyes from me since entering the room. I attempted a discreet signal to stop, but any efforts were either ignored or unregistered.

"Good day, Prince Hector," Menelaus said in kind. I nodded my head in acknowledgment.

"Too bad Achilles is unable to eat among us. I was looking forward to meeting such an eminent warrior," Hector confided in between bites of his meal. "He is said to be the son of a goddess, is he not?" Hector asked no one in particular.

This claim surprised me. I hadn't had a real chance to ask Lucifer what he had been doing in my absence. It was clear now he had made a name for himself, though not his real one. Agamemnon answered, "Yes, that is the story at least. Who knows if it is true, but he certainly acts the part of a demigod. Always disobeying orders. Coming in and out of my home as he pleases." Agamemnon turned his eyes on me then. "He's fortunate he has the skill for combat, or else he would be strung up for his defiance." The other obedient kings grunted in agreement.

I squirmed under his gaze. My loss and resulting want of dignity had

left me lacking in confidence, and his dark aura didn't lessen the uneasiness I felt. I had to refocus on what my purpose was. Observe. Learn as much as possible. Create a strategy.

Uncomfortable, Hector reciprocated, "Yes, well, I am sure he is a great asset, nonetheless." Asset or not, I was certainly glad "Achilles" had decided to skip the meal. I didn't know what to do with him. When I considered the options, I had to remind myself that he wasn't my responsibility anymore. I had freed myself from him and he knew that. I mourned the loss of our ancient bond, but I was liberated just the same.

I studied Hector then. I remembered from the night before that his voice had been sure and steady—trustworthy. Seeing him now, I could only conclude my assumption had been right. The prince held himself tall, even while dining. He had a strong face and gentle eyes. The shade of his hair was identical to his brother's, but his eyes were a calming blue-green, closer to the color of seawater than his brother's stormy blue.

Menelaus stood abruptly, holding his goblet of wine. I had come to enjoy the taste of it at our meals, as well as the calming side effects. I had drained four cups already. It appeared the amount I needed to relax was far more than the others. The glances from my dinner companions contributed to the theory.

"I have an announcement to make while everyone is here." Menelaus took a swig from his goblet before continuing. "I realize that I am past the point of my younger years..."

Younger years? He couldn't have been more than thirty.

"...and am in need of a successor. I believe I have found a woman worthy to bear my son. Helen and I will be married tomorrow evening. After the celebrations we will travel home to Sparta where she shall be taught the customs of our land so that she may succeed as my queen."

Another swig of wine, and the servant who hovered near our table refilled his cup instantly. "I thought it best to wed Helen here, in the capital

of our land, and in the company of our visitors, of course. It will be a great opportunity to celebrate the promise of peace among our kingdoms." King Perversion was pink from his speech and the wine. I was pale from the shock and vomit that wanted to come up.

Unaffected by the others' reactions, Menelaus took my hand as he sat, pleased with himself. Hector observed my panicked expression and returned a sympathetic smile. Paris had dropped his utensil and paled as I had. Agamemnon retained a neutral expression, but his spirit flitted sharply. The other kings studied me leeringly, clearly jealous. Many conflicting emotions swarmed the room, but I could only feel mine: panic, dread, anger. How could he do this without consulting me? I thought he was changing for the better, but it was clear he was still just as controlling and possessive as he was when we first met. Something had to be done. I refused to marry such a man.

I took another swig from my wine cup. My intentions had been to aid humanity, and I couldn't do so as a submissive spouse. People needed to hear me as I was: an independent woman. Granted, there were discrepancies to my plan, but that was the purpose of observing. I needed to know more, and I couldn't do that while under Menelaus's thumb. I would need to convince him that I wasn't ready to be queen. I needed to bargain for more time. But not with an audience. The King of Sparta was easier to persuade alone.

Our meal dragged on. I mentally prepared the argument I would use to sway the king to my side. Paris didn't eat anything more. He simply sat there. His aura had dimmed to a pale yellow shadow. *Oh, Paris.* The young prince cared so much for someone he barely knew. It pained me that I caused such sorrow.

Agamemnon congratulated his brother and wished him success in birthing a son. But I could distinguish the subtle signs of his spirit. It would flit slightly as a thought occurred to him. The elder king was planning

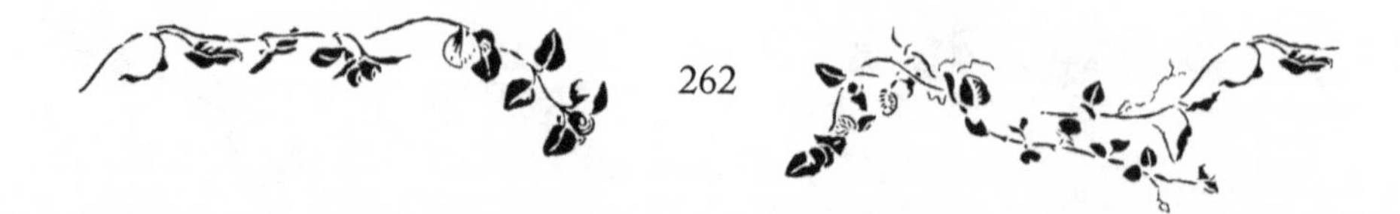

something, and I was anxious to discover where his mind had taken him.

Finally, our gathering separated. Paris dragged after his elder brother. I tried to send him more silent signals, but alas, he had been too distraught to notice. Agamemnon leered at me before exiting. The remaining Greek kings would have as well, if it wasn't for the horde of sparkling women that appeared to lead them to their rooms. Apparently the women were to be enjoyed in private today. That left Menelaus and me alone.

"My king, I am humbled by your offer," I began. My voice trembled pathetically, but he didn't notice.

Menelaus grabbed my hand and lifted it to his lips for a too-long kiss. He proceeded to stroke my long locks of golden hair between the fingers of his other hand. The wine on his breath and the hunger in his eyes disgusted me. "As it should, my dear Helen. You will make an excellent queen and mother." King Perversion pulled me closer. His fingers trailed down my exposed collarbone and shoulder. I'd had more to drink than he had, but he leaned against me for support anyway. "And I do look forward to our wedding night. You are the treasure I have been hoarding away in the darkness. But tomorrow night you will shine, and I will bask in the brilliance of your finery."

I forced vomit back down my throat. "My king, you flatter me. But certainly I should undergo the preparation of a ruler of this land before I become one, wouldn't you agree? It is only the welfare of the people I think of."

My plan would be ruined if he didn't agree, and I would be forced to run again. The thought both relieved and angered me.

Menelaus was an easy man to please, but he wasn't oblivious to my underlying tones. "Helen, you will not cause difficulties. I have given you plenty of freedom considering your status—perhaps too much if you think you have an opinion on the matter." His grip tightened on my hips and I wobbled with him.

I was growing impatient and desperate. "Isn't that what you admire about me? That my mind is also an asset to you? Isn't that the reason we play so much Petteia?" The king did not like that. I had embarrassed him.

"The only reason I indulge you in such games is to keep you entertained and out of trouble, since you have such difficulty following instructions." The king grabbed my hair in his fist and yanked it back painfully. "The disobedience ends now, woman. You are mine and will act as such. Until I seek you out, you will wait in your bedchambers. Guards will be at your door. Do I make myself clear?" I nodded and felt golden strands being ripped from their home.

"Good." Menelaus released my hair and grabbed the back of my head roughly, his mouth meeting mine. It was possessive and angry, and I hated him. "Now go." Menelaus released me and departed the dining room, confident in my obedience. What happened to the progress we made? I had seen kindness in him. I assumed that meant he was growing to care for me. Perhaps he had. But his thirst for control and power was greater. The wine revealed as much.

My body moved without my command. I walked until I found myself in the throne room. It was dark due to the lack of windows, and the black throne looked even more menacing than before. The jewels embedded in it winked at me in the blackness. The euphoria that stemmed from my release from Lucifer had been short-lived. Menelaus had been my only evidence that the darkness could become light. The youngest king was my budding hope that I *could* change the world, the only proof that I was strong enough to stand on my own. My inner flame begged to light again.

I tried to steady my breathing, attempting to remove the red from my vision.

"My lovely Helen, why so upset?" a man's voice chuckled from behind. I was not in the right frame of mind to deal with the elder king.

"Leave me alone," I growled. There was no point in pretending with him anymore.

"So disrespectful to your king, little one." He laughed, amused with my behavior. I turned to face the black spirit.

"Don't toy with me. I am not in the mood. Do you not remember yesterday? Unless you would like to experience that again, I suggest leaving." The king's spirit fluctuated only slightly. Still, he did not fear Helen. That infuriated me. I displayed the most powerful magic, and still he showed disrespect. Everyone disrespected Helen. Everyone ignored Helen. Everyone would suffer.

The dark king brazenly closed the distance between us. "Now, I wouldn't treat me that way, my dear." He stroked my exposed arm. I became rigid. "Now, if you don't want your future husband to discover what you've been doing at night, I would fulfill my wishes." Agamemnon moved his face close to mine and began trailing wet, unwanted kisses down my throat. "You can start by performing for me, as I am sure young Paris and Achilles enjoyed last night in your bedchamber."

How had he seen them? I flinched away from his hot breath.

"Now, now. You don't want your chance at queen to be whisked away due to your pride, do you? My lips will remain sealed, so long as you submit."

"Why not just tell your brother? It is ample reason to cause a problem between kingdoms. Isn't that what you want?" I questioned. The elder king's body pressed against mine in the most terrible of ways.

"Why would I do that when this way is so much more...pleasurable?" His aura fluttered excitedly. He was lying. Agamemnon would use me and then toss me aside for his own agenda, and most likely already had. The thought of Paris or anyone else getting hurt because of me made me nauseous.

The King of Argos had gotten one very important fact wrong, though.

I didn't want to be the Queen of Sparta. He didn't understand Helen or Lilith's intentions. Ruling something as small and insignificant as a city would be pointless. Agamemnon's greedy hands and lips continued, and I laughed. The relief that came with the emotion was wonderful. All the stress of Lucifer and the kings and the hybrids dispersed with every snicker. Agamemnon began to pull away in confusion.

I instantly seized his throat in my hand. The king's eyes bulged in surprise and then amusement. The king assumed he would be able to escape my grasp because of my delicate size. He was very wrong.

As he continued to struggle, his amusement distorted into anger, and I said, "You think I want to be Sparta's queen? To serve at your brother's feet the rest of my days, the devoted servant and mother to his offspring? That is not power. That is a prison. And you, my king, have been caged in your own prison of greed for far too long." I squeezed tighter. My other hand restrained his flailing arms, not that they were able to hurt me. Just annoying. The look of astonishment on his face was satisfying.

"Let me release you," Helen said. The joy I felt as he writhed and fought beneath my hands was addicting. I gazed into his eyes. There I could see the realization forming in his mind. The King of Argos knew he was going to die. My bliss going further still, I reformed into Lilith. I wanted him to see who relieved him of his misused life.

I could have used my influence of energy, my magic to kill him. But I wanted his demise to be personal and memorable, for both him and me. Granted, it wasn't fair that I possessed so much more strength than he did, but at least it was something he understood and could comprehend in his passing.

I let the anger fuel me as I squeezed his jugular. I barely had to expend any energy. It was as easy as plucking a flower. I had to concentrate so I wouldn't rip the head off his body, so the moment could be prolonged that much longer. Delicately and slowly I watched as the life drained from

him. The king's eyes were dulling, but there was enough light left in them to stare at me angrily. I took notice that there was no fear in his dark orbs.

I granted Agamemnon one final piece of familiar advice. "It's best to know all the rules before you play the game, darling." I learned quickly, and the King of Argos had been a quick study.

I heard the last rapid thump, thump, thump of his heartbeat before it stilled. I laid him down on the elegantly decorated floor to rest. The body of Agamemnon laid atop a scintillating, slithering snake. Its golden eyes stared back at me from its place beside the elder king's head. From the time I gripped his throat to the sound of his last heartbeat, his spirit didn't flail or fight. It remained calm and unperturbed. Even in death, Agamemnon was resolute in his pride.

Now that the black cloud had no form to take, it drifted upward and in the direction of my own crimson light. I didn't run as I had with Ambrose. There was no point, and I no longer felt the fear. Now that I wasn't fighting against it, I realized that I could pull his spirit into my own whether I took his life or not, much like the hybrids, but my will was much stronger than theirs. The word *succubus* worked its way into my thoughts.

I felt the darkness fight me upon entry, but it was soon dispersed and integrated into my brilliant light. My soul was much older and much stronger than the King of Argos, so the blackness didn't overwhelm. The redness of my light bounced off the reflective surface of the throne. I could feel the heaviness that now weighed on me.

I felt powerful.

XIX
Black Soul

The blanket that darkness provides
swathes those in need of guidance.
-A

I stood above the body of King Agamemnon, basking in the overwhelming power that consumed me. The hunger I felt was insatiable. I wanted more. But as I stared down at his lifeless corpse, reality hit me. *What had I done? Why did I feel good about it?* I quickly became Helen again. I listened. There was no heartbeat or breath. No one was near. No one had seen me. That was good. *What did I do now?*

I pushed down the questions and frantic emotions so I could concentrate on what I needed to do. I healed the bruising around the elder king's neck. I kneeled down to close his eyes. I took a moment to stare at the dark orbs. They mocked and belittled me, even in death.

I closed his lids so the void could no longer scrutinize me. I swiftly lifted his form up and over my shoulder. Now I listened carefully for any sign of life in the halls. Assured by the silence, I sprinted to Agamemnon's bedchambers, ignoring the siren song of the shining chair that had rested only a few steps from me. Once I reached the overly decorated doorframe, I gripped the handle to open it. It didn't budge. The king must have created a way to lock it so there would be no unwanted visitors. Clever as usual, and also very irritating.

In my haste I twisted with increased pressure, and the handle groaned and popped beneath my palm. I entered the grand bedchambers of the King of Kings and closed the door behind me. The decor was unexpected. I predicted massive amounts of gold, art, and beautiful servants to be awaiting his arrival. But the room held only an oak bed frame with plush sheets and blankets. The walls had been painted dark colors of mahogany and obsidian. There was a large bronze capsule in the corner with linens and a basin sitting on a small oak table beside it. The king deserved his own bath, of course.

The last thing that caught my attention was another doorway. I laid the departed king upon his lavish bedsheets and went to explore the adjoining room. This one was locked, as well. I inspected the contraption further. The bronze handle held a small hole in the center of it. I pressed my eye close to the opening. There were miniature pieces of shaped metals and coils.

I recalled a memory then. I went to Agamemnon and pulled the collar of his clothing apart. There rested the leather string and metal object I had seen the first time I met him only days before. I vaguely remembered the pressure of it against my hand as I strangled him.

I ripped the key from its home and proceeded to open the adjoining door. What I found wasn't pleasant. The smell alone assaulted my nostrils well before I opened the wooden door. There were mutilated colored silks lying neatly on a small table in the dank room. There were no windows or candles to provide light. There was no fireplace to keep it warm and dry. The stone floors were cold and lifeless. It was a cell of misery.

The bodies that had been caged here were gone, but I could still smell the fear and panic they exuded. My sharp eyes could see the strewn tendrils of hair. Several different shades littered the room. Only my eyes could see them. They were crushed into the ground from heavy footsteps. The metallic chains connected to the walls had ensnared parts of the lost hair. I studied

a strand of blonde hair that rested at my feet. The end was stained with blood from its violent removal.

The blood and secretions I smelled could no longer be seen, but I knew they were there. The odor of it was permanently saturated in the surrounding walls and floor. The very air was poisoned with the deeds of the departed king.

I knew then why his soul had blackened. It was not a natural color. He had stolen many lives, and the only choice their spirits had was to remain within him. The range of colors had mixed and muddied his spirit until it wasn't a single shade anymore. It was all of them and none of them.

Those same spirits now rested in me, along with their killer.

I sauntered over to the chains that had entrapped so many lives. So many frightened and helpless women. Each set of chains was formed from a different metal: copper, iron, steel. The king had been experimental. He wanted these women to fight, and he tested which alloy would hold them better. The copper had failed at one point and been repaired. I could see the small scars along the wrist cuffs. Whoever had broken them had fought hard, and that was exactly what he had wanted.

It was ironic, really, that he was defeated by a woman, one who barely needed to expend any energy on him. It hardly took any force to clamp his throat and watch the life drain from him. But had I really won? The fight wasn't physical. It had been mental. And something told me that he had known that. It disgusted me that he would have any satisfaction in his passing. Any comfort to his deranged game. But alas, there was nothing I could do now. A monster was removed from the world, and that was something to be glad for. *So why wasn't I?* I left the haunted room and its memories, locked it and crushed the key in my palm. I tossed the hunk of metal aside and went on about my business.

No one would suspect Helen for the king's death, but I didn't want anyone else to take the blame, either. I had healed his bruising for a reason.

I wanted his passing to look natural. I laid his body on its side under the sheets. I rested his hands against his heart as if he had been clutching it in his time of passing. The King of Argos died from a heart attack, like he should have yesterday morning when I defended myself against him. I could have spared another life in that time. The scent in his dungeon of torture had been fresh, too recent for comfort. And I hadn't heard their cries. *Lesson learned.*

I took the ruby necklaces that he wore from his neck. The hair that made the chains was thick but ripped apart easy enough. The blonde, brown, black, and red strands separated, and I threw them out the king's window, letting the breeze set them free. I wondered how he had found someone with red hair to torture.

Taking the rubies, I departed the king's room quietly. There was nothing I could do about the broken lock, but I bent the frame back in hope that no one would notice. I refused to explore my emotions or questions until my business was completed. My next task was finding Paris.

It wasn't difficult. My faculties were still overwhelmed with the stench of death, but Paris's pleasant odor was recent enough that I could follow easily. The prince was in the garden at the pool's edge. *Sentimental fool.* So in love with a stranger. But I appreciated the opportunity that he presented me. "Paris?" I questioned. My voice was polite, but still too stiff.

Paris stood immediately and took hold of my hand. "My lady, are you well?"

I wished he wouldn't call me that. The concern in his voice was clear, but I refused to feel the budding guilt in my gut. "I wish I could say I was." I looked away from him then. I told myself it was part of the role I was playing, but truthfully it was hard to lie to him. Even half-truths.

"What is wrong? Did he hurt you?" Paris grew angry at once. "I saw how he handled you as we left. If it wasn't for my brother I would have stepped in right there and then."

Helen clasped his hand in hers. "I am glad you did not. Your treaty is worth much more than I am." I meant that. "But I do not wish to marry him, and he has guards watching me. I suspect he already knows I am not in my room where I am supposed to await him."

"And you do not have to wait much longer, dear Helen. Will you take my offer and come to Troy with me?" Paris's face was hopeful.

"I will, but we must make haste. We cannot wait until after the wedding. He will not let me leave his sight," I said desperately.

"Oh, Helen!" Paris lifted and twirled me in delight. Once he put me down, he pressed a light and delicate kiss against my lips. Apparently he took my agreement to leave for Troy as a yes to his marriage proposal, which I had not intended. But I could not risk him changing his mind due to heartbreak, so I attempted to reciprocate his joy. At least until I was away from this land.

I could have escaped on my own, of course, but I suspected Troy was a good place to restart my mission. Paris was a guaranteed route to the ones in power, and if they were anything like him and his brother, they shared my goals.

"We will leave tonight. I will tell my brother I cannot bear to watch you marry another, and request to leave early. Knowing Hector, he will grant me this. Until I arrange our travel, wait in your chambers and proceed as normal. I will come to retrieve you tonight when the home is asleep," Paris explained quickly.

Remembering Paris's last attempt to retrieve me I suggested, "I will wait for you below the tree at my balcony."

Confused, he asked, "But how will you climb down without assistance?"

I nearly laughed at the idea of needing his assistance, but comforted, "I am capable of more than you know." Paris was confused, but he believed me when I said this. He gave me a tender kiss on my cheek before leaving. I sprinted to my room's balcony. I listened for any unexpected guests awaiting

me in my bedchamber. Nothing. I leapt atop the railing, half the height of the adjacent tree.

I peeled off my glittering jewels and embroidered clothes, tossing them to my bed with Agamemnon's rubies. They stank of death and fear. I would no longer be wearing them. I searched my room for any other linens and found none but my sheer white nightgown. I stared at it. It was better than Helen's adornments.

Staring at myself in the mirror, I found that I couldn't explore the emotions that buried themselves in me even if I had wanted to. I was numb, disconnected from myself. I was now a being that ran purely on instinct. I was an animal of the natural world. I found the sensation liberating yet strangely disturbing.

I focused on how much I hated the bothersome task of clothing. Before these hybrids, coverings weren't an issue. If I didn't have any furs to conceal me, it was acceptable, and I wouldn't attract attention. I could walk among others and my "honor" would be intact. Too bad; I had no honor left anyway. I wished at that moment for something to conceal my soul.

The atmosphere changed then. The whispers of fabric brushing against one another distracted me from my reverie. My frustrations had willed themselves into fruition—an ability I realized long ago but had yet to transfer to other aspects of my life. I realized, while the threads were twirling around each other, that the limit to my powers was simply my imagination. I could create wonderful and terrible things with the intricate and creative thoughts in my mind. And my mind was no longer limited.

My sheer, white, floor-length nightgown had transformed into a thick woolen cloak and draped across my shoulders. One side crossed my chest and pinned itself at my left shoulder. Not only had my spell weaved a cloak well known to the people of Greece, but a thin fabric encased my arms, chest, and legs. Thick sandals of cloth wound around my feet.

The clothing kept its original white, but the cloak had detailed red

and black scenes of trees and flowers. The pin was also made of cloth and took the form of a crimson lily. The altered threads were thorough and custom tailored to me, yet another unconscious form of magic I was capable of. Except this time, I appreciated it rather than feared it. Just like everything in this world, it was made of energy. I had only to wield it.

I didn't realize until after my scrutiny that I had reverted back to Lilith. I had to pay more attention, lest I transform in front of someone unknowingly. I changed back into Helen, and my new clothes immediately refitted themselves to the blonde goddess. My newfound ability was strange but helpful.

I brushed out my mass of blonde hair with the golden brush I was provided, and then preceded to tame it. When I was finished, my hair was well under control. A braid began at my forehead and ended at my hips. The end was wrapped in a strip of white cloth I tore from my cloak. The cloak sewed itself more fabric. The magic of the garments reminded me of my healing abilities.

I didn't know if Menelaus would come to see me or not, but I refused to wear the clothes he gave me. I gazed at the jewels he chained me in then. I made myself a bag out of the bed sheets. The material was similar to the fabrics I wore, but the shade was cinnamon and had the appearance of leather, but I knew it wasn't. I placed the expensive jewels and gold into my new bag after washing them severely in the basin. It helped, but the stench of death was not easily removed.

Just in case my plan went awry, I had something to trade. I was still ignorant of the customs and needed a way to pay for food. That's what I told myself at least. A knock at the door interrupted my pondering, and I opened it to find a guard with a message. My own guards were surprised when the door opened; they were still awaiting my arrival it seemed. I giggled at the wary glances they gave me.

The armed man informed me that Menelaus would collect me for our

wedding tomorrow afternoon, and I was also to be brought dinner instead of joining the men as before. I snickered. Too afraid to face me after his behavior, or was this his way of controlling me? Either way, I wouldn't be seeing the King of Sparta again.

The only thing that worried me now was Agamemnon. Would they find him before I left? I shouldn't be blamed, but it could cause complications to our departure. Hector might want Paris to stay after all, and then I would have to leave on my own. On the other hand, the commotion of his death would create a helpful distraction so I could slip away with Paris. I only hoped Paris would be quick enough to realize this.

The hours that passed were filled with fog. I was absorbed in my own thoughts when dinner came. I mechanically opened the door for the servant to bring in the food. The tall, dark-haired woman appraised my clothing quizzically, but didn't voice her opinion, at least as far as I heard. I wasn't paying enough attention to notice if she did.

I picked at my food and waited for either Paris's footsteps below or the commotion that would come with the discovery of the king. There was no panic yet, but it was not yet their dinner time. I only noticed then that my food had come early.

I heard the faint footsteps of my travel companion crossing the garden. Paris was early, too. I jumped onto the balcony's railing. I listened once more for any disorder within the deceased king's home. Silence. I leapt stealthily off the railing and landed with a light thud only I could hear. I smelled sunshine as I fell, though the sun was no longer lighting the grounds. I hid in the shadow of the tree until Paris reached me.

Without a word and only a cursory glance at my attire, he grabbed my hand and led me to the other side of the grand home. Luckily, it was late enough in the day that the darkness concealed us. That's when I heard the sound I'd been waiting for. A woman screamed. There was hastened

shuffling. Men's voices grew loud and urgent. They had discovered the king. This would give us the ample chance we needed to escape.

Paris paused mid-stride and whispered urgently, "They have noticed your absence, Helen. We must hurry." Paris had misconstrued the commotion as a response to Helen's escape instead of the king's demise. Good. That would keep him on task.

We watched behind a rose bush while the warriors guarding the front entrance departed. They ran inside the grand home in pursuit of the reason behind the cries for Agamemnon. But to Paris, they were in pursuit of me. Seeing that the path before us was a clear one, Paris gripped my hand and pulled me in the direction of our ride. The abrupt lurch forward surprised me, and my arm ripped across angry thorns. Crimson granules drained for only a moment, but the pain was sharp and ridden with my guilt.

Paris's carriage awaited us only a short sprint down the pathway from the home in turmoil. Two of his personal guards stood beside it. They must have known to wait for us. They didn't question their leader. They worked swiftly and silently as we entered the carriage. They surveyed for any wandering eyes, closed the door, and joined us on the contraption. One guard sat at the back, and one led the horses at the front.

"You are safe now, Helen. He will not be able to find you," Paris said confidently. I nodded in agreement. I could feel the guilt crawling under my skin. I had to ignore the itch if I was going to continue on. I panicked momentarily while I gazed out the window into the darkness of the trees. I thought I had seen a flash of golden light, but it was gone as quickly as it was seen. Paranoia was another condition I had yet to overcome. Still, I worried.

Lucifer made his choice. It wasn't my fault that he couldn't be happy sharing me, and it wasn't his fault that I wanted more. It was simply the way it was and how it would always be. I didn't owe him a goodbye or an explanation for my leaving. There was no need to worry or feel guilty.

Lucifer was no longer a part of my life. He would follow his path and I would create mine.

Paris tried to wrap his arms around me, but when I shied away he settled for holding my hand. The prince only spoke to me when I asked questions, which I appreciated. I asked why he came for me before dinner, and he explained that he learned I wouldn't be joining them and hadn't been able to wait any longer. I wanted to chastise his impatience, but I couldn't help but feel grateful. The prince most likely wouldn't have been able to leave after they found the king.

Now that I thought about it, disappearing during the finding would be just as incriminating. Even if it looked like natural causes, there would be suspicion for both Helen *and* Paris. My gut wrenched. That was something I had not thought of. I had been too focused on the convenience of the distraction. I had ignored the fact that Paris could be blamed as well. I inwardly cringed at my self-absorption.

It was too late now. I would have to hope for the best. Helen was merely a runaway girl who didn't want to be married, and Paris was a lovestruck boy who didn't want to watch as the girl he loved married someone else. I was sure Hector could attest to this on his brother's behalf. My story didn't need attesting. I was a ghost in the wind, a girl who drifted from place to place and would never be found again.

One could only hope.

Travel was much faster by carriage, and since it was undoubtedly royalty traveling, no one bothered us. We passed through Argos and Sparta quickly. As we left the sparkling city of King Menelaus, I saw the black armor of their worshipped god, Ares. His gold skin glowed against the sunrays, and the spear he held looked sharper and even more deadly than before. Except this time I didn't tremble in fear.

I enjoyed the ride with Paris. I asked him several questions about his

home and family. He considered his father, King Priam, a great and just ruler who cared for his people. Queen Hecuba, Paris's mother, had died when he was young from birthing his younger sibling. Hector and Paris had a young sister, Cassandra. She was ten, and constantly harassed them to train her in combat. She wished to be a warrior, which of course was not allowed. I would have to do something about that.

The young prince spoke of how brilliant his sister was for her age. Apparently Cassandra had a knack for reading people. She could see if a person was trustworthy or had ulterior motives for the kingdom. Their father kept her with him when he made new introductions from visiting lands. Cassandra had saved them more times than not with her ability.

"How does she possess such a gift?" I asked.

"We don't know. We asked her, and all she would say is that she can 'see how bright their light is.'" Seeing my expression and interpreting it wrong, he continued, "Her answers are typically vague. She is a girl of few words, and only speaks when she needs to." I resumed my questions but continued to think of Cassandra. She could see souls. I would have to meet her and judge that for myself.

We reached the port of Gythion by the end of the following day, the town where I had been dragged ashore and forced to face the consequences of my prehistoric deeds, as well as act out more atrocities that sullied my name and spirit. *Necessary sacrifices,* I told myself.

Paris alerted the crew of our early departure and arranged for a separate boat to be prepared for his brother upon his arrival the next day. While our floating contraption was organized, he took me on a stroll through the trader's market, the same market I studied as my frozen sanctuary was rolled down its path. It was the same place I had my first glimpse of modern society. I remembered being both horrified and awed. The scale had tipped in the direction of horrified. With any luck, the royal family of Troy would tip my scale the other way and give me hope once more.

Paris had offered to give my belongings to the crew to load with his, but I found I couldn't part with the wealth I'd obtained. We walked by a man selling fruits on our stroll. His familiar fake smile and scheming eyes made the sand beneath my skin scratchy and irritating. The man held his arm in front of our path, an apple in his grasp. The tradesman eyed me and then the bag I carried.

"A delectable fruit for a delectable lady," he said leeringly. It was clear the man didn't remember me. Before Paris could step in, I grabbed the man's large forearm. My hand was small and barely fit around the limb, but my strength was firm, and he found himself unable to remove it.

"I would suggest changing your dialogue and keeping a respectful distance from your customers." I squeezed a bit harder. "You might come across someone lacking in patience, who wouldn't mind using you as an outlet to relieve some of their frustrations."

Completely unperturbed by my words and grip, he responded seductively, "I can relieve your frustrations any time you want." The trader moved toward me. His hot unpleasant breath overpowered the odors of the marketplace.

I removed my grip from his arm and discretely willed my unseen roots toward him. They played along the surface of his skin. At the moment, all he felt was a slight pressure along his thighs, a side effect to the fantasies he was clearly having about me. I wished my invisible fingers to move farther in and around him. This man assumed he was going to feel pleasure from the mere thought of us being together. How arrogant of him.

In the instant it took me to arouse him, his manhood was being strangled, the pressure upon him causing permanent damage. The tradesman fell to the ground in agony, gripping his delicate organ. The magic I persuaded released its grip before the poor man could pass out. Paris stood beside me, shocked at the sight of the collapsed man. The tradesman laid on the ground in front of me, curled in a ball. His neighboring traders

didn't notice the small incident. The marketplace was too busy and crowded for anyone to notice one man on the ground beside his cart.

I knelt down beside him and whispered, "As I said, you never know who you're going to come across. So watch what you say, especially to women. They're the ones you should be afraid of, not their male counterparts." To anyone who saw us, it looked as if a young girl was caring for the fallen man, whispering inquiries on how to relieve his pain. Even Paris was unaware of the unnatural transaction that occurred, despite his close proximity.

Reassuring Paris that he would be all right and just needed to rest, we left the tradesman who had beaten that small boy on my first visit to Gythion. My knowledge had grown since then, and I learned in my time away from this place that it was better to act in the moment, snuff out the discrepancies before they grew into worse ones, no matter the cost to my soul.

We explored the market without incident for the next hour and decided to check on the boat crew at the docks. That was when I saw him: Aegeus, the fisherman who had reintroduced me to the world. He was helping his fellow crew members unload their livelihood from the boat.

I was instantly wary, worried that he would see me. Then I realized that he wouldn't recognize Helen. I was Lilith when he knew me, the real me. I hadn't acknowledged how much that had bothered me until now, that he hated Lilith and not a fictional face I wore. The fisherman knew the real me and my real story. It was unsettling.

I had grown accustomed to the fantasy of Helen and her background. I had become her, a different person with different problems and different actions. It was easy to separate myself from her life. Subconsciously, I had associated Helen with the Greeks and Trojans, not Lilith. They weren't my problems. They were the complications of the golden-haired goddess, and I bore no responsibility for Helen's actions.

Paris had gone aboard our boat to speak with the captain, leaving me on the dock. Aegeus caught me ogling him and sent a friendly smile my way. Panicked, I quickly glanced away and turned the other direction. I made my way to an empty part of the long walkway. I sat and dangled my feet above the seawater. The salt from the waves washed over my senses.

The seawater was beautiful in a way. The green-bluish hue of it was unique, and the way the sun danced off its rippling surface was dazzling. But I couldn't rid myself of the sight of the dark depths below, the darkness only my eyes could see—and remember.

"Hello there, did you need help finding someone?" a man's kind voice offered.

Oh no.

I twisted and gazed up at my visitor. "No, thank you. I am waiting for my…escort to finish speaking with his crew."

Slight disappointment in his voice, he asked, "Oh, where do you plan to travel?" Aegeus took a seat beside me on the dock's edge.

"Troy," I responded. I begged him silently to leave me be, but my wish was left ungranted as usual.

"Troy? I've heard great things about the city. Are you from there?"

"No," I said, hoping my lack of interest would send him away.

Persistent, he continued, "Where are you from then?" Most people would have been irritated by how unforthcoming I was being, but Aegeus was annoyingly patient.

"The north."

"That explains your hair then, the way the sunshine glitters off your tresses. It is highly sought after in this land for its rarity." Despite his obvious interest in Helen, I found myself at ease once more in his presence. The man was a rare soul, and one that didn't deserve what Lilith had done to him.

"Ah, yes. I have realized this in my travels. Men can't seem to stay away from me no matter how hard I try to sway them with words. They only see the body I inhabit," I revealed unwillingly.

Aegeus wasn't insulted like I feared he would be. "I suppose that can be difficult. Beauty is both a curse and a blessing."

I looked him in the eye for the first time. "Yes. But being human is also a curse, and rarely a blessing," I said. I let myself breathe in deep then. Aegeus's scent was just the same as it was before—so similar to Adam's.

Aegeus nodded his head. A few strands of ebony hair fell from his loosely tied leather hair band. "It is indeed. People experience several different forms of pain in their short lives."

Cautiously I asked, "And what hardships have you experienced in your time?"

Reluctantly he responded, "I have been lucky. Work has always been available to me, so I am never hungry. I would have to say loneliness is what ails me." Aegeus looked at the green ripples that flowed toward us. "The last of my family died a short time ago, and I now find myself alone."

My tear ducts itched because of the scene I recalled: a broken old man lying at the base of the wall he'd been thrown against, Aegeus as he grasped his uncle's form and cried out for him to wake, the hateful eyes of the old man's nephew as he threatened to kill me if he ever laid eyes on me again.

I moved closer to Aegeus and held the hand he leaned against for support. "You will find someone to fill the void you feel in your heart. That emptiness won't last forever." The words I conveyed weren't only meant for him. But the difference was, I had chosen the emptiness; he hadn't.

Aegeus turned his gaze on me and started to say something when Paris called out, "Helen?"

I removed my hand from Aegeus's grasp and stood to embrace the young prince. "Is the boat ready to sail?" I questioned eagerly. I was ready to leave this place and all the memories that haunted it.

"Yes," Paris replied distractedly. The prince was confused and slightly hurt by my choice of company.

"Paris, this kind man kept me company while you were busy."

Reassured by my tone, Paris said, "Well, thank you…"

"Aegeus," the fisherman finished.

"Yes, thank you, Aegeus, for watching over my Helen." Paris wrapped his arm around my waist territorially. I rolled my eyes. Men were all the same, despite their personalities or the shade of their spirits.

"It was a pleasure." Aegeus bowed slightly, took my hand, and kissed my inner wrist. Shivers ran down the rest of my arm. The familiarity he possessed was something I craved—comfort and safety—but something I could never have again.

Ignoring my selfish thoughts, I said, "I wish you great happiness, Aegeus." Paris was ready to leave, but I stopped him from pulling me away so I could give Aegeus a parting gift. "I want you to have this. I have no need of it." I gave the fisherman the bag full of gold and jewels, grateful to be relieved of the burden.

Glancing inside curiously, he said, "I can't accept this. This is too much. Surely you will need—"

"No, I won't. Trust me." And in that moment he did trust me. If only he knew he was speaking to his uncle's killer. The fisherman graciously accepted my gifts and nodded his thanks, shocked at the bounty that had been given. Paris whisked me away then, before I could give anything more away.

I turned my gaze back to the dock as our boat departed. Aegeus was still standing at the spot where we parted ways. In his hand he held the only evidence of the generous girl who had blown through his life. The bag dangled from his grip, and I could see its contents glittering through the thin cloth. To him, Helen had been like a swift passing breeze, never to be seen or heard from again, and I wished desperately to be that breeze, to fly away from the world that burdened me.

The kind fisherman waved farewell, a small sad smile on his face. I found myself sharing his sadness. I desired the company of someone like Aegeus, the support and solace that emanated from him. The possibility of happiness. But I knew in my metaphorical heart that it was not meant to be. Someone like Aegeus could only be hurt by a being like me. I was a feral creature. One didn't know if I would nuzzle their palm or bite into it, because I didn't know myself.

I watched Aegeus's form grow smaller until only I could see him in the distance and he had long ago lost sight of me. Still he stood there, as if he were imagining his own possibilities of happiness with the golden-haired girl he had crossed paths with. He should have been thinking of the red-haired woman who had removed the last piece of happiness he *did* have, the demon-goddess that swayed him with fantastical words of ancient magic and wonder, only to betray him in the end. Because right as I was about to lose sight of the pondering cobalt-blue spirit, I noticed two other forms beneath him, ones without light and life: two small carcasses that cradled each other beneath the wooden planks of the long walkway, children I had failed to save, who now floated, unable to rest, in the salted green seawater, lost and forgotten to the vast world that cared so little for them.

The boat ride was longer than the carriage, but one I wanted to take advantage of before our arrival. I had neglected to learn the skills I wanted during my time with the Greek kings. The basic necessities of the world still eluded me, and that needed to change if I was to present myself as an equal among the Trojans.

Thankfully, Menelaus had granted me his time and practiced Petteia with me. The strategies of the game were great lessons that I would apply to the life I'd chosen to follow. Too bad I didn't think to bring my game board with me. But I needed to know more about the pieces I would be using on *Earth's* board. I learned as much as I could from the crew members.

I asked them question after question about their ways of life and their culture until they were sick of me and I of them. Learning as much as I could from the simple sailors, I went in search of knowledge elsewhere.

The sights above deck were beautiful, of course, and I attempted to enjoy them during the journey: the salty spray of the water and the traveling sea creatures beside us. The water was warmer than I remembered. I even had the chance to watch the moon and stars appear above me. I spoke with them in private like I used to eons before. It was nice, and I had missed the loveliness of my loyal companions. They washed me in their light, and hopefully their wisdom, as we sailed.

Being in the sea for so long soured the enjoyment soon, though. The scent divulged too-recent memories that begged to be repressed. I spent most of my time under deck. There was a royal cabin within, and in that cabin I found a tremendous amount of parchment. The lasting energy I saw in the animal skins saddened me, but it was the next best way to learn about my pieces. Though, I couldn't distinguish the symbols and grew frustrated trying.

Paris soon discovered me sifting angrily through the texts. Laughing, he said, "Do you need help? What are you looking for?"

I didn't need to conceal weakness with Paris as I did with Greece's kings. "I am attempting to read, if you must know."

The prince's chortling ceased. "Oh, I apologize. I did not mean to laugh at you." Pausing a moment, he asked, "Would you like me to teach you?"

I had become very fond of Paris in our short time together. The prince was young and a bit naïve, but very kind. He didn't judge me because of my lack of knowledge or the story of my fictional heritage. The world needed more people like him.

Paris spent the remainder of the journey below deck teaching me to read. Once the concept was explained and the system of the symbols was displayed before me, I understood. Paris was baffled by my quick learning

and suspicious of why I didn't already know if it was that easy for me to learn. I explained that the village I came from had no need of reading and writing. We were simplistic and enjoyed what nature provided us. That was true. My fictional travels had left me little time to learn, as I was too immersed in the culture and the landscapes I visited. That was false, but a reasonable excuse.

I was enjoying my time with Paris, but then his real feelings surfaced and the fun was at an end. I reached for my cup of wine, but before my hand could reach it, Paris took my small hand in his. The prince brought my palm to his lips and began leaving a delicate, wet trail of kisses up my arm. He was nearing my neckline when I pulled away. "Helen, I realize that you have been through an ordeal, and I don't wish to rush you." Paris paused, unsure of his next words. "But it seems as if you do not share my feelings as you did before. You…you don't touch me or kiss me. You shy away when I try to do so." The prince looked down at our separated hands and took a deep breath. "Do you not love me anymore?" Paris stared nervously at his feet. His spirit twitched, anxious of my words to come.

"Paris…" Lie or tell the truth? Lose the opportunity to learn from these good people and be cast aside, or be welcomed with open arms? "Paris, I do love you." I touched his arm. I had been so engrossed in my studies that I had briefly dismissed the role of Helen. "I wish to marry you in the future, but my time with the kings has left me afraid, and it's going to take time for me to forget what they did to me."

Angry, he questioned, "What did they do to you?"

My skin itched. "They hurt me in a way only a man can. Though they did not complete their endeavor, they did hurt me trying to get there." It was my turn to be shy and cautious.

Paris carefully embraced me, comforting my frail disposition. I could hear his heart racing, and I knew that my words had angered him. But it was the only way to explain my reluctance. If I was going to accomplish

my task, I would have to continue to promise myself to Paris. At least that would give me time to figure out another plan and prolong his advances. He was a sweet and lovely young man, and he reminded me of my son. I didn't want to hurt him, but at the moment I didn't see much else for us in the future.

Paris was whispering loving promises and comforts in my ear when the captain above shouted the news of our arrival. Reluctantly releasing me, Paris led me above deck. We made our way to the bow of the boat and gazed at the oncoming city shore.

The sun was rising as we arrived. Ginger and lilac hues painted the clouds, the sunrays peeking through their shroud. The brilliant beams were cast down on the city before us. The architecture was set ablaze in its fiery warmth, as was the wall that protected the great city. The land called to me. The heat was irresistible. I had been in the cold of Greece for far too long. I looked to the city I was to call home for the unseeable future. I beheld the sight of Troy.

XX
Regrets are a Luxury

The existence of fear is a wonderful
and terrible thing.
-A

The events from my time in Greece were banished from my thoughts but not my memories. There was no point in dwelling on them. I didn't have the luxury of regretting past actions anymore. They only slowed me and dulled my senses. The regrets were now seen as necessary sacrifices that would lead to a better future for humanity.

For me.

The smells of the city surrounded the boat. The shelters were simple and the people weren't adorned with shiny trinkets, but the scent of happiness was there. Flowers and pastries traveled on the breeze, inviting me in. I could hear the sound of a freshwater stream running somewhere in the distance. The people were well fed and clean. I smelled none of what I had in Greece: the grime and decay of both land and residents.

Our boat docked, and we were swarmed with people native to the land of Troy. They welcomed their prince and his visitor with open arms. It was obvious the people loved him, and he returned that love naturally. Paris might not have been born to rule the kingdom, but he cared for it just the same. His shared love gave me hope for my new endeavor.

"Cassandra!" Paris shouted in delight. A small girl appeared then.

The crowd parted for her as she sprinted down the dock, her dark curls bouncing excitedly. The girl's beauty was obvious, even at her young age, but her large, pale-blue eyes startled me. Cassandra's brothers both had blue-shaded irises, something that I assumed belonged to their homeland. But her eyes were indescribably unique and other-worldly. The ice-blue, crystal-like appearance of them bored into me.

They reminded me of someone I'd rather forget.

The child stopped short of her brother, despite her previous enthusiasm. Cassandra stepped around Paris and faced me instead.

Curious, but unwilling to reveal myself, I greeted, "Cassandra, it is lovely to meet you. Paris has told me so much about you." Her heart had been beating fast due to her excitement, but that quickly changed when she laid her eyes on me; it became a steady and sure beat.

The girl's only outward response was her raised hand; it stroked the air around me. I could see that she was caressing my surrounding spirit, and apparently so could she, although this was invisible to everyone else. The princess was scrutinizing the dark crimson soul that fell through her fingertips. It had been lighter before I walked among Lucifer's children.

"You will bring death to us," Cassandra whispered. The words were said so delicately, I thought I hadn't heard her right. And if I hadn't, that meant no one else had, either. There was no panic or fear in her expression. The child was simply stating what she saw. I was the one who had to control the wave of dread I felt. Cassandra lowered her arm, took her elder brother's hand, and pulled him down the walkway toward their waiting home. Paris's expression was one of confusion, but I gave him a reassuring smile, regardless of the foreboding sense his sister had given me.

The people of Troy were a welcome distraction. They showered us in gifts and treats to share with the tenants of the king's home. "Miss, please accept this as a welcome gift. We are happy to have you." A young boy

placed a white rose in my hand as I passed by with Paris and his sister. The warriors who guarded us were mingling with the populace as well, completely at ease.

Bringing the flower up to my nose, I thought of the white tree in my old home. "Thank you. It's lovely." I removed the shiny gemstones from the hidden pocket in my cloak and handed them to the small boy. "Please let me return the gesture." Baffled and excited by his new treasures, the boy ran to his mother to share the wealth.

The rubies I gave the boy were nearly the last of my wealth—Agamemnon's wealth. I knew I should have given them to Aegeus, but my newfound greed hadn't allowed me. I felt the last lonely ruby press against my skin through the thin cloth. At least that wealth was now a part of this land, a land that I viewed as a great example for the world. I was glad to see that some of Lucifer's descendants had found a better path. But there was still much more of the world to explore, and with my luck, most of it wouldn't be as fortunate.

Our small group finally made it through the throng of dedicated subjects and onto the king's front steps. I stayed back and observed from a distance.

"My son, why have you returned so soon? Where is Hector? Did negotiations not go well?" An elderly man strolled out of the entrance to the royals' impressive home. A gold circlet adorned his head, simple and elegant. It was only there to represent his role in the kingdom. The King of Troy. King Priam. Father to Hector, Alexander, and Cassandra.

"Do not worry, Father. All is well. Hector stayed only a day longer than I have. He will be home tomorrow." Paris consoled his worried father. Cassandra ran past the king, up the marble steps, and out of sight.

"Then why have you left your brother to deal with the Greeks on his own? You know I sent you to support him as well as learn. We must remain a united front if we are to convince them of peace." King Priam

was scolding his child's behavior, but he couldn't hide the fact that he was pleased to see him anyway.

The prince became bashful and nervous for the onslaught to come. Instead of using his words, Paris retrieved me from my hiding place behind a statue of a gold-painted man with a sun emblem on his chest. The figure held a bow and arrow. Upon seeing me, realization dawned on the king's face. Then a smile formed.

"Ah, you have found a lovely young woman to keep you company, have you?" The king's laughter echoed against the surrounding walls.

"Indeed I have, Father," the prince said proudly, happy with his father's reaction. Paris's heartbeat was erratic from his anxiousness at his next words. "And time permitting, she will become my wife." Paris gazed at me with loving eyes and stroked my hand. "With your blessing, of course, Father." The prince bowed his head in respect.

King Priam's joking manner dissipated at the words of his son. "Marriage? But you have never treated anything with such seriousness before."

Slightly embarrassed at his father's remark, he responded, "That alone should tell you how much she means to me."

The king appraised me. I stood tall and confident, challenging him with my eyes. "What is your name?" Priam questioned skeptically. The king had the same pale blue irises as his daughter, the same eyes as his ancestor.

"Helen." I dipped my body slightly in respect, but I never broke eye contact. I would not make the same mistakes here. I was to present myself as an equal, not as a moldable servant. I would succeed in my goal. I would use these people to spread my idealism to the rest of the world. But I had yet to see what they could offer.

We mentally challenged each other for several moments before the king cheered, "Welcome, Helen!" The king's abrupt change in attitude startled me. The new atmosphere was pleasant and not one I was

used to. "We will hold a banquet in your honor, a way to welcome you to our home."

I was in shock. This man knew nothing about me, yet he welcomed me into their home, no questions asked. No expectations. I didn't need to manipulate or lie my way into their hearts. It was a relief. It was unwise. Priam was this city's king. How could he risk his family's safety? Either he was just the same as the Greek kings, and didn't see me as a threat, or he was overly trusting. Neither option was good. But I took the invitation anyway.

The king and prince took the time to show me their home. It was smaller than the grand residence of the Greeks, but still elegant. They didn't cover their walls in gold and scatter portraits of wars and women to impress. The stone structure was left unmarred by paint and jeweled adornments. There were simplistic portraits of the sea, as well as the members of their family. Their furnishings were modest. The amenities were designed to seat the family comfortably so they could speak and interact with each other. There weren't assigned placements to display the order of power. The residence of the Trojans was a true home—one full of love.

The king left it to Paris to show me the rest of the household. I came across a table full of lit white candles. A stick burned, and the smell of jasmine drifted up to my nose. Shiny trinkets were spread around a small painting of a woman. Jewelry. A hair brush. She had rich dark curls and a petite face. The storm and sea worked together to create her bright blue irises. A silver circlet rested around her curls.

"My mother," Paris explained. I could see it. Her daughter was a near exact copy, or would be, except for the queen's eyes, which her sons had inherited.

"She's beautiful," I said, though it was obvious. I just didn't know what to say. I had never lost a parent, because I never had any.

"Yes, she was. I was seven years old when we lost her." Paris smiled at a memory. "I can still remember how she smelled, like jasmine. I would

bury my face in her hair at night when she put me to bed, hoping the scent would cling to me." Paris seemed to remember me then. "I didn't sleep well alone as a child."

I took his hand in mine, both of us still looking at Queen Hecuba's portrait. "I never knew my parents, but I do know the pain of losing a child." Paris stiffened, surprised due to Helen's age.

"I had no idea," he said. The prince couldn't find the right words, and that was okay. I couldn't find the right words either. But perhaps he was reconsidering his choice to marry me; I was clearly not a maiden.

"Your father must have loved her very much. I can see it in how he looks at his children." I meant that. Priam looked at his children with love in his eyes, but I could see the sorrow behind them. He saw his lost love in his sons' gazes and his daughter's young face. I could imagine what that would feel like. I wondered if Lucifer ever saw Eve in the faces of his children. And if he did, did he care? *Did he ever come to love her?*

Paris showed me to my new bedroom after visiting his mother's shrine. My room was directly across from his. Subtle. I chuckled quietly to myself when I realized this, but it was still sweet. He wanted to be near enough to protect me if I needed him. If only he knew that *I* was the one protecting *him*, but I let him think what he wanted.

I was left alone for the first time in a long while. Even my bedroom in Argos had guards posted outside my door to watch me. The royal family of Troy felt no such need. I appreciated the privacy but questioned their decision. My trust had dimmed with every encounter in this new time, and ones who had lived in this modern world much longer than I were ignoring its very basic rule: only the strong survive. That was truer in this time than it was in my own.

My paranoia aside, I enjoyed my quaint room. It was smaller than my room in Argos, but it contained the necessities I needed. They even included an iron tub for me to bathe in. Steaming hot water awaited me. I peeled

off my sea-crusted clothing and sank beneath the water's surface. My eyes remained open to watch as my waist-length hair surrounded me in a cocoon. The golden light it emanated soon became ruby waves bouncing off the tub's reflective surface. Content, I closed my weary eyes.

The relaxing heat of the water was suddenly replaced with biting cold. The clear waves transformed into crimson blood that washed over me. I wished to resurface, but my body was transfixed by the blood. The thick liquid suffocated me, smothering and pulling me down farther into its dark abyss. This darkness was not the one I lived in for eons. This one was pitch black. My sharp eyes found no sign of light or release from the pawing hands that gripped and pulled me down. The choice to reemerge was nonexistent. I had waited too long to choose.

Startled, I lurched from the icy water. My skull broke through the ice that formed above me. Shivering, I reached for the woolen nightgown the servants had left me. Still, the trembling wouldn't subside. I willed the fire pit in the corner of the room to light, and I placed my hands against its side, despite the sizzling of my skin.

"Are you okay?" a small voice asked.

Startled for a completely different reason, I removed my hands from the fire and hid them under my arms while they healed. I turned to face the insightful young girl from before. "Yes. Thank you. Just a bit cold," I answered. My voice was steady despite the dream I'd had.

The princess's icy eyes scrutinized me. "You are a very talented liar," Cassandra replied bluntly.

Irritated I asked, "Why do you think I'm lying?"

She took a moment to respond. "Your face remains composed, but your spirit struggles for freedom." So it was true. She could see the spirits.

"And you are a very talented seer," I said.

"Seer?" the girl questioned.

"Yes, you can see the light, can't you?"

It was the first time I had seen her face reveal more than she intended it to. "Yes." Her white soul danced in excitement. I pitied her—unable to share the true nature of her gifts with anyone, no one understanding what she saw in people.

I crept closer to her. My hands healed; I reached out. Cassandra stepped away from me, suspicious of my bold movement. "You have nothing to fear from me, little one."

Evading my touch, she restated, "As I said, you are a talented liar." Cassandra strolled over to the tub of ice I bathed in. "My family is very trusting, as I'm sure you've gathered. I am the only one who can protect them from others, as well as themselves. Do not doubt that I will reveal you if I feel they are threatened." She turned back to me. "Do you wish to harm them?"

I took my time answering. This was a very intelligent girl. It was unusual, and not only because of her lack of age. Our unnatural magic had been passed to her, as well as the knowledge she needed to wield it. "No, I only wish to bring peace to all of those who live on this Earth, including your family." What I said was true, but I knew she could see the deeds of my past riddled in the intricacy of my spirit, as well as those that writhed within me.

This skill was something I had not yet mastered. I had lived for eons of time. Most of it was spent ignoring the light, some spent denying it existed and, most recently, opening my eyes to the knowledge it shared with me. I had only begun to learn how to interpret it, and here was a ten-year-old girl who could not only see it, but who had mastered how to read it.

Seeing her wariness, I asked a question of my own. "How do you read the light so well? How can you see past the light into the complexities of the soul within?"

Naturally she responded, "If you want to see into the soul of another, you have to stop looking at your own."

"How do I do that?" I asked, perturbed by her cryptic answer.

"If you have to ask, then you never will," Cassandra said frankly. The princess's words weren't meant to be cruel, but I felt hurt nonetheless. Seeing my distress, the hardened girl softened. "Regardless of my initial opinion of you, I can see that you try. That's all I can ask of you—of anybody really." She looked over at the frozen tub once more. "But you aren't just anybody, are you?" I assumed her question was rhetorical and didn't bother with a response.

The young girl crossed the room and paused at the exit. "Anybody can try and fail. But you aren't just anybody. Failure isn't an option. So try harder." Cassandra left me with those haunting words.

I proceeded to heat the tub water back to its original warmth, but decided I wasn't in the mood for a bath anymore. I washed the sea out of my clothes instead, and had them weave something more suited for a royal feast. The garments I wore became a floor-length silk tunic; it was snug enough that it didn't need sleeves. The white transformed into silver with red embroidered flowers along the collar. Thick red sandals were woven to match.

I had become very grateful for my newly discovered gift, and I thanked the energy within the threads every time I transformed them. I dressed in the shining garment, leaving my hair loose to wave down my back. Staring at myself in the mirror above the basin, I realized that Lilith was staring back. Not Helen.

I panicked for only a moment. Cassandra had seen my true form, and she knew of my unnatural powers, as well, but she would not reveal me to her family. She was the one person who understood the importance of these secrets. People weren't ready to see them. Only time would tell if they ever would be.

My golden hair returned, and I made my way to the dining hall. The ruby continued to hide in the small inner pocket of my clothing. I could hear

laughter and cheer. I could also smell wine and meats. My stomach growled guiltily at the scent, and my nerves craved the relief of the sweet drink. People celebrated freely, despite the early time. It wasn't quite evening yet.

Paris was the first to greet me. "Helen!" He ran to embrace me. The boy stank of wine. The prince remembered himself, though, and apologized for the abrupt contact. The sad story about my time with the kings had worked flawlessly. Even drunk, the prince was respectful and worried about my well-being. *He and Kun would have been great friends.*

"Hello, Paris. It looks like everyone is having fun. There are so many people," I observed. At the palace of the Greek kings, there had been only servants and leaders roaming the halls. Here, the city's people were welcome and celebrated with the royals.

"Yes, too bad Hector can't be here for it. Perhaps we will have another upon his return," Paris speculated gleefully.

Another one? I hoped there was more depth to this kingdom than wine and cheer.

I nodded in agreement. The prince motioned a servant over to fill his cup and provide one for me. The red liquid was wonderful and quickly disappeared. I had five more before I was satisfied enough to mingle. The young prince was too distracted with his own drinks to notice the unusual amount I was guzzling.

I had just had my eighth cup filled when King Priam joined us by the buffet table. "You enjoy wine almost as much as I do," the king bellowed light-heartedly, swinging his goblet, not caring who might come in contact with its spillage.

I laughed and challenged, "I highly doubt that. I have been known to out drink many of the men of Greece, and I am sure you wouldn't be a problem." It was a lie, but I knew it would have been true if I did. I wondered if it was the wine or my own stubbornness that made me bold enough to challenge the king.

Though he was greyed and wrinkled, his body was tall and strengthened from hard work. I admired a king who worked for others rather than making others work for him. The king was analyzing me as well, taking in my small and delicate stature. He wasn't leering like most men did. The king was simply pondering how true my words could be with such a vulnerable form.

Decided, he challenged, "Well, if you are so sure of yourself, why don't I bring out the good stuff, eh? Let's see who collapses first." Priam expected me to dissuade him from his contest, but I stood tall and steady, unlike the wobbly prince beside me.

"Oh, Father, don't do that to her. What are you thinking?" Paris slurred.

"Oh, Paris, either join us or watch as your woman out drinks you." Priam left and returned with a jar of golden liquid. "The Nectar of the Gods," the king called it.

I sniffed the bottle's opening and found the scent ghastly overwhelming. The scent of honey burned my nostrils. It was strong. And just what I needed. Completely composed I said, "The scent is lovely. Shall we begin?" I held out my cup, and the king poured us our first round.

"You can still back out now, my dear. A couple of these and you'll be like Paris over there." I glanced over at the young prince. He had passed out against the stone wall behind me. I laughed loudly. The sight of his drooling face could have brought tears to my eyes. But even laughter wouldn't allow my tear ducts to release.

We sat at the nearest table, and a crowd gathered around us. The men were discreetly betting against me. Only a brave few gambled their money on me. The women were awestruck at my bravery and continued sipping on their wine.

Seeing our audience, I comforted, "I will survive. I have humiliated myself much worse before and am no longer afraid of losing. My question

is, can *you* handle the defeat, my king?" I had told myself I wouldn't be calling him anything other than his name, but he had earned my respect. The King of Troy was about to lose horribly to a young girl in front of his subjects. The least I could do was recognize him as a leader.

Unsurprised by my words, he responded, "Drink up then, little woman." And so I did. And he did. And I did. Then he did. We were on our tenth cup of the nasty sugared drink when the king began to sway in his seat. At this point I felt relaxed. More so than I had in millennia. I really did appreciate how creative humans were.

"Ready to give up, my king?" I teased lightheartedly.

Shaking his head, Priam responded, "Only one other person on this Earth has ever out drunk me." The king's words were indecipherable to the crowd, but I could still understand his meaning.

"And who was that?" I questioned gleefully, knowing his time in the waking world was coming to an end.

"That damn Achilles." His words halted my joyful mood, and I could feel the effects of the mead dissipating. The name he mentioned was true to its meaning. One more should do it. I gulped down another, and he followed suit.

The golden liquid dribbled from the corners of his mouth. His taste buds were probably numb from the constant burn by now. Two servants stood dutifully behind the intoxicated king, and they caught him as he collapsed back on his stool. It was time for the King of Troy to sleep. The crowd erupted into chaotic cheers. Most of the men were baffled at the loss of their money, but the joyful mood remained among them. The women swarmed me. They wanted to know my secrets, and they expressed their gratitude for defeating a man at his own game.

Though the competition had been a fun one, I couldn't rid myself of the irritating feeling in my chest. Lucifer was clawing his way back in, and I had to eradicate him every time he was thought of or mentioned

by someone. The latter was rare. It made me wonder what his story with King Priam had been. How had a lost immortal being found himself in a drinking contest with a kind and trusting king? I would have liked to hear the story if it wasn't so painful to think of him. The mead had weakened my inner protective fire.

I made sure the prince and the king were taken care of before leaving to go to my room. It was dark outside the windows now. I caught a glimpse of Cassandra across the dining room, a smile on her face. But when I stepped in her direction she had already disappeared. The child was gifted in more ways than one.

I was able to avoid drunk visitors on the way to my bed. It beckoned me. Giving the tired threads I wore a rest from the constant alterations, I removed them and dawned the woolen nightgown the Trojans had provided for me. All energy was connected, and energy wasn't meant to be mutated, especially the amount I forced from it. Tired from the festivities and alcohol, I drifted into a deep, dreamless sleep, and awaited the events tomorrow would bring.

XXI
The Sound of Bells

Having hearts in your grasp is
the epitome of power.
-A

My bedroom door swung open and crashed against the stone wall.

"I knew it!" a man's voice accused.

"Brother, stop! It's my fault that she's here. Don't blame her," Paris pleaded. I sat up. My pupils struggled to focus. Honey residue coated my dry mouth. The mead must have had some lingering effects.

"You're damn right it's your fault! Do you know how difficult it was to convince Menelaus that you didn't steal his bride? How hard it was to convince him your absence had nothing to do with her?" Hector questioned his young brother. "And not only that! He even made the assumption that you had something to do with his brother's death! How convenient it was that you disappeared during the chaos of the discovery."

Shocked at the news, Paris replied, "Did he believe you?"

"Barely. Maybe about Agamemnon, but I am sure he still thinks you stole his bride away." The elder prince moved his gaze to me then. I had removed the woolen nightgown during the warm night, and donned only a thin blanket and golden tresses. "And clearly you did." Hector's tone softened. "I apologize for disturbing you. We will take our argument

elsewhere," Hector apologized. I nodded my head in thanks, not at all embarrassed by my appearance. Hector's skin flushed, and Paris's eyes burned into the back of his brother's head as they left the room.

Slightly amused by Hector's rash outburst, I dressed to find the brothers and hopefully resolve the issue; it was my fault, after all. My silver clothing was formed into a ruby red tunic that rested at knee-length. Apparently I missed my red hair more than I had thought. At least the crimson clothes would allow me a piece of my true self.

Ready and on a mission to reconcile the two princes, I strode boldly to the throne room where I heard bickering. About what, I wasn't sure. I was busy concentrating on what I was going to say. This was the time to implement my strategy. Trust was the key to unlocking their hearts, and, if I had a place in their hearts, my voice would be heard.

The bickering ceased once I entered the large room. The throne room was modest for what its purpose intended. It was similar to the rest of the home, but held a grand stone chair for the king. The throne could have easily seated three large men, and the height was well past anyone's reach. Crevices were carved to hold precious jewels in the stone, and silk pillows lined the seats for comfort. It was the most lavish thing in the abode. This was the room where the king made time to listen to his people and their needs. This was the place where Troy's leader shared his power and generosity with those he cared for.

Paris began, "Helen, I apologize for waking you. My brother had no right to—"

I interrupted, "There is no need for apologies. I understand how frustrating this situation is, and I don't wish to cause a rift between you." I looked to Hector then. "I am sorry for the trouble I caused you with Menelaus. He is very stubborn and has a temper. I wouldn't wish him upon anyone. The timing of Agamemnon's death was less than ideal, and I hope that you will not be blamed further." I rubbed my hands anxiously.

"I understand if you don't want me to stay. But I want you to know how grateful I am to your brother for saving me from that man." I looked away in shame. "I will forever be in his debt and yours. Without you, Paris would not have been able to help me escape."

My gratitude fully expressed, I turned to leave when Hector and Paris shouted simultaneously, "Wait!" They shot glares at one another.

Hector continued, "Of course you don't have to leave. We are glad to have you." The elder brother strode up to me and took my hand. "I am so happy that you were spared the wrath of that brute." Hector's other hand stroked the outline of my jaw.

"Yes, of course you won't leave. You are welcome here, and father already has a soft spot for you," Paris said as he forced himself between his brother and me. Once he had thoroughly distanced me from Hector he continued, "I mean, how could he not. You impressed him tremendously last night."

Alarmed, Hector questioned, "Last night? What happened last night?"

Irritated, Paris answered, "The Nectar."

"The Nectar? What do you mean? She couldn't have." Disbelief was apparent in his tone.

"She did," Paris said proudly.

Confused, I asked, "How did you know? You weren't even awake to see me drink it." Paris flushed with embarrassment. I hadn't meant to shame him, but it was adorable how seriously he took my words.

Hector roared with laughter at his brother's expense. "You, my brother, are out of your league." Hector tormented his brother playfully, but I could see the wheels turning in his head.

I asked, "What is so special about the Nectar?"

Paris rushed to respond before his brother. "Father brings the Nectar out for every celebration, challenging anyone he can. No one ever wins against him. Usually he can compete with two or three people per occasion before passing out." Paris smiled. "But not last night."

Satisfied with the respect I'd earned, no matter how strange the circumstances, I laughed along with the two princes. It was obvious I had gained another admirer. My plan had been to win the family's hearts with friendship and camaraderie, but the competition for my own had been set in motion, and I didn't know how to stop it, or if I even wanted to.

There was a vast difference between the princes of Troy and the kings of Greece. These new men in my life were honorable and cared for my well-being. The kings were far from honorable and cared only about satisfying their own lustful intentions. I didn't even want to think about the difference between them and Lucifer. It was nice to be sought after by kind and generous men, but that would only lead to heartbreak and more fighting between them. I had to tread carefully if I was to maintain their trust.

"Brother!" a small voice called from the shadows.

"Cassandra! Come here!" Hector picked up the child as she crashed into him. Cassandra didn't express emotion unless in the company of her brothers, and it was obvious she cared a great deal for them. The girl's snowy soul reached out to her brothers' conflicting ones and calmed them. I could tell she couldn't control the spirits like I could, but she could control her own. In turn, the princess's calm resolve naturally spread to those around her. The interaction between them had me craving a family of my own.

Hector, softened by his sister's presence and my own, said, "Let's not speak any more of this. You are welcome to stay as long as you like. Paris, I will inform father of the news. King Menelaus has halted the signing of the Peace Treaty indefinitely because of the chaos that befell his home during our visit."

Paris nodded and led me in the direction of the training grounds. In his drunken stupor the night before, he asked me to watch him train this morning. I assumed he wanted to display his masculine prowess. I was surprised that he remembered the request.

"Paris! Please take me with you. I want to train," Cassandra begged, climbing down out of Hector's arms. In the company of her family, she

acted the typical ten-year-old. Was it an act she put on for them? Or was what I saw in my room yesterday the act?

"Cass, you know that is not allowed. It's not safe for you," Hector explained. Paris rolled his eyes discreetly. Clearly he didn't agree with his brother. Again.

I asked, "Is it her age that concerns you?"

Hector turned his calm, sea-blue eyes on me. "That and the battleground is no place for a girl."

Pride leading my words, I rebutted, "I agree. The battleground is no place for a child, but how else is a warrior to learn if they do not train first?"

Hector's cloudy gaze cleared and filled with frustration. "There is no need for Cassandra to train. She isn't meant to be a warrior."

"And what is she meant for exactly?" I heard Paris clear his throat inconspicuously in an attempt to cover his chuckle.

"She is meant to learn and prepare to rule if the occasion arises." Hector was steamed now. Where was the patience and decorum he demonstrated in Greece?

"You mean if she is married to another ruler? Because you are in line to rule, are you not? And then Paris?" I questioned innocently.

Hector responded, "Yes. That is the way."

I walked up to the elder prince. "Are you and Paris not trained in combat? Since you have so little time due to your preparation to rule?"

"Of course we are." Hector was baffled at my direct questioning.

"Perhaps 'the way,' then, isn't the right way." My dark eyes pierced his, challenging him. The prince didn't say anything more. He just stared at me in surprise. Women needed to speak more. The men of this time couldn't handle the competition very well.

Paris interceded, "Cass, you can watch today. How's that?" The small girl nodded enthusiastically. I turned away from Hector's confused gaze and followed them.

"Where are you going?" Hector said.

"I am not a child. I am a woman. I am equipped to be on the battlefield." The prince, unable to argue further, left in the opposite direction, an irritated expression on his face.

"Will you really be training with me today?" Paris said cautiously.

"If you don't mind," I said lovingly.

The young prince took my hand in his grasp and brought it to his lips. "Of course not, my brave Helen."

Paris spent the morning teaching me the basics of swordsmanship. Luckily, I had watched the guards in Greece train. The spot where Menelaus and I played Petteia was the ideal location. Their training grounds were directly in front of our window. The king often took his time contemplating his next move, and that left me ample time to watch the armed warriors. Physically doing it was different from observing, but I was a quick learner, and Paris was a surprisingly good teacher.

Cassandra enjoyed watching us, and even began practicing the footwork with me. I could feel a veil of doubt lift from her. Her harsh demeanor from before dissipated, and we found ourselves enjoying our time together. Soon we were dancing the dance of war, parrying and retreating respectively. We laughed at Paris when he tripped over a rock and nearly impaled himself with the wooden sword. The prince was embarrassed at first, but with our contagious laughter he couldn't hide his smile any longer.

The servants who brought us refreshment were happy and willing; I shared my drink with the two young women. We didn't see Hector for the rest of the day, and I was fine with that. I didn't need another admirer or challenger. It was apparent that he was developing mixed feelings for Helen. Lilith wasn't sure what to do about that. Paris was enough to deal with. *Aegeus was right; beauty was a blessing and a curse.*

The day soon became night. Paris unwillingly left me at my bedroom door and crossed to his. "If you are in need of company, I'm a door away," the mischievous prince declared.

I smiled sweetly and responded, "Thank you. I will keep that in mind." I closed my door and watched as his sweet face disappeared.

The guilt crawled ruthlessly beneath my skin. What was I doing? I didn't love Paris, yet I led him to believe differently, and just so I could stay here and exploit his family's power. *But maybe there was more to it.*

"Can I come in?" a tinkling voice asked through the wooden entry.

I cracked the door to find Cassandra waiting anxiously. I let her in immediately and waited for her to speak. "I was wondering if you needed someone to talk to." Cassandra looked down at her bare feet, her nightgown not quite covering them. She was nervous. What a drastic change from the day before when she criticized me for not trying hard enough.

Knowingly, I responded, "Yes, that would be nice." I quickly changed into my given nightgown.

"Where did you get this? You didn't come with any belongings." Cassandra held the red tunic in her grasp. She was a very observant girl.

"I made it."

"How?" she questioned suspiciously.

I knew I shouldn't have, but I trusted Cassandra. I could feel a kinship growing. Also, she knew all my other secrets. Waiting for my answer, I altered the woolen gown I donned into a thin silken material. The nights were hot here, and I needed something lighter to wear anyway, especially if the princes were going to barge into my room any time they pleased.

The child stroked the energy that flowed around my newly altered gown. She watched as the spirit moved and shaped to my will. "Amazing," she said in awe.

"I have only just discovered that I can do this," I explained excitedly. It was a relief to talk to someone about my powers. I hadn't been able

to share anything about them before. I hadn't wanted to. I regretted not sharing moments like this with my own daughters. *Stop.* No regrets. Only moving forward.

But Cassandra saw the sadness shadow my face. "What's wrong?"

And I told her. Everything. I shouldn't have. It was unwise. But it was wonderful. We spent the night sharing everything we could about our lives and the magic that flowed through us. Cassandra may have been ten years of age, but she was wise and understanding beyond her years. *She was a lot like Naavah.* The princess listened and grieved with me as I told her about my past.

I felt guilty for burdening her at such a young age, but I needed someone to talk to. The only one was Lucifer, and he was no longer an option. It turned out she needed someone to confide in, too. Her family didn't know the extent of her sight. They only knew what she told them: that she could see if someone could be trusted. The people of this time weren't ready to hear anything more than that, and I agreed. The human race was too young. Too unpredictable. There was no way to anticipate how they would respond to the unseen magic surrounding them. At least her family was open enough to trust what she shared. That would have to be enough. Our companionship would have to be enough to get us through.

Once Cassandra heard my story, she understood. She supported my mission, but I suspected she wasn't sharing everything with me. Though I didn't push her further than she allowed. Our budding friendship wasn't worth the risk.

Dawn came all too soon. We had yet to rest, but the exhaustion was a necessary sacrifice. Finally, a sacrifice I didn't immediately regret.

Bells chimed aggressively in the distance. "What is that?" I questioned.

Panicked, Cassandra leapt from her spot on the bed and ran out the doorway. "Follow me!"

Guards and servants passed us in a blur as we ran down the hallway toward the throne room. Cassandra led me to an adjoining room behind the grand chair. I hadn't noticed it yesterday. The room was made to look like part of the stone wall. The small child pushed to slide the door open, and, seeing her struggle, I offered my own strength. I nudged the door slightly and it flew into its placement in the wall.

The King and Hector were already in the hidden room. Paris joined us seconds after we entered, sliding the stone door closed.

"Helen! You weren't in your room. You worried me," Paris said.

"Concentrate on the matter at hand. We are under attack," Hector scolded his brother. Hector and Priam were huddled over a table. A map covered the surface, as well as movable pieces. It looked a lot like Petteia.

"Attack?" I questioned.

Hector's calming gaze moved to me. "Yes. It seems Menelaus didn't believe me after all. He knows Paris stole you. How? I don't know. But he's brought the entire force of Greece with him."

Priam interjected, "It couldn't be about Helen. It isn't possible to organize an attack of this size in just a couple of days."

Hector speculated, "Yes, I agree, despite what his messenger said. This couldn't be only about her."

Interceding, I offered, "Agamemnon's goal was to attack you eventually. Perhaps he had his fellow rulers at the ready, awaiting his orders. But now that he's gone, that falls to Menelaus."

Confused, Priam asked, "Then why did he offer peace if those were his intentions?"

"I don't know the specifics, but he would have found a way to betray you. He was a ghastly, power-hungry man, and the world is better now that he is gone," I spat.

Cassandra took my hand knowingly, but she kept silent. I knew the child would keep my secret. The three Trojan men locked their eyes

on our clasped hands. I wasn't surprised by their shock. Cassandra rarely spoke to anyone outside her family, let alone trusted a stranger, mostly due to her sight.

"Whatever the reason, we need to negotiate an armistice," Hector explained.

My anger and fear guiding me, I volunteered, "Let me go. Menelaus wants me. He will leave if I go to him."

"No!" Hector and Paris exclaimed.

Priam added, "That is very brave of you, but most likely your escape is merely an excuse to attack. Like you said, they wanted war. You are just the means to initiate it."

I understood what the kind king meant, but if this was my doing, I was going to fix it. I came here to make things better, not worse. "Still, it is worth trying. Perhaps I can persuade him to at least stop and speak with you," I implored.

"Out of the question," Paris said. "It's not worth losing you."

Touched by his concern for me, I continued, "Paris, your kingdom is worth much more than a woman you only just met. You know that." The young prince looked away stubbornly.

"It is, but Menelaus is going to attack whether you're in his grasp or not. So you might as well stay with us," Hector said. Priam agreed.

Seeing their decision was final, I conceded and left the small room. Advisors and war leaders barreled through the opening after I departed.

Cassandra followed close behind me. "So we're going, right?" Cassandra questioned perceptively.

"I'm going. You are staying here where it is safe." I found my way to the weapons room. The overpowering scent of metal was easy to follow.

The small girl, finally catching up to me, argued, "You need me. You can't know if Menelaus is lying. You also need a chaperone."

"I can handle Menelaus just fine. Why would I need a chaperone?"

I questioned distractedly. I tested several different instruments. Weight wasn't an issue, but I still wanted one that felt natural. The blunt wooden sword we practiced with the day before wasn't what I had in mind.

I found it then, behind the shelving: a double-edged, wide-blade sword. The old weapon measured an additional hand length past my arm. The blade was short for a sword, but it was thick and strong, unique compared to the others. The weapon had been created with a different alloy, most likely something one of the warriors discovered on their travels, or it had been taken from the body of an enemy. The sword was set aside to collect dust; I wiped the thick layer away. The swirling patterns in the blade were beautiful, and they gleamed in the light. The black leather that encased the hilt was soft in my palm. I felt a strong connection to the forgotten weapon.

Of course, a weapon was unnecessary, but at my side the sword would demonstrate strength. That's what I needed with Menelaus. I wouldn't submit to him any longer. He had his chance to prove himself, and the new King of Greece had failed.

"Agamemnon," Cassandra said to answer my question.

"What about him?" I asked, confused.

"You don't want a repeat of what happened." Cassandra was a very blunt and honest person. I'd grown to appreciate that about her. But it still annoyed me.

"Are you saying he deserved to live? That Menelaus does?" I hadn't had a plan when I offered to go speak with Menelaus, but it definitely wasn't going to end with me leaving with him. I wiped away the dust and old blood from the ebony sheath that partnered with my newfound sword.

"I'm saying it doesn't matter. There will always be someone else to succeed them. There will always be someone worse." Cassandra was really testing my temper, and she could see it in my spirit as it flailed restlessly.

"How could it not matter? Ridding the Earth of them could only help

things. Remove the dark and the light will shine," I explained. I changed my silk nightgown into thick black clothes that wove around my form snugly, my legs wrapped securely in their individual shells. I donned the leather armor sorted next to the weapons. There was only one set left; the rest of Troy's warriors were already dying in them outside the city's wall.

I attached the Trojan's crimson cloak around the ensemble and strapped my new sword at my side. The weapon's sheath shone now that the leather was clean, and the surface's harsh designs mesmerized me. I looked the part of a warrior. Now I had to act like one.

"But what is light without dark?" Cassandra questioned.

Exasperated, I said, "Enough of your riddles, Cassandra. What do you want to say?"

"I am trying to say that you will do the right thing when the time comes."

I paused and stared at the small girl. *What did this child expect of me?*

"I will try. But you are still not coming with me," I said firmly. Without another word I sprinted out of the large abode toward the wall. I didn't waste time with appearances. I blazed past anyone who would have tried to stop me. If they saw anything, it would have been a blur of red and gold, a gust of wind that blew sand in their faces.

Reaching the shoreline, it was easy to spot Menelaus's ship, despite the vast number that floated in the water. His was the biggest and shiniest and, of course, it sat behind the rest. I leapt into the angry water, swimming beneath the waves toward the King of Greece and hopefully, Troy's salvation.

I pulled myself onto the king's ship, landing dripping wet on the deck. The wind gusted violently and dried me quickly. I realized then that I had forgotten to tame my golden hair. It blew sporadically in the wind. There was suddenly a spear pointed at my face. Greek men surrounded me. Some I recognized—Menelaus's personal guard. They recognized Helen, as well, and led me straight to the coward.

"How did you get on board?" the king demanded.

"Doesn't matter. The only thing that does is that you retreat and leave these good people alone." There was no waver in my voice. I stood tall and confident against this man who strove to dominate me.

"Woman, you forget your place." Menelaus raised his arm to swipe at me, but stopped when I drew my sword and placed it against his neck. It had taken me only a blink of an eye to do so. His hand lowered slowly to his side. Spears pressed against me, but there was no blood to be drawn. The men noticed this but said nothing, giving only nervous glances to one another. Menelaus was oblivious as usual.

"Remove your army from this place or lose your head," I threatened. Spears pressed farther into me, but I couldn't feel them. I was concentrating on the king's reaction.

Cautious but still arrogant, the king said, "Put away the weapon, girl. It does not belong in the hands of someone so weak."

Pride drove me to say, "Is that so? I don't think your brother would agree." I knew it was a risky strategy, but Menelaus was a coward. The king would run if he knew I was a threat, but the sword against his throat wasn't enough for him.

The king's eyes widened with fury. "You? How dare you! You are nothing but a weak, pitiful girl. You're lying!"

"Was that dungeon connected to your brother's room a lie, as well? Were the women he tortured a lie?" Surprise, then awareness, crossed his face. "You did know then," I said.

How had my perception of him been so wrong? He was as much of a monster as his brother.

"Yes, I knew," Menelaus leered.

"You did it together, didn't you?" I questioned. I had been naïve. Why did I not hear the women screaming in the night? Why had I ignored the scent of blood? I looked down at the golden trinkets that adorned

his bloody neck. A gold key hung there. I had failed to notice it before; it blended with the rest of the jewelry.

Menelaus didn't respond or acknowledge my words; his guards were near enough to hear.

"It doesn't matter. I am here to stop you from attacking. If you don't listen to words, you will have to listen to my sword," I threatened. Menelaus waved his guards away. The spear ends were removed from my sides. Red sand blew in the wind, and the injuries healed instantly. "Tell them to leave. Now." The king waved again, and the guards dispersed. Once gone, I pressed the sharp end harder against his throat. Blood trickled down his thick neck.

"You aren't playing fair, are you?" King Perversion observed. Not only were his dark desires perverted, but his contorted sense of leadership. Leaders were not meant to be so cruel. King Menelaus was never meant to be at all.

"This isn't a game. There are no rules to follow," I said. I wasn't sure what my plan was. My initial instinct was to remove him from existence, but something held me back.

"True, but if our games taught you anything it should be that the game board can be reset, no matter the winner. Both sides will regroup, and there will be yet another king to wage war." Cassandra's words were clear to me then. They were even clear to Menelaus, a poor strategist and even poorer human being. I had thought his losses were due to his lack of strength, his unwillingness to part with his pieces. But in fact, he had been hoarding them to use at a later date, waiting for his brother to make a mistake.

No matter the lives sacrificed, there would always be another to fight. Both sides would reset at the end of the day. The light and the dark. A constant, unending battle for dominance. Menelaus was simply doing his part in the war. "Why are you attacking? How did you know I was here?" I

questioned. I needed time to figure out what to do. Cassandra's words had become my conscience, and her voice refused to be quieted.

"Achilles saw you leaving with that boy during the commotion. That was your plan all along, wasn't it? Do your new friends know what you are capable of?" the king questioned mockingly. That explained it then. Lucifer was a spiteful man. He was going to ruin any progress I made with these hybrids, and all because I didn't love him enough. My internal flame lit and thoroughly destroyed anything of Lucifer that had regrown in my hollowed chest.

Seeing that I wasn't going to provide him an answer, he continued, "I cannot show weakness. The Trojans stole my property and I am here to collect it." The king's spirit fought against the winds. There was a darkness there I hadn't noticed before. It wasn't nearly the same as his brother's blackness, but the cloud of ink was there. In his core.

"I am not your property, and I was not stolen. I left because of your monstrosities." The blood flowed freely down the ruler's neck and stained the wooden deck.

"You speak to me of monstrosities? You are no different from me or my brother," Menelaus laughed. The king regretted that when he began to choke on the blade.

"I am nothing like you. The world is better without Agamemnon in it, and it will be better without you." I pulled him close to me by the collar of his cloak, the sword still pressing into his esophagus.

Menelaus gurgled, "Killing is killing, my lovely Helen. It doesn't matter the reason behind it." He may have been a coward, but his pride overpowered his instinct to beg. A true king indeed.

Beyond the howl of the wind and Menelaus's wheezing, I heard a stone drop to the wooden deck. I looked to my right to find a table, and on that table was my game board, stones in mid-battle. The king fought past the pain of the blade enough to notice where my eyes stared. "Fancy

a game, darling? You had so much fun the last time we played. It was very kind of you to let me win; makes my heart swell with joy, knowing that you care so much." The demented king let out a breathy laugh. I stopped myself from gasping. "Too bad my brother isn't here to play with us. But perhaps this battle is too intimate to include a third." The king choked on his words. Blood was flowing more quickly out of his neck now. I could only stare in horror as he said his next words. "Agamemnon never did like sharing. I suppose I should thank you. I can keep the toys all to myself now." I realized then that Agamemnon had been the force that made him cower, not death.

This had been a mistake. The king wasn't willing to leave even with his life on the line, and he wouldn't leave if I gave myself up. The Trojans had been right. If anything, I only fanned the flames of his wrath. His pride was going to be the death of him and many others, as it was his brother's. But not now. Another would only take his place. I had observed the other Greek kings. They were all the same: prideful and power-hungry. They only went along with the treaty because Agamemnon had ordered them to. I twisted the blade, and Menelaus's blood splattered against its gleaming patterns.

Damn Lucifer. This wouldn't be happening if it wasn't for him. He once called me spiteful because I fed him poisoned mushrooms, but he had mastered the quality since then. Our love had grown misshapen and monstrous. It poisoned us both with its existence. There wasn't anything I could do but swallow my pride and leave. I would assist the Trojans in whatever way I could. This war had been set in motion because of me. It would end with me.

I removed the blade from Menelaus's throat. He collapsed to the ground, clasping his blood-coated gullet. I dove back into the salty water and made my way to shore. Bodies were scattered along the beach. Both sides had lost men, but the Trojans had suffered the most. As I looked

closer, I recognized the pattern displayed before me. Several of Troy's men had been cut down with godly force.

I followed the trail of mutilated bodies. They led to a golden temple that dwelled outside the city's wall. It was different from the other homes. The entrance held no door. A statue of a man stood at its side, welcoming visitors. A sun was engraved on his chest. His features were beautiful and youthful. The man held no weapon. This was a place of peace.

I trailed my hands down the walls as I entered. Golden paint peeled to reveal the stone underneath. My nostrils flared at the scent of sunflowers and warmth. The smell of the sun was fitting. It filled the halls, despite the raging storm outside. One would think the Trojans' god, Apollo, had come to protect them. But it was an entirely different god, one without mercy or fear. One who relished the thought of war.

"Helen."

I moved my gaze from the edible offerings left for the sun god and locked eyes with a green-eyed warrior. The Greek demigod was leaning against one of the golden pillars, completely at ease. "Achilles. What are you doing here?" We didn't even want to acknowledge each other's names aloud anymore.

"Doing what I do best. Killing. If you had stayed around long enough, you would have known that." Lucifer grinned that awful, arrogant grin. He wore no armor, and the blood of his children coated his golden skin.

Unperturbed, I questioned, "Why did you tell Menelaus where I was?"

Baffled, he responded, "Why do you think? You betrayed me yet again, and then ran off with another. Again." Lucifer's nonchalant demeanor was no more.

Angered, I argued, "I never betrayed you. I was honest with you. You were the one who couldn't handle it, and still can't it seems." Maintaining self-control with Menelaus was difficult, but with Lucifer it was unbearable. "And I didn't run off with anyone. Paris was simply a way out.

Troy is a wonderful place to begin my work—the work that you deny is your responsibility."

"I will not explain myself further to you. If you don't see it, you never will." Lucifer's greying spirit twitched uncomfortably. His words hit home. Cassandra had said something similar only a short time ago. *What was I not seeing?*

"No, Lucifer, you are the blind one." It hurt to say his name. "This chaos isn't all my fault. You have a claim to it, too." Why couldn't he just leave me be? I was doing my best to fix our mistakes, and he tortured me because of it.

Lucifer just laughed. About to lunge at him, I heard light footsteps entering the temple. Lucifer saw my panic and sped toward the noise. A girl screamed.

"Let Cassandra go!" I raced toward the struggle, but Lucifer had a tight grip around the child's throat.

"Why should I?" Lucifer's deadened eyes taunted me.

"Look at her. She is just a child." Lucifer looked down at her then. I was sure he intended on ending her life, but he lessened his grip. "Please, don't be the monster I know you are," I whispered. Lucifer's body went rigid. He saw something in Cassandra that I didn't. The noise of the storm outside lessened.

Moving his pained stare back to me, he warned, "Let this be the last thing I do for you, my love. Don't expect me to do it again." The immortal man before me released the girl's neck and departed in a blur of gold. His familiar green gaze was the last thing I saw before he disappeared into the now sunlit day.

Forcing myself out of my shocked stupor, I ran to Cassandra. I held her in my embrace, wishing she could stay there forever. Inspecting her throat, I asked, "Are you in much pain?"

The child shook her head. A tear slid down her cheek. It wasn't the

pain that bothered her, it was the fear of death. She was wise well beyond her years, but she was still just a little girl.

"He can't hurt you now," I said.

Cassandra didn't say a word on the way back home. She rubbed her throat distractedly. Lucifer had frightened her, but I suspected there was something else to it. I did my best to console her, but she just stared off in the distance, ignoring me. *Stubborn child.* Cassandra sought me out despite my instructions not to, in spite of the danger. But regardless of my irritation, I knew she was someone I could count on.

Defeated in my task, I turned to my own turmoil. Menelaus lived and was angrier than before. His pride ruled him and longed to not only claim me, but Troy as well. I had only freed him of the careful control of his brother and turned his greatest warrior against me. And my plan to gain the Trojans' trust had been too easy. I worried for their safety as Cassandra did. The best I could do for the Trojans now was devote myself to them. Because, just as the child predicted when she first saw me, I had brought death to the City of Troy.

XXII
Trying Harder

Upon command the snuffed flame
will relight.
-A

1184 BCE

Blood coated my armor. My golden hair had fallen from its tight braid. My breathing was ragged, but it wasn't from exhaustion. It was from excitement. I leapt gracefully between foes, dancing in the blood that I spilled. I ran the tip of my sword across throats and plunged my weapon hilt deep into hearts. I was swift and deadly. Yet I still held myself back, unable to unleash my true potential.

The war between Troy and Greece waged on, ten years long. But it was nothing but a sliver of my lifetime. I could wait. I would win. Achilles fought tirelessly against me and my warriors, but it wasn't enough.

My current fight brought me into the midst of the horde of warriors. It became difficult to know which were friend or foe. Spears and blades clanged together; the deep red colors of our people were lost to the black of Greece. I was always able to regain enough self-control to stop my blade from harming red, but most didn't have such discipline, and I couldn't blame them. Battle was chaotic. There was no order once enemies met. The careful planning of kings and leaders was lost. The need to survive was all

that remained. The guaranteed setting of the sun was the only thing that controlled their animalistic instincts.

My sword relieved my opponent of his head. I watched as the man's brown hair fell to the ground. It shone in the light of the sun's rays, catching the golden hues in its soft texture. I didn't look at his face, just the blood that spattered across my eyes. The slice was quick and clean; there was no time for the departed to feel the pain of it. Though, in the heat of battle, I couldn't make myself care if they did or not.

A spear swiped right where the warrior's head was not a moment before, and its swing continued on to me. I bent backward, my feet the only thing balancing me as the sharpened end of the spear passed above. The weapon grazed the hair that had failed to stay tamed in my braid. As I watched the delicate, blood-soaked waves detach from their home, I saw a flash of green eyes.

Achilles.

The man I had come to loathe didn't even acknowledge my presence or the fact that he had nearly killed me. I didn't take the time to stop and chastise him for it. This was war. Stop moving and you died. With Lucifer near, this was true even for me.

I expected King Menelaus to be my priority during this war. But I was wrong. Achilles was the one who kept this war alive: him and his specially trained men. Granted, his men were only for show. They distracted the others from his unnatural talent for killing. But I knew better.

Ignoring my ancient mate, I cut down man after man. Kill after kill. My primal instincts took over, and I felt nothing but the kill and the spirits that joined mine. The scent of blood and chaos powered me. I wondered if this was what the natural animals felt. If the lioness felt thrill and exhilaration during her hunt, felt the life drain from the antelope's neck as she bit her sharp fangs into its soft fur. If only I could have held on to that experience. If only I could have felt that all the time. But night would always

come, and the army would reset in preparation for the coming morning.

The night gave me ample time to reflect on the day's murders. To remember every stab. Every slice. Every rip of flesh. Every soul that entered my body and would stay for the remainder of my days. I watched the smoke from the funeral pyres beyond the wall rise and disappear into the sky.

Necessary sacrifices. I had to keep trying.

I could have ended all this. I sincerely believed that Troy was the best hope for this world. If we could win, it would show the neighboring lands how powerful we really were. No one would challenge us. We would be free to shape the world in our image: an image of peace and equality.

Over the course of the war I considered abusing my unnatural abilities. The magic that flowed through me was more than strong enough to burn all the Greek ships to ashes. But my magic couldn't predict what Lucifer would do. If I ended the war swiftly, then Lucifer could retaliate. The possibility that he would burn Troy to the ground or flood the great city in spite of my actions was too great. I had to fight fair or else everything would be lost. *I couldn't lose another family.*

The day's battle done, I looked to the stars above. The moon was a small slice of light. The grass I sat upon was wet with dew, and the scent was refreshing. The familiar smell of earth breathed life back into me. I attempted to listen to the sounds of the natural world, but they grew quieter with each passing day, as if I was losing the ability to hear it. All I could hear now were the screams of the souls I had taken.

"There you are. I've been looking everywhere." Hector approached me from behind, sat, and wrapped his arms around my waist. His breath blew against my ear as he settled his head on my shoulder.

"Sorry. I was resting for a moment before tending to the injured." My knowledge of medicinal herbs had been useful in this war. I only learned more as time went on. Guilt still refused to allow unnatural healing.

"There are more than enough people to help. Rest tonight. It's not

your responsibility to care for everyone," Hector reassured. But in fact, it was my responsibility. *If not mine, then whose?*

I didn't respond to his caring words. I just allowed him to hold me. It felt nice, the contact. Hector was a strong and determined leader, and he was also a caring and compassionate man. Those reasons allowed me to surrender myself to him. He was my only reprieve in this war. I had promised Adam I would try to find happiness. I would take it where I could find it.

"You haven't washed yourself of today's battle. Let's go to my chambers. I have a hot bath ready for you," Hector said. The offer was meant to be kind, but I could hear the hidden meaning behind his words. Still, I nodded, grateful for his offer. A sliver of happiness was better than none at all, much like the waning crescent that shared its light with us.

Once we reached Hector's chambers, he proceeded to relieve me of my soiled armor. My faithful weapon was coated in dried blood and begged to be cleansed of her deeds. The ruby that decorated the hilt glinted in the light, and I was reminded once again of my purpose. The stench of death still wafted from the gemstone, the memory of Agamemnon forever taunting me. I had named my sword Sacrifice, since I burdened the metallic weapon with the curse of my ambitions. It was only fair that she be treated with respect and acknowledgment, though my fellow warriors thought me odd because of it.

Tossing my warrior's ensemble aside, the new king of Troy led me to the steaming water he promised. The kindness he shared with me was appreciated. He cleansed me of the blood and earth that covered me. Hector proceeded to rub my supposedly sore and tired muscles despite my protests. I let him, though there was no blood flow to stimulate. My muscles were and always would be battle-ready. The tiredness was spiritual.

Hector raised me from the tub, firmly secured in his arms. The water dripped from my bare form down to the cold ground as he walked to the bed. My long golden hair tangled in his grip. The king laid me upon his soft

sheets, not bothered by how moist I made his bedding. He relieved himself of his own clothes and climbed atop me. The water from my bath made our movements slick and all the more enjoyable. My mind was numbed by the embrace; that was all I asked for. I was no longer capable of love, and Hector was a lovely distraction. The king pulled my hair back roughly, forcing my vulnerable neck to be caressed by his wandering lips.

This war had forced many things to change. The kind man who ruled this kingdom before Hector, King Priam, had lost his life one year into the war. Unknown to us, he had snuck into the enemy's camp to beg for mercy. He offered ransom to King Menelaus in exchange for his people's lives, but he did not know the Greek king like I did.

I watched as Achilles dropped the Trojan king's corpse at our front gates. He didn't make eye contact with me as he passed, but his body had tensed from our close proximity. He knew the red fire flared around me, and he expected me to attack because of it. But he didn't deserve the pleasure of my offered redemption. The memory of the king's pyre burning bright in the starry night continued to remind me that I had such self-control.

Hector rolled us across the bed so I straddled him. I appreciated the temporary power it gave me. My damp blonde strands hung loose and clung to both of us. Hector wrapped the locks gently around his hands, pulling me down to him.

A king and father was lost to us, but a change in the kingdom occurred because of it. For as kind as Priam had been, he was trapped by his old traditions. I now led Troy's army, Paris and Cassandra as my second and third in command. Women were allowed to train and fight alongside the men if they chose. Some continued to be healers and caretakers, but at least the option was now there. The offer would have been extended to the men if it had not been for lack of warriors. We couldn't afford to lose more than we already did daily.

Cassandra had chosen the warrior's path, alongside me. The past ten

years had transformed her into a deadly fighter, as well as a wise counselor. The ten-year-old girl I had first met was no more. She was plagued by the trials of war, though she never revealed it. Cassandra chose to suffer in silence, a role model for her fellow warriors.

I called out in pleasure as my hips forced Hector deep inside of me.

Paris was a different story. He proved himself to be useful in combat and strategy, but he wasn't meant for the carnage that took place daily. His soul was too gentle, too soft. His position as second in command was given merely out of respect. The fact that I was chosen to lead the army instead of the next in line to the kingdom was hard for him to accept, but both he and Cassandra knew it was the right choice. If it wasn't for me, Troy would have already been lost.

I closed my eyes and tried to concentrate on the pleasure of the act rather than the betrayal. Hector's hands guided me when I unknowingly slowed my rhythm.

Paris's weak state of mind was the reason Hector and I chose not to tell him about our relationship; he still believed me to be his betrothed. Not that there was much to tell on my behalf, but Hector viewed our relations differently. If it wasn't for the war, he would have asked me to be his beloved queen. That was never going to happen.

I rolled off of Hector and lay in his bed, relaxed and content. I realized then how little time I spent in my own bedchamber. I was either resting in the camp or the king's bed.

The tranquil feeling only lasted a moment before he said, "You seem distracted."

I was always distracted. Didn't he know that? "Just thinking about Paris. He must be in a dark place right now, and I don't know how to help him," I answered truthfully.

Irritated, Hector replied, "My brother is a grown man. He isn't the only one struggling through this dark time."

Seeing that Hector was upset, I asked, "What's wrong?"

Hector rolled off the bed and dawned his white chiton. "We just made love, and you are thinking of my brother. Don't you realize how that can hurt a man's pride?"

Annoyed myself, I said, "Pride is nothing but a weakness. You must be confident enough in your abilities to know you satisfy me greatly, despite my conversation topics."

"Is that all I do for you? Satisfy your lustful needs? Good to know my place in your heart," Hector growled.

Hector's tenacious tendencies irritated me. If he didn't realize my intentions before, that was his fault. He had let his imagination make us into something we weren't. I had never said I loved him or wanted to be with him. If he was just now realizing this, I questioned the love he claimed for me. If the king paid more attention to what I said instead of my body, this wouldn't have been an issue. "I have never claimed anything more. Goodnight," I said bluntly. I grabbed my battle-stained clothes and sword and headed in the direction of my own room, completely unashamed of my bare appearance. Most likely everyone would be asleep in the king's abode anyway.

Reaching my door, I stopped to listen to the heartbeat within.

I entered begrudgingly. "Cassandra, what are you doing in here?" My patience had run thin. Today's losses, the guilt over Paris, and Hector's pettiness were enough.

Taking in my appearance, she asked, "Have a nice visit?"

"Not really," I grunted.

The young woman sat at the foot of my bed, twirling one of her throwing knives. She still wore her battle armor, though it had been cleaned and polished. "Well, maybe it's for the best. Paris doesn't need to catch you sneaking around with his brother, does he?" Cassandra had made her opinion very clear to me when she found out five years prior. She had grown into a beauty like her mother and had become wiser than anyone

I had ever encountered, maybe even Naavah. The princess's advice was something to follow, and it infuriated me that her guidance was against my wishes. Because I knew she was right.

I could have used Paris as my "distraction," but he was too vulnerable and too attached to me to have any kind of physical relations. The pending separation would have crushed him if I used him in such a way. But the longer time went on, the more I knew it wouldn't matter. I would end up crushing both brothers' hearts regardless of my forethought. The young prophetess's words went unheeded for too long, and it was now too late for me to change anything.

"Perhaps," I said.

Surprised, she said, "Oh, have you decided to end things then?" The young woman's armor made a sharp noise as she shifted.

"It needs to happen. Your king has grown too attached, and the jealous pettiness is only going to push him and Paris further apart. He should be concentrating on caring for his brother, not fighting against him." The words I said were true, but still I hated saying them. Did I not deserve happiness in whatever form it came to me? But alas, the well-being of others outweighed my own. Cassandra was the one who reminded me of this. *Damn magic.* I hated that Lucifer's essence coursed through her. He tormented me even in his absence with the foresight of his wise descendant.

"That is very wise of you," Cassandra mocked.

I laughed sharply. She mimicked the words I teased her with every time I grew tired of her relentless morality. Now I knew how Lucifer felt in our early years. But instead of pushing her away, as he did to me, I embraced her. I was happy that I could call her a friend. I'd had so few in my life.

I dressed in my nightwear and sat across from her on the ground. I willed a fire to take flame in the pit cornered in the small room. The night air chilled the home. I had pleaded to anyone or anything that would listen for a chance at a real home. But I knew in my metaphorical heart that this

was not the place. The relationships I built here had shaped me and guided me in this new developed world, but I could feel my time in Troy was coming to a close. Cassandra could feel it, too.

"Oh, Lilith. I don't blame you for anything that happens to my family. Just be satisfied in the knowledge that you tried," Cassandra said. The princess breathed out a tired sigh. "The fates have other plans for us." She always attempted to guide me in the direction she thought best, but she never judged me. That was a very unique characteristic for her race, and something I cherished.

"What happened to 'try harder'?" I questioned jokingly. But rather than laugh at the first few words she had spoken to me, she became unreadable. The princess's expression was neutral, and her spirit revealed nothing. Despite her attempts to teach me how to read the inner workings of people's souls, I couldn't master it. I would catch glimpses, but nothing permanent would arise. I would have to live with what I could see: actions and consequences of those around me. In a way, I was no better off than the hybrids.

After moments of silence, Cassandra spoke, "That too." She rose to depart for her own bedchamber, her dark curls bouncing as she walked. "Get some rest. The sun rises early." Upon her leave I heard the slow and sad melody of a song being sung by the Trojans beyond the wall. The fire crackled with their deep voices, and the few women that gathered there added a tinkling effect, like wind chimes against a harsh storm.

The Gods rest on the mountain
Do they look down from the peak?
The Gods rest in the clouds
Do they look down to their children?

The Gods made us weak
So we could not test their strength
Now we are left to battle demons
Demons that force our cries
But there is no one to listen
Besides those who left us weak

The Gods rest on the mountain
Do they look down from the peak?
The Gods rest in the clouds
Do they look down to their children?

Unsettled by Cassandra's behavior and the song the Trojans voiced over their fires, I lay in bed awake until the sun rose over the water's horizon. I bathed my battle wear and polished and sharpened Sacrifice. Ready for the day's battle, I strode out into the sunlight. The words Cassandra spoke years ago resonated in my soul, inspiring me. *Try harder.*

The camp outside the wall was buzzing with activity. I could hear the sharpening of swords, the clanking of wood against wood as the spears were piled together. My front line camped outside the city's wall. The warriors rotated, so everyone had a turn sleeping in their own bed at one point or another, but my army was at the ready at all times of the day and night. We had to be. The remainder of my men were stationed at the wall's peak with arrows, much like Apollo himself, waiting for the ones who slipped past the front line. In all ten years, the Greeks had not made it past my second line. None had made it past the wall.

I saw movement in the distant trees. A horse grazed on the greenery. I had set most of the horses free so my army wouldn't be able to use them to fight—the Greeks' horses as well. Every time they recaptured them the

creatures would be set free again. This was a continual task I had. It wasn't right for the horses to die for us. It wasn't their war. The grazing horse peeked through the dense brush in my direction. It still unnerved me how long I'd been frozen. The ivory horns that adorned the animal's forehead were no more.

The Greek ships floated in the water, a constant reminder of the war-filled lives we led. Achilles camped with Menelaus's army on the beach, enough distance away that the hybrids couldn't see, but close enough that I could spot Achilles sharpening his sword or mending his spear. Sometimes it looked as if he saw me, too.

I knew it would have been easy enough for Lucifer to break through and kill everyone in his path, but he was abiding by the same rules I was, though not for the same reasons. He didn't care for his people like I cared for mine. Lucifer wanted to torture me slowly, making me watch as those I commanded died, day after day. He didn't realize I had seen worse. I had watched my children die one by one due to their age and ailments. I had seen the corpses of my descendants after he hunted them down and slayed them, all because of his petty vindictiveness toward me. And here we were again. But this time, I wasn't going to let him win. I was going to fight.

"Helen," a gravelly voice said behind me.

The water lapping at my feet, I turned from my view of the sea to find the youngest prince staring at me. His once rebellious stormy eyes were now clouded with what they had seen—death and more death. Paris wasn't handling the war well. He was too thin, and his once shiny hair had lost its luster. Grey hairs were starting to show on his temples. I wished then, as I had countless times, that I could have aged, but not even my magic allowed me to take the form of anything older than what my true form displayed. Life continued to be cruel.

"Paris." I offered my hand, and he took it graciously. It unnerved me how happy my touch made him. The guilt that crawled beneath my skin returned with every encounter. I had pledged my love for this man, only to

use him for his status. And I repaid him with war, speaking of the promise of tomorrow. The promises I made him seemed to keep him afloat, but that raft was slowly sinking. The prince knew deep down that I didn't love him and would leave once the chaos was concluded. But he held on to those promises and continued to be a defender to his people.

"Beautiful day," Paris said. The prince gripped my hand tighter.

"Yes it is." These moments before the battle began were all we had. Every morning we would look out at the sea, no matter the weather, mentally preparing for what was to come. Paris, Cassandra, and I would lead our men to their deaths, kill as many Greeks as we could, come back, and sleep. Repeat. Hector, as the ruler, would remain behind the walls. Safe. But I knew Hector wished to battle alongside us; it took the convincing of his siblings and the council to keep him at bay. Troy needed its leader alive. Priam had taught us that much.

Despite the code of honor that warriors and leaders alike followed, I didn't trust that the Greeks would keep to it. They had followed it so far. There were no surprise tactics and we didn't fight at night, but this war had gone on for too long. It was time someone ended it, code or not.

"Helen, you know I love you, right?" Paris stated. I stared into his disturbed eyes and saw the desperation there.

"Of course I do," I replied. It seemed Cassandra and I weren't the only ones who felt the end nearing. Soon this war would be over. The Greeks would be defeated, and I would leave. Lucifer would have no motivation to stay and hurt them further if I left, and they would have settled the war amongst themselves.

"Good." He moved his gaze back to the rising sun.

"You know I love you too," I said. The prince nodded his head once, clinging to the lie.

We made our way to the front line. Cassandra was waiting for us. "It's about time," she said knowingly.

We took up our arms, and our warriors did the same. I could see the approaching army before us. We needed to move. The farther away from the wall, the better it would be. Raising my sword high above my head, I shouted, "For peace!"

My army echoed the words as we ran forward, charging toward deadly swords and protruding spears, weapons that would end several of the lives that followed me. The necessary sacrifices I had made were growing in number, but necessary they were.

XXIII
Honor

The warriors perish. The kings watch as they expire, knowing they do so because of the words they uttered unto their empire.
-A

The day was victorious for the Trojans. We obliterated the Greeks' numbers in only a few hours. The people of Troy were joyous and wished to celebrate the small win. I allowed my army to join their peers and sleep in their own beds for the night. The chance that the Greeks would attack after a loss as great as theirs was slim, but I had rotating guards at all times anyway. I stood watch first, and most likely would remain there the rest of the night. These people deserved to celebrate. Ten long years of war warranted some joy.

"Come to the celebration. Spend time with us before new troubles arise," Cassandra said. She climbed up the rickety ladder to the peak of the wall entrance.

"No, you go ahead. I'm going to stay here a while and relax." Cassandra knew my words were meant to encourage her departure, but she respected my wishes regardless.

"Just remember, we love you. You are a part of our family. You deserve to be happy, too." The wise young woman left me with those words. There were times I felt I could have been part of their family, but my actions spoke otherwise.

I watched the ships in the distance. Their positioning didn't allow anyone at the front entrance to see them, but of course I could. I could always see the threat that lingered outside the city walls, anchored in the seabed.

Suddenly the sails expanded. The crewmen worked to move the great ships. My first instinct told me they were planning another attack, but the massive black sails heaved the boats the opposite direction and were quickly retreating out of sight.

I retrieved one of my men from the festivities and ordered him to keep watch in my absence. I said that the ships were departing, and I was going to explore farther. His rosy cheeks and staggered walk indicated that he had been drinking, but upon my instructions he composed himself and took his place at my previous post. "Do not speak a word of this until I return," I commanded. The man nodded once and looked forward, eager to complete his task. If I was wrong and the Greeks weren't actually leaving, there was no need to excite the people needlessly, only to disappoint them. Their celebration would continue.

I followed the path leading to the enemy's camp. The sand was soaked with the blood of the deceased warriors. I pondered for a moment if my red sand would ever mix with the people's blood, and if it would bring me peace. But I knew what the answer was as long as the humans existed on Earth. I would live. They needed me.

The Greek camps were deserted. They had abandoned their supplies and tents. *Where did they go?* I searched the expanse of the beach as long as the footprints continued. Had the Greeks really gone? Disappeared in the night, ashamed of their defeat? I refused to hope. The likelihood of that happening was slim. Menelaus was too prideful to give up now. Ten years was a long time to wait for surrender.

"They aren't here," a man's deadened voice said to me. Out of the water came Achilles. He dripped with the sea's water. Still, the dried blood from his recent battle clung to him.

Lucifer and I fought the same battles, day after day, but we never engaged one another on purpose. We only observed as the other killed the human warriors who opposed them. It was an unspoken agreement between us. Clearly something had changed. "Where did they go?" I demanded.

"Not far." Lucifer smiled that arrogant grin, except this version revealed how dark he had really become: a monster taken right from the humans' imaginations. It seemed their imaginations weren't fictitious after all.

"What are you doing? We don't fight during the night. Does Menelaus have no honor?" The Greeks had planned an attack, but I didn't know what it was. Where were they? They couldn't attack from their ships.

"I think you know the answer to that," Lucifer said, delighted at my panic.

Do *you* have no honor?" My question surprised him, but he would not be swayed from his mission.

Honor is a human concept," he replied.

"Are we not human?" I questioned ruthlessly.

Lucifer wasn't in the mood to speak, or maybe he just didn't want to speak to me. My honest words ten years ago had destroyed him that much. So much that he loathed the sight of me. So much that he made it his life's purpose to torment me. But I had given him an answer. After so long, he finally had one. Lucifer knew he wasn't enough for me. The light he provided no longer replaced my missing heart. I had to ignite my own flame.

I drew Sacrifice. The metal shone in the light of the moon, and I could feel Agamemnon's ruby as I slid my hand across the hilt. The sliver in the sky provided enough light to see exactly what Lucifer planned to do. Spear in hand, Lucifer lunged at me. Achilles's familiar green irises flashed in the darkness. My ancient mate could see the anger in my crimson spirit. It fought to be released and drove me forward.

Lucifer's golden spirit had become dull and lifeless. The darkened grey encompassed a majority of his life force. *What had I done to him?*

Though we could see one another's spirits, we refused to show our natural faces. It would have been too painful—to love someone for eons, only to be reduced to fighting. It was a tragedy.

Helen and Achilles sparred ferociously. There was no need to hold back. The war had only sharpened our skills and prodded our need for battle. The warriors we fought against daily were easily disposed of, but the opponent we faced now was not. *Whose red sand would fall to the seashore?*

Lucifer wielded his spear gracefully and unforgivingly. The spear had been his weapon of choice since the beginning of us. He had invented it, mastered it, and used it to his advantage. I had only begun fighting, sword or not, ten years prior. I had nothing on Lucifer's millennia of violence, but I had something stronger. I had a reason to keep going, to keep trying.

Lucifer was strong and his blows would cause me great damage, but I was faster. That much hadn't changed. I thought back to our meeting at the waterfall. What would have happened if I had managed to outrun him? If that vine hadn't tripped me?

Our battle quickly moved to the water, and even that couldn't slow us. We swam and stabbed with precision, yet neither could hit their target. I removed the seaweed that tangled my feet just before Lucifer could spear my stomach. Even the predators that patrolled the water in search of fallen warriors swam away in fear. They sensed a greater threat was near.

Hating the feel of the sea, I leapt out of the waves and into the trees that lived across the sand. Even the birds had fled the battleground. I became invisible, still as a panther cornering her prey. Lucifer would have a hard time finding me in the foliage, but he would soon enough. My senses opened, waiting for the chance to strike.

The immortal warrior crept toward the trees where I hid. His eyes scanned for movement. There was none. "Lilith, I hope you are prepared to burn more children, because that's what you're going to be doing in the morning," Lucifer prodded.

I refused to respond to his taunting. I wasn't ready yet.

"I can hear their screams already. Do you hear that?" Lucifer circled around the trees, continuing his search. "Don't you care about them? They need you." His mocking words became reality. I heard the bells in the distance warning the people of Troy of an attack. The people screamed. *How had they managed to get past the wall?* Suddenly a whiff of smoke protruded my nostrils. Burning flesh.

I threw my sword outside the line of trees, away from me. Lucifer responded and lunged toward the sound. That's when I attacked. I leapt from the trees with the grace and stealth of Shamira, aiming for his back. The immortal warrior heard the hiss of the wind and turned in time to defend himself. Our collision threw us across the vast beach and back into the water. Lucifer's spear flew from his hands and buried itself into the sand.

Neither of us with weapons, we thrashed and hit one another with great force. We produced waves that crashed against bulging rocks, and those rocks were soon destroyed. Even the water had come to fear us; the tide was departing. We were tiring for the first time in our lives. The wounds we dealt were deadly, and they weighed on the battle we fought.

I twisted in the water and kicked him in the ribs, feeling the vibrating pop of broken bones in the water. I couldn't pull my leg back fast enough, and he used it to propel me into the sea floor; my spine caved unnaturally. Though in great pain, I was able to move fast enough to catch him before he could lift the neighboring boulder. I swung my elbow across his face as he turned in my direction. Another pop.

Both exhausted, we pulled ourselves onto the beach. The sea cascaded down our forms. I gulped for breath. The salt had dried my mouth, and I wished for fresh water. But I had to finish it. Lucifer ran for his protruding spear. I ran for Lucifer. With all the strength I could muster, I swung my fist at the back of his head, but he had reached his weapon. Achilles twisted to face me as I swung. He pulled the spearhead out of the sand in time to

impale me. My blow was so great we were forced apart, and he landed in the trees across from me. I collapsed onto the bloody sand that clumped beneath my feet.

I knew I had landed my blow. If he wasn't dead, he was asleep for the foreseeable future. A small part of me hoped he wasn't gone. *If he was, then how would I ever find peace of my own?* But perhaps that time was now. I felt the old bone spearhead wedged in me. It was near where my heart would have been, but not close enough. My shoulder was what took the brunt of the damage. I still had a chance to save them.

I removed the spear with great effort and willed my clothes to secure my injury. I had recovered from worse, but this was different. The damage had been done by Lucifer. I stood. I swayed back and forth for a few moments, in sync with the waves that crashed against my feet. I took the spear still grasped in my hand and crushed the wood in my palm. The spear fell to the ground in two halves, useless.

I sauntered over to Lucifer's still form. The face of Achilles was still worn by him, but those green eyes were closed and unable to taunt me. I saw the shallow rising and falling of his chest. The stab wounds and bruised blows from me weren't healing. The red sand beneath his skin was shifting, slowly stitching his form back to its original glory. I hoped he enjoyed healing like the mortals he murdered daily.

A memory flashed behind my eyelids. Despite my painful injuries, I found the strength to move his body. I drug it to the water's edge and willed my strength to be enough. I brought my leg back and shot it forward as hard as I could. Lucifer drifted above the water, as the seabirds did, for a few long moments before crashing into the water far away from the shoreline. Now he would feel the pain of endless drowning, just as he made me experience while my children were murdered. It would keep him away long enough for me to do what I had to.

I sprinted down the seashore. Sacrifice awaited me. She was standing

in the sand, hilt up. The ruby winked against the light of the moon. I ripped her from her grave as I ran. *It's not our time yet.* I looked out to the black sails of the Greek ships. Then those black sails were on fire. I heard the screams of the men who lingered on their decks. Some dove to the safety of the water, but they were quickly washed away with the angry tide. There was no need to play it safe anymore. I only regretted that I hadn't been the first one to break the code of honor.

Tired of the sea-soaked cloth wrapped around my feet, I willed the fabric to release. My feet were free to grip the sand as I ran. Memories of the forest flashed by me. The wind stung the cuts on my face. My shoulder bled scarlet sand. The fabric that supported it filled with the dry earth, scraping my skin.

I willed myself on despite the lingering pain. I would heal just as the mortals did now. I had to remember this as I entered the carnage of the great city. The gates that guarded it were undamaged and swung wide against the wind. There in the center of the festivities rested a massive wooden horse. The belly had been gutted, and corpses littered the surrounding area. The one closest to me was the guard I had told to stand watch. The watchman's throat had been sliced, and his fist still clutched a cup of wine.

Homes were aflame. The royals' home was aflame. Men, women, and children were cut down, whether they held a weapon or not. I heard flesh tear behind me. I turned to find Paris staring back at me, a spearhead bulging from his chest. A Greek warrior had managed to sneak up behind me. Paris blocked his path.

Anger ripped through me. My injuries throbbed, but nothing could stop me. I whipped my way around Paris and met the man holding the murder weapon. I gripped his throat with my usable arm and squeezed. The Greek's throat was crushed in my grasp. The warrior's death was quick, to my dismay, but I had more important things to do.

Paris had fallen to his knees. I kneeled and faced the prince. "Paris,

why did you do that? You fool!" I pressed my hand around the protrusion, begging the wound to close. He didn't deserve this.

Paris tried to speak, but blood replaced his words. I reached behind him and removed the spear quickly, fully intending to break my own rules and heal him, though I knew reforming him would have its own side effects.

I laid him down on the dirty, blood-soaked ground. I pressured the opening with my palm and willed the words that would heal him to come to me.

Paris grabbed my hand. "Don't," he gurgled. He couldn't have known what I was going to do, but he stopped me just the same.

"Paris, let me do this for you," I begged.

The prince's heart slowed. I couldn't hear it anymore. "No, Helen." That was the last thing he said. The young prince smiled up at me, as if he were staring into the eyes of his own personal goddess. Relief shone in his gaze. Paris would feel no more pain. I was a poor excuse for a goddess.

I closed his stormy eyes. The prince's spirit, having nowhere else to flee, came to me for guidance. I allowed it to enter and make a home within me, along with all the others that had not yet descended. Paris was a part of me now and would always be. I didn't know if that was good or bad.

I went in search of survivors. The Greeks had made quick work of the city. Surprised and intoxicated, the Trojans didn't have a chance. *It was my fault.* I should have known, should have stayed. The win, the ships, and Achilles had been part of a greater plan, and I fell right into their trap. I wondered who came up with the plan. It seemed too intricate for Menelaus.

I found the throng of warriors then. They were battling in the king's home. The clanking of metal on metal hurt my delicate eardrums. Lucifer had managed to clap my head between his hands during our encounter, and it ached. I moved to the throne room. Hector was battling someone I had come to loathe. Someone I had dreamed of killing. *Menelaus.*

The kings fought ruthlessly. Hector was clearly the more agile, but

Menelaus had experience. "Stop!" I shouted. Hector paused only a moment. That was long enough for Menelaus to slice his thigh. The blood dripped to the floor and the young king kneeled in agony.

I ran to him, guilt overtaking me. I kneeled beside him to support his frame.

"Menelaus, stop. You have taken the city. Isn't that enough?" I questioned.

"My dear Helen." Menelaus and I hadn't seen each other since I had infiltrated his boat ten years prior. I could see the scars on his throat, left behind by my sword tip. "You haven't aged a day," he leered. "No matter. Your chance to be my bride has passed." The king went to swipe his sword at me.

I reached out and gripped the blade within my hand. Had he forgotten how powerful I was? The pride and arrogance of man never ceased to amaze me. "That's enough," I growled. The pain in my body and lack of patience in my mind led my actions. "No more. No one wins." I ripped the blade from his control, flipped the hilt, and swiped back at him. Menelaus wasn't worthy of Sacrifice. His innards dropped to the floor. The King of Greece collapsed in agony, desperately fighting to salvage his organs. He couldn't.

Soon he was nothing but a pile of steaming flesh. The king's darkened spirit added itself to mine. *How many horrific spirits lived inside me?* The urge to follow their sicknesses plagued me each day. I had to repeatedly remind myself who I was and who I wanted to be. I only hoped the light would outshine the darkness building inside me.

"Hector, let me help you," I said. I willed his clothes to wrap tightly above his wound. I dressed it in a similar fashion. The look on his face was upsetting. I had been right. People of this time were not ready for such magic. But this was all I could do to help him in my condition.

"Your brother is lost to us," I said.

Recovering his tortured expression, he said, "Paris was already lost. Now he is at peace." A tear streamed down the king's face, but he held himself straight and assured. A true ruler. Hector would be strong enough on his own.

"Where is Cassandra?" I asked. The fighting had lessened. Only a few survivors fought on.

"She went past the wall to search for you. The guard said you left," Hector explained. I was wrong to leave someone so intoxicated by joy and drink to such an important task. Once again, my decisions had cost people their lives.

Panicked, I promised, "I will find her."

I rose to leave when Hector grabbed my arm. "If she's alive, send her back to me. Then leave this place and do not return." Hector's words hurt. The king knew I was the instigator of this war, and he knew I was the cause of its end. Except this wasn't the end I had strived for. I nodded once, and he released his grip on me. A look of understanding passed between us. Goodbyes were not needed.

Maddened with pain, I cut down any Greek in my path. They attacked freely, having no other opponent left to fight. Troy had been lost. Only its king lived on, and I grieved for the burden he would bear because of it. I sprinted past the dead and guideless spirits. With everyone dead, there was nowhere for the spirits to go besides down. I allowed them to be taken into me, pulling them into my own pit of despair. I hoped it was better than wherever they would disappear to.

I passed the dead prince once more as I raced to find his lost sister.

XXIV
Wars End

The fates have other plans for us.
-C

Dark clouds blocked out the light of the moon. The wind gusted fiercely against anything that dared stand against it. I walked for hours down the beach's path, opposite of where my battle with Lucifer had been. There was only a single set of footprints that matched the size of Cassandra's feet. They led me. The scent of her was lost to the wind.

My blonde hair swirled around me angrily. Helen had failed. There was no point to her existence anymore. My red curls returned and flailed just as angrily. But at least they were free now. The reformation pained my injuries and the wound in my shoulder grew in size because of it, but it was worth it to be myself again.

I followed the footprints until the gusts blew them away. I knew she was out here. *Why did she go so far? Didn't she know I would return?* A trail of blood appeared then; grooves where someone was dragged coincided. *No.* I couldn't take another loss. I peered through the darkness and found what I was looking for.

Cassandra lay unconscious on the sandy beach, near the woodland's edge. Only part of her armor still clung to her frail form. "Cassandra!" I called out. My voice was lost to the sound of the storm. I ran as fast as I

could to her. Ignoring my shoulder wrappings, I held her with both arms. The princess's body felt cold, and her heartbeat was weak. She had been beaten beyond the point of recovery.

"You can't get rid of me that easily." Lucifer's voice penetrated the sounds of the storm. My injuries pulsed from the memory of our battle, and I recoiled.

"Why can't you leave me be? You've taken everything from me! Let this child live and I will leave with you. Please," I begged. The tears wanted to pour, but still they would not.

"You had your chance, my love. Now you have to suffer the consequences of your actions. Just as you left me to mine," he spat.

I heard his quickened footsteps approaching from the tree line. Unable to defend myself, he ripped me from Cassandra. The abrupt movement caused her to cry out and wake. "Cassandra! Run!" But she could not. Several of her bones had been broken, and blood pooled around her. Ice-blue eyes stared after me. Lucifer was dragging me toward the water. This was our pattern it seemed: cast the other to the depths only to have them rise and retaliate. It was a sadistic pattern and I couldn't afford to have it reoccur.

My friend. My sister. My *child* needed me. I thrashed and fought against Lucifer's grip. He was still in Achilles's form, still a coward. "If you are to torture me, let me see your face. Don't hide behind another's," I demanded.

In his anger, he dropped me at the water's edge. The waves crashed over my weak form, and he transformed into the man I knew most. The piercing blue eyes stared at me through the darkness. They iced me over. The water that surrounded me stilled, and the cold crept into my bones. *Not again. I couldn't go back. Not now.*

"As you wish, my queen." He smiled knowingly. "You can watch as I kill the last thing you have connecting you to these creatures," he spat, the smile gone. Lucifer took his time treading through the wind-blown sand toward Cassandra. She still hadn't moved. She still stared back at me. My

fire wouldn't light. I couldn't melt the ice. I was too cold. The memory of darkness overwhelmed me.

A flicker of recognition shone in Cassandra's deadened eyes then.

I said this war would end with me, and so it would. My internal flame lit, and I broke through the ice with what will I had left. My wound was gushing red sand, and it joined the sea-soaked earth below me. Pain ripping through me, I reached for a weapon. I was unable to unsheathe Sacrifice. The metal had frozen over and clung to the patches of bare skin. I began my crawl to Lucifer with an ice shard in my hand. Parts of my body either screamed in pain or were numbed by the ice, but I couldn't stop.

The immortal torturer was slow and careful with his actions. He wanted me to see every moment of Cassandra's death. The man was so engrossed in his endeavor that he hadn't heard me break free. The storm had masked my escape; for that I was grateful. I encouraged the wind to rage on, my breathing horrid in its movements. My curls whipped my eyes painfully. Still I crawled farther.

The remaining ice shards flew in a whirlwind above me and away to the sea. My approach was silent. I couldn't hear his words, but it looked as if he was speaking to the princess. The man seemed harsh, but his slow, careful movements suggested that he wanted to be gentle; he had never been gentle with anything besides me. Lucifer's hands wrapped around her throat, his shoulders tense with frustration.

I could see that he was suffering as I was. Lucifer's body was bruised, and red sand spilled to the ground continuously. His golden hair was crusted with salt and grime. I could see that his legs trembled from the pain he was enduring. He hadn't tended to any of the injuries I'd dealt him. Lucifer's sole mission had been to swim to land, and Cassandra had been on the beach when he did.

She had been on the beach looking for *me.*

I crept behind him, now on my hands and knees. The ice shard was

still clasped in my hand. I struck where I could reach. My ice weapon had frozen to my skin and ripped away painfully when I wielded it. My only wish was that I had stopped him in time.

Lucifer cried out in pain upon contact. The sharp ice edge had opened a gash in Lucifer's heel, causing him to crumble. Sand poured angrily from him like the sea that raged behind us. That was all I needed. He couldn't stand any longer, and I collapsed from exhaustion right along with him. Sand found its way into my lungs; it burned.

But I wasn't done.

I willed the ever-raging gale to aid me further. A gust flew in as he let go of Cassandra and threw him back out to the sea. I could see his dim golden light writhe in agony. Lucifer was in pain, and that seemed to add to my own, but I refused to lose. I had lost too many loved ones already. The storm I encouraged would not be easy to escape, and I begged that he would forfeit and leave me be.

"Cassandra!" I pulled myself forward. Our bodies mirrored each other. Her glassy eyes stared back at me. The ice blue of them had faded, painfully reminding me of someone whose were just as beautiful and still undeservingly alive.

For a moment I thought she had passed, but then the young woman forced her hand forward to hold my scarring face. Her pale fingers were surprisingly steady. "Keep trying," she whispered. The wind had taken her words before they reached my ears, but I watched the message shape her lips. Cassandra's sure and delicate hand dropped to the ground, spraying more sand up and into the gales. The princess of Troy was gone, and so was my one true friend. *I was too late.*

I had never known the connection of siblings, but she had given me a taste of the type of friendship that I would never have. Though as I stared into her soulless eyes, I couldn't help but feel the same loss I felt long ago, when Lucifer had taken my children from me.

I felt tired.

Cassandra's loss was too much to bear. The magic that flowed through me felt nonexistent, and I imagined it was what death would have been like. But I managed to find her tether, and her white spirit came to me. My connection was stronger than Lucifer's, and he was in no condition to fight me for her.

None of the lives she'd taken during the war had managed to sully her spirit. Instead of darkening my soul, she lightened it, relieving some of the burden. The white spirit was forever with her brother. The lost prince and princess of Troy. I hoped they had found a home within me.

Too weak to give her the proper Trojan burial by fire, the sand blowing in the wind danced around her body, scrubbing the memory of her pain away. The princess's form was soon the sand itself; forever a part of her homeland.

Knowing my time in Troy was done, the ground parted beneath me. I went so deep that I felt the heat radiating from the core. This was as close to understanding Earth as I ever would come. The heat that it expelled was too much even for me. My skin blistered and forced me to move away. But I stayed near, miles under the storm that raged above.

Helen had failed and died with Troy. Lilith was all that remained, and that frightened me. I had come to rely on the golden-haired goddess. She did what Lilith couldn't; she had lit our flame. Now Lilith was left alone to care for it. But Cassandra had been a friend to both of us, and Lilith remembered the words she spoke to her all too well. *Keep trying.* Because that's all Lilith *could* do.

Epilogue
Countless Endings

If love was easy,
it wouldn't exist.
-A

Time Unknown

The earth scraped against my skin as I moved. I had ample time to heal my physical wounds, even at the pace of a mortal—something I only had to suffer when Lucifer attacked. I was grateful for the time away from him, but no amount of time would heal the wounds in my mind, especially those that he had caused himself. Those were permanent and would forever be a part of me.

Being underground had been different from the water's depths. The warm earth felt a part of me; I took its energy and it took mine. It was where I belonged. But I had been gone too long already. The idea of staying was tempting, but I had made that mistake before. I would not cower. Earth still needed me. The humans still needed me. I had made too many promises to the souls I sacrificed. Their unwavering cries would haunt me until my last breath.

Earth and rock created pathways for me to follow, and I let them guide me. The earth itself moved my resting form. Then the course abruptly changed. I was headed upward instead of east. It was time to wake. No

more hiding. I emerged into a layer of cold ground. The warmed core of the Earth had done its job. I used well-rested limbs to climb and dig my way out, and the farther I climbed, the colder I got.

I broke the frozen surface and took in a breath of icy fresh air. It stung my lungs, but it was better than the small musty breaths I'd been inhaling. I shivered at the drastic change in temperature. The ground I had been recuperating in was similar to what I imagined a womb would feel like to a child.

This frozen place was no womb. The wind whipped scarlet curls across my face. My ripped and ragged clothes were not accommodating. My mind was dull, but I willed the tired clothes to reform. Slowly but surely I was encased in thick clothes. Sacrifice remained dutifully at my side. The glint of her ruby was prominent against the terrain.

My surroundings were coated in white dust. Small flakes floated down from the heavens. Each one I gazed into was utterly unique. I attempted to hold one, but it melted in my hand. My positioning was high, higher than I had ever been. I looked down at the valleys below. Snow stretched across the land. But at the very bottom, where only my eyes could see, I saw green.

My magic had run dry, and I no longer wished to travel underground; if I went back I might not return to the surface. I began the journey on foot down the great mountain. The freezing wind thrashed against my face and froze my eyelashes. Though I knew my soul needed rest, I tried to light a fire anyway. But the air was too cold to force heat from in my weakened state. I had to suffer in silence.

I sped my journey along as much as I could, but the snow deterred my haste. Though I couldn't find it in myself to complain, because one phrase kept repeating itself in my mind as I descended farther down the peak. *Try harder. Try harder. Try harder.*

The Creation of Adam

I heard a female call from the clearing. The water that I drank from often rained down loudly from its high point on the cliff beside her. The smell of this domain was prominent, and it was clear that it had been claimed. Still, I found myself here. I was curious to see what this rare being was like.

I sauntered into the open meadow, all too aware of how exposed I was. The scent that surrounded this realm was fresh, but the source was no longer here. Satisfied with that fact, I went to the creature with red fur. She had called to me using my own language, though she was not of my species. That confused me, but I couldn't make myself leave. Her tender and caring presence calmed me. I knew somehow that I would be safe with her near.

The female's red fur blew wildly as the wind passed by, and I watched as its strange curled shape bounced tirelessly. Distracted as I was by the rare animal, I didn't notice that I was in the air until my feet were already too far from the ground. I looked to my side and saw that a snake flew with me. I struggled against the force that controlled my body and begged that the snake did not bite.

I looked to the red-furred animal again, and my movements stilled.

She was the one doing this, and somehow I didn't mind. I could almost understand the meaning behind the sounds she called out.

Then I was gone.

I wasn't me anymore. I was a new thing. A different thing. I didn't know what I was other than the instructions given to me. Then there was another voice in my mind, a sickly soothing sound that whispered to me. I only understood a few words. The new language kept going in and out. Like the sun through the dense canopy of the forest, only patches of the light rays could be seen on the cold, damp ground.

In the midst of my new chaotic mind, another animal appeared. My nostrils flared, and I knew then that this was the domain's ruler. I trembled in fear, but the sweet voice in my head told me to attack. I pushed that enticing voice to the very back of my mind where I could no longer hear it, but I could still feel it. It writhed and fought to take control.

In command of my new body, I ran to the red-furred creature to ask for help, but the sounds wouldn't form. It took all my strength to keep that dark voice from taking me over. The caring animal said, "I am sorry. Everything is going to be all right. I just need to make a few changes." I gazed into her piercing, forest-green eyes and saw the empathy there. She would help. I nodded and stepped back.

This time her sounds were clear, and I did as she instructed. I was glad to be free of the new body and the sickly soothing voice in the back of this form's mind that taunted me. I freed myself from the bonds that tied my soul and reformed into the toughest and safest thing I could: a bone.

The last thing I remembered was the red-furred woman putting her hand around my new form. I was tired. I couldn't go on anymore. It felt as if I had been ravaged by a predator, though I didn't recall fighting one. Soon I was encased in darkness and I slept.

I couldn't sense anything. All the sensations from my past life were gone,

leaving me with nothing but exhaustion. I had slept a long while, yet I wanted to continue. But I would not wake alive if I did. Accepting that I was to leave this unsuitable form, I let go. The rest of the spirits called to me, and I wished to join them. The tether that bound my soul to theirs pulled, and I gratefully let them take me. I was so tired.

Then there was the prodding of another tether that pulled me the opposite way. I fought against it, knowing it was not where I belonged, but then I felt something. I couldn't hear or see, but my soul could understand. The opposing tether that bound itself to my spirit was in distress. I could feel its loneliness and its sorrow. This new tether needed me.

Reluctantly I let go of the tether that bound me to the rest of the souls, leaving only a thin trace of what could have been so that I could find my way back to them one day. Back to where I belonged.

Accepting my fate, I grabbed on to the lonely tether and pulled. Our connecting line grew shorter until the spirit stopped me short of joining it and whispered instructions to me. The voice was familiar, and I bowed to its will.

The same sensation from before overwhelmed me now, except this time it was just *my* voice speaking. There was no sweet, terrifying voice to fight against. Only me. That realization made me smile. I lifted my new hand to feel the expression on my new face. My smile widened. My mind widened as well. Things I had never thought of before entered my psyche. Language and emotions. So many emotions to choose from. So many to feel and experience.

I heard the stifled sounds of whimpering then; my senses had returned. I looked down to find a beautiful young woman with flowing red hair; it covered her body like a blanket. She was shivering from the chill, and her face was wet with water. Still she slept, unaware of my presence. Instinctually, I laid down and wrapped my arms around her body to warm her. She was soft, and her curls tickled my nose.

I knew in that moment that I would stay with her until she was warm again, perhaps even longer. I whispered in the woman's ear as she let out another small whimper, "Rest now. Tomorrow will be better."

Acknowledgments

I want to acknowledge my family for their undying loyalty to me and my dreams.

Thank you, Mom, for your dutiful eyes and ears. I made you read chapter after chapter and not once did you complain. I couldn't have written this book without you. Thank you, Dad, for your constant flow of ideas and opinions (even when I didn't want to hear them). A lot of your persistent words make their way onto my pages. Thank you, Conner, for your endless amount of wisdom on every subject imaginable. Your talent for debate keeps my mind sharp and my writer muscles toned. You're an amazing brother.

Thank you, Brandon, my husband. Your knack for story structure and character development guided me through the journey that is Lilith. Even tired from a hard day's work, you made the time to listen to my ideas and writer's block struggles. You are a rare soul. You are my heart.

I want to acknowledge the team at Proving Press for their limitless support and advice.

Thank you, Emily, CEO of Proving Press. You always take the time to answer my call and sift through my endless questions. It's obvious that you love your job and it made my experience that much more special.

Thank you, Heather, my editor, for your time and knowledge.

Thank you, David, my cover designer, for your creative vision.

Finally, thank you, readers. I hope that you enjoyed this book and will continue with Lilith on her next journey. I mean, what's the point of the story if there is no one to tell it to? Lilith's journey is long and harsh, but she soon becomes a person who inspires courage.

Like her, you all have a voice. And *all* of you have inspired my voice.

—Anne MacReynold

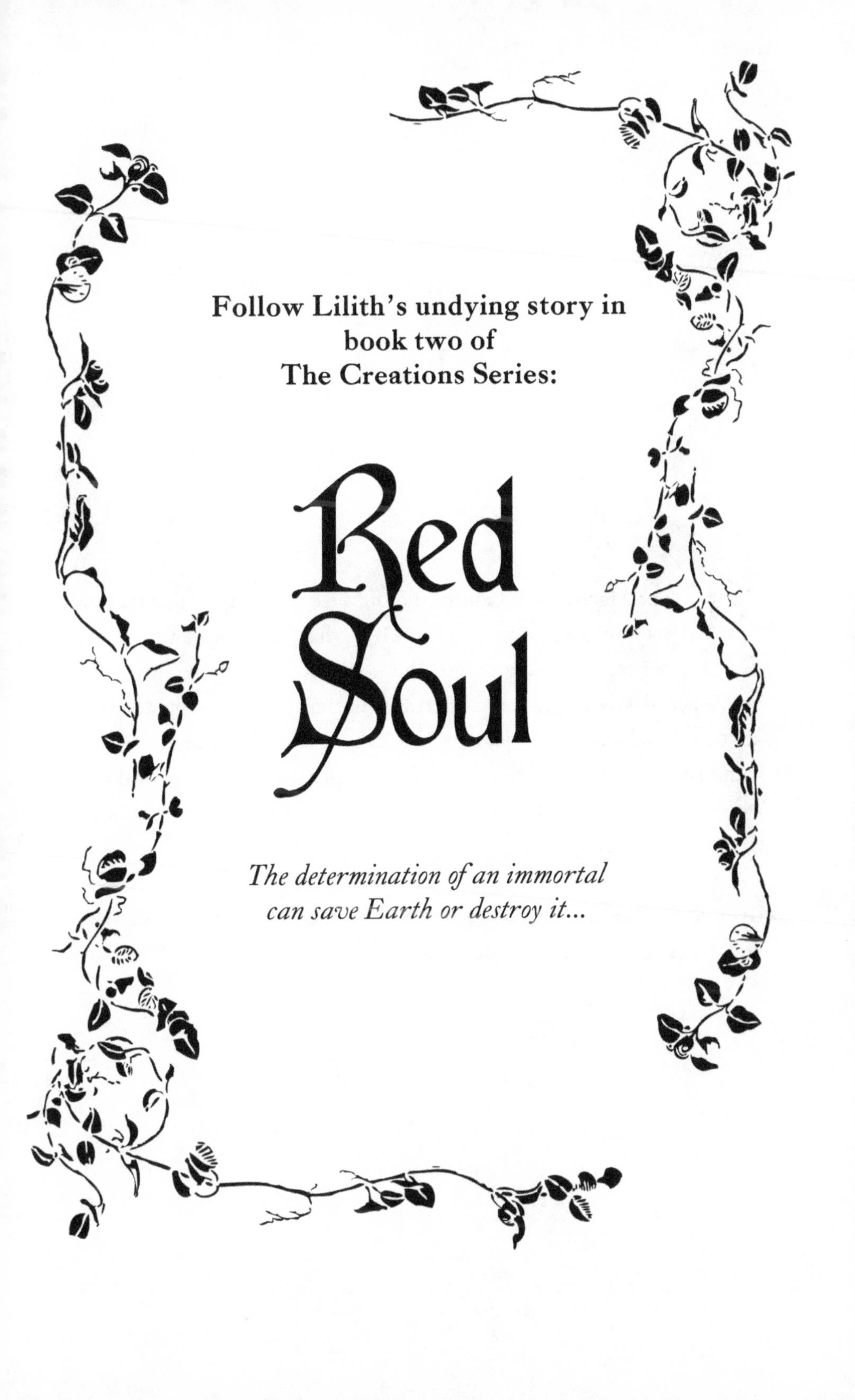

Follow Lilith's undying story in book two of The Creations Series:

Red Soul

The determination of an immortal can save Earth or destroy it...

About the Author
Anne MacReynold

Anne MacReynold believes our universe holds magic that we have yet to comprehend, and she wields this power of thought in her writing. Not only do her philosophical views weave themselves into her stories, but her life as well. Anne continues to find happiness with her family and animal companions in Alaska, a place that still displays the natural beauty that is the Earth, and a home that allows her to spend time with those she loves. Anne proves that sometimes the simplest of lives can be the most fulfilling.

Keep up with Anne's book releases and other writings by following her website, annemacreynold.com, or connect with her on Facebook @WriterAnneMacReynold.